Needing Her

By Allie Everhart

Needing Her
By Allie Everhart

Copyright © 2015 Allie Everhart
All rights reserved.
Published by Waltham Publishing, LLC
Cover design by Okay Creations
ISBN: 978-1-942781-02-8

CHAPTER ONE

PEARCE

The limo drives through a part of New Haven I've never been to before. Police sirens are going off in the distance and I see nothing but old brick buildings with windows that are either shattered or boarded up with cardboard. Graffiti covers almost every surface; benches, billboards, traffic signs. We pass a woman pushing a shopping cart filled with cardboard boxes and ratty blankets. Her hair is wiry and matted and it looks like she hasn't showered in weeks.

"What are we doing here?" I ask my father.

He has a slight smile on his face. "You'll see."

I don't like it when he smiles. When other people smile, it's good. It means they're happy. But when my father smiles, it's either because he's in public and has to comply with the rules of proper social interaction, or it means something bad's going to happen. Since I'm the only person in the back of the limo, there's no need for him to smile. Which means he's up to something.

My stomach knots and my muscles tense. I don't know what he's planning to do, but he took me here for a reason. And I know it's not good.

I look at him sitting across from me. "Tell me what we're doing here."

He points out the side window. "You see those people? The two men and the woman?"

He's pointing to some homeless people, dressed in ragged clothes, their skin sweaty from the sweltering August heat and humidity. The woman is sifting through a trash can, and the two men are talking closely, likely doing some kind of drug deal.

"What about them?" I ask.

His gaze remains out the window as we pass by more homeless people. "They're dregs of society. The remnants that bring us all down. Taking up space and resources. Straining our economy by their dependence on our government." His gaze returns to me. "And yet they serve a purpose. They allow people like us to look good in the eyes of the masses. We donate money to the shelters. Fund job programs. Host charity events. And in return, we're put on a pedestal for our good deeds."

I'm getting more nervous as he talks. Something's about to happen. Something bad.

"Tell me what we're doing. Please, Father. Just tell me."

We're sitting at a stoplight and he watches as a homeless man carrying a duffle bag crosses the street. "They serve another purpose. One that I'm about to show you."

"I want to get out of here," I say. "Let's go home."

"We will." His eyes are still on the man crossing the street. "But first we must accomplish our mission."

"Which is what?" My heart's pumping fast, my hand gripping the seat.

My father looks at me. "Relax, son. It gets easier each time."

"What gets easier? Please, just tell me what we're doing here."

My father reaches up and lightly taps on the glass that separates us from the driver. The limo slows down as we pass a homeless shelter. It's evening and people are lined up out front, likely waiting to get a meal. Our driver makes a right-hand turn down an alley. And then he stops, but leaves the limo running.

"It's time, Pearce." My father gives me a full smile now, but his eyes are dark, almost black. I watch him reach into a compartment in the side of the limo. He pulls out a handgun with a silencer attached.

My heart pumps harder, fear prickling the back of my neck. "Father, what are you doing?"

He doesn't answer. He presses the button to lower the window. I look out and see a man with his back to us, urinating on the side of the building. His gray hair is spiked up all different directions and he has on torn jeans spattered with mud, and a dingy white t-shirt covered in stains.

I flick my eyes back to my father and see the gun pointed at the man. And then, as if in slow motion, I watch my father's hand depress the trigger and then release.

"No!" I hear myself yell.

But it's too late. The gun already went off. The sound it made was just a blunt pop instead of the loud, echoing cry that it would've been without the silencer attached. I shift my eyes to the man standing by the building, but his body is now crumpled on the ground, the back of his shirt displaying a circle of blood that's growing outward from the hole made by the bullet that went through his back and straight to his heart.

My view is disrupted when the tinted glass from the window rises. I feel the limo pulling away. I slowly turn to look at my father. The gun is put away and he's pouring himself a glass of scotch.

He looks at me, a smile still on his face. "And that, my son, is what it means to be a Kensington."

CHAPTER TWO
Early 1990's

PEARCE

I bolt up in bed, my bare chest slick with sweat, my heart pumping hard and fast. I squeeze my eyes shut, then open them and see the artwork across from my bed, the dark wood dresser just beneath it. And then the sound of Beethoven fills the room. It's my alarm going off.

I squeeze my eyes shut again and rub my forehead. It was just a dream, or more like a nightmare. I haven't thought about that day for years. But yesterday, on my way to meet a client, I was sitting at a stoplight and looked to my right and saw a homeless man urinating on the side of a building and the memory of that day came flooding back.

I was 16 when that happened, and after that day, my life changed. *I* changed. My father said that was my first step in becoming a man. Little did I know back then that my remaining steps to manhood would be even worse than what happened that day. And that I wouldn't have a choice in the matter.

My life has been planned for me since the day I was born. Probably even before I was born. And so far, I've followed the plan. Resisting it got me nowhere. Even if I was somehow able to escape this life, I'm not sure what I would do. This is the only life I know. I wouldn't even know how to live as a normal person. A person who just goes about their daily life without all these secrets. Without knowing they've killed for nothing more than to prove a point. To show you're a man. A member. A Kensington.

"Shut it off," a voice mumbles beside me. "It's too early."

4

I turn to find a woman next to me in bed. She's facing me, her long blond hair spread out over the pillow. Her eyes are closed and she's smiling.

"Shut off the alarm and get over here," she says, her hand moving up my leg, heading to my crotch. "I'm not finished with you yet."

Anger swells inside me. What the hell is she still doing here? I don't allow women to spend the night. It's not just *their* rule. It's *my* rule. But apparently I broke it last night. I'd had too much to drink and must've fallen asleep and this woman took it upon herself to sleep in my bed.

I take her hand off me. "You need to leave. I have to get to work."

She flips the covers back, exposing her naked body. "Can't you be late to work?"

My eyes drift over her. She's gorgeous. Large breasts, flat stomach, long legs, golden tan skin. She could easily be a model. That body could sell most anything. Clothing. Perfume. Purses. Shoes. She's the type of woman other women would kill to look like. I'm not sure how much of her is real. I know she's had at least some work done to look that way. Her breasts are definitely fake, but whoever did them did an excellent job. They look natural. It's the feel that gave them away.

"I can't be late," I tell her as I get out of bed. "I need to get ready. You can use the guest bathroom if you'd like."

She's staring at my naked body and it makes me uncomfortable. I don't like feeling exposed. My life is all about covering things up. Secrets. Lies. The truth about who I am and what I do. I turn away from her and go to my closet to get my robe.

"Don't cover up," I hear her say. "A body like that needs to be on display. Tall. Muscular." She pauses. "Well-endowed."

I ignore her compliments. I know she only says them because she's supposed to. I'm sure she says the same thing to the members who are old and out of shape.

5

I put my robe on and turn back to find her in front of me. Naked. Her hand sneaks under my robe, just below my waist, moving downward. "Come on. Just one more time?"

She starts stroking me, showing off her skills. And she definitely has skills in this area. Then again, she does this all the time so she has plenty of practice in knowing how to please a man, physically. If she wasn't good at it, they wouldn't keep her on staff.

I don't know this girl's name but she works for us. For the organization, the secret group I'm part of. A small but select group of rich, powerful men who control the world. Or at least that's what we like to think.

"Doesn't that feel good?" she whispers, her soft hand still stroking me.

My shoulders relax and I tip my head back. "Yes."

The organization hires girls like this to take care of the members' needs. Most of the members have arranged marriages so wives are nothing more than display objects. They take their place on the arms of their husbands at high society events or whenever people are watching. Then behind closed doors, both husband and wife lead their separate lives, fulfilling their needs outside the marital bed. But the majority of the men don't have time to go find a woman to sleep with, at least not the *right* woman. We can't choose some random woman at a bar. We have to be careful. When you're rich and powerful, you trust no one, especially a woman you just met.

So to make things easier on us, women are provided as a benefit to membership. The women are screened, both mentally and physically, to ensure they're suitable for the job. The pool of candidates includes beautiful women of all races and nationalities. Some would say they're high-end call girls but we call them associates. It's a code word we can use in everyday conversation without anyone knowing what we're talking about. Only the members know and it's become somewhat of an inside joke. *I'm having drinks with one of my associates tonight.* We all know what it means. Even the wives know.

Unlike the associates, the wives are one of us. They have the right name, the right education, the right lineage. Most have

6

fathers or brothers who are members. That's why they're paired up with us. They know their place. They know their purpose. And most are happy to accept their role, even though it means a life in a loveless marriage.

"God, you feel good," I hear her say as she grinds into me, her legs straddling me.

I wasn't going to do this, but she got me started and now we're back in bed so she can finish me off. Her breasts are bouncing over my face but I close my eyes and try to imagine myself somewhere else. With someone I care about. Someone I feel something for. I don't know why I do it. Why I imagine these things I'll never have. I'm not even sure real love exists. If it does, I know I'll never experience it.

This is my future. A woman like this. Someone I don't know. Someone who's more than happy to get me off, but doesn't give a damn about me. She's just doing a job. And tomorrow night, she'll be doing it to someone else.

It'll be like this for the rest of my life. I'll always be with women like her, even if I'm forced to get married again.

My wife was chosen for me when I was 22. She was also 22 and had just graduated from Vassar with a degree in Russian Literature. I had just graduated from Yale with a degree in Finance. Neither one of us wanted to get married but we were young and obedient and did as we were told.

Her name was Kristina and she had dreams of spending her twenties traveling overseas, not playing the role of Pearce Kensington's wife. And I had no desire to play the role of her husband. My sole focus was to attend graduate school at Harvard and learn as much as possible so I could someday prove to my father that I was better at running our company than he was.

After Kristina and I got married in what was a ridiculously over-the-topic summer wedding, attended by six hundred of our parents' closest friends, we moved to Boston and I attended Harvard and began working on my MBA. As with other couples who had arranged marriages, Kristina and I led separate lives. She spent her time either reading or partaking in high-end charity events, trying to establish her place as a socialite. And I went to school and spent my free time going out with my classmates, some of whom were also members of the organization.

My marriage to Kristina was not even close to being real. She and I only had sex one time, on our wedding night. We thought we should at least try, given that we were husband and wife. But it was awkward and uncomfortable and ended with us both deciding to never do it again. I had zero attraction to her. She's average height with shoulder-length reddish blond hair that she always pulled back behind her head and pinned up in a style that made her look much older than she was. She didn't like the outdoors or any kind of physical activity, preferring to stay inside and read, a lifestyle that wasn't kind to her body. Her skin was pale and she was very thin with almost no muscle tone.

The marriage ended a year later, after Kristina admitted she was a lesbian. I suspected she was when I first met her, but she didn't tell anyone until ten months into our marriage. The members didn't think Kristina would be able to adequately fake being my wife, given her sexual preference, and therefore allowed us to get a divorce. It was the best news I'd had in years. Kristina was a nice enough girl, but I was relieved to be out of the marriage, and so was she.

I never want to get married again but I know they'll force me to. Being a bachelor isn't accepted in my world. Not just among my wealthy friends but also in my business life. Someday I'll be CEO of Kensington Chemical and our clients and business partners are more likely to trust a CEO with a stable married life than a single bachelor. And I need someone to accompany me to social events.

But since my divorce almost two years ago, I haven't been set up with anyone. I think they want me to be more settled in my career before they push me into another marriage. Or maybe they think it's too soon. My world is all about appearances and it would look better if I waited a few years before getting married again.

After my divorce from Kristina, I completed my MBA, then returned to Connecticut to work for Kensington Chemical under the direction of my father, the CEO. I'm now 25 and have spent the past year working at the company, learning the business.

My mind returns to the woman on top of me who's doing what she's trained to do. My body instinctively tenses up as I get my release, then relaxes as I come down from it. She moves herself off me and lies back on the bed.

"You're not going to tell them, are you?" she asks.

"You shouldn't have done it." I get out of bed, putting my robe back on. "You know the rules. No sleeping over."

She sits up on her knees, pleading with me. "I had too much to drink. I was tired. I fell asleep. It was an accident. I didn't mean to. And I tried to make it up to you this morning by—"

"I didn't ask for that. And as for the alcohol, it's your job to limit yourself so things like this don't happen."

She nods and looks down at the bed.

I feel bad for her. She's young and beautiful and yet somehow got stuck doing this job. I wonder how long ago she was recruited. Recruitment can be done by any of the members, although I haven't done it myself. The way it works is that a member will see a beautiful young woman and offer to make her dreams come true for a price. For some of these girls, the dream is to become a model or an actress. Others just want large sums of money to spend as they please.

Whatever the dream, the price is that they have to take care of the members' physical needs. I'm sure this girl doesn't want to be doing this. But now she can't get out. She'll never be out. When her looks fade, making her undesirable to the members, she'll still be monitored to make sure she never reveals our secrets.

"What's your name?" I ask her. I never know their names.

She cautiously looks up. "Sophia."

"Sophia, I need you to leave now. And I don't want to see you again. If you see my name listed, let another girl take the job. I will not tell them that you spent the night, but you have to be more careful next time. They're very strict about the rules. If it had been anyone else, well, you know what could've happened."

She shakes her head. "No. I don't. What could've happened?"

Did they not tell her? Maybe she's new. This is the first time I've been with her and she looks like she's about 20 or 21. Maybe

9

she just started. Still, they should've told her the rules and the punishment for not following those rules.

"You could get hurt." I need to be honest with her. Breaking the rules has gotten other girls killed. I don't know that for sure, but I assumed that's what happened to them when I never saw those girls again.

She moves off the bed, holding the sheet up to cover herself. "They never told me that. When I started, nobody ever said anything about—"

"Sophia, I don't have time to discuss this with you. I need to get to work."

She nods. "Yes. I'm sorry. I'll leave." She picks her lingerie off the floor and starts putting it on.

I walk past her toward the bathroom. "The driver is waiting downstairs to take you back."

"Thank you," she says.

I look back and see her trying to zip her dress up. I go over and zip it up the rest of the way.

She turns and puts her hand on my arm. "You're a nice man, Pearce. You're not like the others."

And then she reaches down to grab her high heels and scurries out of the room and out the door.

A nice man. She couldn't be more wrong. If she only knew the things I've done.

I am not a nice man. I'm a Kensington.

CHAPTER THREE

RACHEL

I haul my groceries up the three flights of stairs to my apartment, sweat dripping off my forehead. It's times like this I really wish this place had an elevator. It's an old, charming building and I love living here, except for the stair issue. And normally I don't mind, but today it's brutally hot and humid outside and the stairwell is even hotter.

It's fall in Connecticut, so why is it so hot? I guess it's technically not fall yet. It's only the first of September. Maybe in a week or two it'll cool down.

My phone rings just as I reach my apartment. I quickly open the door and race to the kitchen, dropping the four heavy bags on the counter.

I grab the phone from the wall, yanking on the cord to untangle it. "Hello?"

"Hi, honey, it's Mom."

"Hey, Mom. I just walked in the door. I'm a little out of breath."

"You should move to a better place. One that has an elevator."

"I don't need one. It's good exercise to walk up the stairs. And this place is close to school."

I'm a grad student at Hirshfield College, a small liberal arts college in New Haven. It doesn't have much for student housing and the apartments around there were all full, so I ended up getting an apartment close to Yale, but Hirshfield is only a few miles away.

"Your dad and I sure miss you," my mom says. "Two weeks just wasn't enough time."

"I know." I start unloading my groceries, starting with the freezer food. "I miss you guys too, but classes are starting and I couldn't take any more time off from work."

I'm a history major and work part-time at a museum. I work at the front desk, but I also give tours, which is my favorite part of the job.

"I'll be back at Thanksgiving, Mom. That's only a few months away. I hope Dad isn't planning on frying the turkey again."

My parents live on a farm, and last year my dad almost burned the barn down while trying to make the turkey. My mom wouldn't let him have the fryer anywhere near the house so he took it out near the barn and it caught on fire. Luckily, he stopped the fire before it did any real damage.

"Your father's turkey frying days are over." She laughs. "The turkey will be going in the oven this year. Oh, before I forget, your father wants me to get the plane tickets for your graduation. But if you're moving back, I was thinking maybe your father and I should just drive out there and help you with the move."

I graduate in December and my mom's comment right now was her not-so-subtle hint that I should move back to Indiana after graduation. She wants me to live close by so she can constantly watch over me. She's been extremely overprotective of me ever since my twin sister died of cancer. She died when I was six, and after it happened, my mom thought I'd get cancer too, so she took me to the doctor whenever I had even the slightest hint of a cold.

Even now, she worries about me constantly. And not just about my health. About everything. She doesn't like me driving alone. She doesn't want me going out after dark. She doesn't want me dating a guy unless she knows his family.

She has so many rules and so many restrictions that I felt suffocated living under her roof. I love her and I know she means well, but I needed some space, which is why I was secretly thrilled when Hirshfield offered me a scholarship that covers half of my tuition. It gave me an excuse to leave Indiana and finally live on my own.

I've lived here for a year now and I love it. It's new and different and I feel like I'm on my own mini adventure. I just turned 24 and finally feel my age. Living with my parents I always felt like a kid because they refused to let me grow up.

"Mom, go ahead and get the plane tickets. I don't know what I'm doing after graduation. My lease goes until the end of December and I'm hoping to have a job by then, so I'll be moving to wherever that ends up being."

"They have history museums in Indiana. You should at least apply."

She suggested this when I was home last week. She even gave me some brochures for Indiana museums. She drove all the way to a tourist information booth off the highway to get them. I just took them and didn't say anything. She knows I don't want to go back there. I want to get a job at a large history museum in a big city, like New York.

When I don't respond, she says, "Well, I guess I'll get the tickets. Your father and I can always drive out later and help you move."

I reach in the bottom of my grocery sack to get my ice cream. The sides of the box squish in my hand, causing the top to pop off and ice cream to spill out all over. "Mom, my ice cream melted and made a huge mess. I need to clean this up. I'll call you later. Tell Dad I said hi."

"I will, honey. Bye."

The ice cream is now in the sink. I rinse my hand off and grab a paper towel to dry my hands, then go to the air conditioning unit that's wedged in the window and turn it to high. The fan speeds up but the air coming out of it isn't very cold.

I unload the remaining two grocery bags, putting everything away except for a package of chocolate chip cookies. I get a bowl out and scoop some of the melted ice cream in it, then rip open the package of cookies and crumble some over the ice cream, making a cookie sundae. It's my favorite dessert. I especially love it when the ice cream melts into the cookies, so the fact that my ice cream melted is actually a good thing. It's just the way I like it. It's 6:15 so I should be eating an actual meal, but for now, this is good enough.

I go to the couch and turn on the TV. I don't have cable so my options are limited. As I'm flipping through the channels, sirens blare outside my window. That happens a lot. Police sirens are always going off. My apartment isn't in the safest area. It's run-down and has its fair share of crime. But I've never had any problems, maybe because I'm always careful and keep my doors locked and don't go out much at night.

My parents have been here a few times to visit and when my mom saw where I lived, she became even more worried about me. She's convinced I'm going to be murdered living here.

There are a lot of homeless people that hang out in my neighborhood. I'm guessing at least some of them have been in prison and had nowhere to go when they got out so ended up on the streets. And there are some guys who live in my building who look like your average college guys but I'm almost positive they're drug dealers.

I know it's a dangerous area, but I don't let it bother me. Maybe I'm naive or overly optimistic, but I choose to believe people are inherently good, but then something happens and they get down the wrong path. Not that I think criminals are good. I'm just saying that everyone deserves a second chance and we shouldn't judge people based on mistakes they made in the past. Doing so just keeps them going down that wrong path and they never find their way off it.

That's why I volunteer at the homeless shelter one day a week. I teach reading and writing to whoever wants to learn. A lot of these people never finished school and never even learned how to read, so they can't find work and are stuck living on the streets. Some of them have been in prison but now they're trying to turn their lives around and I want to help them do that.

I haven't told my parents about my volunteer job. They'd approve of me helping people, but not if they saw the area where the shelter is located. It's in a really bad part of town.

The air conditioner is starting to cool down my apartment but I still feel hot and sweaty so I take a quick shower. After the shower I'm hungry for some real food. As a graduate student who only works part-time, I don't have much money, so I try not to eat out or get takeout. But tonight I'm too hot and tired to fix anything and I'm really craving a pizza. It's the night before classes start so I might as well enjoy my last night of freedom with a pizza splurge.

I order a large combo, then wait on the couch, flipping through channels, trying to find a movie to watch. I've seen every movie I flip past. Back in high school, my friends and I watched a ton of movies. There wasn't much else to do in a small farm town.

"Shit!" I hear a girl yell it out in the hall. "Dammit!"

I spring from the couch and race over to look out the peephole. A girl around my age appears to be moving in next door. Boxes are lined up next to her. All of the apartments come furnished, which makes moving in easy since you don't have to mess with furniture.

I go out into the hall. "Need some help?"

The girl jumps a little when I say it. She must not have seen me come out of my apartment.

"Maybe." She's jiggling the door handle, trying to open it.

"Those doors are tricky. You have to hold the handle really still and then turn the key."

She laughs. "So I'm doing the exact opposite of what you're supposed to do?"

I laugh too. "Yeah, kind of. Want me to show you?"

She hands me the key and I open the door without a problem. "You just have to practice a few times."

"Thanks." She takes the key back and shoves it in the pocket of her shorts. "I'm Shelby. Your new neighbor."

"I'm Rachel. I've lived here for a little over a year. I'm a grad student at Hirshfield."

"Oh, yeah?" She smiles. "So I'm living next to a genius."

I smile back. "I said Hirshfield, not Yale. I'm not a genius."

"Hirshfield is just as good as Yale, so if you go to Hirshfield, you're a genius. Hardly anyone gets accepted there. And I know that because I used to work in admissions. I was a secretary. Now I work at a law firm. Still as a secretary."

"How do you like it?"

She shrugs. "It's okay. It's just a job. Something that pays the bills. I only work there three days a week."

I glance at the stack of boxes by her door. "You want some help with the boxes?"

"Sure. Thanks." She moves her hair behind her ear, then tugs on her earlobe. "Shit. I lost my earring."

"What does it look like?"

She shows me her other ear, which has the remaining earring. It's an angel wing with a fake diamond in the center. "They were cheap earrings so it's no big deal."

"I can help you find it."

"That's okay. I think it fell off in the car. I'll look for it later." She points to the floor. "Watch out for the glass. My vase fell out of one of the boxes. That's why you heard me yelling out here."

I look down and see green shattered glass surrounding her sandaled feet. "I can clean it up. I have a dustpan."

"Don't worry about it. I'll get it later. Come inside."

We each take a box and go into her apartment. It looks just like mine, but it's hotter and stuffier in here because her air conditioning's not running.

She goes over and turns it on, then stands in front of it, the fan blowing her long blond hair around. She's wearing tight red shorts that show off her long legs. She's about 5'9, same height as me. We have a similar body type; thin, but we still have curves, although she has way bigger boobs than me. Her tight white tank top can barely hold them in.

"What's with this weather?" she asks. "Why is it so freaking hot?"

"If you want, you can come over to my place until yours cools off."

She stares at me. "Where are you from?"

"Indiana. Why?"

"I knew you weren't from around here. You're way too nice. So…Indiana. That's considered the Midwest, right?"

"Yeah. I grew up on a farm. My parents still live there."

"A farm girl from Indiana," she says with a fake Southern drawl. "Well, that's just about as wholesome as they come."

I know she's kidding, but I don't like it. I hate it when people joke about where I'm from. I get enough disrespect from my professors who act like I'm not as smart or as driven as the students from the East Coast. It's not at all true. I work harder than anyone else in my graduate program and I have the highest grades to show for it. I also have a job, whereas my classmates don't work at all. Most come from wealthy families and don't need to work.

"I'll go get some more of the boxes." I walk to the door.

"Hey!" She runs after me, stopping me. "I'm sorry. That was rude, wasn't it? I didn't mean it that way. Really. I just get nervous when I meet smart people because I didn't even finish high school. I have my GED. Anyway, I shouldn't have said that. I don't know anything about people from Indiana. You're the first person I've met from there. For all I know you're not wholesome at all. You could be a crazy whore who sells drugs on the side."

I laugh. "Okay, now *that* was insulting. Do I look like a crazy drug-selling whore?"

I'm wearing tan shorts, a white t-shirt, and sneakers, my long brown hair still wet from the shower and no makeup on.

She runs her eyes over me and taps her lips with her finger. "Hmm. I'd say no on the drugs. But with a body like that, you could easily—"

"Stop." I jab her shoulder, kiddingly. "I'm not selling my body on the streets. I don't even sleep around. I'm not that kind of girl. You're right. I'm a wholesome Midwest girl."

She tilts her head and gets this sly grin on her face. "How wholesome? Wholesome as in you've never done it before?"

I roll my eyes. "Not *that* wholesome. I mean, come on, I'm 24."

"Did you do it with a farm boy? What are they like? Are they any good?"

I walk out in the hall and grab a box.

She follows me out there. "Shit! Did I offend you again? I'm such an idiot."

"You didn't offend me. It's just that I don't kiss and tell." I go back in and set the box on the living room floor, then sit on her couch. "But yes, I have been with a farm boy. Several actually."

"What does that mean?" She drops the box she was carrying and races over to the couch. "You can't say something like that and not tell me."

"Nope. Sorry." I put my feet on her coffee table. "I can't tell you anything."

"Was it a threesome? With two guys?" She scrunches up her face. "Now *that* would not be wholesome at all."

I laugh. "It wasn't a threesome. I was just letting you think it was more scandalous than it was, in order to dirty up my wholesome image." I pick up a throw pillow from the couch, tugging at a loose string along the seam. "I just meant that I've had boyfriends who grew up on farms."

She lifts her legs up and crosses them in front of her on the couch. "Were you serious with any of these guys?"

"Um, yeah, I guess. I dated one of them for almost a year."

"Tell me about him."

I set the pillow aside. "I'd rather not."

"Why? Did he cheat on you?"

"No. I just don't like talking about him."

Someone knocks on a door out in the hallway. I get up from the couch. "I have to go. The pizza guy's here. Hey, do you want to join me? I got a large."

"You're offering me dinner?" She jumps up from the couch. "You're so sweet! I've decided I love people from Indiana."

I laugh. "And where are *you* from?"

She sighs. "New Haven. I've never left. Probably never will."

I walk toward the door. "Come on. Don't worry about drinks. I've got cold pop in the fridge."

"What's pop?" I hear her say as I go out in the hall.

"Soda!" I call out behind me.

I always forget and say 'pop' and people here have no idea what I'm talking about. Once I ordered a pop at a diner by

18

campus and the waiter told me they don't sell popsicles. From then on, I made sure to always ask for a soda, but in everyday conversation I sometimes forget and call it 'pop.'

The pizza guy's waiting impatiently at my door. "It's $11.59."

"Yeah, sorry." I squeeze past him when he doesn't move and unlock my door. I go inside, grab some cash, and hand it to him. "Keep the change."

I take the pizza and he turns and walks down the stairs, counting the money as he does.

Shelby appears in the hall and we go inside my apartment.

"Nice place," she says jokingly, since mine looks the exact same as hers. Same layout. Same furniture. Same wall color.

"Yeah, I thought you'd like it." I set the pizza on the kitchen counter. "If you want, I can help you design yours."

She laughs as she finds some glasses in the cabinet. She fills them with ice as I grab the soda from the fridge.

"Do you want to eat in front of the TV?" she asks.

"Sure, that's fine." I grab some plates and napkins.

She takes a slice of pizza. "Thanks for dinner. I was starving."

We bring our plates and glasses of soda to the couch. I hand her the remote. "You're my guest so you can pick what we watch."

"Seriously?" She shakes her head. "You are way too sweet. I can't believe you're still like this after being here a year."

I shrug. "I'm just being nice. That's all."

She flips through the channels, stopping on a movie. "Look. It's one of those made-for-TV romance movies. These are so bad and yet for some reason I love them."

"Me too. Let's watch it."

After a few minutes, we both say, "Love triangle."

She laughs, pointing at the screen. "I knew as soon as that guy got hired at the restaurant."

"I know. He was totally flirting with her."

"Why do these movies always have a love triangle? Most girls have enough trouble finding just one guy. Who the hell has two trying to date them?"

19

"I guess that's why it's in the movies. It doesn't actually happen in real life." The movie goes to commercial break and I turn to Shelby. "So do you have a boyfriend?"

"No." She takes a sip of her soda. "I'm not really into relationships. I just date."

"When was the last date you went on?"

"I don't remember." She picks up the remote and flips to a different channel. "I hate waiting for commercials to end."

"Was it that long ago?"

"What?"

"The last time you went on a date."

She flips back to the movie. "I don't go on many dates. Most guys are assholes. It's hard to find the good ones." Her eyes remain on the TV.

She doesn't seem comfortable talking about this. I wonder why. Maybe she's been hurt in the past and is taking a break from dating.

I kind of am too. After Adam and I broke up, I wanted to give up on dating. I didn't see the point. It could never get serious. Not once the guy found out I couldn't give him what he would eventually want. But then I thought that if a guy really likes me, maybe it wouldn't matter. Maybe he'd be okay with it.

Despite telling myself that, I still have a hard time dating. I went out with a guy from Yale last year but it didn't go past a couple dates. Then I went out with a guy who came into the museum. He's a teacher and brought his second grade class there for a tour. He was a great guy, but on our third date he told me how much he loves kids and wants at least four of his own someday. So that ended that.

It's fine. I don't need a boyfriend. I don't really have time for one anyway. I'm too busy with school and work.

Shelby points to the TV. The movie just ended and the credits are rolling. "Do you think she should've picked Luke?"

Luke is the childhood friend of the main character and part of the love triangle.

"No. She's not attracted to him. She loves him, but only as a friend."

"Yeah, you have to have chemistry with a person or it won't work."

"And if you only have chemistry but nothing else, it doesn't work either."

I've had both those scenarios. I had nothing but sparks with my first serious boyfriend but we weren't really friends. And then with Adam, we had friendship but no sparks.

"How do the right people ever get together?" she asks.

"What do you mean?"

"It just seems impossible to find someone you like as a friend but who you're also insanely attracted to. And that person just happens to live in the same town as you? And you just happen to somehow meet him?"

"When you put it that way, it *does* seem impossible."

"Maybe our perfect matches are halfway across the world and we'll never meet them."

"That's depressing."

She sighs. "Yeah. Totally."

"We need ice cream. And cookies. You want some? I had some earlier but I'm splurging tonight."

"Cookies and ice cream?" She's laughing. "You're so damn wholesome."

I'm laughing too. "Stop calling me that!"

"Okay, but can I call you Farm Girl?" She cowers like I'm going to hit her.

I playfully swat at her. "No! You can call me Rachel. That's it."

As I go to get the ice cream, she heads for the door.

"Shelby, where are you going?"

She stops, halfway out the door. "I need some alcohol. All this sweetness is making me crave a shot of hard liquor. But I'll bring over some wine for your more sophisticated palate."

"Sophisticated? I'm not sophisticated."

"You go to Hirshfield, daahling." She says it like rich people talk on TV. "That means you're sophisticated."

I shake my head, smiling, as she disappears in the hall. I like Shelby. She's funny. I can already tell we'll get along. Not just as neighbors but as friends. I don't have a lot of friends here. Last year I hung out with the people in my masters program. We'd go out for dinner or drinks but I wouldn't call them friends. More like classmates. And they all finished the program last May, so by now they've found jobs and moved away. My graduate program is only supposed to be a year, but because I had to work, I wasn't able to take enough classes to finish on time.

"Sorry, I only have beer." Shelby appears with a six-pack.

"Beer doesn't go with ice cream."

"Then we'll eat our ice cream and then have the beer. It needs to chill anyway." She puts it in my fridge, then pulls out a pager. She checks it and her face drops, her eyes glazed over.

"What's wrong?"

She snaps out of it. "Nothing."

"Why do you have a pager?"

"My mom made me get one. I'm not home much and she likes to be able to reach me."

And I thought *my* mom was overprotective. I'd hate it if she made me bring a pager with me everywhere I go.

"So what should we watch next?" she asks. "Do you have any movies?"

"Yeah, in the basket next to the TV."

She walks over there and I notice the tension in her body, the stiffness of her shoulders. Whoever paged her must've been someone she didn't want to hear from. Maybe an ex?

As she's looking through the movies, her pager goes off again. She checks it and her body becomes even more tense.

"Shit," she mumbles.

"What happened?"

She comes back to the kitchen. "I have to go."

"What about the ice cream?" I point to the two bowls which are piled high with ice cream and crumbled cookies.

She picks up the spoon and takes a big bite. "I love it, but I can't eat it right now. Can you put it in the freezer and I'll have it tomorrow?"

"Um, sure."

"Thanks for the pizza. I'll pay for the next one. I'll see you later."

She races out the door. I check the clock. It's after ten. Where would she be going this late? And why did she react that way when she got paged? Her hand was shaking when she picked up the spoon to eat her ice cream. Something's going on with her.

CHAPTER FOUR

PEARCE

My attention drifts as my father drones on about a contract dispute we're having with one of our distributors. I'm sitting in a board room with eight other men, all of whom are at least thirty years older than me. But as the owner's son, I'm allowed to sit in on these meetings. Actually, 'allowed' would imply I want to be here. 'Forced' is a more accurate term.

I have zero interest in chemicals, or the manufacturing or distribution of them. But that's the business we're in and therefore I'm expected to be part of it and someday take it over. The last thing I want to do is run my father's company but I don't have a choice. Even if my father let me out of my obligation, the secret organization I belong to would force me to run the company.

Since my father and I are members, the organization is given full access to the products we produce. They can take whatever chemicals they want and use them for whatever purposes they choose. Sometimes we're told what those purposes are and sometimes we're not. It's not our place to ask and so we don't.

If anyone other than my father or me were to run Kensington Chemical, they'd find out what was going on and wouldn't allow it to continue. That's why the company must stay in the family, but I'm not planning to have children so when I'm gone, another one of the members will have to take it over.

"I'm not negotiating with him any further," my father says to Richard, the man sitting next to me. "Tell him those are the terms.

And if he doesn't agree, tell him our relationship ends when the contract ends."

"But he's our only option in the Southwest," Richard says. "And he knows that, which is why he's playing hardball."

My father slams his fist on the table. "I am NOT backing down. You force him to agree to our terms or you're fired!"

The men at the table look at my father with fear in their eyes. Richard is too afraid to speak. I'm the only one who's relaxed, making notes on a legal pad. I'm used to my father acting this way and his employees should be used to it too, but from their reaction they're clearly not.

"What are his demands?" I ask Richard.

He pauses like he's afraid to answer, but then says, "He wants us to contribute to his insurance costs. The costs to insure trucks transporting hazardous chemicals are extremely high and continue to go up every year."

I turn to my father. "It doesn't seem that unreasonable of a request."

My father shoots me a look to keep quiet. He'll yell at me later for this. I'm never supposed to undermine his authority, especially in front of other people. But if I'm going to get any respect at this company, I need to start sharing my opinions and ideas. I can't just sit in these meetings and never say anything.

"We could offer to pay twenty percent of his insurance costs," I say. "But in return, he needs to find us however many new customers it will take to cover our costs for the insurance. Perhaps we could do more than cover our costs. Perhaps we could make money on this."

The room is silent. My father lets the silence continue for several very long moments, then directs his attention to the CFO, who's sitting at the end of the table.

"Cavenaugh, run a cost-benefit analysis of the scenario Pearce just described. Get it back to me within the hour." He looks at the man next to Cavenaugh. "Saunders, I need a detailed breakdown of our sales and profits in the Southwest and a timeline of when our contracts expire." Lastly, he looks at Richard. "Don't think this means you'll keep your job. Pearce has just bought you some time. If we decide to move forward with this, you'll need to get the distributor to agree to our revised terms. If he doesn't, you'll be out on the street." He stands up. "Pearce, come with me."

I follow him out of the room and down the hall to his office. When we get there I remain standing, prepared for the fight we're about to have. I know he's furious with me, but I had to say something in that meeting. I can't continue to work here and never offer my opinion. I can't remain quiet until my father retires and then take over as CEO. Nobody will ever listen to me.

He closes the door and walks over to the window, his back to me. "That was an interesting approach you took just now. Offering your opinion when it wasn't solicited."

"I simply asked a question and provided an opinion on the matter. It was just a suggestion. The final decision on the matter is still yours."

"It was a viable suggestion. One that deserves to be considered." He turns to face me, his eyes narrowed. "That said, you will never again challenge me in front of our employees."

"I wasn't challenging you. I was—"

"I am NOT done speaking!" He steps closer to me. "You caught me off guard and I do not tolerate such behavior. I will not be made to look like a fool! I am the owner and CEO of this company and my authority will not be challenged! Especially by some inexperienced child."

"I am not a child. I'm a grown man with an MBA from Harvard. I'm not stupid and I'm not going to act like I am. I have ideas for how to make this company better and I'm not going to wait until you're retired to offer up those ideas."

My father takes a deep breath, trying to calm down. He doesn't like showing emotion, even anger. He thinks doing so shows a lack of self control and he's a man who has to be in control. So when he *does* show anger, it means he's beyond furious. But right now, he's not at that point.

"If you have something to share," he says. "An idea. A proposal. I am open to hearing it. But you will not offer it up in a public setting. You will discuss it here, in my office, or in another private location."

"If I'm going to be CEO someday, I need to start earning some respect, not just with our employees, but with our clients and the industry as a whole. And I'll never gain that respect if you don't allow me to share my opinions or recommendations with others. I need to own those. I need people to know they came from me."

He ponders that for a moment, then says, "Going forward, you will offer up any and all thoughts and ideas with me privately. If I agree to them, we will discuss ways to present them in a public setting that will not harm my reputation or undermine my authority. If I choose to present them as my own, I will. And you will not say otherwise. Do you understand?"

It's not what I want but it's a start. At least now I'll get credit for a few of my ideas.

"Yes. Understood."

"Tomorrow we will meet for lunch in the private dining room and go over any other suggestions you have."

He never asks if I'm available. He always just schedules things as if my time is his.

"I can't tomorrow. I'm speaking at Yale over the noon hour."

"Why are you speaking at Yale?"

"They asked me to take part in their lecture series. They asked several of their alums, all from different fields."

"What is the topic of your lecture?"

"Ethics in business and how they've evolved over time."

He laughs, but it's a short laugh. He normally doesn't laugh. "Ethics. Interesting."

He says that because our company lacks ethics. We cheat and lie and do whatever else we have to do to make money.

"Good for you, son." He takes a seat behind his desk. "That will be good PR for us. Make them think we're following the rules. When these students go out in the real world, they'll learn for themselves that having ethics is the fastest way to put your company out of business."

"Yes, well, I need to get back to work." I leave while he's still in a halfway decent mood. I didn't expect that to go so well. He

27

seemed to agree that I need to start taking a stand at work, making my opinions known.

My father rarely agrees with me. Or if he does, he tries to hide the fact that he agrees with me. To him, agreeing with me means he's giving up control and he never gives up control. That's why he made those conditions, telling me I had to meet with him privately before I presented my ideas in public. But earlier at that meeting, I took charge. I did what I wanted to do, despite knowing there would be consequences. It was a small victory for me. I stood up to my father. And I won.

It felt damn good. I finally felt like I was my own person for once instead of just Holton Kensington's son. It felt good to challenge him. And to win. I need to do that again.

I replay that meeting in my head and it gives me such an adrenaline rush that I can no longer sit at my desk. It's 5:30 and I'd normally be at work until eight or nine, but tonight I need to get out of here and celebrate my small but important victory.

I drive down to Westport to one of my favorite seafood restaurants.

"Would you like your usual table, Mr. Kensington?" the hostess asks when I arrive.

"Yes, but I'm going to have a drink in the bar first."

"Of course." She smiles. "Go ahead."

The restaurant is busy for a Tuesday night so I'm surprised she's letting me have the table without a reservation. It just shows the power that comes with being a Kensington.

"Scotch, please," I tell the bartender. "Neat."

He nods like he already knows. I don't usually sit in the bar but I've seen this bartender before. He's a man about my age. I've noticed he never looks directly at me. He always seems nervous around me. I don't know why.

"Pearce Kensington." I hear a woman's voice and feel her hand on my shoulder.

I turn to see a woman slightly older than me wearing a black dress and extremely high heels. Her blond hair is cut short, outlining her petite face.

"Yes. And you are?"

"Rielle Hanniford. Future CEO of The Hanniford Group."

I smile at her confidence. "Is that so?"

The Hanniford Group is a very successful investment firm, headquartered in Greenwich. Rielle's father is the CEO and she has three older brothers who want the position when he retires. I met her brothers at a party in the Hamptons a few years ago but I've never met Rielle.

She takes the chair next to me at the bar. "Are you doubting my abilities?"

"Not at all. Is your father retiring soon?"

"He's considering it. He'd like to get into politics."

"In what capacity?"

"He's hoping to run for president."

"That's ambitious." I take a drink. If she only knew what a waste of effort that would be, she could save her father a lot of time and money.

"We're an ambitious family." Her leg brushes against mine. "We set the bar high and go after what we want, which is why I plan to take over as CEO."

"You'll have to compete with your brothers for that. I've heard they're very competitive."

"Too competitive for their own good. That's why I'll overtake them and get the company. I'm also much more persuasive with clients." She rubs my arm and smiles.

I turn toward the bar, swishing my scotch around in my glass. "My investment needs are already taken care of."

"Are your other needs being taken care of?"

I take a drink. I've barely been here five minutes and I'm already being offered sex. Another perk of being a Kensington.

She's still waiting for an answer so I say, "I don't do relationships."

"Good. Because I don't either." She waves the bartender over. "Scotch and water."

He pours the drink, and as he does, I consider her offer. The safe thing to do is to stick with the girls who've been pre-approved. The ones who work for us. But I know plenty of members who go outside the pre-approved list. And tonight, I feel like trying something new.

I swig my scotch. "Let me see your ID."

"What?" She laughs. "What are you talking about?"

"I need to know you are who you say you are. I need your ID before we continue."

"Are you serious?"

I'm a person who takes risks but I'm not stupid. For all I know, this woman could be a prostitute or someone trying to get money or trying to get pregnant so she can get money later on.

I wait for her to get her wallet out. She shows me her driver's license and the ID badge she uses to access her father's office building. It has her name and photo on it.

"Happy now?" She pretends to be offended but I think she's turned on. Some women might think I'm an ass, but a lot of women like a man who says what he thinks.

I don't play games with women. I tell them what I want and leave no room for interpretation. If they don't like it, they can leave. I'm not looking for a girlfriend or a wife. This is just two people meeting each other's needs.

"Let's go." I toss a fifty on the counter, then stand next to Rielle, grasping her elbow as I lean over to talk in her ear. "I don't like to wait."

She smiles as I help her off the barstool. We leave the restaurant and go out to our cars. I follow her to her place instead of mine. I don't want her knowing where I live, and going to her place will be another check to see if she's a Hanniford. When we arrive, I find she lives at the Hanniford estate, but in a guest house, not the main house.

"Was this another test?" she asks as I get out of my car. "Going to my place instead of yours?"

"You can never be too careful."

We walk into her house, which is large for a guest house. It's decorated in all white. White walls, white chairs, a plush white rug, and an overstuffed white couch. It's too much white.

"Can I get you anything?" She's standing in front me, loosening my tie. "Maybe another scotch?"

"I'm not here to drink." I take my suit jacket off and toss it on the back of the couch. I spot the master bedroom in the back. "Let's go."

"You're all business, aren't you?"

I lead her to the bedroom, and once we're there I remove the rest of my clothes before Rielle attempts to do it. I don't like women undressing me. It's too intimate. Same with kissing. I try to avoid it whenever possible, which isn't a problem when I'm with one of the associates. They'll go along with anything. But Rielle will expect a kiss.

She turns around and I unzip her dress. Underneath she's wearing very expensive lingerie. I know because we buy the same lingerie for the associates. The members don't want them looking like cheap hookers so we provide them with high-end lingerie and clothes that are only to be worn with us.

Rielle turns back to me and reaches up to kiss me as I slip her lingerie off. She has a great body but her breasts are definitely fake. I don't think I've ever been with a woman who didn't have fake breasts, other than Kristina, but I don't count her.

Rielle is giving me hard, frantic kisses, her tongue whipping around in my mouth. She's an awful kisser. And I'm tensing up the longer this continues. I don't kiss, and I don't like *being* kissed, especially by someone who doesn't even know how to do it.

I need to move things along so I pick her up and set her on the bed. The condom is already in my hand. I put it in my pants pocket before I got out of the car so I wouldn't have to dig through my wallet later. I always provide the condoms. I don't want a woman making holes in a condom in the hopes of getting pregnant. This happened to one of the members years ago, which is why my father taught me to bring my own condoms.

I rip the packet open and put it on.

"Pearce, not yet." Rielle pouts, which I find annoying. "You've barely kissed me."

She's needy. I hate needy. If I'd known this about her, I wouldn't have come here. I consider leaving, but I could really use this right now.

31

"I can't help what you do to me," I say, boosting her ego. "I can't hold back any longer."

She smiles. "Then go ahead."

I put myself inside her, moving slowly to give her time to warm up. We had a deal and we both need to get pleasure out of this. I reach down and touch her. But she pulls my hand away and yanks me closer, her nails digging in my back, her legs circling my waist. She starts telling me to go faster, so I do, and before I know it she's done. Either she faked it or she's really fast at getting off. I wait for her to remove her fingernails from my back, then finish what I came here to do.

The sex was okay. Nothing great. Then again, when you're used to doing it with professionals you have higher expectations.

"That was incredible." Rielle picks up my arm and settles herself beneath it, her body pressed against my side. I don't like it. Again, it's too intimate. I came here for sex, not to cuddle. I'm not the type to lie in bed and hold a woman in my arms. When the sex is over, I get up and leave. Or if I'm with an associate, she knows to leave when it's done. Except for Sophia, who didn't follow protocol.

"I need to go." I take my arm back and get out of bed.

She scrambles to get up, the sheet catching on her legs. "Why don't we have dinner, then do this again later?"

"I can't," I say, pulling on my pants. "I need to prepare for a meeting I have tomorrow."

I'm now regretting this. It wasn't worth it. Rielle's looking at me like I'm an ass for leaving. It's wrong for her to do that. I was up front about what this was and she can't go and change the rules after the fact.

As soon as I'm dressed, I go back out to the living room.

Rielle follows me, wearing a white robe. "Can I give you my number?"

"I told you I don't do relationships." I pick my suit jacket off the chair and slip my shoes on.

"Okay. Then, goodbye. Have a nice life."

She looks down at the floor. She wants me to feel sorry for her, hoping that'll make me agree to see her again. Girls did this to me in college and I fell for it several times. But I'm smarter than that now. Rielle knew what this was.

"Goodbye, Rielle." I leave and go straight to my car.

I'm famished from missing dinner earlier, so I stop at a restaurant, quickly eat my meal, then go back to my loft.

This is not how I wanted this evening to go. I was supposed to be out celebrating my triumph at work, but instead I'm home, feeling guilty over something I shouldn't feel guilty about. This is why I use the service and avoid real dating and real relationships.

The next day I arrive at work early to get some things done before I have to leave for Yale. The event starts at noon, but it's a forty-five minute drive to New Haven and I don't want to be late.

I'm looking forward to this. Unlike most people, I actually enjoy public speaking. I've done it for years for various events and I was on the debate team in high school. I've never given a speech about business ethics, but I'm not worried about it. I'll just say the things that appear in all the business books about ethics. As my father said, few people actually do business ethically, but business students are still forced to learn about it.

I get to Yale at 11:45, which is later than I'd planned but I hit traffic on the way here. I set my things up at the podium, which is at the front of a large lecture hall with tiered seating. Students have already filled in the first five rows, eating their lunches as they wait for me to begin. This lecture series is open for anyone to attend but I'm assuming everyone here is in the business school.

It seems like forever since I was a student here. I've seen and done a lot the past few years. Things that have matured me far beyond my twenty-five years.

At noon, one of the business professors introduces me and I begin my speech. Ethics is a dull topic so I try to make it interesting by adding real world examples, citing companies who just recently found themselves in hot water due to ethical violations. It seems to hold the attention of the eighty or so students who are in the audience. The speech is only a half hour, followed by questions, but at 12:15 I see the door to the lecture hall open and someone walking in. People are allowed to come and go as they please, but I'm still annoyed by the interruption.

I continue talking, but my eye catches the person who walked in late. It's a young woman, probably in her early twenties. She's tall, with long, dark brown hair, wearing a yellow dress. She finds a seat near the back.

"And with the recent incidents in the accounting—" I stop when I see the woman's face. She's incredibly beautiful. Stunning. To the point that I can't seem to take my eyes off her.

Her attention is focused on the podium and I realize I'm no longer speaking.

"Pardon me." I clear my throat and take a drink of water, acting like the pause was intentional. "As I was saying, the recent scandals in the—"

She leans forward to get a pen from her bag, her hair falling over her shoulders. She tosses it back as she sits up, her eyes returning to the stage and meeting up with mine. She smiles slightly and I find myself doing the same.

Someone coughs in the front row, returning my attention to the other people in the room. Shit. I stopped again and I didn't mean to. What is wrong with me today? I normally don't lose my focus like this. And why do I feel so out of breath? It feels like my heart is racing. Maybe I had too much coffee this morning.

My gaze keeps returning to that woman, but I force myself to look away so I can finish the speech without distraction.

At 12:30 it's time for questions and a student up front raises his hand.

"Go ahead," I tell him.

"How far do you think the government should go in punishing the unethical practices of private companies?"

As he's talking, my eyes wander back to that woman and I forget the question. "Could you repeat that, please?"

He does, and this time I keep my eyes on the front row and answer him.

A few more questions are asked and then the professor says there's time for only one more. The woman in the yellow dress raises her hand. I ignore all the other raised hands and call on her to speak.

"Why do you think companies find it so hard to be ethical?"

She has a nice voice. It matches her face. Soft. Innocent. Yet alluring.

I need to respond to her question but I don't have an answer, at least not one that's politically correct.

"I don't mean to sound naive," she says since I didn't answer her. "I just find it sad that we have to teach a class and give lectures on how to act ethically. It should just be a given. Not something that has to be taught."

"I agree," I say. "But unfortunately, money is a powerful driving force of behavior, and money fuels business. When money is involved, ethics can sometimes come into question and people have trouble discerning right from wrong, so we teach ethics in order to take away any uncertainty. Of course, in the end, people will do what they want to do."

She nods and the professor approaches the podium, signaling the end of the lecture. He thanks me for my time and dismisses the students.

Everyone leaves the room except the woman in the yellow dress. She writes something down in her notebook, then stuffs it in her backpack. I gather my things and make my way to the exit, meeting her there. I hold the door open for her.

"Thank you." She smiles and something jerks in my chest. I ignore it.

"Are you in the business program?" I ask, stopping her before she walks away.

"No. I'm getting my masters in American History at Hirshfield College. But I live near here, so sometimes I have lunch on the Yale campus."

"And you're interested in business?"

She looks to the side, her cheeks blushing a little. "Actually, I had some time to kill and I noticed this lecture was open to the public so I decided to check it out." Her eyes return to mine. They're the most gorgeous shade of blue. Like a bright blue sky on a sunny day. "I'm really sorry about walking in late. I read the sign wrong. I thought the lecture started at 12:15."

"It's an informal event. People can come and go." I can't stop staring at her face. Those big blue eyes. Those high cheekbones.

Those soft pink lips. And that smile that could light up a room. Or maybe it's *her* that's lighting up the area around me. She gives off an energy that must be contagious because now I'm feeling it too.

"Well, it was very nice meeting you, Mr. Kensington." She holds her hand out.

I shake her hand and smile. "It's Pearce. I'm only 25. I'm too young to be a Mr., unless you're one of my employees. Everyone else calls me Pearce."

"You're only 25? You seem older." When she sees my expression, questioning her comment, she puts her hand on my arm. "I mean, not that you look old." She notices she's touching me and quickly takes her hand away. "It's just that you've accomplished a lot for someone who's only 25." She looks up at me and we hold gazes for a moment. "Well, I should go. Have a nice day."

She starts to leave and my heart races in my chest, like it did when I was giving my speech. What is going on with me? Do I have heart problems now?

"Wait." I take one of my cards from my suit jacket and hand it to her. "If you ever have any questions about business, feel free to call me. I'm usually at the office from six to ten so that's the best place to catch me."

"Six in the morning until ten at night? That's sixteen hours. You really work that long? Every day?"

"Yes, but I work fewer hours on the weekends."

"You work the weekends too? Wow. I feel lazy now." She's still smiling. She must smile a lot. "Thanks for the card. Bye, Pearce."

"Goodbye. Wait, what's your name?"

She turns back but continues walking. "Rachel. Rachel Evans."

Rachel. I even like her name.

I watch her walk away, waves of dark brown hair flowing down the back of her yellow cotton sundress. My eyes trail down to her narrow waist and her long tan legs.

My heart speeds up again. I think I need to see a doctor.

Or maybe I just need to see Rachel again.

CHAPTER FIVE

RACHEL

I walk outside the business building and head over to a bench to sit down. I'm completely out of breath, my heart racing from being so nervous.

I just talked to what I have now decided is the hottest man on the planet. Oh my God. The absolutely hottest. No doubt about it. I didn't know they made men like that.

According to the poster promoting the lecture series, Pearce is a graduate of both Harvard and Yale and has an executive level position at Kensington Chemical, his family's company. I don't know much about that company other than that it's very large and that the family who owns it is very wealthy. The poster also listed all the magazines Pearce has been interviewed for. He's even been interviewed on TV. So he's a smart, rich, well-known businessman. Why would someone like him talk to someone like me? I'm not saying there's anything wrong with me. I'm just saying that I can't believe a guy like that would even notice me. He's probably surrounded by rich, beautiful, powerful women every day and I'm just a plain ordinary grad student.

Why did I ask him that question? He must think I'm completely naive. I obviously know why companies aren't ethical. I only asked him that because I wanted to see what he'd say. But now I regret saying it. I should've come up with a better question.

And then I walked in late. How embarrassing! No wonder he kept staring at me when I got there. He seems very professional. I bet he's never late to anything and he probably gets very annoyed when other people show up late.

What a horrible impression I made. I usually make a much better first impression.

Oh, well. I'll never see him again. Later today, he'll have forgotten I even exist. Just as I'm thinking that, I see him walking out of the business building down the sidewalk toward the parking lot.

He's very tall. Maybe 6'5? He's also wide, built like a football player. When I touched his arm, it was solid. All muscle. I love tall, strong men. I also love dark hair, and he has thick, dark brown hair that's short, but not too short. His face is rugged, manly, with a strong jawline. And his eyes. I couldn't stop staring at them. They're this incredible shade of blue. Almost a grayish blue. Steely blue.

He's now at the parking lot and my eyes haven't left him. He's wearing a black suit that fits every part of him perfectly. I love a man in a suit. But *this* man in a suit? Too hot for words. I watch as he gets into a black Mercedes. He puts his sunglasses on and I swear, he got even hotter. I'm not even near him and my heart's still beating fast.

This is ridiculous. I never react this way over a guy. As he drives off, I get up from the bench and walk back to my apartment. I drive to Hirshfield for my afternoon class, then go to the museum and give a tour to a group of seniors from a nursing home. I talked really loud during the tour but I don't think many of them heard me. But they smiled and were really nice, so maybe they at least enjoyed the parts they heard.

When I get home I watch TV, then do the reading that was assigned for class tomorrow. But I find it difficult to concentrate because I can't stop thinking about Pearce. I'm sure he has this affect on *all* women, not just me. He's smart, sophisticated, and extremely handsome.

I use that excuse the next day as well to explain why he's still in my head. It's not just his appearance I keep thinking about, but also his demeanor. In our short encounter, he came off as being very confident, yet not in an arrogant way. It's more like he knows what he wants and goes after it, which I find to be very sexy. He kept his eyes on me the entire time we talked, while my eyes kept wandering away from his. Maybe that's why my heart beat so fast around him. Maybe he made me nervous, staring at me like that.

I take his card out and get the urge to call him. But what would I say? He's probably already forgotten about me. And why would I call him? It's not like I'd ask him out. If I did, he'd probably say no. A guy as good looking as him is probably already dating someone. Besides, I'm not looking for a boyfriend. Even though it's been over a year since Adam and I broke up, I'm not ready for another relationship. Not yet. Maybe not ever.

The week goes by and my classes get busier as the professors give out more assignments, including a group project I have to do with five other people. I don't like group projects but they're common in graduate school. The professors like to force us to work with our classmates but it's nearly impossible to find a time we can all meet outside of class. We have our first meeting on Sunday but one person doesn't show up. I'm already dreading this group project.

It's now been seven days since I went to that lecture at Yale and I'm still thinking about Pearce. I have no idea why. I have so much stuff going on I shouldn't be wasting time thinking about a guy I'll never see again. But my mind just keeps imagining those steely blue eyes, those broad shoulders, that deep voice, that confident demeanor. It gets me all worked up to the point I can't think straight.

I haven't told Shelby about him. I don't want her thinking I'm one of those girls who becomes obsessed with a guy, especially a guy I met one time and haven't spoken to since. Even so, I'm dying to tell her about him. Maybe if I do, he'll finally get out of my head.

I'm going over to Shelby's place for dinner tonight. I like spending time with her. She's funny but also sweet, in her own unique way. She tries to pretend she's tough but she's really not. I think she does the tough act because she's been hurt in the past.

We're becoming good friends, but not good enough that she'll tell me what's going on with her. We've been hanging out together every night but she keeps doing that thing where she gets up and leaves suddenly.

I've asked her repeatedly if she has a boyfriend and she keeps saying she doesn't. She won't tell me anything about her exes, either. Whenever the topic comes up, she changes the subject. I'm wondering if maybe she really does have a boyfriend and that's who keeps paging her every night. But why wouldn't she tell me that? Maybe it's not a good relationship. She always seems nervous when her pager goes off. Maybe the guy is controlling or abusive and she feels like she can't leave him. I hope that's not true. But the way she gets that panicked look and drops everything and leaves whenever her pager goes off makes me think that's what's going on.

I haven't pushed her to talk about it because I haven't told her about my own dating history so it's not really fair to force her to talk about hers. But I'm worried about her. If she's in danger I want to help her, but I can't do that if she doesn't tell me the truth. Maybe if I tell her about *me* she'll open up and tell me who keeps paging her and why she leaves almost every night.

At 6:30 I knock on Shelby's door. When she opens it I toss her a package of hotdogs to go with the mac and cheese she's making. It's the only meal either one of us can afford right now. I need to get another job. I don't get enough hours at the museum to make enough money to pay my bills. I saw a help wanted sign at the grocery store. I might go fill out an application.

"Hey." Shelby smiles and hands me a beer.

"We're drinking tonight?" I sit on the stool next to the high counter that's attached to the kitchen island.

"We're celebrating." She swigs her beer as she stirs the pasta in the pot of boiling water. She's wearing a tank top and her usual very short shorts. I wish she'd cover up more. I've seen guys on the street outside our apartment staring at her and it makes me worried for her safety, especially since she's always going out at night.

"What are we celebrating?" I ask, sipping my beer.

She shrugs. "I don't know. I just felt like having a beer and I knew Miss Wholesome wouldn't want to drink in the middle of the week unless we're celebrating something."

"Just because *I* don't drink during the week doesn't mean *you* can't. Alcohol just makes me tired and I can't be tired during the week. I have too much to do."

She grabs a box of cheese crackers from the cupboard and sets them down between us. She opens the box and pours some out on the counter. "Appetizers." She pops a few in her mouth. "Now what should we celebrate? Make something up."

I take another drink of my beer, then smile. "Okay, this is totally stupid, and not really anything to celebrate, but..."

I shouldn't tell her this. I'm embarrassed to admit I've been obsessed with some guy for the past week.

"But what?" She pops some more crackers in her mouth. "Spill it, Rachel. I can tell you're dying to say whatever it is you're about to say."

I'm still smiling. I smile whenever I think about Pearce. It's so pathetic. I don't know what's wrong with me.

"I met a guy last week," I say, my eyes on the crackers. I pick one up and eat it.

"Rachel!" She reaches over and kiddingly shoves my shoulder back. "You've been going out with some guy and you didn't tell me?"

"I'm not going out with him. That's why it's stupid to even talk about. But the thing is, I can't stop thinking about him and it's driving me crazy. I figured if I told someone about him, maybe I could get him out of my head."

"What's he look like?"

"He's hot. Really hot. As in the hottest guy I've ever seen. Guy's not even the right word. He's a man. All man. One hundred percent man. Tall. Dark hair. Steely blue eyes. Really deep voice."

She drags me to the living room to sit down with her on the couch. "Where did you meet this guy? I mean, man?"

"He was at Yale last week giving a speech as part of a lecture series at the school of business."

"And you went to the speech? You go to Hirshfield."

"Anyone can go to the lecture series. It's open to the public. I didn't plan on going. I was only there because it was a nice day out so I walked over to the Yale campus to eat my lunch."

"I thought you were a history major."

"I am, but I had some time to kill and saw this poster about the lecture series when I was walking past the business building so I decided to stop by and check it out. But I misread the time on the poster and ended up walking in fifteen minutes late, right in the middle of his speech. I was mortified."

"So this guy was the speaker? So how did you meet him?"

"We were both leaving the lecture hall at the same time and he held the door open for me and followed me out. Then he asked if I was a business major and we talked for a couple minutes. I was so nervous. I don't even remember what I said to him."

"Why were you nervous?"

"If you saw this man, you'd understand. He's the type of man women go speechless around. And he smelled good. I don't know what cologne he wears, but he smelled amazing."

"Did you ask him out?"

I look at her like she's lost her mind. "No, I didn't ask him out."

"Why not? He seems to get your panties wet just talking about him."

"Shelby! Must you be so crude?"

She laughs. "Yes. I must. My crude comments balance out your wholesomeness." She smiles at me. "So does he?"

"Does he what?"

"Make your panties wet?" She can barely hold in her laughter.

"Stop saying that!" I feel my cheeks blushing as I laugh.

"Okay, I'll stop. But you need to ask this guy out."

"Even if I wanted to, I don't know if I could. I've never asked a guy out. It seems kind of forward."

She rolls her eyes. "This isn't 1950, Rachel. It's the Nineties. Girls ask guys out all the time."

A loud sizzling noise comes from the kitchen. We both jump up from the couch.

"The pasta!" She runs back to the stove and turns the burner off. "Good enough. I'm sure it's cooked."

"You need some help?"

"No, I've got it." She drains the pasta in a colander in the sink. "Going back to this guy, I think you should ask him out."

I sit on the barstool and grab some crackers. "I'm not asking him out."

"Why not? It sounds like you have serious chemistry with him."

"He's not interested in me that way. I'm sure he has a girlfriend, or maybe several. A man like him could have any woman. He probably only dates models or actresses. He's not only hot, but he's also wealthy and somewhat famous in the business world."

"So you think you're not good enough for him?"

"It's not that. It's just that I'm not glamorous like the women he normally dates, who wear expensive clothes and jewelry and get their hair done at expensive salons."

"How do you know what type of women he dates?"

"I don't. I'm just—"

"Making assumptions when you shouldn't be. Just because he's rich and super hot doesn't mean he wouldn't go out with you. And besides, why should only rich girls get to date guys like him? We should all get a chance. I say go for it."

The mac and cheese is done now and she's divided it onto two plates. She forgot the hotdogs but that's okay. We'll have them some other night.

She sets our plates down on the counter, grabs some forks, and comes around to sit on the stool next to mine.

"So what do you think?" She hands me a fork.

"I haven't tried it yet but I'm sure it's good."

"Not about the mac and cheese. About this guy you met. Are you going to ask him out?"

I laugh. "No. I met him one time. And we talked for like two minutes."

"But you're still thinking about him. That has to mean something, right?"

"It means he's hot. That's it. Besides, I'm not looking for a boyfriend." I regret saying it. Now she's going to ask why.

She reaches over for the paper towels and rips two from the roll. She sets one next to me and takes the other one for herself. "Why don't you want a boyfriend? Are you trying to get over someone? I thought your last serious relationship was over a year ago."

"It was. It's just..." I move my pasta around on my plate. "Something happened during my last relationship and I'm not quite over it yet."

She turns to face me. "What happened?"

I set my fork down. "It's hard to talk about."

And yet I want to. I *need* to talk about it. I talked to a counselor after it happened but that didn't help. The counselor was an older man, and although he was nice, he didn't understand what I was going through. The doctor didn't help either. He just used medical jargon which made the whole thing clinical and impersonal.

"You can tell me, Rachel." She's watching me, concern in her eyes. "Whatever happened, you can tell me. I'm a really good listener."

My gaze drops to the counter. "In my senior year of college...I got pregnant."

CHAPTER SIX

RACHEL

"Oh." Shelby speaks softly. "So you gave the baby up?"

"No." I squeeze my eyes shut as a tear escapes. "I lost it. Ten weeks into the pregnancy."

"I'm sorry," I hear her say.

I open my eyes, wiping the wetness away. "There's more. I didn't just lose the baby. I—" I swallow hard and take a breath.

"What is it, Rachel?"

"After I lost it, my doctor ran all these tests and found out that I…that I can't have children."

She hesitates, then says, "I don't understand. You just said you were pregnant."

"He said I can get pregnant. I just can't carry a baby to term." More tears run down my cheeks. I haven't cried about this for months. I try not to think about it, because when I do, this is what happens. I'm filled with this overwhelming sadness and loss for what I'll never have. I love children and I wanted at least two or three of my own, so to be told it'll never happen was devastating.

Shelby gently rubs my arm. "Maybe the doctor was wrong. Doctors are wrong all the time. Like on the news, I've seen people who were in car accidents and the doctor tells them they'll never walk again but then they do."

I nod. "I know. And I've thought about getting a second opinion but I haven't been able to do it yet. I'm afraid another doctor will tell me the same thing and I don't want to hear it. I'm not ready to."

She lowers her hand back to her side. "What did your boyfriend say when it happened? I mean, when you lost the baby."

"He was sad. When we found out I was pregnant, I was six weeks along. After the shock wore off, we were both excited about it. We started preparing for it. We even got engaged a few days after we found out. I wasn't ready to get married but I felt like I should. Like it was the right thing to do. Our parents expected us to get married, and so did everyone else we knew. Adam and I grew up together. We went to the same church. Our families are friends. It's a small town with conservative values. We didn't really have a choice but to get engaged."

"So you didn't want to marry him?"

"No. He was okay as a boyfriend, but I didn't want him as my husband. I didn't want to get married. I'd already applied to graduate schools. I'd planned to move away in the fall. I wasn't even thinking about marriage. Adam and I were just dating. It wasn't anything serious. We went to the same college. We started going out the summer before our senior year and when we went back to campus in the fall, we just continued dating for the rest of the school year. We never talked about marriage and he knew I planned to go to graduate school. Then in May, two weeks before graduation, I found out I was pregnant. We weren't being careful and it just happened."

"And he broke up with you after you lost the baby?"

"No." I get up and walk to the living room, my back to her. "He broke up with me when he found out I can't have children." My voice cracks and more tears slip down my cheek.

Shelby comes over, putting her arm around me and leading me to the couch to sit down. She doesn't say anything. She's probably not sure what to say. This is awkward to talk about and she probably doesn't want to. We usually joke around and have fun. We don't talk about the serious stuff. And maybe I should've kept it that way. But it's too late now.

I wipe my face and fake a smile. "Sorry, I didn't mean to break down like that." I motion to the kitchen. "Let's go finish dinner."

Shelby has a sad look on her face. "I'm sorry, Rachel. I'm not very good at this. I never know the right thing to say." She smiles a little. "What I want to say is that your ex is a total jackass, dumping you like that. I just wasn't sure if I should say that because I don't know if you still have feelings for him."

I shake my head. "I don't have feelings for him. I used to, but I don't now. I'm just glad I didn't end up marrying him. It would've been a mistake."

"Did *he* want to get married? Or was he only doing it because of the baby?"

"He wanted to get married. He told me he bought the engagement ring a month before we found out about the pregnancy. He was going to propose in June and wanted to get married a year later. He had it all planned out and thought I felt the same way and wanted the same thing. He never even bothered to ask. He just assumed I'd forget about graduate school and give up my dreams and marry him." I pause. "When we lost the baby and found out I couldn't have children, Adam said he needed time to think. We didn't talk for a week, and when I saw him again, I was going to tell him the engagement was off. I knew I didn't want to marry him. But before I could tell him, he called off the engagement himself, telling me he couldn't marry someone who can't have children."

Tears run down my face but I quickly wipe them away and try to smile. "Anyway, that's why I haven't dated much the past year. I'm not ready to get into another relationship. I don't know if I want to. What's the point?"

"What do you mean?"

"Every guy wants children someday, and I can't give him that. If I get serious with a guy, I'll have to tell him this, and then he'll break up with me, just like Adam did."

"Rachel, that's not true. First of all, you need to get a second opinion so you know for sure whether or not you can have kids. And even if the results are the same, doctors are always finding new ways to treat stuff. By the time you're ready to have kids, maybe they can do something so that you can have them."

"Maybe." I smile at her, because she's trying so hard to make me feel better.

"And as for guys, not every guy wants kids. And if a guy really loves you, he won't care about the kid thing."

"I wish that were true, but I don't think it is." I gaze down at the floor. "Adam said he loved me. And he left me after he found out."

"Rachel." She waits for me to look at her. "Did he *really* love you?"

I hesitate, not sure how to answer. I've never really thought about that. When Adam told me he loved me, I believed him. He said the words and I assumed he meant them. But looking back, I honestly don't think he did. I never really felt like he did. Then again, I've never been in love so I don't know the signs. But I know Adam, and I know he's the type of guy who would marry me because it was the next logical step in our relationship. He's a very logical person. He acts with his brain, not his heart. He'd invested a year with me, we'd both finished college, our families knew each other, we're from the same town. To him, it made sense to marry me, then get a house and have kids. But when the kid part wasn't possible, it disrupted his plan and he no longer saw a future with me.

"No," I say quietly as I realize this for the first time.

"No, what?"

"You're right. Adam didn't love me. He just thought he should marry me."

She puts her hand on mine. "I'm sorry, Rachel. I really am."

"It's okay." I wipe my eyes and look at her. "Actually, I'm glad you asked me that. You made me see something I should've seen a long time ago. Adam never loved me."

"But someday, someone will. And when you find him, he'll want to marry you no matter what."

I smile. "I didn't know you were such a romantic."

She shrugs. "It's from watching my parents. They've been married thirty years and are still totally in love with each other. And if my mom had told my dad thirty years ago that she couldn't have kids, he would've still married her. She's the only woman for him. There's no way he would've let her go."

"Your mom's lucky. Most men aren't like that."

"Some of them are. You just need to find the right one."

"Why are you telling me all this?"

"Because I don't want you to end up an old maid with fifty cats because of some asshole who dumped you back in college." She pulls me up from the couch. "Come on. Let's eat."

I laugh. "I'm not going to end up an old maid. I'm just taking a break from dating."

"Which is a horrible idea." She drags me to the counter and takes a seat on the stool next to mine. "You're in your prime, Rachel. This is the time to find a man." She picks up her fork and waves it at me. "Look how gorgeous you are. Any guy would love to go out with you."

"Yeah, right. I hardly ever get asked out."

"Because you've closed yourself off and guys sense that. Men are like dogs. They sniff around and if they get the sense you're not interested, they move on."

I take a sip of my now warm beer. "Trust me, Shelby. Nobody's been sniffing around."

"You need to ask that guy out."

"What guy?"

"The one from the lecture series. The hot rich guy."

"I am *not* asking him out. He'd probably laugh at me."

She jumps up and goes around the kitchen counter and takes the phone book out of the drawer. "What's his name? I'll look up his number."

"I already have his number. He gave it to me that day I met him."

She drops the phonebook. "He gave you his number? That means he wants to go out with you!"

"No, it doesn't. He just gave me his business card. He probably hands them out all the time."

"Rachel." She comes back around the counter, turning me toward her. "This man is interested in you. He gave you his number because he wants you to call him."

"No. It's not like that. He just said if I have any business questions, I could call him. He was just being nice."

She steps back, her hands on her hips. "Did you tell him you're a history major?"

"Yes."

"Then he *knows* you wouldn't call him with a business question. He gave you his number hoping you'd call him for some other reason. Like for a date."

"That's not why he gave it to me. He seems like someone who's used to being the one in control, which means he's not the type of man who wants a woman asking him out."

"I'm telling you, Rachel. He wouldn't give you that card unless he wanted you to call him. He wanted to see you again. And from the look on your face, I can tell you want to see him too."

"What look on my face? I don't have a look on my face."

She rolls her eyes. "When you talk about him you get this dreamy look on your face and you can't stop smiling."

"I smile all the time."

"Not like that." She points to my face. "That's a different kind of smile and you only do it when you talk about this guy. You need to ask him out. Then you'll know for sure why he gave you that card, and if you find out he's not interested, you'll be able to stop thinking about him."

"Hmm." I chew on my lip and look off to the side. "It's not the worst idea. But instead of asking him out, maybe I could take a less direct approach. Like maybe invite him to have coffee. Tell him I'd like to learn more about what he does at his job. That's kind of like asking him business questions but more personal. And honestly, I *am* interested in his job and his family's company. I've never met anyone who runs a company that large. Well, his father runs it, but he'll probably take it over someday."

"So you're going to ask him out?"

"Yes, but it's not a date. It's just two people having a conversation at a coffee shop."

"Call him right now. You can use my phone."

"I'm not calling him now. We need to eat. I'm starving."

We reheat our food in the microwave and finish our dinner. Afterward, as we're cleaning up, I notice Shelby's pager on the counter. I wonder if that guy's going to page her again tonight. I guess I shouldn't assume it's a guy but why else would she leave late at night like that? It has to be for a guy.

As I'm putting the plates away, I say, "So do you want to go out Friday night? Maybe to a club or something?"

I never go to clubs. I don't have money for drinks and even if I did, I don't drink much. But I'm thinking if we go out, maybe Shelby will meet someone and forget about this guy who keeps paging her every night.

She dries her hands on the dishtowel. "I can't imagine you at a club."

"Why?" I point my finger at her. "And don't you dare say it's because I'm a wholesome farm girl."

She laughs. "That's exactly what I was going to say."

I shake my head, smiling. "Do you want to go or not?"

"Why would you want to go to a club?"

"Because you might meet someone there."

"Yeah. Guys who are drunk or high and looking for a quick hook-up in the bathroom."

That's probably true. The few times I've been to a club, they did seem to be filled with people just looking to hook up.

"How about someone at work? Is there anyone you're interested in?"

"Why are you trying to find me a guy?"

"I just thought you might want to go on a date. If you're pushing *me* to go on one, *you* should have to go on one too. You said it's been a while. By the way, why's it been so long? I'm sure you get asked out a lot."

"I do, but I turn them down. The guys I attract don't want to date me. To them, I'm just a one night stand. That's it."

"Then you're dating the wrong guys. Why don't you try dating one of the Yale guys? Start having lunch on campus. Guys are always hanging out on the benches there between classes."

She rolls her eyes. "Yeah, that's hilarious."

"Why?"

"Rachel, I have a GED. A Yale guy is not going to date a girl with a GED."

"And a rich, successful businessman is not going to date a farm girl from Indiana. But you still told me to ask him out."

"Our situations are not at all comparable. You're in grad school at a fancy private college. It doesn't matter where you grew up. You're smart and successful and you have a future. The only thing you don't have is money. And that's not enough of a reason for this guy to turn you down."

"Shelby, why won't you date?" I ask cautiously. "Is it because you're already seeing someone?"

She wipes down the counter with a paper towel. "What makes you think I'm seeing someone?"

"Because you disappear all the time at night. And sometimes I don't hear you get home until three or four in the morning."

She throws the paper towel down on the counter. "Are you my babysitter now? Waiting up all night to see when I get home?"

"No. But the walls are thin and I can hear the door open and close. It wakes me up."

She crosses her arms over her chest. "Then I'll be sure to be quieter next time."

"Shelby, I don't care about the noise. I'm just worried about you. If some guy is making you do things you don't want to do, or hurting you, or threatening you if you leave, then—"

"What are you talking about?" She storms into the living room. "Nobody is making me do anything! Would you just drop it?"

I follow her. "I'm just trying to help. There's a women's center near campus. They have people there who could help you get away from this guy. You can't let him control you like this."

She puts her hand up. "Okay, stop. There is no guy. Nobody is controlling me or abusing me."

"Then why do you keep leaving at night? And why do you have a pager?"

She hesitates. "Because my mom needs to be able to reach me." She turns away but I go around to face her.

"Why? I don't understand."

She sighs. "My dad is sick, okay? He has cancer. It's terminal. They can't do anything for him so he's at home and he needs constant care. Sometimes my mom needs a break, especially at

52

night, so I go over there and keep an eye on my dad so she can sleep."

Now it makes sense why Shelby always gets nervous and panicked whenever her pager goes off. She thinks it's her mom paging her to say something bad happened to her dad.

I take her to the couch to sit down. "Shelby, I'm so sorry. Why didn't you tell me?"

"Because I like to pretend it's not happening. My dad and I are really close and I'm not ready for him to go, which is selfish of me because he's in a lot of pain and it'd probably be better if he passed away." Two big tears roll down her cheeks. "But I don't want him to. I'm not ready."

I reach over and hug her. "I'm so sorry. I had no idea you were going through all this. Can I do something? Anything you need. Just tell me."

She pulls away. "I need you to act normal. Pretend you don't know what's going on. I can't be sad and depressed twenty-four hours a day. I'm serious, Rachel. I can't do it. It's too much. Having you as a neighbor has been great because you're funny and you smile constantly and laugh all the time. And although your constant need to hug me can be annoying, I've learned to look past it. We all have our flaws." She smiles.

"Hey!" I sit up straight. "Hugging is not a flaw."

"It is when you can't control it."

"I *can* control it."

"No, you can't. You hug *everyone*. People you don't even know. Is that some Midwest thing? Because I'll be honest with you, people here will think you're crazy for doing that."

"I do not hug people I don't know."

"You hugged the mailman yesterday!"

"Because he delivered that package from my mom. She sent me homemade cookies and I was excited when the box arrived."

"Then you call and thank your mom for sending it. You don't hug the mailman."

"He's old and he had to carry that box up three flights of stairs and I thought he could use a hug."

She laughs. "I swear, you are just too damn sweet. I've seriously never met anyone like you."

I put my hand on her arm. "Are you sure you're okay?"

"What did I just say? You're supposed to act like I never told you this. Let's just watch TV."

"Okay, but if you ever need anything, just ask. Or if you just need to talk, I'm here. I kind of know what you're going through."

"Your dad had cancer?"

"My sister did. My twin sister." It's another topic I avoid talking about. Another painful memory from my past. But if it comforts Shelby in any way, then I'm willing to share it. "My sister had leukemia and she died when we were six." I blink away the tears and take a breath. "Even though I was young, I still knew what was happening, and it killed me to watch her go through that. And then to lose her. She was my other half and then she was gone. I don't even like talking about it, but I thought it might help you to know I've been there. I know it's not the same situation, but still. I understand how hard it is…and how much it hurts. So if you ever want to talk, I'm here."

"Thanks."

She seems uncomfortable so I leave her alone and don't say any more. She flips through the channels, looking for something to watch. I wish she'd let me help, but then again, I don't know how I could. When my sister died, there was nothing anyone could say or do to make it better. And it took a really long time to get past it.

Shelby and I watch a movie and when it's over I go back to my apartment. I need to get some reading done for class. But first, I take Pearce's business card out of my backpack. On one side is the company logo and on the other side it reads as follows.

Pearce Kensington
Director of Strategic Development
Kensington Chemical, Inc.

Below that is his number. Should I call it? I wasn't going to. I only told Shelby I would so she'd stop bugging me to ask him out. But now I think I might do it. I really want to see him again.

Maybe it's too late. I should've called him right away. Will he think it's weird if I call him a week later?

I take the card and go over to the phone in the kitchen. I'm doing this. I'm calling him before I change my mind.

The phone rings at least seven times and I'm about to hang up, but then he answers. "Hello."

"Pearce?" My throat is already dry and I've only said one word. Why am I so nervous?

"Yes. This is Pearce Kensington." He sounds very serious. Maybe this was a bad time to call. "Can I help you?"

"You might not remember me, but we met last week at Yale. You gave me your card and—"

"Rachel. Rachel Evans." His tone lightens, the seriousness gone. "The girl who arrived at 12:15. How could I forget?"

I cringe. That's what he remembers me for? Being late? I should just hang up now.

"Yeah. Again, I'm really sorry about walking in so late."

He laughs, a short but deep laugh. "I was just kidding. How are you doing, Rachel?"

He's asking how I'm doing? I wasn't prepared for that. I thought he'd just sit quietly on the phone while I asked him out and then he'd tell me no, but in a nice way. He seems nice.

"I'm okay," I answer.

"How are your classes going?"

"They're going well. I meant to call you earlier but I've been busy with school and work."

"Where do you work?"

"At a small museum near campus. I sit at the front desk and also give tours."

"I would love to take part in one of these tours. Do you give them every day?"

He wants to go on one of my tours? Is he serious? The man has probably been to museums all over the world and he wants to go to my teeny, tiny museum that hardly has a collection?

"The tours are just for special groups, like school groups or senior outings. They're usually not every day."

"I see. So could I arrange for a special tour? I'd be happy to make a generous donation to the museum."

"The tours are free, but yes, you could certainly make a donation if you'd like. We limit the tours to twenty people. How many people do you plan to have in your group?"

"Two. Or if you don't count yourself, then one."

"Oh. So you're saying you want a private tour?"

Did that sound dirty? Like I was implying something? God, I hope not. But for some reason it sounded dirty when I said it.

"Yes. I would like a private tour with you as my tour guide. I'm available this Friday at 4 p.m. Would that work?"

This is happening so fast I can't think. Did he just ask me out?

"Rachel, are you still there?"

"Yes. Four would be perfect."

"Excellent. Now, as for the reason you called, did you have a business question you've been dying to ask?" He sounds like he's kidding again. When I met him at Yale, he didn't seem like the type of person who jokes around. He was so serious. But I like this side of him. It makes me feel not so nervous.

"Yes. I mean, no, I don't have a business question, at least not a specific one. I called because I thought maybe we could meet for coffee. I'd love to learn what you do and learn more about your company."

"You're interested in the company? You do know we make chemicals, right?"

He's joking again and this time I laugh. "Yes. But I'm still interested in learning more about it. And about you."

I cringe again. I shouldn't have said that last part. It sounded like I was flirting and I'm not. Okay, maybe I am, but I shouldn't be because I don't know him and he may not like me that way. But he did invite himself on a tour with me, so maybe he *does* like me that way.

"I would very much like to have coffee with you, Rachel. Would you like to meet tomorrow?"

"I would very much like to meet tomorrow, Pearce." I say it in the same formal tone he used.

He chuckles. "Very well, then. Tomorrow it is. Shall we meet at six?"

"Sure. There's a coffee shop downtown called Barista's. It's not as crowded as the ones near campus."

"Yes, I've been there."

"Are you coming from work? Because if it's too far to drive, I can meet you somewhere else."

"No, it's fine. New Haven is only a forty-five minute drive from the office."

"That's a long ways. I could meet you halfway."

"Don't worry about it. I don't mind the drive. I'll see you then."

"Wait. I thought you said you worked until ten at night."

"Not when I have something better to do. Goodnight, Rachel."

He hangs up and I set the phone down. I'm sweating from being so nervous, or maybe it's because his voice got me all hot inside. His voice is so deep and sexy. I could listen to it for hours.

I can't believe I just did that. That I asked a guy out. I've never done that before. But I'm glad I did. There's something about this guy that I really like. And it's not just his looks. It's something else that I can't identify. It's like when you meet someone and you instantly click, kind of like when I met Shelby. I had a feeling we'd be friends and I was right. So maybe I'm right about Pearce too. Maybe this coffee date will lead to something more.

What am I thinking? It can't be more. I'm not looking for a relationship. This is just a date. Not even a date. Just coffee. We're just going to talk business. That's all this is.

CHAPTER SEVEN

PEARCE

I don't date. And yet I have a date tonight. Technically it's not a date. Rachel called me last night, saying she wants to meet for coffee. She said she's interested in the company. Maybe she's hoping to get an internship here, although she's getting a degree in history so that doesn't make sense. So why does she want to meet?

My mind lists out all the possible reasons and they all come back to money. I don't like that I think that way, but my family constantly has scam artists trying to get our money so my mind naturally goes there.

Trust no one. Even those closest to you. I've learned that's how I have to live in order to survive. I don't even trust my own parents, especially my father.

So as much as I'd like to believe Rachel just wants to talk over a cup of coffee, I'm wary of her motives. I have to be. I don't know this woman, and even if I did, I still couldn't trust her.

Trust no one. It's all I know.

It's 2:30 and I just got out of a meeting and am now sitting at my desk reviewing a stack of contracts. But I can't seem to stay focused. As soon as I start reading I get distracted, my thoughts wandering to Rachel. Her bright blue eyes. That warm smile. She's been in my head for a week now and I don't understand it. I met her one time. Yet I haven't been able to stop thinking about her.

This is not good. I can't let myself be distracted by a woman. And I never have been. Until now.

I focus on the paperwork in front of me. Line after line of legal jargon that all sounds the same. So Rachel works at a museum. I don't think she told me the name of it. I wonder how long the tour will be. She seemed surprised I wanted a tour. *I'm* surprised I asked her for one, but I really want to see her again and that was the only excuse I could come up with when she called.

I didn't think she'd call. Many women are intimidated by me, or more likely my wealth or the Kensington name. But Rachel didn't seem to be. She seemed a little nervous at the start of the call last night but then she relaxed.

I wonder why she took so long to contact me. I gave her my card a week ago, and when she didn't call after a few days, I assumed she never would. That's when I made a conscious effort to stop thinking about her, but I couldn't. As hard as I tried, she continued to consume my thoughts.

When she called me, I was surprised but also pleased. Just hearing her voice again caused that strange, rapid heart movement again. I should really see a doctor. That can't be normal.

Dammit! My mind is wandering again. I need to stay on task. I go to the break room and get a cup of coffee, then return to my desk, grab a pen, and begin marking up the contract in front of me.

I check my watch. It's only 2:45. This day is going by very slowly. Usually I'm so busy I don't even notice the time, but today I'm acutely aware of it, wishing it were later. Wishing it was six o'clock.

My cell phone rings, which can only mean one thing. It's from them. Nobody else calls that phone. Nobody knows the number except my fellow members. Each of us were given a cell phone so we could be contacted at all times. I try to keep the phone hidden because cell phones are such an oddity that letting people see I have one causes too many questions. I'm sure someday everyone will have a cell phone, but as of now, they're rare, so tend to draw attention.

"Yes, it's Pearce," I say as I answer.

A recorded voice says, "Input your member number."

I type it into the phone; 1479.

The voice speaks again. "Meeting notice. This Saturday, 11 a.m. Eastern Standard Time. Exit 128. This concludes the call."

The phone goes silent and I hide it back in my suit jacket. It's been a month since we had a meeting so I assumed we'd be having one soon. It's unfortunate it's this Saturday. I have so much work to catch up on that I had planned to be here all of Saturday as well as Sunday. But you're not allowed to miss the meetings. They would punish you if you did.

The 'they' I'm referring to is the organization. The secret society I belong to. It's extremely exclusive. We have members located around the world, but the majority of them are in the United States. Although the organization doesn't consider itself a secret society, that's exactly what it is. We operate in secrecy, cloaked among the masses while working behind the scenes to control how countries operate. How money exchanges hands. How currencies are valued. How leaders are chosen. We control how the world functions, or at least we think we do.

The organization was formed in the 1700s when European investors realized the potential for immense wealth in the land that would soon become the United States of America. The people making these investments were already wealthy but they wanted more. More money but also power. Power that would come from controlling the rich and vast resources of this new land, and the transport of those resources. They wanted to be the first to develop the cities, dictating the architecture and planning the layout of the streets. They wanted to build the companies that would attract people to live in these cities, and once the cities were built, they wanted to establish the newspapers that would control the messages they wanted to convey.

Only a select few can afford to do all these things, and those people became the founding members of the organization. Over time, other members were added based on how they could benefit the group. The organization recruited the owners of large companies in different industries—oil, electricity, railroads, banking—so that the group's power was diversified. As these industries became more regulated, the organization saw the need to have control measures in place within the government, so they used their money and power to get some of the members elected into Congress which caused their power and influence to grow exponentially. They could do what they wanted without government interference.

Not everyone in the government is part of the organization. If they were, we'd be found out. Politicians are constantly watched, their backgrounds studied and dissected by reporters hungry for a story. So for that reason, there are only a handful of members currently in office. But that's all you need if they're strategically placed.

Those placements include positions on key Congressional committees, such as the Appropriations Committee, which controls where the money is spent, or the Defense Committee, which controls not only our involvement in wars, but also the collection and storage of information on almost every person on the planet. Having people on the inside of these two very influential government entities has proven to be quite useful and is what has made us the most powerful secret society in the world. There's also the fact that we now control the presidency as well. This took years to accomplish but we've now successfully seated the past three presidents.

Although this group started in the United States, it grew to include members around the world because they needed their influence to reach beyond U.S. borders. World leaders were not willing to simply hand over power to this group, so it took some negotiation, specifically bribes and blackmail, to get it done. But since membership is limited to the select few families who have the proper lineage, our members in foreign countries were carefully chosen and then given positions of power in those nations.

The reason I'm a member and my father is a member is because my ancestors were some of those early investors in America. They had money, and their money allowed them to start a business. They decided to make that business the manufacturing of chemicals necessary for producing materials vital to many industries. As soon as our first plant was built, it was already overcapacity and we had to build another. And since those early days, we've just continued to grow.

Chemicals are used in many useful ways, but they can also be used in destructive ways. They can kill. Destroy things. Take down buildings. Blow up cars. Knowing this, the members saw the benefit of including a Kensington in their group. And since membership is passed down to sons, my father is a member and so am I.

Membership isn't a choice. You're a member from the day you're born, but you don't find out until you're older, usually around 20 or 21, when you're mature enough to keep a secret as great as this. My father chose to tell me when I was 16. The day he took me to New Haven and shot that homeless man was the day I learned about the organization and my membership in it.

The organization is not the real name. It's the name we use with outsiders. Freelancers. The people we hire to do the things that need to be done. Sometimes they make us do these things ourselves, but in most instances, we use a freelancer. As members, we need to keep our hands clean. We can't have anything being traced back to us.

Keeping our secrets is difficult, especially as technology continues to become more sophisticated. Hidden cameras, microphones, and other equipment could all be used against us to provide proof to the public that we exist. We've been caught many times, sometimes by accident by someone who was at the wrong place at the wrong time. When that happens, the person must be 'taken care of.' That's the phrase we use because it's more civilized than coming out and saying what actually happens to the person. The truth is that the person is killed. Murdered. By one of our freelancers.

Given what we do, you'd think some people wouldn't want to be a member, but surprisingly many people consider it an honor. It's exclusive, for one, which makes people feel special. But it also has perks, such as access to the Clinic, a secret medical group reserved for only the wealthiest and most powerful people in the world.

The Clinic has treatments and medicines that aren't shared with the masses. If they were, certain illnesses would disappear off the planet and we can't have that. Treating illness is a business. A very profitable business. And it provides a lot of jobs. In fact, many members feel we're doing the world a favor by keeping these treatments a secret. Millions of people would be out of work if these illnesses didn't exist.

I don't agree with this philosophy. I think everyone should have access to these treatments, but I would never admit that. As a member, I need to go along with their ideals. Keep quiet. Arguing with them wouldn't change anything. And as for the Clinic, I really don't know what they're capable of. What they can treat and what they can't. I don't think they can cure cancer. I think their treatments are just slightly better than what's available. At least that's what I tell myself so I'm not consumed with the guilt I would feel if I knew they really could cure a fatal illness.

Dunamis. That's the name of the group I belong to. The name is never to be spoken outside of official meetings. Even the generic name, the organization, is not supposed to be uttered to anyone but our freelancers, but I hear members say it at other times so that rule isn't always followed. But as for the real name, you'd be severely punished if you ever said it outside the company of other members.

Dunamis is the Greek word for power. Not just any power, but extreme power. Some even associate it with divine power, as in the power of God. That just shows you what the founding members thought of themselves when they named this group. They considered themselves God. Maybe not THE God but a group with god-like powers. By definition, those with dunamis have power but also strength and ability. They are capable of most anything.

So yes, the name is fitting, maybe even more so now than back then.

Despite the perks, the power, the prestige—I hate being a member of this group. Dunamis has destroyed my life. Destroyed who I am, and who I used to be before I knew they existed. They're the reason I don't have a normal life and never will. They're the reason I'll spend my life running this company I have no interest in running. They're the reason I don't sleep at night, and why I always have splitting headaches, a knotted-up stomach, and tense muscles that never relax. They're the reason I have no hope.

And they're the reason I'll never know love.

CHAPTER EIGHT

RACHEL

I arrive at the coffee shop at 5:45. I wanted to get here early because it's hard to find parking downtown and I needed to leave time to circle the block a few times to find a spot. There was no way I was going to risk being late after my late arrival at the lecture last week. Luckily, I found a spot right out front and now I'm sitting inside, waiting.

I wasn't sure what to wear so I just put on a casual summer dress. It's hot out today and the dress is lightweight and cool. It's periwinkle blue, sleeveless, and fitted on top, then flares out into a full skirt. As I'm sitting here looking at it, I'm realizing it has kind of a retro feel, but I don't think this style ever really goes out of fashion. At least I'm telling myself that because it's too late to change and I don't have a large wardrobe to choose from. For shoes, I wore white sandals that have a slight heel. I kept my makeup simple, like I always do. Just some blush and mascara. I don't like lipstick so I don't wear it much. Plus, I think it's gross when it leaves that mark on your coffee cup.

If this were a date I might've added more makeup, but I didn't want to get too glammed up just for coffee. Glamorous isn't really my thing. I have more of a natural, girl-next door look. Pearce is probably used to a more glamorous type of woman but I'm not going to pretend I'm something I'm not. Doing so would make me uncomfortable and I'm nervous enough as it is.

Pearce walks in at 5:55. I knew he was the type of person who arrives early to everything. I stand up so he can see me. I picked a table that was off to the side so we could have privacy. I guess we don't really need privacy. This isn't a date. Or is it?

I watch as he approaches the table. He has a suit on. A dark gray one this time. His shirt is bright white and doesn't have a single wrinkle. And his tie is silvery blue like his eyes.

"Rachel. It's a pleasure seeing you again." He holds his hand out.

"You as well." I extend my hand to him, but instead of shaking it, he brings it to his mouth and kisses it, his eyes fixed on mine.

That might be the hottest thing a guy has ever done to me. It was just a hand kiss, but the way he did it was...I don't know how to describe it other than...perfect.

It was completely unexpected. I mean, who *does* that? Do guys still kiss a girl's hand? A girl they just met? Maybe, but I've never had it happen before. And although I'm sure it wasn't that slow, in my mind it seemed like slow motion. Him lifting my hand to his mouth, his lips gently kissing the top of it. And his eyes. He kept that intense gaze going the entire time.

He's now behind me, waiting for me to sit down. As I do, he slides the chair in. Again, it's perfect. Flawless. Other guys have tried this and their timing is completely off. They either push the chair in too fast and hurt my legs or push it too slowly and I almost fall off the chair.

"Were you waiting long?" he asks as he takes the seat across from me.

"Just a few minutes. I got here early. I promise you, I'm not normally late to things. Last week was an anomaly."

He smiles as he reaches over and puts his hand on mine. "Rachel. There's no need to bring that up again. I shouldn't have teased you about it. Please, forgive me."

I nod, my focus on his hand, which is still covering mine. "So you said you've been here before?"

"Yes." He takes his hand away. "I'd sometimes study here when I was a student at Yale."

"I don't come here very often but I've heard they have good cappuccinos."

"Is that what you would like?"

I glance back at the menu board. The cappuccinos are expensive. I should probably stick with coffee. "I think I'll just have coffee."

"I think you'd rather have the cappuccino. It's on me, so have whatever you'd like."

"Oh, no, you don't have to pay. I made you come all the way here to meet with me. I'm not going to make you buy my coffee."

He leans back, smiling. "I'm not buying you coffee. I'm buying you a cappuccino. Would you like anything else?"

I smile back. "No. Just the cappuccino. Thank you."

He motions the waiter over. "We'll have a cappuccino and a double espresso. Thank you."

I'm staring at Pearce across the table. Last time I saw him he was cleanly shaved, but today he has a thick five o'clock shadow that I find extremely sexy.

"Rachel, is something wrong?"

I snap to attention. "Um, no. Everything's fine."

"You're not upset that I ordered for you, are you? Some women are offended by that. That's not my intention. It's simply a habit. I'm somewhat old-fashioned. Opening doors for women, pulling out chairs, taking their coat, ordering for them at a restaurant. It's what I've been taught, but if you take offense to that, please let me know."

"I don't find it offensive. Actually, I like it. I think it's kind of romantic."

He smiles. "I suppose it could be considered romantic, couldn't it? To me, it's just basic manners."

So he's just being polite. I knew this wasn't a date. I should focus on why we're here.

"I'm sure your time is limited so we should get started. Tell me about Kensington Chemical."

"Rachel." He waits until I look at him. "You don't really want to hear about a chemical company, do you?"

"Yes. I mean, I don't have specific questions, but it's your family's business and I'm sure you're very proud of it and like talking about it."

"I don't like talking about it. I spend so much of my life there that I need a break from it. So unless you really want to hear about it, I'd prefer to talk about something else."

"I *would* like to hear about it. I've never met anyone who owns a business of that scale. But maybe you could tell me about it some other time. Not that you plan to meet with me again, but—"

"I would be happy to meet again. That will give me time to prepare something interesting to say about the company, because at this moment, I can't think of anything."

He's doing that thing again where he's joking, but it's subtle. He's been smiling since he got here but it's a partial smile, not a full one. It's somewhat mysterious, keeping me guessing as to whether he's being serious or kidding around.

The waiter brings our drinks. I see the foam on my cappuccino and realize it's going to be all over of my face when I drink it. I didn't even think about that.

Pearce sips his espresso elegantly, like he's had lessons in it. Then he sets his cup down. "I should mention that your earlier statement about my time being limited is true. But tonight I've taken the evening off and it would be my pleasure to spend it with you. Unless you have somewhere you need to be."

He wants to spend his evening with me? Drinking coffee? So I guess this *is* a date.

"Perhaps I should explain," he says when I don't answer. "I felt rather odd meeting you here just for coffee, given that it's nearly the dinner hour. If you wouldn't mind, I would like to take you to dinner after we're done here."

"Dinner. Yes, that would be nice." I sound nervous. Why am I so nervous? I glance down at my dress. "Is what I'm wearing okay? Because I could go home and change."

His smile gets slightly wider. "What you're wearing is perfect. You look beautiful."

"Thank you." I feel my face blushing. I wasn't expecting the compliment. I barely have any makeup on and I didn't do much with my hair. I wore it down and left it in its naturally wavy state instead of blow-drying it straight.

I sip my cappuccino and feel the foam on my nose.

Before I can get my napkin, Pearce reaches over with his and blots the foam away. "Cappuccinos can be messy."

"I should've ordered something else." I blot my lips with my napkin. "This is embarrassing."

"There's no reason to be embarrassed." He sips his espresso, then says, "So tell me about yourself. Where are you from?"

"A small town in Indiana."

"I've never been to Indiana. What's it like?"

"The area where I grew up is mostly agricultural land. My parents are farmers." I glance down, my face heating up. I shouldn't be embarrassed about where I'm from or the fact that my parents are farmers, but I am, because I've found that sometimes the people here make fun of me for it.

"You're blushing," Pearce says. "Can I ask why? It's not the cappuccino this time."

I look up at him. "It's just that the people out here, at least the ones at my college, tend to judge me for growing up on a farm."

"Judge you how?"

"They just assume things. They act like I'm not as smart as them or not as sophisticated."

"Rachel, I'm not judging you," he says in a serious tone. "And I never would. People who do so are either misinformed or just plain ignorant. I'm sure none of them have even been on a farm, so making any kind of judgment regarding such matters simply highlights their ignorance."

I smile. "I've never heard it put that way. I might have to write that down and use it on one of my classmates."

"So did you like growing up on a farm?"

"Maybe we could talk about that some other time."

"You don't like talking about it?"

"It's not that. I'd just rather not talk about it tonight."

Truthfully, talking about home reminds of my overprotective mother and Adam and the pregnancy, and I don't want to think about those things. Not while I'm here with Pearce. I just met him and it's too soon to bring up such personal topics.

"Tell me about *you*," I say. "Are you from Connecticut?"

"Yes. I grew up in a rather small town along the shoreline. My parents still live there. It's about a half hour from here."

"And where do you live now?"

"I have a loft in Weston."

I've driven through Weston. It's a very wealthy area. Even an apartment would be expensive there.

I run a spoon through my cup, then tamp down the foam a little so I can drink my cappuccino without making a mess of my face. "Tell me about your parents. Do you see them much?"

"I see my father every day."

"That's right. He's your boss. Is that weird for you, or do you like it?"

He clears his throat. "I'd rather not talk about my parents."

"Maybe some other time?" I smile.

"Yes." He nods. "When you tell me about growing up on a farm, I'll tell you about my parents."

"It's a deal." I extend my hand, just jokingly, but instead of shaking it, he takes my hand in his and doesn't let go. Instead he rests our joined hands on the table like it's the most natural thing in the world. But it's got my heart beating like crazy. And yet he seems perfectly calm. He's probably been out with so many women that this is no big deal. He probably does this all the time. Holding hands with a woman he just met. He did it with complete confidence so he's clearly done it many times before.

Our hands remain joined on the table as we continue to talk. I tell him about my classes at Hirshfield and he talks about his years at Yale and before I know it, it's eight and we realize we should probably head to dinner.

We find a place a block down from the coffee shop. It's just a casual restaurant so I wasn't sure if he'd want to go there, but he did. I'm sure he's used to eating at much fancier restaurants, but he didn't act like this place was beneath him.

After we order, he says, "Are you nervous around me, Rachel?"

I hesitate. "Yes. A little."

"Is it the suit? I should've changed into something more casual. Suits can be intimidating. Too corporate."

"No, it's not the suit. I like the suit."

"Then what is it that makes you nervous around me?"

"Just the fact that you're well-known and used to being around important people and beautiful women."

That was brutally honest. Why was I so honest with him? I must be feeling more comfortable around him if I was that honest.

"And you're not important? Or beautiful?"

"I'm not saying that. It's just a different kind of—"

"Rachel." He reaches over for my hand, which is resting on the table. "You are extremely beautiful, which is why I haven't been able to take my eyes off you the past two hours. And as for your importance, *everyone* is important. While it's true that money can buy importance, it's fake and can be taken away as quickly as it's given. I've only just met you and yet I already consider you to be one of the most important people I know."

"Really? Why?"

He pauses to think, his hand rubbing his jawline. "You seem to be able to bring something out in me. A different side I honestly almost forgot was there. The less serious side. The side that isn't consumed with work. I haven't even thought about work the past two hours."

I smile. "This is your less serious side?"

"Yes. Why do you ask?"

"You still seem pretty serious."

"I'm usually far more serious. I rarely crack a smile."

"Then I guess I *am* seeing your other side because you've smiled a lot tonight."

"So what else makes you nervous around me?"

"The fact that you're so put together. The way you speak. Your clothes. Your impeccable manners."

He laughs. "The manners were instilled in me from a young age. It's merely habit now. And I knew the suit was a bad choice. I should've changed." He rubs his jawline again. "But I didn't shave so you can take some points off for that. I was going to before I left to meet with you but I forgot. My mother would die if she'd known I'd taken a woman to dinner without shaving first."

"I think you look good. You didn't need to shave."

"That's nice of you to say but I should've shaved."

The waitress arrives with our salads.

As we're eating, I say, "You're not really going on that tour on Friday, are you?"

"Why wouldn't I go?" He was about to take a bite of his salad but stops, his fork held over his plate.

"Because it's at this really tiny museum with not much of a collection. I only work there because it lets me practice giving tours and it's close to campus. I'm sure you've been to the greatest museums in the world so it'll be a waste of time for you to see this one."

"It's not a waste of time. I'm going because *you'll* be there. And I'm looking forward to this tour. How long is it?"

I don't answer. I'm still stuck on what he just said. *I'm going because you'll be there.* I guess I assumed that was the reason he was going, but I can't believe he just came right out and admitted it. That was bold. And very sexy. I admire his confidence. I'm far too shy to admit when I like someone. Instead I drop hints that guys never seem to get.

"Rachel?"

"Yes. Sorry. The tours usually last a half hour."

"If the museum doesn't have much of a collection, how do you fill a half hour?"

"I go off script and add my own hand-selected collection of historical facts I find interesting, tailoring them to the audience of course."

He sets his fork down and leans back in his chair. "And what types of audiences do you get?"

"All kinds. A lot of elementary school kids. They're my favorite. I love children. They ask the funniest questions. And then there's the high school kids, who are probably my least favorite because they don't want to be there so they don't pay attention. Sometimes we have people from a group home who have Down syndrome. Some of them don't understand what I'm saying so I try to make the tour more visual for them. I use pictures, maps, drawings, and photos instead of just talking. And

72

then the other main group is the seniors from the nursing homes. They're always super nice and smile a lot, even when I mess up."

Pearce is staring at me, not saying anything.

"Did I totally bore you just now?"

He smiles. "Not at all. I found it fascinating. So you just took it upon yourself to devise all these different tours? Catering them to each group?"

"Yes, because sometimes history can be boring. My goal is to make it less boring. And in order to do that, I need to consider what different people find interesting. For example, little kids like hearing about stuff that's gross or outrageous. Or they like hearing about what it was like being a kid a hundred years ago."

"You should've gone into business. Identifying your customers. Assessing their needs. Tailoring your product to meet those needs. Some of my fellow Harvard MBA grads can't even figure out how to do that. And yet you seem to be doing it flawlessly."

"I don't know about that, but I like what I do. And really, my goal is just to get people interested in history and wanting to learn more about it. Because as cliché as it sounds, history does repeat itself. Yet we continue to make the same mistakes over and over again. We don't learn from the past. And maybe the reason for that is because nobody wants to go back and look at those mistakes and figure out how we can avoid repeating them in the future." I pick up my water glass. "That's an idealist's view, I know. On a more realistic level, my goal is just to make people more interested in history."

He's still staring at me as I take a sip of my water. He's barely touched his salad. "You're very smart."

"Thank you." I look down and adjust my napkin in my lap.

I feel his hand on my arm. "Is something wrong?"

My eyes meet up with his again. "No. I'm just not used to getting so many compliments. You've given me a lot of them tonight."

"They're not really compliments. I'm simply stating the facts. You're beautiful. Intelligent. Hard-working. You're quite an amazing woman."

I smile. "Now you're making me blush. Let's change the subject."

We talk all through dinner and dessert. We're at the restaurant until ten, but the time went so fast I wasn't ready to leave. I finally relaxed around Pearce and found myself talking about all kinds of things, from childhood stories to current events. I never ran out of things to say and neither did he. The conversation just flowed. It was easy and natural and I didn't want it to end.

But at ten we leave and he walks me back to my car.

"I had a really great time tonight," I say as we stand by the car. "Thank you for dinner."

"Certainly. Thank you for agreeing to go with me. Forgive me for not giving you more notice."

"I'm glad you suggested it. It gave us more time to talk." I smile. "But you still didn't tell me about your company."

He nods. "Some other time."

"So I'll see you on Friday? At four?"

"Yes. I've already cleared my schedule."

"Which tour would you like?"

"What would you recommend?"

"The senior citizen tour is probably the one you'd find most interesting." I laugh when I see his face. "Not that you're old. I didn't mean it that way. Maybe I should create a new tour. The businessman tour. Then you could tell all your friends and I'd have a whole new set of customers."

"I don't want you having to do all that work. The senior tour will be fine."

"No. I'm going to make a new one just for you. I'm trying to get you to like history, remember?"

"Very well, then. I look forward to it." He pauses. "And I look forward to seeing you again."

I feel my heart race when he says it. We're standing close, our bodies almost touching but not quite. He's kept a small distance between us, probably so I wouldn't feel uncomfortable. I've learned tonight that Pearce is very much a gentleman. And I like that. These days, it's rare to meet a guy with such good manners.

74

We've been staring at each other the whole time we've been standing here. It's like we can't look away. Like we don't want to leave. I think he's waiting for *me* to, but I can't. Not yet.

With his eyes still on mine, he steps closer and slips his arm around my waist, his hand lightly gripping it. His other hand lifts to the side of my face. Then he leans down and presses his lips to mine. His lips are soft and warm, his touch gentle, and I relax into his arm that's now wrapped tighter around me. He pauses a moment, his breath over my lips. I wait for him to continue, but then I feel his hold on me loosen as he slowly backs away.

Our eyes meet and I can tell he feels it. That wasn't just any kiss. That was different. There was an intimacy there that I don't normally feel with a first kiss. Usually I don't feel much of anything with a first kiss because I don't know the person that well. And although I don't know Pearce that well, I still felt something with that kiss. Something I've never felt with anyone else. It's hard to explain in words. It's more of a feeling.

And even though he only used his lips and not his tongue, his kiss ignited a heat inside me. A desire to do more. There is serious chemistry between us. I felt it when we met at Yale that day, and then again tonight, the moment he arrived at the coffee shop. It's like there's this energy emanating off us. An attraction that's so strong that if we weren't standing in the street right now, we might end up doing things we shouldn't be doing on a first date.

"Can I escort you home?" he asks.

It takes me a moment to wake up from the aftereffects of his kiss. "Um, no. I have my car."

Obviously my mind is still not intact. We're standing right next to my car.

He smiles a little. "What I meant is, could I follow you to your place and walk you to your door?"

"Oh. No. That's not necessary."

"Are you sure?"

"Yes, but thank you for offering."

He opens my car door, but before I get in, I ask, "After the museum on Friday, are you busy?"

His lips move up into a slightly bigger smile. "Why do you ask?"

"I just wondered if maybe you'd like to have dinner afterward. But if you had plans, don't worry about it."

He lifts my chin up and looks me in the eye. "I will clear whatever plans I had. Because I would love to have dinner with you again."

"Great! Then I'll see you on Friday." I try to sound casual, but inside my heart's beating so fast I feel out of breath.

His hand is still cupping my chin, lifting my face up to his. Our gazes meet and he slowly leans down and gives me another kiss. It's a soft, gentle kiss but it sets off more sparks inside me.

He backs away. "Goodnight, Rachel."

I can barely breathe, still recovering from that kiss.

"Goodnight." I say it quickly, then get in my car. He watches as I drive off.

That was the best date I've ever been on. Pearce was kind. Generous. A good listener. A gentleman. An excellent kisser. I could go on and on.

It's only our first date and I'm already falling hard for this guy. What am I doing? This wasn't supposed to be a date. I wasn't supposed to like him this much. I was hoping we'd meet and I wouldn't like him and I'd finally get him out of my head. But now I'll be thinking about him even more.

I didn't think this would go anywhere. And maybe it won't. But I think I want it to.

CHAPTER NINE

PEARCE

I don't know what just happened. I think I just went on a date. A date with an incredibly smart, incredibly beautiful woman. This wasn't supposed to be a date. It was just going to be a conversation over coffee. But then I invited her to dinner. I hadn't planned on that, but as soon as I saw her again, I knew an hour at a coffee shop wouldn't be enough. I wanted more time with her. And even after four hours, it still wasn't enough.

Tonight was definitely a date. I haven't been on a date since college and I promised myself I would never go on a date again. At least not a real one. Why would I? I have plenty of women to fulfill my sexual needs and it's pointless to date when I know I'll eventually have to marry whoever they choose.

So what was I doing tonight? I can't be with someone like Rachel. I know this and yet I made another date with her for Friday night. And even more troubling is that Friday night now seems very far away. It's Wednesday night so it's only a day away but I already want to see her again.

I need to stop this. End it before it starts. But I can't. I have to see her. I've never been out with a woman like Rachel. Someone who's kind and generous and real. Those are qualities that are lacking in the women I've been with in the past or in any of the women I'm used to being around. I'm surrounded by socialites, women who care only about how they look and their standing among their society friends. That's true for my mother as well, so I grew up thinking all women are like that. Of course, as I got older,

I encountered many women outside of that world but I have still never met anyone like Rachel.

She looked beautiful tonight. She looked beautiful when I saw her at Yale that day too. She has a natural beauty that is simply stunning. No plastic surgeon could ever replicate that type of beauty. I know women who've spent thousands of dollars trying to achieve that look and yet it always comes out looking fake. A nose that's too small or too pointy. Eyes that are pulled too tight. Overly puffy lips. You just can't replicate pure, natural beauty like Rachel has.

I didn't mean to stare at her all night, but I couldn't take my eyes off her. Her dark hair hung in long, soft waves, framing her face. And I loved her dress. So simple and yet she made it look elegant. It was a sleeveless dress that showed off her arms. She has lean, toned arms. I wonder if she plays some type of sport. She didn't mention it, but I don't know how else she could be in such good shape. The dress was in a shade of blue that matched her eyes. Those eyes. I can't get enough of them. It's not just the color but the warmth and emotion they convey. And her smile. It lights up the room. I've heard that expression before but never believed it until I actually saw it for myself.

Our conversation held my interest the entire four hours we were together. That never happens. Usually when people are talking for that long, my mind drifts in and out and I have to work to stay focused. But Rachel captivated my attention the entire time.

And that kiss. I broke my own rule. No kissing. But then I put my arm around her narrow waist and looked into her eyes and before I could stop myself, I kissed her. And I don't know what happened, but that kiss did something to me. Obviously, given my attraction to her, it caused a sexual response, but it was more than that. I felt this closeness to her that I've never felt when kissing a woman. I didn't want the kiss to end. I don't think she did either. But I felt that it should and so I backed away.

I limited the kiss to only her lips. I would've liked for it to be a more intimate kiss, but I didn't think that would be right since we just met. That makes absolutely no sense since I normally skip the

78

kiss and have sex with a woman within a half hour of meeting her. In fact, I did just that the other night with Rielle. But I wouldn't do that with Rachel. I wouldn't feel right about it.

I also held her hand. I never hold hands with a woman. It's another rule and I broke it. But I couldn't help myself. I had to touch her, and when I did, I couldn't let go.

I'm so consumed with thoughts of Rachel that I missed the entrance into my building. I turn around and drive back to the gate, stopping at the security guard station. I roll my window down.

"Welcome back, Mr. Kensington." The guard smiles at me as he presses the button to open the gate.

"Thank you, George."

"Just getting home from work?"

"No. I was out having dinner."

He nods. "Must've been one very special girl."

I raise my brows. "Why do you say that?"

"I've just never seen you smile like that before. I figured it had to be a girl."

I clear my throat. "Yes, well, have a good evening, George."

"You as well, Mr. Kensington."

I drive through the gate to the underground garage and park in my assigned spot. I check my reflection in the rearview mirror. I'm not smiling. What was he talking about? Was I smiling when I drove up to the gate? When my mind was still on Rachel?

This is very concerning. I do not let women affect me this way. I have sex with them. I take them to dinner or the opera or the ballet or a charity ball. But that's where it ends. I do not get involved with them. I like to remain in control at all times. So why does it feel like I'm already losing control when it comes to Rachel?

The next day at work, I try to concentrate on spreadsheets showing our latest sales numbers and projected earnings for next quarter but none of it is making sense. It's just a sea of columns with numbers in them.

Every time I try to focus on a certain column, my mind shifts to last night. I keep trying to analyze what's going on with me when it comes to Rachel. There has to be a logical explanation for why I feel so strongly about her.

I'm very logical and when I can't find a rational explanation for something, it infuriates me. And there is nothing rational about my feelings for Rachel. The only thing I can come up with is that she's forbidden, and when a person is denied something, they want it all the more. It's simply human nature. Basic psychology.

Rachel is forbidden on many levels. For one, going out with her breaks my self-imposed rule never to date. Two, she does not fit in my world and never will. She's not wealthy. She doesn't have the right last name. She didn't attend the proper schools growing up. Three, she's not *allowed* in my world. My parents would kill me if they knew I went out with her, and Dunamis would punish me. And lastly, if I continued to see her and was somehow allowed to be with her, it would never last because she would never be able to truly know me. She can't ever see the side of me I keep hidden. The dark side. She can't ever find out what I've done. She can't know about Dunamis and what they do, or who the members are, or how I'm forced to do things I don't want to do. She can't know any of that, which is why I can't pursue whatever this is I started with her.

It's noon and I decide to call her. I need to cancel our date tomorrow and tell her I'm busy. If she calls me again after that, I'll keep telling her I'm busy and eventually she'll get the message. It's not what I want to do, but I have to. It's for the best.

She answers on the third ring. "Hello, this is Rachel."

Just hearing her voice I feel myself smiling. Dammit! I straighten up in my chair and try to maintain a businesslike tone.

"Hello, Rachel, it's Pearce."

"Hi, Pearce." Her voice shifts to a slightly higher octave. "I didn't expect you to call. You're not canceling on me, are you? Because I did some research and came up with some interesting facts on the Civil War that even *I* hadn't heard before. And I have a really fascinating story about one of the soldiers that very few people know about. I can't wait to share it with you. I'm really looking forward to this tour. And, well, I really want to see you again."

There goes my plan. I can't tell her no. Not now. Not after she said all that. I generally have no problem telling people no, but I can't make myself do it with Rachel. She's such a sweet girl and it was kind of her to do all that work preparing for my tour. And when she said she wants to see me again, I smiled even wider. A full-on smile, which I never do. But I couldn't control it. I feel the exact same way about her. I can't wait to see her again. Even if she hadn't said all that just now, I still wouldn't have been able to cancel our date tomorrow. Logically, I know it's what I need to do, but logic seems to get thrown out the window when it comes to this girl.

"I want to see you too," I tell her, that damn smile still on my face. I hope nobody walks by. They'll think I've lost my mind. "And for dinner, you pick the place. Wherever you'd like to go."

"Okay." She pauses. "So were you just calling to say hello? I never gave you a chance to say why you called."

"I was thinking about you and wanted to see how your day was going."

"It's going well. Thank you. And yours?"

"It's slow, but it's going fine."

"By the way, I was thinking about you too, so I'm glad you called. I wanted to call you, but I know you're busy at work and I didn't want to interrupt anything."

"Call whenever you'd like. If I'm not here, just leave a message and I'll call you back when I can."

"Okay, well, enjoy the rest of your day."

"You as well. Goodbye, Rachel."

"Bye, Pearce."

One of the secretaries appears at the door to my office. "Mr. Kensington, Jack Ellit just called. He said he's been trying to reach you. You were supposed to meet him for lunch ten minutes ago."

I jump up from my chair. "Yes. I completely forgot. Thank you for letting me know. I'll head over there right now."

Jack is my mentor at Dunamis. Every young man is assigned a mentor when we learn of our membership in this group. I learned about it when I was 16 but I wasn't allowed to attend meetings until I was 20. That's the age when most young men are told. But my father felt the need to tell me early. He said it would make me a man sooner if I learned the truth about how the world works.

I hate him for that. He stole the last remaining years of my childhood. While everyone else my age was leading a carefree life, going to dances and parties and football games, I had to live with the fact that my father had killed an innocent stranger right in front of me, then listen to him tell me how this is done every day and nobody knows. Horrible crimes are committed by him and the other members. Leaders of society, who tell themselves they're doing it for the good of the nation. The good of the world. After hearing that, what little innocence I had left from my childhood was destroyed. And when my father told me I'd soon be part of it, any hope I'd had for my future was gone.

I wasn't assigned a mentor until just this past year. I couldn't have one before that because I wasn't around. I was at Yale until I was 22 and then I went straight to grad school at Harvard. When I graduated and started working full-time at Kensington Chemical, I was finally introduced to Jack Ellit, my mentor. He's 58, married, with two grown daughters, both of whom are married to members.

So far, I haven't spent much time with Jack. He owns a large telecommunications company and travels a lot for work. I see him at meetings and we meet for lunch once a month but that's about it.

The mentors are supposed to teach us how to follow through on our assignments and complete them successfully. They teach us the rules and make sure we follow them. They're also there so we have someone to talk to when we're struggling with being part of the organization. Being a member involves ethical dilemmas that can cause psychological and emotional stress. That's not true for everyone, but it's true for many, especially the younger members who haven't been doing this for very long. Sometimes you just need someone to talk to, and since we can't talk about this to anyone outside Dunamis, we have to talk to a fellow member.

My father was angry when I was assigned a mentor. He wanted to train me himself, but it's against the rules. Mentors can't be relatives. Of course, that doesn't stop my father from teaching me things he believes are important, mainly how to shut off all emotion in order to successfully complete your assignments so you can someday reach a higher position in Dunamis. I have no desire to be promoted to a higher level but I don't tell my father that. I just let him tell me these things and pretend to listen.

I meet Jack in the private dining room next to his office, which is in his company's corporate headquarters. We have to meet in private dining rooms like this, because in a restaurant we risk someone overhearing what we're saying. We need complete privacy and a secure location.

"Jack, I'm sorry I'm late." I walk in and see him standing beside a small round table covered in a white linen tablecloth.

Jack is shorter than me, around six feet, and has a stocky build. His thick hair is all white and he has a tan from all the time he spends in the sun, golfing or sailing. He's wearing a navy suit with a blue and yellow striped tie. He's one of the few members who wears bright colors like that. Most everyone else wears ties that are silver or dark gray. And most of us wear black suits, sometimes mixing it up with gray, but rarely navy.

Jack smiles as we shake hands. "It's no problem, Pearce. We all get busy and time slips away."

"That's not an excuse. I should've been on time. Again, I apologize. It won't happen again."

He motions me to the table. "Shall we sit down?"

We take our seats. On the table are two goblets of water next to two short fat glasses filled with scotch. Our meals are also sitting there, covered by a silver dome. The wait staff isn't allowed in here during our meetings so we remove the domes ourselves and set them on the tray that's next to the table.

Our lunch consists of a small steak with a side of roasted potatoes and asparagus. Jack has a simple palate, another way he's different than the other members. A good meal to him is an expensive cut of meat prepared to his specifications and served with a side of potatoes. The other members prefer gourmet meals made with ingredients that are difficult to obtain and therefore very expensive.

Whenever Dunamis has meetings or parties, Jack always complains about the food. His complaints are not well received. The other members look at him with annoyance, but he gets those looks a lot so he's used to it.

Jack is a bit of a rebel. He pushes the rules to their limits and he isn't afraid to voice his opinion when he doesn't agree with something. His rebellious attitude is what I like most about him. Deep down, I'm a rebel too. My father constantly tries to get rid of that trait in me and make me more obedient, and for the most part he's succeeded, but not completely. I still go behind his back and do things he wouldn't approve of. Like going out with Rachel. He would be furious if he knew I was seeing a woman like her.

My father knows Jack's reputation as a trouble maker who challenges the rules, so he was outraged when he found out Jack was my mentor. He tried to get them to pick someone else but they wouldn't do it. I'm a little surprised myself that they would pair me with Jack, given that we both have that rebellious streak. But then again, I keep that side of myself mostly hidden, so other than my father, the other members probably don't realize it's there.

"So what have you been up to, Pearce?" Jack cuts into his steak, which is seared on the outside but so rare on the inside that blood is dripping out.

"I've been busy with work. Sixteen hour days, seven days a week." I cut into my own steak, which is cooked to a perfect medium-rare. The first time he meets you, Jack asks how you like your steak cooked. Then when he invites you for a meal, he makes sure his chef prepares it exactly the way you like it.

"You need to get some hobbies," he says. "Maybe take flying lessons. Get your pilot's license. Or take up sailing. I could get you into my yacht club."

"My father doesn't allow me to have hobbies unless it will benefit the company. Golfing is on his approved list, but only because it's an activity we do with clients."

Jack takes a bite of his bloody steak, not bothering to finish chewing it before he speaks again. "When are you going to stop listening to your father? You're a grown man. Holton shouldn't be telling you what to do."

I laugh a little because if my father heard Jack say that, he'd probably strangle him. *You never outgrow your obedience to your father's authority.* That's what my father told me when I tried to use the I'm-an-adult argument. Telling him I was a grown man who could make my own choices did nothing more than cause a fight between us.

"Jack, I think you know my father well enough to know that he will never stop telling me what to do. Over the years, I've learned that *not* following his orders is more difficult than following them."

"That may be true for some things, but for other things, you need to take a stand." He stabs a chunk of potato with his fork. "Pick your battles. Isn't that what they say?"

"Yes. But it's not that simple with him."

He takes a swig of his scotch. "What else? You got a girl in your life?"

I smile at his sudden change of topics. That's typical for him but I'm never prepared for it. Sometimes his topics or the things he says are inappropriate, or his timing is inappropriate. The other members call him out on this, but Jack just ignores them. He doesn't care what people think of him.

"No, I'm not seeing anyone." I can't tell Jack about Rachel. I can't tell anyone about her.

"I heard you had a date with Rielle Hanniford." He stuffs a wedge of steak in his mouth and gnaws on it.

"Where did you hear that?"

"I've got eyes everywhere, Pearce. I have to. And as for Rielle, I gave her father some money to invest and now I have to keep an eye on him and his family to make sure they're actually investing it and not squandering it. Years ago, I trusted a man with my money and ended up losing it in a Ponzi scheme. Since then, I've been more careful. Plus, spying on Hanniford gives me an opportunity to test out my latest surveillance equipment."

Jack's telecommunications company doesn't just deal with telephone lines. They also make equipment used to spy on people. His company is one of the leading producers of this type of equipment and has all the latest technology. That's why Jack's so useful to our group. I'm sure if the rules allowed it, the other members would try to take away his membership, but that'll never happen. They need him in order to access his company and its technology.

"I wouldn't call it a date," I say.

He chuckles. "Yes, I know what it was. Are the associates not good enough for you? Or did you just want to try something new?"

This is an example of what the other members would consider to be inappropriate conversation to be having over lunch, but I don't mind. Jack is who he is and you can't change him. I find him rather humorous.

"She found me sitting at the bar and wouldn't take no for an answer."

He winks. "I'm sure you could've fought her off if you tried."

I smile. "I suppose you're right."

"It's hard to turn down a beautiful woman, isn't it?" He swigs his scotch.

I panic, thinking his question implies he knows about Rachel. If he saw me with Rielle, did he also see me with Rachel? What if he's spying on me?

"Rielle is a very beautiful woman," he says. "Far too young for me, but I'm sure she's very appealing to a man your age."

"I'm not seeing her again. It was a one-time thing."

Jack wipes his mouth and chin with his white cloth napkin, then sets it on the table. "There's a meeting this Saturday."

Again, I find his rapid change of topics amusing. From sex to meetings without any kind of transition.

"Yes, I received the call. Do you know what's on the agenda?"

"The usual. Nothing too exciting. Things are typically slow when we're this far out from an election. But slow is good in our line of work." He picks up his plate and sets it on the tray next to us. Then he goes to take mine. "Are you finished?"

"Yes. Thank you."

He adds my plate to the tray.

I watch him, noticing how his mood changed just now. It became dark and somewhat regretful. When he said things were slow, he means we aren't as busy trying to cover things up or take care of people who see too much. Even though he's done it for years, I can tell Jack isn't comfortable doing the things they make him do. That's why I like him. He seems to have maintained that part of himself that many of the members have lost. The human side. The side that feels emotion. The side that sees people as people and not just problems that have to be taken care of. Before I met Jack, I thought I would someday lose that side of myself. I could feel it slipping away. But after meeting Jack, I realized that if he can keep that side of himself alive after all these years, maybe I could too. Because I don't want to lose it. If I do, I'll become my father, and my worst fear is becoming him.

"Do you have any questions for me?" Jack asks.

"No. Sorry, I should've been more prepared."

"Nonsense. You didn't need to prepare anything. I was just asking if you had any questions."

"I guess I do have one."

"Go ahead."

I try to figure out how to say this without offending him. I'm only asking because I find it odd that every time we meet we just make small talk. We never really discuss anything.

"My father mentioned that mentors generally go over specifics on how to best complete an assignment."

"You've already had assignments and carried them out successfully." He swishes his drink around in the glass, the ice clanging against it. "So what do you need to know?"

"I'm not sure. That's why I'm asking you. My father said something about the rules regarding assignments. I wasn't sure what he meant."

"Here are the rules." Jack drinks the last of his scotch, then sets the glass down. "You hire competent people. You tell them what to do. You confirm that it was done. Then you pay them. That's all you need to know." He sits back in his chair.

He's right. It really is that simple and yet my father makes it sound so complicated.

Jack leans forward again. "Pearce, we may not know each other that well, but I think you've figured out that I take a rather unconventional approach to things."

I nod, trying not to laugh.

"As your mentor, I will be teaching you things the other members don't teach their students. I do things differently than they do. Any other member would teach you the rules and how to follow them, but that's not what I'm going to do. I don't like the rules. I never have. Fuck the rules."

I can't believe he said that. My father lives by those rules. If he heard Jack say that just now, he'd tell the organization and make sure Jack was punished.

"Are you going to finish that?" Jack points to my scotch, which I haven't drank.

"No, it's a little early in the day to—"

"Another rule." He reaches over and takes my scotch. "Who was the idiot who made that rule about no drinking before five?" He swigs the scotch. All of it. Then he slams the glass down on the table and sits back. "First thing you need to know? Rules are made to be broken."

"If you break them, they punish you."

"I didn't say to break all of them. You pick and choose which rules to follow. And when you break one, you make sure they never find out."

"How do you do that?"

"We'll get to that when the time comes." He grins just slightly. "As Holton Kensington's son, I'm sure you won't be breaking any rules anytime soon. I'm sure that man has beaten you down to the point you don't dare challenge him or the rules he's established. Am I correct?"

I clear my throat and glance away from his stare. "Could you continue, please?"

"That's your first mistake."

"Mistake?" I look at him and see that his smile has been replaced by a stern, serious expression. "I don't know what you're referring to."

"If you're going to be strong, you can't deny your weaknesses. You need to acknowledge them so you can overcome them. And your father is one of your greatest weaknesses."

It's true but I hate admitting it.

"Pearce. Would you agree?"

I nod. "Yes."

"My goal as your mentor is to make you strong. To teach you things that will empower you. As a group, Dunamis is all about gaining power and strength so we can continue our dominance over others and control outcomes of important events. But when you think about it, as individual members, we lack the very things we strive so hard to achieve as a group. As individuals we have no power. No control. No strength. Those things are beaten out of us in order to keep us in line. It's ironic, really."

His explanation is true, yet I'd never thought of it that way.

"We're soldiers," he says. "We do as we're told. We follow orders. We're not allowed to ask questions. We're expected to speak only when spoken to. And it will always be that way."

"What do you mean when you say you're going to empower me?"

"I'm going to teach you to be a fighter. Because if you're not, you'll never survive."

"Who am I fighting?"

"Your fellow members. Any one of them could be your enemy at any given time. Even your father could be your enemy. Or me. But your greatest enemy isn't a person. It's the organization as a whole. Being part of this group and carrying out your assignments can steal your humanity. But only if you allow it to happen."

"What about other enemies? Ones outside Dunamis?"

He nods. "Yes. You will also learn how to fight outside enemies, but fighting criminals is much easier than fighting the people who claim to be your allies, and a thousand times easier than fighting the enemy that is yourself. Everyone has two sides, Pearce, the good and the bad. Being in this business, the bad tends to win out unless you fight it. Some of us have, and we've survived with both sides still intact. Others have lost the battle or never even tried fighting it. You seem like a fighter, Pearce. Am I correct?"

I'm so mesmerized by his words, trying to take them all in, it takes me a moment to respond. "Yes. I want to fight."

"Excellent." He stands up from the table. "I hope you enjoyed your lunch. I need to get back to work. I'll see you on Saturday. Please see yourself out."

And then he leaves. I'm still sitting in the chair trying to his process what he said. As I do, I feel this sense of hope I haven't felt since finding out about Dunamis. I'll always be part of this group but I don't have to become them. I can fight. I can keep alive that part of me I thought was dying.

Just knowing that, having that tiny glimmer of hope, is like a bright beacon of light in my very dark world.

CHAPTER TEN

RACHEL

My tour with Pearce is at four and it's now 3:45. I feel nervous. Excited nervous. The kind of nervous that makes your stomach fluttery.

This is not typical for me. I don't usually react this way over a guy. But Pearce is not the average guy. I've never met someone like him. I've never been this attracted to a guy. I've never had anyone consume my thoughts this much.

I'm working the front desk until he gets here. Nobody else is in the museum. Friday afternoons are really slow so I always bring my books and study. We close at 4:30 so after I give Pearce the tour, I'll just need to lock up and then we can go find something to do before dinner.

Today isn't as hot as it was earlier in the week, but it's still warm outside so I wore another sleeveless dress. This one is fitted, not flared out at the waist. It's a casual knit dress I got on clearance last year for $10. Total steal. I think nobody wanted it because it's orange and people have a fear of wearing orange. But with my dark hair and the tan I still have from the summer, the orange looks good on me. I brought a lightweight white sweater to put over my arms in case I get cold later tonight.

Pearce comes through the door at 3:55. Instead of his usual suit, he has on black dress pants, a white shirt, and a blue silk tie. His ties are gorgeous. I bet they cost a fortune.

My eyes move up to his face. He shaved this time, probably right before he left to come here. His face is smooth, and as he approaches me, I smell a hint of aftershave or maybe cologne. Whatever it is, it smells really good.

He looks so hot I'd like to just take a few moments to stare at him, but that would be weird.

I pop up from my chair and go around the desk. "Welcome to the museum."

He smiles. "Thank you. You weren't kidding. It's very small."

"It's good to see you again." I hug him but he just stands there, rigid, his arms at his side. Oh, God, this is awkward. Why did I hug him? Shelby's right. I need to get control of the hugging thing.

I release him and step back, my cheeks heating up. "Sorry. I kind of have a hugging problem."

He's still smiling. "It's not a problem. It's fine. I just wasn't expecting it. I'm not used to people hugging me."

"You're not?"

"No. I honestly can't remember the last time someone hugged me. Childhood, maybe?"

"Are you serious?" He doesn't answer so I say, "Well, that's just wrong. Of course, this is coming from someone who hugs everyone. Even the mailman. Even people I don't know. Anyway, I'm sorry if I made you uncomfortable."

"You didn't make me uncomfortable." He motions me toward him. "Come here. Let's do it right this time."

I step forward and hug him again. This time, he hugs me back. For someone who doesn't hug much, he's pretty good.

When he lets go, I say, "Next time, maybe do it a little tighter."

He laughs. "Did you just critique my hug?"

"No, I'm just making a suggestion. It's strictly personal preference. I tend to like a tight hug."

"The few hugs I've had have been very distant hugs, limited to the upper body only. So to me, that was a tight hug."

"Okay, well, ready to start the tour?" I walk over to the first display.

"Get back over here."

I look at him, confused. "Why?"

92

"Because I don't like not being good at things. I need to do the hug again."

I'm trying not to laugh because this is really funny. He's taking this so seriously. But it's fine with me. I'll take another hug. I like being in his arms.

I hug him again and this time he hugs me tighter. It's almost perfect, but then he lets go.

"How was that?" he asks.

"It was good." I take his hand and lead him over to the display case. "But next time, don't let go so soon. Let me, or whatever girl you're hugging, let go first, and then you can let go."

"I wasn't aware there were so many rules to hugging." He leans down and talks in my ear. "And just so we're clear, the only woman I will be hugging is you."

I freeze, my fluttery stomach now doing flip flops. He slowly backs away, the scent of his cologne lingering around me. I don't know if I can do this tour. I'm far too distracted by him.

I take a moment to collect myself, then motion to the display case. "So this is a Civil War era gun that was used by..." I continue on for the next half hour. Pearce stays engaged the entire time. He asks lots of questions and he even laughs at my ridiculously corny jokes. Those are a big hit with the senior citizens, but I included them on Pearce's tour to see if he'd laugh. He's so serious all the time that I like seeing him laugh.

We're back at the front desk again. "That concludes the tour. Did you like it?"

"Yes. It was excellent." He reaches over and takes a comment card from the box on the desk.

"You're filling out a comment card?"

"I'm going to tell your boss what a stellar job you did." He sticks the card in his pocket.

"You don't have to do that. I'll only be working here a few more months."

"Your boss should still be told. Maybe you'll get a raise."

"I doubt it. They can barely afford to pay minimum wage."

He gets that serious look again. "They only pay you minimum wage?"

"I know it's not much, but I wanted the experience of working at a museum, giving tours. I'm going to apply for a job at the grocery store to get some extra income." I grab my purse from behind the desk. "I just need to close up and then we can leave."

We go outside and I lock the door. "So what should we do? It's too early for dinner. There's a park nearby. We could take a walk."

He's looking at me like I'm crazy. Does he not take walks? Or maybe he doesn't want to walk in his nice clothes.

"I suppose we could do that," he says. "Do you mean the park right over there?" He points to it.

"Yes. We can just leave our cars here."

We walk over to the park, which is just a paved walking path surrounded by shade trees and lined with benches. The weather is a lot cooler than it was earlier and there's a light breeze. It's finally starting to feel like fall.

As we stroll through the park, I tell Pearce about a tour I gave this morning to a group of first graders.

"When the tour was over, one of the little boys came up to me and told me I was pretty and gave me a lollipop from his pocket. It wasn't wrapped so it was covered with lint and who knows what else, but I took it because he really wanted me to have it. And then he asked if I'd go to the movies with him."

"Did you tell him you already had a date for tonight?"

"No, but I did refocus his attention on one of the girls from the class who had her eye on him the entire tour. The little girl reminded me of my sister. She was always looking at boys."

"Where does your sister live? Is she still in Indiana?"

"No. She died when she was six. She had leukemia."

"Oh. I'm sorry to hear that."

"We were twins. We did everything together. When she was gone, I felt like she took half of me with her." I wipe the corners of my eyes. Even today, I still tear up when I talk about her. I don't want to bring the mood down so I force out a smile and say, "Sorry. Being with all those kids today just reminded me of her."

We're still walking, but we've slowed our pace. I feel Pearce's hand brush against mine and I glance over at him. He's looking at me with the sweetest, most caring expression. Like he senses the pain that still lingers inside me from the loss of my sister and wishes he could make it go away. He notices me watching him, and looks away, but his hand wraps gently around mine as we continue walking down the tree-lined path.

In the short time I've spent with him, I've learned Pearce is very reserved with his feelings. I think he's more comfortable expressing himself without words, which he did just now by holding my hand. It's such a small gesture, but I felt like it meant something. Like he was telling me he cares. And to me it was better than words.

We're quiet after that, and I like the silence. I like just walking beside him, hand-in-hand, listening to the leaves rustle around our feet. It doesn't feel awkward or strange that we're not talking. It's like when you know someone so well that you can be together without words having to be spoken. But given that we just met, it's surprising that we're already this comfortable with each other.

When we reach the end of the park, we walk back. This time we talk, but not about anything serious. Just random things. And then he suddenly stops and leads me off to the side. Before I can ask what he's doing, he leans down and kisses me.

It takes me by surprise and when we break apart, he explains. "It had been far too long since I'd done that. I hope you don't mind."

I smile. "I don't mind. Actually, I was wondering what took you so long."

He kisses me again, longer this time, then says, "That should last me until we get to the car."

I laugh. I'm glad I'm not the only one who felt that way. I've wanted to kiss him this whole time but I didn't want to appear too forward. I'm someone who prefers the guy to make the move. And Pearce keeps doing it when I'm least expecting it, which I find to be a total turn on. So that unexpected kiss just now? Extremely hot.

We return to the paved trail and walk back, hand-in-hand, to our cars.

"I know it's still early," I say, "but I'm really hungry. Would you mind if we eat now?"

"Not at all. What did you pick for dinner?"

"A little Italian place not far from here. It's family owned. They have really good food."

"Then that's where we'll go." He leads me to his car and opens the door for me. I've never been in a Mercedes. This one's brand new. It even smells new. And it's immaculate inside.

I show him where to go and when he sees the restaurant he looks concerned. The outside does look kind of bad but it's cute inside, with checkered tablecloths and candles on each table.

When we're seated, I say, "This place isn't very fancy, but like I said, the food is good."

"I don't need fancy." He points to himself. "See? I didn't even dress up this time. I ditched the suit and went casual."

I start laughing. I didn't mean to. It just happened. "That's casual? Dress pants, a dress shirt, and a tie?"

"This isn't casual?" He's completely serious.

"No." I calm my laughter, but I'm smiling. "I would say what you're wearing would be considered dressed up. Not casual."

"What do you consider casual?"

"Jeans and a t-shirt."

"I don't own jeans. And I only wear t-shirts when I'm at the gym."

"You really don't own a pair of jeans? Not one pair?"

He shakes his head. "No."

"Have you ever owned a pair?"

He stops to think, then says, "No."

"You just don't like them? Or what's the reason?"

"They're not proper attire for social gatherings."

I almost laugh again but I hold it in. "What kind of social gatherings do you go to?"

"Fundraisers. Charity events. Auctions."

"What about when you go out just for fun, like to the movies?"

"I don't go to the movies."

"What do you mean? Like recently? Or ever?"

96

"I've never gone to the movies."

"How is that possible? Why haven't you gone?"

"It's just something I've never had the desire to do. It's not that I haven't seen movies. One of my friends in high school had a theater room in his house so I'd watch movies there. I just haven't been to an actual movie theater."

"So if you're not into movies, what do you like to do for fun?"

"I go to the opera. The symphony. Plays."

That doesn't sound very fun but I don't tell him that.

He smiles. "I know what you're thinking. Those things aren't exactly fun. And you're right. They can be quite boring, although I do enjoy the symphony and I've seen several good plays."

The waiter keeps walking by, like he wants us to order so I open my menu and Pearce does the same.

When I close my menu, Pearce says, "What would you like?"

"I'm getting the lasagna, but you don't have to order for me. I can do it."

"So you *do* find it offensive?"

"No, it's not that. It just feels kind of strange. I'm not used it. Is that really an etiquette rule? That the man orders for the woman?"

"Yes, but like I said, it's rather old-fashioned so if you'd like to order for yourself, go ahead."

The waiter returns, and out of habit, Pearce starts to say my order but then stops and motions me to continue.

We have another perfect dinner in which the conversation flows seamlessly from one topic to another. I find Pearce to be very funny in his own unique way. I like his sense of humor. His funny comments come out of nowhere and are sometimes so subtle it takes me a moment to get it, but when I do it's always really funny. He's very smart. Even his humor is smart.

As we're waiting for the check, I tell him the idea that's been brewing in my head all night. "So I had this idea, but first I need to know something."

"Okay. What is it?"

"Will you be asking me out again?"

97

He grins and reaches over to hold my hand. "I will most definitely be asking you out again."

I sit there, quietly.

His smile fades. "Did you not want me to ask you out again?"

"I want you to ask me, but I'm waiting for you to do it."

He smiles as he brings my hand up for a kiss. "Rachel Evans, would you go out with me tomorrow night?"

"I would love to, but I would like to pick the place we go."

"And what place is that?"

"I would like to go to a movie. At a theater. And split a bucket of popcorn."

"They sell food in a bucket?" He looks horrified.

I laugh. "Yes. They do."

He nods. "If that's what you would like, then that's what we shall do."

I swear, I've never heard the word 'shall' used so much in my entire life. Pearce uses it all the time.

"And before the movies, maybe we could go to the mall?"

"The mall?" The horrified look reappears. "Do you mean a shopping mall?"

"Yes." I laugh again. "Please tell me you've been to a mall before."

"I'm not sure that I have. I have a personal shopper who buys all my clothes and delivers them to my loft." He pauses to think. "Actually, now that I think about it, yes. Back in college, I took a girl to the mall. But it was just one time and I haven't been back since."

"We don't have to spend long there, unless you want to eat dinner there. They have a lot of restaurants to choose from."

"Since you seem to be planning this date, you go ahead and pick. I'll plan the next date."

I smile. "So you're asking me on another date?"

"I am. Are you accepting?"

"Yes. I find you quite charming, Pearce Kensington. Although the fact that you've never been to the movies is a bit concerning. But we'll remedy that tomorrow."

The waiter brings the check and Pearce sets some cash out. "So earlier you said you had an idea. What was your idea?"

"I want to introduce you to some things you haven't done before, like going to the movies. But that's just a start. I have all kind of things in mind for you."

Dammit. That sounded dirty and I didn't mean for it to. Maybe he didn't take it that way.

"I'm intrigued." His sly smile says that he took it that way.

"I didn't mean that—"

"I know you didn't. Go ahead."

"I'm not going to tell you what I've got planned. You just have to go with it. Are you up for it?"

"I will try most anything once, so yes."

"Great! So should we get out of here? It's still early. We could go back to my apartment."

I hope he doesn't take that as an invitation for sex. That's not what I meant. I just didn't want to say goodbye to him yet, so I thought we could hang out at my apartment.

He agrees to it, not showing any signs that he's expecting anything. I guess I'm not sure what those signs would be, but he's been a complete gentleman the whole time I've known him so I don't think he'd pressure me into doing anything I wasn't ready for.

"Just drop me off at my car and then follow me," I say as we're driving away from the restaurant. "My apartment doesn't have a parking lot so you'll have to park on the street."

We go back to the museum and I get in my car and drive the short distance back to my apartment, with Pearce following behind me. When we arrive at my building, Pearce scans the neighborhood.

"Just lock your car," I tell him. "It should be fine."

He meets me on the sidewalk. "I'm not worried about the car. I'm worried about *you*. I don't like this neighborhood, Rachel. It's not safe."

"There's always police patrolling the area, so it's usually okay. I try not to go out at night."

I let him into the building and we walk up the three flights of stairs.

"There's no elevator?" he asks as I unlock my door.

"No, it's an old building."

When we get inside, he inspects my door. "These locks aren't adequate. Someone could easily break in."

"What are you, a security expert?"

"I know a lot about security. When you have my kind of money, you have to be extremely cautious."

I pull him into my apartment and close the door. "Well, I have almost no money and nothing valuable so no criminal would want to break in here unless he wants my cupboard full of mac and cheese."

"Rachel, I'm not joking about this. You need to get better locks. And an alarm system." He walks over to the window. "And in a neighborhood like this, you should have bars on the windows."

"Pearce, I don't need any of that. I've lived here for over a year and never had any problems. I don't have anything to steal."

"Yes, but there are other reasons a man may try to break in."

I know what he means and it makes me shudder. "That won't happen. I keep my doors locked."

"Let me get you some better locks and an alarm system."

"No. I'm fine. Really. I'm good friends with the girl next door and we keep an eye out for each other. Speaking of her, I wanted to introduce you to her. She's been gone a lot lately. I'm not sure if she's home. I'll call her quick." I do, but she doesn't answer. "I guess she's not there."

When I hang the phone up, I turn and see Pearce looking at the trophies on my bookcase.

"Those are for swimming," I tell him.

"When you told me you like to swim, I thought you just meant in the summers at the local pool. I didn't know you swam competitively. And won." He points to my medals. "Why didn't you tell me about this?"

I meet him by the bookcase. "Because I really miss it, so I don't like talking about it."

"You don't swim anymore?"

"I do, but not as much as I used to. In high school, swimming was my life. It's all I did. And I swam all through college, and as you can see, I did pretty well. But then I moved here, and between school and work and other stuff, I don't have time to swim. And if I get that grocery store job, I'll have even less time."

He leads me over to the couch to sit down. "Rachel, don't take another job. One is enough."

"The museum doesn't pay enough. I need something else."

"Would you consider letting me give you some money?"

"No. I'm not taking your money. You didn't think that's what I meant when I said I didn't have money, did you? Because I wasn't asking for money. I swear, that is not what I meant."

"Of course not. But if you need some help—"

"I don't need help. I'm good."

My parents taught me to never take handouts. To work hard and only buy what you can afford. So although I'm struggling to pay my bills, I wouldn't feel right taking money from Pearce, or anyone else.

"Well, the offer is always there."

I pick up the remote. "You want to watch TV? This place doesn't have cable but I can usually find something to watch."

I turn to see him looking at me. It's more than a look. It's heat. Desire. Attraction. I know because I feel it too. I was trying to ignore it all night because it's very distracting, but now it's front and center, lingering between us.

He hasn't answered me about the TV. And before I can say anything, his hand slides under my hair, around the back of my neck, and he leans in and kisses me. I drop the remote and kiss him back, letting him know I don't want him to stop at just one. I want more. I *need* more. His kisses are amazing.

I lie back on the couch and he follows, not breaking the kiss. I feel his breath over my lips and I part them, inviting him in. His tongue moves slowly over mine as his hand trails from my neck down to my breast, gently cupping it while teasing the center with his thumb. A tingling heat fills my core, concentrating between my legs.

I undo his tie and slip it off, then unbutton his shirt. As I do, he kisses the side of my neck. I glance down at his chest. It's smooth and muscular. I run my hands over the defined ridges of his abs, then make my way up to his broad shoulders and slide his shirt off. He sits up enough to take it off, then lies over me again.

We continue to kiss, my body heating up even more as the minutes go by. His kisses are slow, deep, sensual. Combine his expert kisses with the way his hand is moving skillfully over the fabric of my dress and it's almost too much. I've never been this turned on before, an aching need building inside me.

He's holding himself up with one arm but our bodies are still touching and I feel his arousal against my leg. Out of instinct or pure desire, I push my hips into him. He shifts so he's between my legs and presses into me. It only intensifies that aching need, making me want more of him. All of him. I've never done it this soon after meeting someone. I used to think it was wrong. Part of me still does. But right now, with Pearce, it doesn't feel wrong.

I reach between us to undo his belt.

"Rachel." He says it over my lips. "No."

No, as in he doesn't want to do it? I'm confused.

"You don't want to?" I stop and look at him.

He squeezes his eyes shut, then opens them again. "I want to more than anything, but…it's too soon."

I sigh. "I know. And I normally don't do this, but something about this feels right."

"I agree, but I still think we should wait." He raises his brows. "Maybe just a few more dates?"

I smile. "I don't know what difference that would make."

He sits up on the couch and pulls me up next to him and looks into my eyes. "I know we just met, but I feel something for you that I'm not quite sure how to explain. But it's good and I like it and I don't want it to end. I don't want to mess it up. But sex can sometimes do that. So I think we should wait a little longer before we go there. Even if it's just a few more dates."

I nod. "You're right. We should wait. I just got carried away. I wasn't lying when I said I normally don't move that fast. It took six months before I did it with my first real boyfriend. And that

102

was in college. It was my first time." I look away, embarrassed I just admitted that.

He turns my face back to his, smiling at me. "Did you really wait that long?"

I glance away again. "Yes. And I only did it because I felt like I had to. I didn't think my boyfriend would keep waiting. Of course, later I found out he was cheating on me the whole time. After that I decided I should wait until I'm in love. My next serious boyfriend didn't come along until senior year and even then, we waited several months before...you know."

Why am I telling him this? He doesn't need to know this!

"So you were in love?" he asks.

"No. I just thought I was."

"Have you ever been in love?" he asks in a cautious tone, like he doesn't really want the answer.

"No. I haven't."

A week ago I would've answered differently. Before I had that talk with Shelby, I'd convinced myself I used to be in love with Adam. I did so because I thought I *had* to have loved him. Why else would I have dated him for that long? And agreed to marry him?

"Have *you*?" I ask Pearce. "Ever been in love?"

"No. Never."

"Good." I say it without even thinking. Why did I say that?

"Good?" Pearce is smiling at me. "And why is that good?"

"I didn't mean to say that. I don't know why I did."

He holds my hand. "You're right. It's good neither one of us has been in love. If we had been, it's likely we never would've met."

I smile at him. "I'm really glad we met."

"I am too. I've never met anyone like you."

"Shelby said the same thing."

"Who's Shelby?"

"My neighbor. She's crazy, but in a good way. We're friends. We hang out a lot." I hear a door close in the hall. "Hey, that's her. Do you want to meet her? I really want you to meet her."

"Then, yes, but I need to put a shirt on." He stands up and starts putting it on.

I watch him button it up. "I really like you without the shirt."

He leans down and gives me a kiss. "I guarantee I'd like you without that dress. But that'll have to wait for another time."

He helps me up and we walk out in the hall. I knock on Shelby's door and she answers.

"Hi, Shelby, is this a bad time? I know you've been gone a lot so—"

"It's not a bad time. Come on in."

"I brought someone with me. I wanted you to meet him." I step aside and Pearce appears next to me. "Shelby, this is Pearce Kensington. The man I met at the lecture series. And Pearce, this is Shelby. My friend and neighbor."

They look at each other but don't say anything. I understand why Shelby doesn't. Pearce is so hot he tends to make you forget to speak. But I don't know why Pearce is so quiet.

"Are you two going to say anything?"

Pearce clears his throat. "Yes, sorry. It's very nice to meet you, Shelby."

He shakes her hand.

"Nice to meet you too," she says.

And then more silence. This isn't going how I thought it would.

CHAPTER ELEVEN

PEARCE

Rachel's neighbor and new best friend is one of our associates. I slept with her a couple weeks ago. She's the girl who spent the night at my place when she wasn't supposed to.

When Rachel introduced me to her, I didn't know what to say. I was too shocked. What the hell is she doing living in this run-down building? She makes more than enough money to live in a decent apartment. Most of our associates live in luxury condos. Some have their own house. I know this girl is new, but still. She would've received money up front when she signed the contract.

I wonder if Shelby is her real name or another fake name like the one she gave me before she left that morning. Sophia. That's what she said her name was. All the girls use fake names but sometimes they do so in their real lives as well, trying to escape whatever dark past led them to the point where they would succumb to working for people like us.

"Let's go inside," Rachel says as she leads me into Shelby's apartment. It looks the same as Rachel's. It even has the same furniture. The apartments must come furnished. Rachel's apartment was neat and clean but Shelby's place has clothes strewn everywhere and dirty dishes sitting out.

"Sorry about the mess," Shelby says when she sees me looking around. "I didn't have time to clean before I left the other day."

"Where have you been?" Rachel asks her. "At your mom's house?

"Um, yeah."

It's a lie. I can tell by the way she hesitated before answering and the way she's staring down at the floor.

We hear a phone ring and Rachel says, "That's my phone. I'll be right back."

She leaves and I wait until I hear her apartment door close, then say to Shelby, "What the hell are you doing here?"

"ME?" Shelby talks just above a whisper. "What are YOU doing here? And what are you doing with Rachel?"

"We're seeing each other. We were on a date tonight."

"No!" She shoves me back. "Stay away from her! She's not one of your whores. She's a nice girl. A really nice girl. And she deserves better than you."

Her words hit me hard because it's true. Rachel *does* deserve better than me. But I can strive to be better. And I will.

"You said I wasn't like the rest of them."

Shelby huffs. "Obviously I was wrong. Now that I know you use people like Rachel, I realize you're just like the rest of them."

"I'm not using her. We're dating. Getting to know each other."

"Yeah, so you can have sex with her, if you haven't already. Why are you doing this? You can pick from any of the associates. They're all beautiful and they'll do whatever you ask."

"This isn't about sex. I like Rachel. I like her a lot. I care about her."

Shelby glares at me. "If you care about her, then leave her the fuck alone!"

Now I'm getting angry. "I will do as I please and you will keep your mouth shut."

"Rachel's my friend. And I'm not letting her get involved with someone like you."

"She's a grown woman. She can make her own choices."

"Not when she doesn't have all the facts. I'll tell her who you are and then we'll see if she wants to be with you."

I step closer to her and lower my voice. "If you do that, you know what will happen."

"Are you threatening me?"

"It's not a threat. It's a fact. When you accepted the deal, you made a contract with the devil. You were in danger from that

106

point forward. One slip-up and it's over. And telling Rachel about me, or about any of us, is more than a slip-up. It would be the end for you. If you do that, I can't protect you. I won't be able to control what they do to you."

"Yeah, I get it. I won't tell." Shelby's voice is shaky. I scared her. But she needs to know the reality of her situation. I don't know why she doesn't already know. Are they not telling the girls this?

"I'm sorry to have frightened you. I'm just trying to protect you."

She rolls her eyes. "Yeah, right. Like you give a damn about me. Or about any of the girls."

"Of course I do, but I can't do anything about the rules. And if you didn't want to be part of this, you shouldn't have signed up."

"I needed the money," she mutters.

I shake my head. "That's what they all say. I don't understand it. Is having designer shoes and handbags really worth giving up your freedom?"

"I'm not doing it so I can afford expensive things." She says it too loud, then lowers her voice. "Obviously if I was using the money on myself, I wouldn't live in this shithole."

I want to know why she needs the money but I don't ask. The less I know about her the better.

"Rachel said you've been gone a lot. Is it because of a job?"

"Yes, but I don't want to talk about it."

"That doesn't make sense. It shouldn't take that long."

"Well, it did, okay?" She rubs her arm.

"How long were you there?"

She sighs. "I said I don't want to talk about it."

I lower my voice. "Just tell me. How long were you there?"

"All day," she says quietly. "I missed work yesterday and now my boss is mad at me for not coming in."

"What boss? You have another job?"

"I work at a law firm a few days a week. I'm a secretary. When I was hired by the organization, I was told I'd only have to work in the evenings. But this last job went longer than planned."

"Why? Was it an out of town job?"

107

I shouldn't be asking these questions. It's none of my business and I get the feeling I won't like the answers.

"It wasn't out of town. It's just…he wouldn't let me leave. I went to his place the other night and when I went to leave, he—he insisted I stay."

"All night?"

"Yes." She pauses. "And the next day."

"That's against the rules. You're supposed to leave when you're done. You're not supposed to be seen in public with us."

"We didn't go out. We stayed in all day and—you know."

"Still, the rule says you do what you're there to do and leave. It's a very strict rule, which is why I didn't tell them you spent the night. We could've both been punished."

"You're not listening to me. I tried to leave but—" She keeps her eyes on me as she rolls her sleeves up. "He wouldn't let me."

I glance down at her arms. There are red marks around both her wrists. He tied her up and kept her there against her will. Shit.

"Who did this?" I'm furious. The members are not supposed to harm these girls. And they are most definitely not to hold them against their will, tied up like an animal.

"I can't tell you," she whispers. "I'd get in trouble. You know that."

"Did he hurt you?"

She lowers her sleeves, covering her wrists. "Only when he tightened the restraints. Other than that, not really."

"He should never have done that. If you tell me who it was, I promise you, I will make sure he's punished."

She thinks about it, then says, "No. But thank you for offering."

We stand there in silence. The walls are thin and I can hear Rachel talking on the phone in the other apartment.

"Pearce, I know there's a part of you that's not like the rest of them and doesn't want to be. But the fact is you *are* one of them and you always will be. So please, I'm begging you, leave Rachel alone. She's sweet and generous and has the biggest heart of anyone I've ever known. She still thinks the world is a good place and she believes people are good. Don't take that away from her.

Let her have a normal life. Let her be with someone who isn't part of this. She wants a family and a house with a white picket fence. And she deserves that. She doesn't belong in your world and if you put her there, she won't be happy." Shelby holds my forearm with both her hands, her eyes pleading. "Please. Just let her be happy."

"Sorry I took so long." Rachel walks in and Shelby quickly takes her hands off my arm and pretends to adjust her ponytail. "Did you guys get to know each other?"

"Yes," I say, keeping my eyes on Shelby. "Shelby was telling me about her family."

"How's your dad?" Rachel sounds sad as she addresses Shelby. "Is he getting worse?"

Shelby glances at me, then back at Rachel. "He's the same. No change."

"Is your father ill?" I ask her.

She nods, avoiding my gaze. She obviously didn't want me to know this.

"He has cancer," Rachel says. "Shelby goes home a lot to help her mom take care of him." She notices Shelby's face. "I'm sorry. Was I not supposed to tell him?"

"No, it's fine," she says.

So that's why Shelby needs the money? To help take care of her father? Help pay his medical bills?

Guilt fills me as I remember what I said to her. I accused her of wanting money to buy clothes and purses when she really needed it for her family. She shouldn't have to do this. She shouldn't have to sell her body to take care of her father.

"I'm really tired," she says. "I need to get to sleep. It was nice meeting you, Pearce."

"Yes. And you as well."

Rachel gives her a quick hug. "Bye, Shelby."

When we get back to Rachel's apartment, I pick up my tie from the floor. "I should go."

"But it's only ten. And it's Friday. You sure you don't want to stay?"

I lean down to kiss her. "If I stay, chances are I'll never leave. And I think we both know where that would lead."

She smiles. "Then I'll see you tomorrow."

I give her one last kiss, "Goodnight, Rachel."

When I get to my car I take some deep breaths, trying to clear my head of what I just heard, but it's no use. Shelby's words are haunting me, reminding me that what I'm doing is wrong.

She doesn't belong in your world and if you put her there, she won't be happy.

Shelby's right. Rachel doesn't belong in my world. But it's not the world I want to live in. I want out. And maybe I could find a way out. Maybe Jack could help.

I know that's wishful thinking but I let my mind go there because I don't want to stop seeing her. I don't want to lose her. She makes me feel something. Something good. I'm used to feeling nothing but pain and anger and when I can't take it anymore, I use alcohol or sex to numb it.

This is the first time I've felt something good and I want to feel it again. Rachel makes me forget about the pain and anger. She lightens my mood. She makes me happy. Since meeting her, I've laughed more than I have in years. And I can't seem to wipe that idiotic smile off my face whenever I'm with her, or even just thinking about her.

So what do I do? Is it selfish of me to keep seeing her? Am I just leading her on, knowing it won't last?

Maybe so, but I'm not ready to end things between us. Which means I'm either a selfish bastard or Rachel's optimistic attitude is rubbing off on me because a part of me believes we could make this work. I don't know how, but I want to believe it could happen.

I'm back at my apartment building now and I almost missed the turn again but I slammed on the brakes just in time. As I pull up to the gate, I wait for George to push the button.

"Welcome back, Mr. Kensington," he says. "You've got that smile again. You must've been out with that special lady."

I wave, but don't answer him as I drive forward through the gate. I can't be so obvious. If George notices something's up with me, others will too. I have a Dunamis meeting tomorrow and I can't have people suspecting something's going on with me.

Saturday morning I drive to Greenwich, which is where the meeting is today. We rotate meeting locations, and this time it's at the Bianchi estate, which belongs to one of our members. Inside the estate is a hidden door that leads to an underground tunnel and the room we use for our meetings. Many of our members build these underground rooms beneath their estates. They're as luxurious as the rooms in the main part of the house, with ornate rugs lining the floor and priceless artwork hung on the walls.

"Kensington." Royce Sinclair greets me as I enter the room. It's 10:40 in the morning and he already has a drink in his hand. Several other members are there and they also have drinks. Most of us drink too much. We joke that it's just men being men, drinking to excess. But it's really a coping mechanism we use so we can live with ourselves.

"Hello, Royce." I shake his hand.

I went to college with Royce Sinclair. Freshman year, we lived in the same dorm at Yale, on the same floor. I've never really liked Royce but I had to be friends with him because our fathers are friends and the Sinclair family is very rich and very powerful, even more so than *my* family. In my world, you're taught to befriend those who can help boost the status of your family's name, and being friends with a Sinclair will do that.

Royce's family owns Sinclair Pharmaceuticals, an international corporation that holds the patents to some of the world's most popular drugs. They're also a leader in the research and development of new drugs. Dunamis uses Sinclair Pharmaceuticals to create drugs for various purposes. Some are used by the Clinic. Most of those drugs will never be shared with the general public because our members like exclusivity and this allows them to have that. Other drugs are created to harm. To kill our enemies but make it look like an accident. We have drugs that induce heart attacks, strokes, aneurisms. These drugs are especially useful for killing leaders of foreign nations who don't cooperate with our demands.

111

Although the Sinclair family is forced to create these drugs, the fact that they do so makes me leery of them. I shouldn't judge them that way because they're no different than anyone else here. We're all forced to do bad things, but I know Royce and I know what he's done and because of that, I judge the rest of his family the same way.

Like me, Royce doesn't like following the rules, but he's far riskier than I am. I only break the rules now and then. Royce does it all the time. He basically does whatever he wants but tries to keep it hidden from his family and the other members. But he's openly breaking the rule that says he has to take over his family's company. He's made it clear he wants nothing to do with Sinclair Pharmaceuticals. Royce aspires to be a politician and so his brother, William, is going to take over the company once his father retires. Typically, both sons would be expected to work for the company but Arlin, Royce's father, allowed his son to take a different path, probably because he wasn't given a choice.

Dunamis is always trying to recruit politicians from among the ranks of our members, but most of us aren't suited for the job. Being a politician takes certain skills, like being an excellent liar during interviews and in debates. Lies must be spoken with utmost confidence; your face, tone, and mannerisms must never give you away. Royce is very good at that, so he's currently being primed to be a senator. In the next election, he'll be working alongside a current senator so that he becomes known in the political world.

"It's been far too long since we've gotten together." Royce motions me to the bar. "Come have a drink."

I agree to it because I need a drink to help me relax. These meetings always make me uptight. I never know what's going to happen.

"So how's business?" he asks as I pour myself some bourbon.

"Good. We'll soon be acquiring some new clients in the Southwest."

"Have you been doing anything besides work?"

"Not really."

"I don't know how you do it, Pearce. Working all those hours. I can't even get my ass out of bed in the morning. And I definitely

112

couldn't sit at a desk all day and night like you do. What are you working now, like ten hours a day?"

"Sixteen."

He shakes his head. "That's absurd. Again, I don't know how you do it."

"You'll be working just as much when you start campaigning."

"That's years from now. And I'll let my campaign staff do all the work. I just need to smile for the cameras. Put on a show." He steps closer and nudges my side. "Just imagine all the women I'll get once I'm on TV all the time. I already get my fair share, but the celebrity angle will have them flocking to me." He smiles. "I'm looking forward to being on the road."

"You better not get caught. People will be watching your every move. You'll have reporters following you. You need to be careful, Royce. The last thing we need is a scandal."

He refills his drink. "Pearce, your father has had far too much influence on you. You need to stop being so obedient and live a little."

"There are consequences to that."

He smirks. "That's what makes it fun. Knowing you could get caught. It's an adrenaline rush. It gives you a high you crave to feel again and again."

As he talks, I wonder if he was the one who was with Shelby. I wouldn't put it past him to tie up a woman like that. Royce takes what he wants and he doesn't take no for an answer.

"Where were you on Thursday?"

He stares at me. "Thursday? What are you talking about? What was Thursday? Did I miss a meeting or something?"

"No. Just tell me where you were."

"I don't know. I can't remember. I was probably at home coming down off something."

Royce does drugs sometimes, but he doesn't get in trouble for it because a lot of our members do drugs. It's another coping mechanism. But they've told Royce he needs to stop the drug use when he starts campaigning. I'm sure he won't.

"Pearce." Jack comes over, smiling at me. "How are you this morning?"

"I'm fine. Could I talk to you for a minute?"

"Certainly. Just let me get a drink."

After he does, we excuse ourselves from Royce and go into an empty room to talk.

"What is it?" Jack takes a drink of his bourbon.

"It's about one of our associates. Someone used her the other night, then made her stay and wouldn't let her go. He tied her up and kept her there the entire day."

"And what do you want *me* to do about it?"

"It's against the rules. This person needs to be punished. Otherwise he'll do it again."

"Who was it?"

"I don't know but I thought you could help me find out."

"No." He takes a drink. "I can't do that. And you need to stay out of it."

"But it's not right. We're not in the business of tying up girls and holding them hostage for our personal pleasure."

"Was she hurt?"

"She had red marks on her wrists where he tied her up. Other than that, she said she wasn't hurt, but she could've been lying to protect him."

"Who is this girl? And why was she telling you this? Each encounter is to be strictly confidential."

"I can't tell you who it was. Besides, if you're not going to do anything, it doesn't matter." I sound angry, because I am. "I thought you would care about this, Jack. You have two daughters. Would you want them to be treated this way?"

"This girl is not my daughter. And what these girls are doing is a job. There are hazards to all jobs and when these girls signed up, they knew what they were getting into."

"No, they don't. I don't think they're telling the girls all the rules when they hire them. This girl wasn't even aware of the punishments or the severity of them."

He sighs heavily. "That might be true. They've been having trouble recruiting girls, so it wouldn't surprise me if they've been leaving out important details when the girls sign up, such as what the punishments will be for breaking the rules. If they told them, chances are they wouldn't take the job."

"That's not fair. They have to be told. We have to do something. Bring it up at the meeting today."

"No. Absolutely not." He lowers his voice and narrows his eyes at me. "Like I told you the other day, you pick your battles, and this is NOT a battle worth fighting. They won't do anything about it and you'll have a target on your back for bringing it up. They'll grow suspicious of you, wondering why you're sticking up for this girl, and then they'll begin tracking your every move, listening in on your calls, bugging your car. Is that what you want?"

"No."

"Then stay out of it. You're young and still new to the group. You don't know much, so right now, they'll leave you alone. They won't even pay attention to you if you just keep quiet and don't make waves. There will come a time when you can voice your opinion, but that time is not now. And when you finally are able to voice your opinion, think long and hard before doing so. Only do it for something you feel strongly enough about to risk your life for, because that's what you're doing every time you challenge them." He pats me on the back. "We need to get in there. The meeting will be starting shortly."

The meeting is mostly just updates on things that are already in the works. My father talks about his progress on the development of a new chemical compound that can be used in explosives and not be traced. I don't even want to know what that's about, but I'm sure I'll find out eventually.

We break for lunch, then the meeting continues. It concludes at four. My father approaches me as I'm leaving. I haven't spoken to him since I got here. That would seem odd to anyone else, but to us it's normal. We only speak to each other when necessary. That's the way our relationship is and always has been. Growing up, there were no father-son talks, unless I was in trouble for something. And now, as an adult, he talks to me only when he wants something or feels the need to lecture me about my behavior.

"Several of us are going into the city for dinner," he says. "Would you like to join us?"

"I can't. I need to go to the office. I'm behind on work."

"Is that because you left early on Friday?" He smirks, happy with himself for knowing something he knew I wanted to hide from him.

"No. I just need to get some things done while the office is quiet."

"So where were you yesterday afternoon?"

I quickly try to come up with a lie he'll believe.

"I went golfing. I know I shouldn't have left early, but it was a nice day and I needed to work on my swing."

He nods. "I agree. We have several client golf outings coming up. You should work on your game so you don't embarrass us like you have in the past. I'd like to practice my swing as well. Perhaps we should go together next week. We'll go to the country club."

"Yes, we'll do that. Enjoy your dinner."

I leave without saying goodbye to Jack, who's at the bar getting another drink. I have to get out of here. My body is wound so tight my muscles ache. I hate these meetings and I hate being around these people.

The only thing keeping me sane right now is knowing I'm going to see Rachel. Her beautiful face. That kind smile. I want to hold her in my arms, in one of those hugs she likes so well. Tightly this time so I don't get yelled at. I laugh as I think about that. Out of all the things I could be reprimanded for, I never once thought it would be for how I hugged.

I speed on the way back to my loft. I'm supposed to meet Rachel at seven, but I'm going to call and see if I can go over there earlier than that. I have to see her. I *need* to see her. And I don't want to wait another minute.

CHAPTER TWELVE

RACHEL

Pearce called and asked if he could come over now instead of waiting until seven. I told him yes, but I'm not quite ready so I'm hurrying to finish up.

I'm glad he's coming over early. Even though I just saw him last night, I already miss him. Thinking back, I realize that I never missed Adam, even when we were apart for days. I should've taken that as a sign we weren't meant to be together.

I'm not saying Pearce and I are meant to be together, but the fact that I miss him this much when he's not around has to mean something. I can't believe how much I like him. And it's not just because he's good-looking. It's more than that. I like that he's polite and a gentleman and that he's always so attentive. When I'm talking, he gives me his full attention, which is rare for anyone, but especially guys. I like his subtle humor and how he hides it behind his serious demeanor. Just being around Pearce, I get this happy, excited feeling that I haven't felt with other guys I've dated.

I'm in the bathroom now, drying my hair. Blow-drying it always makes it frizz a little but I can't go out with wet hair so after I dry it, I put it up in a ponytail.

The cool fall weather from last night has remained so I'm wearing jeans and a white v-neck sweater. I do my makeup quick, and just as I finish up, Pearce is knocking on the door.

I open it and see him standing there, wearing black dress pants, a crisp white button-up, and a blue, black, and gray striped tie. His shirt is taut over his broad shoulders with no bunching or wrinkling, like it was made for him. I bet it was. His clothes are probably custom made and that's why they fit him so well. My gaze lifts up to his face, which is freshly shaved, accentuating his well-defined jawline. Just the sight of him causes that fluttery feeling to take over my stomach again.

He hands me a bouquet of flowers, a dozen long stem red roses.

"Pearce, they're beautiful. Thank you."

He leans down and kisses me. "You're quite welcome. I wasn't sure what your favorite flower was but I assumed I couldn't go wrong with roses."

"I love roses." I take them to the kitchen.

"But they're not your favorite," he says.

How did he know that? Did I not sound excited enough about the roses? He's very perceptive. I've noticed he seems to pick up on the smallest things, like changes in my facial expression or tone. I'm not used to that. In my past relationships I had to come out and tell a guy what I thought or how I felt about something, and after I did, he usually didn't listen or remember.

"Tulips are my favorite, but roses are a close second." I set the flowers down on the counter. I feel Pearce's arms around me and I turn and see him smiling at me.

"Then I will bring you tulips next time." His hand sweeps down the side of my face, settling by my ear and holding me in place as he lowers his lips to mine for another kiss. This time it's a slow, sensual kiss like he gave me the other night. I love how his kisses aren't rushed. How he takes his time, his soft lips moving slowly over mine. And when I part my lips, he doesn't shove his tongue in like most men do. Instead, I feel his breath and then his tongue, as his kiss gradually becomes deeper.

We remain by the counter, and I feel my insides heating up as everything else around me fades away. We're just kissing, but the way he does it affects me in such a way that I lose myself in the moment. Like I can't remember where I am or what I was doing before he got here. It's not just his kisses making me this way. It's him. His large stature. His commanding presence. The way he holds me in such a strong, powerful way. He distracts me from

118

everything else and all I can focus on is him and what he's doing to me.

When we pause to take a breath, I back away, knowing if we continue this, we'll end up in the bedroom. And we shouldn't do that. Not yet. It's too soon. But it's not like I don't want to. I'm just not someone who moves that fast. But damn, I wish I was, because I really want to take this farther.

I nod toward the flowers. "I should probably put those in water." He lets me go and I take a big plastic pitcher from the cupboard. "I don't have a vase. This will have to do."

As I'm trimming the roses in the sink, Pearce comes up behind me and wraps his arms around my waist and kisses my cheek. "I missed you today."

"I missed you too."

His strong arms surround me and I feel the heat from his body. I breathe him in because he smells good; fresh and clean with a hint of cologne that mixes well with his skin. He kisses the side of my neck, making me shiver.

I keep my eyes on the roses. "You better stop that or I'll cut myself."

"Then let me do it." His kisses continue as he takes the scissors from my hand.

"Pearce," I whisper, my eyes closing as I savor the feel of his lips on my skin. "You'll hurt yourself. I'll cut them later."

"Don't worry about me. Just relax." He says it soft and low, his warm breath tickling my neck.

He's doing it again. Making me so aroused I want to drag him to the bedroom and give in to my urges. This is so unlike me. Wanting to do it this soon. But I feel like I've known him longer than it's been. And this attraction I have to him is off the charts.

I hear him drop the scissors and I open my eyes to see the roses now propped in the pitcher that's sitting in the sink.

"How did you do that?" I ask him. "You weren't even looking."

"I'm good with my hands," he whispers in my ear.

My heart's beating fast, wetness pooling between my legs. I tilt my head to the side, begging for more of his feather-light kisses along my neck. He does what I want, kissing the side of my neck as he tightens his grip around my waist. His other hand moves up to my breast, gently squeezing it.

I softly moan and feel his lips smile slightly against my skin. His hand moves to the waistband of my jeans and he undoes the button, then tugs the zipper down. My breath quickens as I feel his warm hand on my skin, sliding down my lower abs and slipping under my panties.

"Pearce," I whisper.

"Yes," he whispers back, his hand knowing exactly where to go, moving in slow, purposeful movements.

"Maybe we should..." I was going to say stop or slow down but it's not what I want. It's what I *think* I should want because it's what I'm supposed to do. Be the good girl. Take things slow. But I'm tired of being that way. I want to do what I want. What feels right to me. And right now, what Pearce is doing feels very right.

"Would you like me to stop?" I hear him ask in his deep sexy voice.

"No." I breathe out the word, unable to say any more, lost in the feel of his touch.

I moan again, tipping my head back against his chest. My body is flooded with sensations, from head to toe. I'm still facing the sink and he presses into me from behind as he pulls me closer. I feel him, fully aroused, and wanting this as much as I do.

I'm thinking he'll back away and take me to the bedroom. But he doesn't let me go. Instead, he continues what he started, his hand between my legs, igniting the sensitive bundle of nerves and quickly bringing me to the edge. As I pass over it, waves of intense pleasure hit me with such a force that I have to grab onto the sink to hold myself up. He holds me tighter as the waves continue, over and over until they eventually subside.

He slowly removes his hand and talks low and soft into my ear. "Are you glad I came over early?"

I turn around and see him smiling at me.

"If I'd known *that* was going to happen, I would've had you come over this morning."

He chuckles. "I told you I was good with my hands."

"Let's go to the bedroom." I run my hand over the front of his pants.

"Not yet." He takes my hand and brings it to his mouth for a kiss. "I'm still getting to know you."

"I think you got to know me quite intimately just now."

"True. But I need to know more."

"But you didn't get any enjoyment out of that."

"Trust me. I enjoyed it. I think you could feel how much I enjoyed myself." He kisses me again. "Are you ready to go?"

"I just need to finish my makeup."

"Go ahead. I'll wait here."

I go in the bathroom, my body still recovering from what he did to me. That was amazing. I've never felt anything like that before, which is sad, because by the age of 24, you'd think I would have by now. But apparently the guys I've been with didn't know what they were doing. Pearce *definitely* knows what he's doing.

When I come back out to the living room, he's watching TV.

"Okay, I'm ready." I grab my purse and keys.

He shuts the TV off and meets me by the door. He puts his hand on my lower back and kisses me. "You look beautiful."

"Thank you. And you look very handsome. All dressed up again, I see."

He holds out his tie. "This is a very casual tie."

"A tie is never casual." I pull him into the hall and lock my door.

"Sure it is." He takes my hand as we walk down the stairs. "When you go beyond two colors in a tie, it becomes casual. That's the rule."

"Who made that rule?"

"I did." We reach his car and he opens my door. "Are we still going to the shopping mall?" From the look on his face, you'd think I was taking him for a root canal.

I laugh. "Yes, and you're going to love it."

He shakes his head as he walks around the front of the car. He gets in and says, "So where is this mall?"

I give him directions and ten minutes later we're there. We go inside and I lead him to the Gap and take him to the men's side of the store, placing him in front of the wall of jeans.

"What kind do you want? They have all different kinds."

He looks at me. "Rachel, I cannot wear these."

"Why not?"

"It's not appropriate attire."

I set my hands on my hips. "Excuse me, but I'm wearing jeans right now. Are you saying I'm inappropriate?"

"No, of course not. They look great on you, but they wouldn't look good on me."

"How do you know? You've never even worn them."

"All of my clothes are tailored to fit. I can't buy clothes off the rack. They won't fit right."

"Sure they will. You just have to try them on."

He eyes the stack of jeans, his expression wary.

I get up close and whisper in his ear. "The thought of you in jeans really turns me on. And if I saw you actually in them, I may not be able to keep my hands off you."

He slowly smiles. "You're very clever. And very persuasive." He takes a pair of jeans from the stack. "I'll try these on."

"You have to try on more than one. Let's get a few more styles. What's your size?"

Unfortunately, the store doesn't have many options in his size because he's so tall. But we find four pairs and go back to the dressing room. He walks out and shows me the first pair and, wow, he looks hot. He's got a tight ass that looks great in jeans.

"I like those," I tell him. "You should get them."

"They feel strange. The fabric is so heavy. I'm not used to denim."

"You'll get used to it. Try on the next pair."

"Why? If you like this pair, I don't need to try on any more."

"I want to see you in the other ones. And it's good to have more than one pair."

He sighs and goes back in the dressing room. I poke my head in before he closes the door. "You look really hot in those jeans. Really, really hot."

122

He smiles. "You're just saying that so I'll try on the other ones."

"No. It's the truth. You look great. Really."

I kiss him quick, then close the door and wait outside the dressing room. Shopping together like this, I feel like we're boyfriend and girlfriend and have been dating for months. I don't know what it is about Pearce, but I feel this connection with him that I haven't felt with anyone else. Not even Adam.

And I'm much more comfortable around Pearce now than I was just a few days ago. I think it helps that he's not acting so formal anymore. He's more relaxed and casual, or at least what's considered casual for him. He still speaks in a very formal way but I'm used to it now and have come to like it.

Pearce steps out of the dressing room and shows me the next pair of jeans, which also look good. The next two he tries on look good too. By the time he's done, I can't decide which he should get so I let him decide. He picks the first two he tried on. After that, I don't think he was paying attention. Like most men, shopping bores him.

Next we go to the stacks of t-shirts.

"I don't need any more t-shirts," he says.

"But these aren't for working out. They're to be worn out on our casual dates."

"I have to wear a collared shirt in public." He points to the rack behind us. "How about a polo shirt?"

He *would* look good in a polo shirt with his broad shoulders and muscular build. He'd look good in a t-shirt too. He'd look good in anything.

"Okay, but we're getting you a t-shirt to wear for when we're home watching TV or making dinner."

He's smiling at me and I can't figure out why until I replay what I said. Home. Watching TV. Making dinner. We've just started dating and I've already assumed we'll be spending all this time together.

He slips his hand around my waist and leans down to me. "It sounds like we'll be seeing each other a lot."

"Would you be okay with that?"

"I would be *more* than okay with that."

He lets me go and I focus my attention back on the t-shirts. I pick out a dark blue one. Then I get a white polo shirt and a black one. I chose basic colors that I've seen him wear before. The shirt style is a big enough change. He wouldn't wear the shirts if I picked ones in colors he doesn't normally wear.

We go to the register, and after he pays I take a pair of jeans and the white polo shirt and hand them to him. "Okay, go change."

"I'm already dressed."

"You're too dressed up for a movie. I feel underdressed. I'd feel better if we were both wearing jeans." I reach up and kiss him. "Please?"

He sighs, then takes my hand and we walk back to the dressing room. Before he goes in there, he gives me a kiss. "I'm only doing this because I find you extremely irresistible and hard to say no to, which is a dangerous combination by the way."

I laugh as he goes in the dressing room again. He comes out in the new outfit. He looks like a super hot college guy. His dress clothes make him look older than 25, but in the casual clothes he could pass for 22 or 23.

I take the clothes he had on and neatly fold them up and place them in the sack.

"What do you think?" He stands in front of me. "Because I feel very uncomfortable right now so I hope you like it."

"I love it. You look great. But why are you uncomfortable? Do the clothes not fit right?"

"They fit fine. I've just never been out in public in clothes like this. In college I occasionally wore polo shirts but with regular pants, not jeans."

"Well, relax, because you look really hot." I thread my hand with his and we walk out of the store.

"Now I need to get something for *you*." He glances around the mall. "They don't appear to have any designer stores here but I'm sure we could find something nice at that department store."

"I don't need anything. I'm good."

"Come on. Let me buy you a dress. Or jewelry. Whatever you want."

"Really, Pearce. You don't need to buy me anything."

"I have to get you something." He scans the stores again. "I know what to get." He takes me over to a jewelry store.

"Pearce, no. I don't want you buying me jewelry."

"I'm not. I'm buying you this." He holds up a tall crystal vase. "Do you like it?"

"Yes. It's beautiful. But don't buy me that. It's too much."

He cocks his head, a grin on his face. "You do know I have money, right?"

"Yes, but that doesn't mean you should buy me expensive gifts."

"I want to." He takes the vase to the register. While he's up there, I check the price. It's $250. He shouldn't be spending that much on me but I can't seem to stop him and at least now I'll have something to put my flowers in.

We take our shopping bags to the car. "Thank you for the vase. That was a very nice gift."

He wraps his arms around me. "You're welcome. But it was more of a necessity than a gift. You'll be getting a lot more flowers from me and you needed something to put them in."

"Now I need to do something nice for you. I don't have money to buy you a gift but I could make you dinner sometime. Or I could make you brownies or pie or banana bread. Not to brag, but I'm a really good baker."

"You bake?" His brows rise. "I didn't know people our age bake. Or that *anyone* still bakes."

"I guess a lot of people don't, but *I* do. I find it relaxing and I love the way the house smells when something's baking in the oven." I check my watch. "Do you want to head inside to the theater? I was thinking we should go to the movie now and have dinner later."

"Good idea. Let's get the movie over with."

"Hey!" I playfully hit him. "Movies are fun. You promised to be positive about trying new things."

"I never promised that."

125

"Well, then just pretend you like it, for my sake."

We go back inside and walk down to the theater. He lets me pick the movie so I pick an action film. If I'm making him go to the movies, I thought I should pick something he might like.

After we get our tickets, we stop at the concession stand and I order a bucket of popcorn and two large sodas. Pearce tells me he doesn't drink soda, but I explained that soda and popcorn go together and that he had to at least try it.

We snack on the popcorn while waiting for the movie to start.

"Sorry," he says when his hand bumps mine in the bucket.

I nudge his side. "That's supposed to happen. Hands meeting in the popcorn bucket? It's a form of flirting. Actually, that's more true for 12-year-olds than people our age, but since you're new to this you should practice. Go ahead."

He plays along, dipping his hand in the bucket and finding mine. But instead of leaving it there, he picks it up and kisses it.

"I'll pass on the popcorn trick. I can find better ways to flirt." He puts his arm around my shoulder. "Are you having fun?"

I move closer to him. "Yes. Are you? And don't say no. You have to be positive."

He kisses me. "I think I'd have fun doing most anything with you. And that's saying a lot because I don't normally have fun."

"Then I need to change that, because everyone should have fun. Even stuffy old businessmen."

"Hey." He takes his arm back. "I'm not old! Or stuffy!"

I shrug. "You will be if you don't add some fun to your life."

He smiles and puts his arm around me again.

The movie starts and I shift a little so that I can rest my head on his shoulder. He lightly rubs my arm, and just like when he held my hand in the park, I get the feeling he's telling me something with that simple gesture. I feel like he's telling me he's starting to care about me or maybe he already does. I hope so, because I care about him too.

After the movie, I take him to a sports bar. It's one of those places with giant TVs everywhere and pool tables and dart boards. It's Saturday night so football is on and it's loud and crowded. That doesn't bother me, but I was worried it might bother Pearce because he's not used to places like this. I only suggested it because I thought it would be fun to watch some of the game. My dad and I used to watch football together on the weekends and I miss it. I don't have anyone to watch games with anymore.

"Do you like football?" I ask Pearce. We just ordered. We both got a burger and beer. I was a little surprised Pearce would order that. I thought he'd order something more sophisticated, like a steak and a glass of wine.

"I love football," he says, "but I don't have much time to watch it with my work schedule."

"You work too much. It's not good for you."

"I don't have a choice. There's a lot to be done." The waitress drops off our beers and he takes a drink.

"You're not working *tonight*."

"Because I had someplace better to be." He holds my hand across the table. "Someone I had to see."

"So you're saying I should hang out with you more so you don't go into the office so much?"

"I hadn't thought about that, but yes, that would work."

As he takes another drink of his beer, I glance over at the table next to us where four women around my age are sitting and talking. I do a double-take when I notice they're all looking at Pearce. Looking at him like they'd like to take him home and, well...do things. They look away when they see me watching them. I scan the rest of the bar and see some other women checking him out. Does this always happen when he goes out?

Pearce is definitely the hottest guy here, but he's also with me so these women need to back off. I'm usually not the jealous type, but for whatever reason, I just felt a twinge of jealousy seeing other women look at Pearce that way.

Pearce doesn't even notice this is going on. His eyes are on the TV, watching the game, his hand holding mine on the table.

I rub his hand to get his attention. "So you never told me what you did today. Were you at the office this morning?"

His eyes shift from the TV back to me. "Yes. I spent the entire day there. What did *you* do?"

"I went to my volunteer job from nine to noon, then I worked on a paper that's due next week."

"Where do you volunteer?"

"I thought I already told you this, but I guess not. Every Saturday I volunteer at a homeless shelter. I teach people how to read. Today I had this older man who—"

He stops me, his hand gripping my forearm. "What shelter? Where is it?"

I glance down at my arm. Why is he gripping my arm like that?

"It's near downtown, close to the bus station. It's kind of a run-down area, but I heard the city has plans to fix it up."

"Don't go there anymore." He uses this strict tone that makes me feel like he's telling me what to do.

I don't like that tone. At all. I already have a controlling mother. I don't need a controlling boyfriend as well.

"Pearce, I volunteer there. I have for a year. I'm not going to stop going."

"I'm sorry, but you'll have to tell them you're done volunteering. I can't let you go there."

"LET me?" I yank my arm away from him. "You don't get a say in it. And the fact that you *think* you do makes me wonder if you're not the man I thought you were."

"Rachel, I'm telling you this for your own good. You shouldn't be going to that part of town."

"We've been going out for a week and you're already telling me what to do? Yeah, I don't think so."

"You didn't have a problem telling *me* what to *wear*." He sits back and motions to himself. "And now look at me. I look ridiculous."

I feel my temper rising. "First of all, every guy in here is dressed like you. You would've looked ridiculous wearing a shirt and tie. And second, if you didn't want to wear the clothes I picked out, you could've just said no." I get up and grab my purse. "I need some air."

"Rachel, wait!"

I storm out the door, angry and confused. Why is he trying to control me like this? He hasn't done this before. This is why I

128

don't rush into relationships. You think the person is normal, but after a few dates they turn out to be crazy and controlling.

"Rachel." Pearce comes out of the restaurant and stands in front of me. "Rachel, I'm sorry. I shouldn't have said that about the clothes. I like the clothes."

"No, you don't," I mutter.

He half smiles. "Okay, maybe not, but you're right. I would've looked strange wearing a tie in a sports bar. Or the movies. And I appreciate the fact that you took the time to help me pick something out. And maybe eventually I'll come to like these clothes."

When I don't say anything, he continues. "You have to understand, this is all new for me. Movies. Sports bars. Jeans. Shopping malls. It's a lot of change all at once."

My lips creep up. "I did kind of make you do a lot of new stuff in one night. I didn't realize that. Next time, I'll just pick one or two new things."

He lifts my chin up. "So there's going to be a next time?"

"Yes. Why?"

"When you stormed out of there like that, I wasn't sure."

"I'm not good at arguing. If I feel myself getting really angry, I have to leave and calm down before I can talk to the person again. I've always been that way."

"And I'm the type of person who likes to talk it out and end it as soon as possible."

I smile. "That's going to make for some interesting fights. I'll leave and you'll be left talking to yourself."

He smiles back. "Yes, I suppose that's what will happen. But since that's a very ineffective way to argue, let's try to avoid letting it get to that point."

"Pearce, why did you react that way when I told you I worked at the shelter?"

"Because it's not safe and I don't want you to get hurt."

"I only go there during the day. And I'm not alone. There are plenty of people around."

"Maybe *inside* the building, but outside is a different story. I've driven through that area. I've seen what's it like. There are drug deals taking place on the street. Men lurking in the alleys. Even the police won't go there."

"What were you doing in that part of town?"

"I was on the way to meet with one of our distributors and I accidentally made a wrong turn and ended up going down that street where the shelter is."

"I know it's dangerous, but I only go there once a week and I'm making a real difference with those people. The first person I taught to read was a man named Raymond, and now a year later, he can read entire books. It's changed his life. He has all this confidence now. And he got a job and just moved into an apartment. Do you know how great it feels to be able to help someone like that? When he read his first sentence we were both crying. I still cry when one of my students reads their first sentence."

Pearce is smiling at me. "You're very special, you know that?"

"*I'm* not. My students are. You wouldn't believe the horrible lives they've had. But they made it through all that and they're trying to get a better life by learning to read so they can get a job. And I want to help them do that, which is why I keep going to the shelter."

"Maybe you could meet somewhere else. There's a bus stop at the shelter. They could take the bus to a library and you could meet them there."

"Pearce, you need to let this go. I know you're concerned about me, but you don't need to be. I can take care of myself. And you need to know right now that you can't tell me what to do. I can't be in a relationship like that. You can express your opinions and concerns, but in the end, I'll make my own decisions."

He opens his mouth to say something, but then stops before he does.

"We should go inside and have dinner," I tell him. "They probably thought we left."

We go back to our table just as our food arrives. After that fight we had, we keep our dinner conversation light. I ask him what he thought of the movie and then we talk about football and watch the game on TV. I feel like I'm on a date with just a normal guy and not a billionaire. Pearce is relaxed and smiling and laughing. In just a week, he's really loosened up around me. And I like it. I like seeing him not so serious and having fun. He needs that. He needs more fun in his life. And I'm going to make sure that happens.

"Do you play darts?" I ask Pearce after the waitress clears our plates.

"I can't say that I ever have."

"Do you think you can handle one more new thing tonight?"

"I think I could." He drops some money on the table for the check, then follows me to the dart board.

I quickly explain the rules and then we start. He struggles on the first game, but gets better in the second. And by the third, he's getting really good.

"You're a fast learner." I step in front of the board for game number four.

He hugs me from behind and kisses my cheek. "I had a good teacher."

That must be true because he wins game four. We make that our last game, then head back to the car.

Another awesome date. The fight wasn't good but it was over quickly.

It's late, but I don't want the night to end. And maybe it won't. I'd kind of like Pearce to finish what he started in my kitchen. This time with both of us enjoying it.

CHAPTER THIRTEEN

PEARCE

"Would you like to go my place?" I ask as we're driving away from the restaurant. "I have cable TV, so consider that before you answer."

"Hmm. All those channels are pretty tempting. Do I get to pick what we watch?"

"Of course. The guest always picks."

"Your place is like a half hour away. And then you'll have to drive me all the way back to my place."

I glance at her. "I don't see the problem here."

"It's just a lot of driving."

"I don't mind. I like driving. But you need to make a decision fast because if we're going to my place I need to take the next exit."

"Okay, let's go to your place. I'd like to see it. Do you keep it clean or is it messy like the stereotypical bachelor pad?"

"I have a cleaning staff that comes in, so it's clean."

As we're driving, I try to figure out what I'm doing. Bringing her back to my place? After a night of nonstop flirting, kissing, and touching? The sexual tension so thick I can feel it in the air? This is going to lead to sex and I told her we would wait. But I know she wants it. After I touched her like that in her kitchen, she was ready to do it right then and there. And as for me, I've wanted to have sex with her since the moment I saw her sitting in that lecture hall. I've never felt this level of attraction to a woman in my entire life. Every time I'm with her I have to work to hold myself back. So why am I even questioning this? We both want it and we've waited long enough. Longer than I've ever waited with anyone else.

The problem is there's this war going on inside me. It's been going on since I met her, telling me I need to leave her alone before this gets too far. I think it already has gone too far, and if we have sex tonight, it will definitely have gone too far.

Unlike the other women I've been with, I don't think sex with Rachel will be purely physical. I have feelings for her, which complicate matters. I've never had sex with someone I actually cared about. This is all new for me and I'm not sure I'm ready for this.

We're at my building now and I pull up to the guard station.

George is there and says his usual line. "Welcome back, Mr. Kensington." He leans down a little, trying to get a better look into the car.

"Have a nice evening, George."

I drive forward before he can look too closely at Rachel.

"He seems like a nice man," she says.

"He is, but I had to hurry through because he was checking you out."

She swats at my arm. "He wasn't checking me out. He's like 70 years old."

"And yet he was checking you out. Dirty old man." I act annoyed as I pull into my parking space. "I'll have to speak to his supervisor about that."

"Pearce, don't get him in trouble."

I go around and open her door. I put my arm around her as we walk to the elevator. "I was kidding. George and I are friends. And I can't blame him for checking you out. You're gorgeous. Men can't help themselves. We have to look at beautiful women."

"And women can't help but look at a hot man. You had plenty of women checking you out at the restaurant."

"I didn't notice." I kiss her. "The only woman I noticed was you."

We ride the elevator to the top floor, which can only be accessed by a security code. The elevator opens right into my loft apartment, which takes up the entire top floor of the building.

133

"Is this your place?" Rachel asks.

"This is it."

She steps into the living room. "It's huge. Look at all this space."

"I'm a big guy. I need a lot of space."

She walks into the kitchen. "I like the open layout. I like how the kitchen and living room are all one big room."

The kitchen and living room make up the middle of the loft. Then off to one side, down the hall, there are two bedrooms, one of which I use as an office. On the other end of the loft, just off the kitchen, is the master bedroom. The bedroom door is placed so that I can see the elevator and living room from my bed. I had it built that way so that if someone's in there, trying to rob me or attack me, I'll see them coming. I keep a gun in my nightstand just in case.

We're in the kitchen and I go over to the refrigerated glass case that holds an assortment of beverages. "Would you like something to drink?"

"Just water is fine."

"I have several kinds of water in here. You have to be more specific. Or just pick one."

She comes over and takes out a bottle of citrus flavored water. I grab a plain water for myself. I don't buy any of this. The cleaning staff stocks it for me.

We're both standing by the counter, holding our waters. I take a sip of mine and she drinks some of hers. Our eyes meet and I feel it again. The tension that's been hovering between us all night. Pure, raw sexual tension that's stronger than I've ever felt before.

I step closer to her, setting my water on the counter behind her. I take her water and set it next to mine. I shouldn't do this. Doing this will only move this relationship forward, taking it to a place I said I wouldn't go. But God, I want it. I want it so bad. I want *her*, and not just sexually. I want her in my life. I want this to go somewhere. Someplace real. For the first time in my life, I want a real relationship and I want it with her. Maybe it won't work out, but I at least want to try.

Our bodies are just inches apart, our eyes locked on each other, the sexual tension ready to burst. I don't know what the hell I'm waiting for.

I haul her into me, my other hand buried in her hair as I crash my lips to hers. I wanted our first time together to be slow and gentle, but we're way past that point. Slow and gentle will have to wait until later.

She yanks up my polo shirt and I break from her lips just long enough to rip the shirt off. I take her sweater off next, getting even more aroused when I see her breasts overflowing a white, lacy push-up bra. She's already working on my belt so I work on her jeans, unbuttoning them and tugging down the zipper. It reminds me of when I did this earlier and she moaned in pleasure at my touch. I want to make her moan again and yell out my name.

It's taking too long to get her jeans off while standing, so I pick her up and carry her to my bed. Once she's lying down, I'm easily able to slip off her jeans, then slide her white, lacy string bikinis down her long, lean legs. I strip off my jeans and boxers, and while I'm doing that, she whips off her bra. I'm left with the sight of her naked body. And damn, she's beautiful. If I wasn't so desperate to be with her, I'd just stand here and stare at her.

I get a condom from my nightstand and put it on, then lie over her and kiss her, my tongue tasting her. She runs her hands down my back.

"Are you sure about this?" I ask.

"Yes," she says breathless.

I line myself up and push inside her. Fuck. She feels incredible. Like she was made for me. A perfect damn fit. I didn't think that was possible. She must feel it too, because she's moaning even more than she was earlier. I'm trying not to go too fast, but I've lost all control of it. It's like there's this momentum driving us forward and I can't slow down. And I don't think she wants me to. She's matching my movements, holding onto me as I thrust into her, harder and faster.

I'm so close, but I'm trying to hold out longer for her.

She tells me to keep going, and then I feel her as she comes. I follow seconds later, then lie over her a moment, catching my breath while softly kissing her.

"I'll be right back," I say, getting up. I go in the bathroom and dispose of the condom. This is when I'd normally tell the woman to leave. But instead, I return to the bed and lie on my back, putting my arm out. Rachel moves under it and against my side and I lower my arm around her.

As we lie there, I go over in my head what just happened. That wasn't just sex. I've had sex many times and it's never felt like that. With all the other women I've been with, it's always felt like we were two separate people, our bodies briefly connected but never really together. But with Rachel, I felt like we were truly one. Our minds, our thoughts, our need for each other. It was intense. And emotional. I actually felt emotion during sex. Shit, that can't be good.

I can't let this move forward. I can't keep leading her on when I know it's going to end. I can't get her involved in my life. It's too dangerous.

And yet…I can't let her go.

"Pearce." Her hand moves over my chest in a slow, circular pattern. It's warm and comforting and not what I'm used to. Women always touch me in a sexual way, not a loving, caring way like Rachel is doing right now.

I kiss her forehead. "Yes, Rachel."

"That was amazing."

"I agree." I smile, happy that she got as much pleasure out of it as I did.

"I mean, I've never had it that…good. We're going to have to do that again."

"I couldn't agree more."

"But not right now. Right now I just want to lie here." She moves closer, snuggling up against my side. "I like being in your arms."

"I like having you there." I kiss her forehead again. "I want you to stay here tonight. I don't want you to go."

She lifts her head up and kisses me. "Then I won't go." She rests her head on my shoulder and hugs my chest.

I tighten my arm around her, securing her in place. I'm breaking my own rules again. Never hold a woman after sex. Or ever. And never let her spend the night. Yet here I am, holding her in my arms after asking her to stay.

I don't know why I'm acting this way. I know it's wrong. I know it's against the rules, both theirs and mine. Maybe I'll come to my senses tomorrow and end this. Tell her I can't see her anymore.

I look down and see her resting on my chest, her eyes shut, her arm over me. She has a slight smile on her face and looks peaceful. Content. I feel the same way. It's a feeling I've never had before. That feeling of being at peace.

How does she do it? How does she bring out these feelings in me? I never feel anything. It's what I've been taught. Think. Don't feel. Use your brain, not your heart. Shut off all emotion. Feeling emotion makes you weak. And *showing* emotion is even worse. It makes you vulnerable. Open to attack. So I do everything possible to keep my emotions hidden, burying them so deep I can't feel them. But with Rachel, my emotions keep rising to the surface and I can't seem to control it.

I glance down at her body; those lean long legs, those curvy hips, that narrow waist and those soft full breasts. God, she's beautiful.

She's also intelligent. Compassionate. Amusing. Easy to talk to.

Dammit! I'm getting way too attached to her. I need to end this. Soon.

But then I feel her in my arms, and think about how I feel when I'm with her, and I can't do it. I can't end this. I know I need to, but I can't.

I lift the covers over us and minutes later she falls asleep on me. I find myself drifting off as well. But before I do, I check the clock. It's only 11:30. I haven't gone to sleep this early in years. Probably not since high school. I usually go to bed at two or three in the morning, then get up at five for work. I'm always too wound up to sleep. But the feel of Rachel next to me calms my mind and my body and I fall asleep.

A noise in the bathroom wakes me. I bolt up, my head whipping right and left as I yank open my nightstand to get my gun.

The door to the bathroom opens and I see Rachel standing there. I'm not used to having someone in my apartment and my instincts just took over. I slowly close the nightstand drawer as she walks over to me.

"I didn't wake you, did I?"

She has on the white dress shirt I wore yesterday, and damn, it looks sexy on her. She only has the middle section buttoned, giving me a glimpse of her breasts. My shirt is long, but she's tall so I still see plenty of her lean, toned legs.

"No, I was awake," I tell her. "What time is it?"

"Nine."

"Nine?" I check the clock. "I haven't slept that long in—" I pause to think. "I don't think I've ever slept that long."

"I guess you were tired." She climbs on top of me, straddling me and pushing me back down on the bed. "I must've wore you out last night with all those new activities." She leans down until her face is just over mine. "Or it could've been that incredibly hot, amazing, best-I've-ever-had sex."

I smile. "That was probably it." I reach up and start unbuttoning the shirt she's wearing. "I should let you know, I have serious insomnia. Perhaps you could help me out."

She kisses me, her mouth minty. She must've found my toothpaste. "Are you saying you want me to come over and do that every night?"

"Is that a problem?" I undo the last button and slip my hands under the shirt, over her hips, and around her firm, round ass.

She closes her eyes, smiling and becoming breathless at the feel of my touch. "Every night might be too much." My hand moves up to her breast and she gasps. "Or maybe not."

I'm still naked from last night and she has nothing on under the shirt. She feels the hard length of me beneath her and starts rubbing herself against me.

I push the shirt off her shoulders and she slips it down her arms and tosses it aside. She kisses me while still rubbing against me. I can barely hold myself back. I'm so hard, it's throbbing, desperate to be inside her again.

I need to get a condom, but they're in the drawer with my gun. I don't know her stance on guns, but I'm going to assume she won't like it.

"Let me get a condom," I whisper between kisses.

"Are you clean?"

"What?"

"Do you have any diseases? Like STDs?"

"No."

"Then we don't need one. I'm on the pill."

She reaches down and takes me in her hand, positioning me. Just as the tip touches her, I hold her back.

"Wait. We need a condom."

"Why? I don't have any diseases."

I've never done it without a condom. It's too risky. What if she's lying about not having diseases? What if she's not really on the pill? I've only known her a week, and although I have feelings for her and don't think she's the type of woman who would lie to me or try to trick me, I can't trust her. I trust no one.

"I can't do this without a condom," I say.

She doesn't seem mad or hurt by the request. "Um, okay. Are they in the drawer?"

"I'll get it." I lift her off me and set her next to me on the bed. Then I open the drawer just barely and take out a condom and slip it on.

"If you don't want to do this, we don't have to," she says.

I lie over her. "Believe me, I want to do this."

I kiss her, then put myself inside her. Shit, she feels good. It's almost unbelievable how compatible we are this way. She arches up and I lean down and kiss her breast. I didn't have a chance to do that last night so I'm taking time now. She has full, round, perfect breasts. And the best part is that they're all real. When I felt them, they were soft, natural. And knowing that makes them even more beautiful.

She grips my hair, keeping me at her breast while she wraps her legs around my waist. I go slower this time. I want this to last. I bring my mouth to hers and we kiss. Her hands slide down to my shoulders, holding onto them as my hips move faster. I attempt to slow down but she tells me not to, so I keep going, and moments later we're both there, over the peak and riding it down together until our bodies collapse. I roll off her, sweat beading up on my chest.

The sex was just like last night. Powerful. Intense.

"I think we've now confirmed that we're definitely compatible that way," she says, out of breath.

"I already came to that conclusion last night."

"I didn't. I thought it was too good to be true. A fluke. Like maybe you were just having a good night."

"Hey." I laugh and nudge her side. "I know what I'm doing."

"I know, but it's more than that. It's like we just fit. Like our bodies are made for each other."

I'm starting to think it's more than just our bodies that are made for each other. There's something else between us that's drawing us to each other on a deeper level. I hate admitting that to myself because I don't believe in fate or destiny or love at first sight. But I *am* the type of person who trusts my instincts. And if my instincts tell me to do something, I don't question it. I just do it. I make decisions fast. I can't stand it when people take forever to make a decision, analyzing every detail then wavering on what to do. I make a decision and go for it. And as much as I've tried to ignore my instincts when it comes to Rachel, if I listen to them, they tell me to be with her. To not let her go.

"Pearce, are you laughing at me?" She's lying on her side, facing me.

I look at her. "No. I'm not laughing."

"Yeah, but you're smiling like you think I'm crazy for saying that."

"Saying what?"

"That we're made for each other. Well, our bodies, not us."

"Why not *us*?"

140

Her smile turns into a shy grin. "Because we haven't known each other very long."

"You don't think there's anything else between us besides sex?" I act offended.

She gives me a kiss. "That's not what I meant. Truthfully, yes, I think there *is* something between us, but I'm not ready to admit that yet. It seems too soon."

I slip my hand under her waist and pull her against my side. "Is it too soon for me to consider you my girlfriend?"

"No. I would like that."

I kiss her. "Then would my girlfriend like breakfast?"

"Yes. I'm starving. Are there any good breakfast places around here?"

The answer to her question is yes, but I don't think we should go out. I know a lot of people in this town and if they see me with Rachel, the news will get back to my father or one of the members.

"Why don't we stay here and I'll make us something? It'll be the first time I've ever used the kitchen."

"Really?" She sits up a little. "How long have you lived here?"

"About a year."

"And you've never used the kitchen?"

"I always eat out. I don't cook."

"That oven you have in there costs a fortune. It's top of the line. And you've never used it?"

"No. Never. I don't even know if it works. I've never tried turning it on."

"What?" Her eyes widen in shock. "How is that possible? If I had an oven like that, I'd use it all the time. I think I even saw it had a convection setting."

"When were you checking out my oven? You were supposed to be checking out *me* last night, not my oven."

She laughs. "I wasn't checking it out. I just glanced at it and noticed the settings. Would you care if I used it sometime?"

"My oven?"

141

"Yeah. The one in my apartment doesn't work right. It cooks unevenly. It burns my baked goods before they're even done inside."

"You can use it whenever you want. What are you going to make?"

"Well, first I'm going to make you dinner like I told you I would, so pick a night and I'll come over. And since it's fall, I'd love to do some baking, like maybe an apple pie, some pumpkin bread, an apple crisp. Fall is my favorite baking season. I'd bake for days if I had someone who could eat everything I made."

"I can't eat *all* of it, but I could help you out. I don't think I've ever had pumpkin bread or that apple dish you mentioned."

"Are you serious?"

"Completely serious."

"What about caramel apples?"

"No."

"Caramel corn?"

"No."

"You didn't even have it as a kid?"

"You don't seem to be getting the fact that I live a rather unusual life." I say it jokingly, but it's true. "My childhood was atypical. There were no trips to the movies or the park or the shopping mall. I've worn suits for as long as I can remember, even as a young child. And I didn't eat things like caramel apples or popcorn. When I was growing up, I had no idea what we ate for dinner every night. The chef would announce what we were having but it was nothing you'd recognize and definitely not something that would appeal to children. But my peers had similar lifestyles so none of us knew what we were missing."

"Well, that settles it. I have to make you one of my pies. I've been in the mood to bake so this is great. Do you think I could come over next weekend? If you need to go to work, that's fine. I can be here alone. I'll be sure to make more than we can eat so you can share some with your parents. In fact, I'll make them their own pie."

The mention of my parents drags me back to reality. My other life. My real life. Not the fantasy life I'm currently living with the kind, smart, beautiful woman lying beside me.

"Don't worry about my parents. They have their own chef and they're very picky eaters."

"Maybe I could bake something for George. I bet he'd like an apple pie."

"Yes, I'm sure he would." I lean over and kiss her. "Now let's go find some breakfast. All this talk about baked goods has made me hungry."

We go to the kitchen, only to find I have no ingredients. So I call up a local restaurant and have breakfast delivered. We get dressed while we wait for it to arrive.

I should be at work right now but I don't want to go. I want to spend the day with Rachel.

"What are you doing today?" I ask her as we're finishing breakfast.

"I have to study, but I was thinking I might take an hour or so to go on a drive and check out the leaves. They're starting to turn color and I want to see them before they're gone."

"Why don't we take a drive together? I've lived here my whole life. I know the best spots to go."

"That'd be great. Could we go right now? That way I could get back this afternoon to study."

"Let me just grab my keys."

As I'm walking over to the table to get them, the phone rings. I stop to answer it. "This is Pearce."

"Pearce, it's your father."

I turn away from Rachel. "What do you need?"

"I need to know why you weren't at the office last night. You said you were going to work after the meeting, but I stopped by and you weren't there."

I can't stand the way he keeps tabs on me, like I'm a child.

"What time did you come by?"

"Around eight."

"I'd already left by then."

"I asked the janitor where you were and he said you hadn't been there all night."

Great. Now he's got the janitor spying on me?

"Actually, I wasn't feeling well so I went home to rest."

"Why didn't you say that before?"

I lower my voice. "Because you always say illness is a sign of weakness and I didn't want a lecture about how I needed to be stronger."

"You'll be getting a lecture if you don't get in the office. It's already 10:30 and you're not here."

"It's Sunday. Maybe I decided to take the day off."

"You don't get to decide that. I'm your boss. Get in the office."

"I'll just wait downstairs," Rachel says as she walks toward the elevator.

I hold my hand up, telling her to wait.

"Who was that?" I hear my father say.

"No one."

"So you're not sick. I knew you were lying. I can always tell with you, Pearce. Who are you with?"

Rachel's standing a few feet away, looking for something in her purse.

"I can't talk right now. I need to go."

"That woman shouldn't be there. The associates are not allowed to spend the night. Tell me her name and I'll take care of it."

If I *did* have an associate here, my father would be more than happy to report her and make sure she's punished. He likes punishing people, including me. It makes him feel powerful.

"It's not one of them," I say.

"You found someone else? Was it Rielle? I heard you were with her recently."

What the hell? Is everyone spying on me? Or did Rielle go tell the entire world we had sex?

"Yes," I lie. "That's correct."

I say it's Rielle because my father would approve of someone like Rielle. He would not at all approve of Rachel.

144

"Well, get rid of her. We have work to do. I expect to see you in the office in a half hour."

He hangs up and I set the phone down.

"Is something wrong?" Rachel asks.

"I need to go into the office. We'll have to postpone our drive to another day."

"Okay, that's fine. Maybe I can talk Shelby into going for a drive."

I take Rachel back to her apartment. It's out of the way from the office, which means I'll get there late and have to listen to my father scold me and probably punish me by piling on even more work.

Why do I let him continue to treat me this way? Because he knows how to get in my head. That's why. He knows my weaknesses. He knows how to control me. And I can't seem to stop it.

CHAPTER FOURTEEN

RACHEL

Pearce has been quiet the entire drive back to my apartment. Now we're parked in front of my building, but the car's still running and his seatbelt is still on.

"Do you want to come in for a minute?" I ask as I release my seatbelt and open my door.

"I can't. I'm already late for work."

Late for work? It's Sunday. It's not even a work day. How can he be late on a Sunday?

"So, um, do you want to do anything this week?" I ask him.

"I'm not sure. I'll call you." He looks straight ahead as he says it.

"Then I guess I'll see you later. Bye."

I wait for him to say it back, but he doesn't. He's not even looking at me, his eyes still straight ahead.

I shut the door and he speeds off.

A sick feeling hits my stomach as I watch him drive away. Why was he being so quiet and cold? We were having such a great time and then he just shut down. When he left just now, he was almost acting like he wanted nothing to do with me. Like he was done with me. He didn't even walk me to the door or kiss me goodbye.

Maybe I made a mistake being with him last night. Maybe he was just using me for sex and now that we've done it, he never wants to see me again. Dammit! This is why I don't have sex this early in a relationship. I never should've done that.

I go upstairs to my apartment. Shelby comes out in the hall as I'm unlocking my door.

"Hey, are you just getting home?" she asks.

Now I feel ashamed. I don't want her knowing I spent the night with Pearce. I know some girls would think nothing of having sex after just a few dates, but to me, it's a big deal and something I never thought I'd do. And now I regret it.

"It was too late to come back here last night so I just stayed over," I say as I go inside my apartment.

Shelby follows me. "So you must really like him."

"I do, but...I don't know." I hang my purse on the hook by the door.

"You don't know *what?* Whether you still like him? Did something happen?"

We go over to the couch and sit down. "He was acting weird when he dropped me off. He didn't talk to me at all on the drive here and he didn't walk me to the door, which is fine but usually he does so. . . . I don't know. Maybe he was just in a hurry."

"I know what's going on here. You slept with him, didn't you?"

I nod.

"And now that he got what he wanted you think he's lost interest in you."

I look down at my hands. "Yeah."

"Rachel." She touches my arm and I look up again. "Don't feel bad about this. Just forget about him and move on. You don't want to be with a guy like Pearce Kensington."

"What do you mean? You don't even know him."

She straightens up and sits back a little. "No, but I know he's hot and super rich, which means he can have a different girl every night."

"I just thought—"

"You were different than the others?"

"Yeah." I lean forward, my elbows resting on my knees as I cover my face with my hands. "How could I be that stupid? I never move this fast with a guy. And I never thought I would. I feel like such an idiot."

"Hey." She nudges me. "It happens to all of us. There isn't a girl out there who hasn't fallen for the wrong guy."

"But he didn't seem like the wrong guy. He seemed like the *right* guy." I sit up. "I guess I just got caught up in the fantasy of being with someone like him. He's handsome, charming, polite, smart, successful. He's like my dream man. But I guess he's everyone else's too." I take a throw pillow from the couch and hug it to my chest, resting my chin on it.

"You'll find someone else. Why don't we go out this week? We'll go to a club and dance and have drinks. If we happen to meet some guys, great. But if not, we'll just have a girls' night."

"I don't really feel like going out. And I'm not ready to find another guy." I look at her. "Shelby, I really liked Pearce. There was something about him. Something that drew me to him in a way I've never felt before."

"He's super hot, super rich, and knows exactly what to say. That's why you felt that way."

"No. It was more than that. I mean, yes, he complimented me and bought me gifts, so I guess you could say that was just him trying to get me to sleep with him. But I didn't feel like that's what it was. I really felt like he was starting to care about me. And *I* care about *him*. I worry about him. I know he's rich, but I don't think he's happy. There's this sadness to him that he tries to hide but I know it's there. I can tell it's hard for him to let his guard down and open up to people but he was starting to do that with me. He was loosening up and smiling more. He was letting me see this other side of him that I don't think he shows many people, not even himself. He's always so serious and he never does anything fun. He'd never even been to the movies until last night. And he didn't own a pair of jeans. I took him shopping and picked out two pairs, along with some casual shirts. He'll probably never wear them again but at least he wore them last night." I smile. "You should've seen him at—"

"Rachel, what the hell?" Shelby's staring at me.

"What?"

"Are you in love with this guy?"

"No! Of course not. I just met him."

"Oh my God." She throws her hands up.

"What? What's wrong?"

"The way you answered my question just now. Total denial."

"Denial about what?"

"The fact that you're in love with Pearce Kensington."

"I am NOT in love with him. In lust with him, maybe. But not love."

"It's definitely love. You should've seen your face when you were talking about him. I've seen that look before. No wonder you feel like shit. How did this happen so fast?" She sighs. "I don't know what Pearce did or said to make you all crazy about him but you've gotta stop this before it goes any farther. You need to stop calling him, stop seeing him. You need to end this."

"First of all, I'm not in love. And second, I think it's already ended."

"Good. But knowing him, he'll probably stop by some night and try to lure you back. You can't fall for it, Rachel. If you do, you'll end up right back where you're at now. Feeling hurt and used, while Pearce moves on with someone else."

"Why do you keep acting like you know him so well? You met him one time."

"I don't need to know him. I know his type. Guys like him are all the same. Spoiled, rich guys who will do anything to get what they want. They keep secrets. They lie. They never tell you about their past. You can't trust them."

"I don't think Pearce lied to me. And I don't feel like he's been hiding anything from me. In fact, he's told me a lot about himself."

She crosses her arms over her chest. "Did he tell you he used to be married?"

"He was married?" There's that sick feeling again, knotting up my stomach.

"See? He's been hiding his past. Keeping secrets. Exactly what I said."

"When was he married? And how do you know this?"

"It was in the newspaper and on TV. It was a huge wedding. It was a few years ago, right after he graduated from Yale."

"Who was the girl?"

"Some rich socialite. Kind of an ugly girl. Skinny with really pale skin. I don't think she ever went in the sun."

"Why would Pearce marry an unattractive girl when he could pick anyone?"

"Because she's rich and comes from the right family. That's how it works with guys like Pearce. They don't marry for love. He probably never even had sex with her. The whole marriage was a sham. A lot of rich people have fake marriages."

"That's really sad."

"I guess, but the guys probably like it. They can sleep around with whoever they want and their wives don't care."

"I don't think Pearce would do that."

She laughs. "God, Rachel, you're so naive. I'm not trying to be mean, but sometimes I think you have no idea how the world works."

I roll my eyes. "I understand that sometimes people marry for the wrong reasons. All people, not just rich people. But that doesn't mean Pearce is like that. I think he'd rather be single than marry someone he didn't love."

"Rachel. Did you not hear what I just said? Pearce married that woman. So yeah, he IS like that. He married a girl he didn't love because she was rich and had the right last name."

I sigh. "Fine. But he obviously realized it was a mistake because he's no longer married to her."

"He only divorced her because it turned out she was a lesbian. At least that's the rumor, according to the tabloids."

"That shouldn't have mattered if your theory is true. You just said he didn't need to have sex with her to be married."

"Whatever. I didn't say I was an expert in this." She stands up. "Let's go do something. You don't want to sit here alone and depressed all day."

"I can't go out. I need to work on a paper and get some reading done."

"Okay, but come over and get me if you change your mind."

I walk her to the door. "You never told me what happened the other day with your dad. It must've been bad if you missed work."

"Actually, my mom had some appointments that day and she just needed me to go over there and stay with him. I'll see you later." She opens the door but then stops and turns back around. "Hey, I'm sorry about Pearce. I know you really liked him. But trust me, you're better off without him."

She leaves, closing the door behind her. I go to the kitchen and get a glass of water. I spot the roses Pearce gave me, sitting in the plastic pitcher next to the sink. The vase he bought me is still in the trunk of his car. He was in such a hurry to leave this morning, I forgot to get the vase. He'll probably give it to some other girl.

I pick up the flowers to toss them out, but then put them back. I might as well keep them. I don't get flowers very often and I can't afford to buy them myself.

What if Pearce wasn't breaking up with me this morning? What if he was just in a bad mood? When he got that phone call before we left, he sounded angry with whoever had called him. And he didn't seem happy about having to go to work. So maybe his behavior this morning had nothing to do with me.

If he was just using me for sex, why did he let me spend the night? Why did he invite me for breakfast? And suggest we take a drive together?

What Shelby said is true. A man like Pearce could have a different woman every night, and it's possible I was just one of those women. But I don't want to believe that. The Pearce I've gotten to know has been caring and thoughtful and a gentleman, and it didn't feel like an act. It felt real.

To keep my mind off him, I clean my apartment, then work on my paper. Then I call my parents, which I do every Sunday. My mom wants me to call her every day, but it's too much. Every time we talk she tells me how I should move back home. Then I feel guilty for moving away, which I shouldn't. This is *my* life and I have to live it for me, not my parents. But my mom doesn't get that. Ever since my sister died, my mom acts like I owe it to her to live next door and be with her as her only remaining daughter. And as much as I love her, I hate that she puts that burden on me.

Today on our call, I tell her about school and then she gives me the town gossip. We always start our calls this way. After that, she starts in with her motherly advice.

"Did you get a chance to look at some other apartments?" She just asked me this the other day. Even though I only call my parents on Sundays, my mom calls *me* several times a week to remind me of everything I'm doing wrong and what I should be doing instead. It drives me crazy.

"Mom, I told you I'm not moving. The rent here is cheap. It's all I can afford."

"You'd get a lot more for the money in Indiana."

Here we go. Let the guilt trip begin.

"I don't live in Indiana. I live here and I like my apartment."

"It's not a safe area. I saw on the news last week that some girl in Connecticut got attacked while walking to school. And that was in the nice part of Connecticut. You live in a dangerous neighborhood."

It gets to the point I tune her out sometimes. It's the only way I can keep my sanity.

"Adam stopped by the other day," she says. My mom loves Adam. She wanted us to get married, even after I lost the baby.

"Why was Adam there?"

"Because he wanted to ask about you." Her voice lifts, like she's excited for me. "He said he never hears from you."

"I'm not dating him anymore. I have no reason to stay in touch with him."

"He has a bright future. I heard he plans to open his own accounting firm. And he's very handsome."

I roll my eyes. "Mom, I'm not interested in him. Set him up with someone else."

"I gave him your phone number."

I sigh. "Why did you do that? I don't want to talk to him."

"He's a nice young man and there's no reason why you two can't still be friends. And who knows? Maybe it'll turn into more. Just talk to him, Rachel."

"I should go. I have a lot of stuff to do."

"Okay, honey. I'll call you later this week. Love you."

"Love you too."

That wasn't too bad of a call. Usually my mom goes on and on about what I need to be doing with my life. I swear she makes a list before she calls so she doesn't forget anything. And now she's adding something new to the list: Get back together with Adam.

I never told my mom the truth about why Adam and I broke up. She thinks *I* was the one who ended the engagement. She doesn't know Adam did. If she knew, she wouldn't like him so much. But I don't want to tell her. I still have a hard time accepting the reason he broke up with me. I know he didn't love me, but I wish he'd just said that instead of telling me I was useless to him because I can't have kids.

That still hurts. And it hurts even more that Adam moved away after he broke off the engagement. He didn't even stick around to help me get over the loss of our baby. He never called me after that. He knew I was devastated when I lost the baby and was told I'd never have children, and yet Adam never even tried to comfort me. Instead, he treated me like damaged goods. So why the hell does he think I'd want to talk to him? If he calls, I won't even pick up the phone. I don't want to talk to him ever again.

What if every other guy is just like Adam and rejects me when he finds out I can't have children? Would Pearce do that? I'm not sure. I don't know him well enough to say. He's an only child so I'm sure his parents expect him to have children. They need someone to pass all that money to and carry on the family name. And I'm sure Pearce wants a child, at least one. Maybe not now, but in the future.

That's another reason I shouldn't have pursued a relationship with him. Even if he wanted to be with me, and wanted to get more serious, I can't, because there could never be a future with us. I can't give him a child.

In the afternoon, I study some more, then go knock on Shelby's door to see if she wants to have dinner together. She's not there. I don't know where she goes all the time. It seems like she's always gone. She doesn't have many friends and she doesn't have a boyfriend. She must've gone to her parents' house.

153

I'm not that hungry so I just make a peanut butter sandwich and eat it in front of the TV. It's 5:30 and I thought by now Pearce might've called just to say hi. But the phone hasn't rung all day.

I already miss him. I miss talking to him. I miss making him laugh. I miss the feel of his arms around me.

Not seeing him anymore is going to be hard. Really hard.

There's a knock on the door and I pop up from the couch, assuming it's Shelby. She probably just got back and is coming over to ask if I want to eat dinner with her.

"I already ate," I say as I open the door.

But it's not Shelby at the door. It's an older man with thick white hair. His skin is tan and he's wearing light-colored pants and a white polo shirt.

He gives me a big, wide smile. "I wasn't planning to ask you to dinner, but maybe some other time."

I smile back. "No, I thought you were someone else. Do I know you?"

He looks kind of like a professor, but he doesn't teach any of my classes.

"We haven't met, but you volunteer for the literacy program I run at the homeless shelter. Actually, I don't run it. I just fund it."

I shake his hand. "It's nice to meet you. I'm Rachel. I've been working with the program for a year now."

"Yes, that's what Laura said. She told me a little about you."

So he knows Laura, the woman who runs the shelter. Then why didn't she tell me about him? And why didn't she tell me he'd be coming over?

"Laura didn't mention you," I say. "What's your name?"

"Jack Ellit."

"Hi, Jack. Would you like to come in?"

I step aside and let him in. I'm not sure why he's here. At first I was leery of him just showing up at my door, but I feel better about him knowing that he funds the reading program.

"I can't stay long," he says. "And pardon my appearance. I just finished a round of golf."

"Would you like something to drink?"

154

"No, thank you." He's glancing around my apartment, his eyes pausing on certain spots. "So Laura said you're a student."

"Yes. At Hirshfield. I'm in graduate school."

"What are you studying?"

"American History."

"And what interests you about American History?"

"I like learning about the past, especially the time when our country was forming. I like learning about how cities were made. How industries grew."

"That *was* an interesting time, wasn't it?" He walks over to my bookshelf.

I don't want to be rude, but I need to know why he's here. His questions are starting to make me uncomfortable. "So why did you-"

"You're a swimmer?" He holds up one of my medals.

"I was on the swim team in high school and college. Now I just swim when I have time, which isn't very often. So anyway, why again are you here? I'm not sure you said."

He turns to me and smiles. "Forgive me for not explaining. I came by to meet you. I'm trying to be more connected to the literacy program, rather than just writing a check. I wanted to get your feedback on how the program is run."

He came all the way here for *that*? He could've just showed up at the shelter on Saturday. If he'd done that, he could've met all the volunteers at once. It'd be better than showing up at their homes, unannounced.

"I think the program is good," I tell him. "I guess my only suggestion would be to have an actual classroom for us to meet in rather than the dining area, which can be really loud. The building next to the shelter is vacant. Maybe part of it could be renovated and turned into classrooms."

"That's a good idea. I'll look into that. Anything else?"

"This isn't related to the program, but it would be good to install better lighting along that street. I know that's the city's responsibility, but if you were able to make some calls to the right people, maybe they would listen. It's a very dangerous area and better lighting might help deter crime."

He's quiet, his eyes on mine. I don't know why, but it's kind of creeping me out.

Finally, he says, "I'll see what I can do." He does another quick glance around my apartment. "Well, I've taken up enough of your time. I should be going."

I escort him to the door.

"Do you have a business card you could give me?"

"I'm afraid I don't." He smiles. "I don't usually carry them with me when I'm golfing." He puts his hand out. "It was a pleasure meeting you."

I shake his hand. "You as well."

I watch as he walks away. That whole encounter was very strange. I'm not sure what to make of it. He seemed like a nice man, but he asked me a lot of questions that had nothing to do with the literacy program. He was trying to get information about me, but why? Was he just being friendly? Making conversation? Or was it more than that?

CHAPTER FIFTEEN

PEARCE

When I dropped off Rachel this morning, I was in such a hurry I don't even remember telling her goodbye. And I haven't had a chance to call her all day. Since the moment I arrived at the office, I've been in a conference room with my father and three of the company's lawyers, trying to finalize the contracts I've been working on.

I have no interest in reading through contracts, which is why my father makes me do it. He thinks it builds character to do things you don't want to do. My father is not a happy man and he doesn't want others to be happy either. He knows I'd rather spend my Sunday doing anything but be here, and yet here I am, doing as the boss ordered.

It's now eight at night and I haven't had dinner. I know it's late but I'm going to call Rachel and see if she'd like to get something to eat. We'll have to go to a place where people I know won't see us.

Dating her is going to be difficult, but it's what I want. I never thought I'd meet someone like her, but now that I have, I plan to do everything in my power to keep this relationship going. Which means I need to make time for her. Given my work schedule, I don't know how I'm going to do that yet, but I'll find a way. Because I have to spend more time with her. Whenever we're together, it's never enough. I've thought about her ever since I dropped her off this morning. I miss her and I need to see her.

I get up and shut the door to my office so I can have privacy. But just as I'm about to call her, my phone rings. Not my regular phone, but my cell phone. We can't possibly have another Dunamis meeting this soon. We just had one yesterday.

I answer and hear the recorded voice ask for my member number. I punch it in, then hear the recording again.

"This is an assignment notice. An assignment has been issued to you. You will receive your assignment within the next six weeks. Please be aware that you should not travel during these weeks as you need to be available in case the assignment cannot be carried out by the freelancer. Details of the assignment are forthcoming. This concludes the message."

"Fuck." I say it out loud as I slam the phone on my desk. I haven't had an assignment for months but the last one I did still haunts me. I've only had five assignments so far, one for each year I've been a member. But now that I'm out of college and being mentored, I'll be getting more assignments. A lot more. Some of our older members, like my father, get one a month.

The assignments vary, but the end goal is the same; to maintain the power and influence we've worked so hard to achieve. Much of our power is derived from controlling key political positions, so during election years, assignments often involve feeding fake stories to the media to make our candidates look good. On non-election years, our focus is finding and grooming candidates for future elections. We also work to grow the companies owned by our members so that we dominate every industry.

Accomplishing these tasks almost always involves illegal activities; bribes, blackmail, theft, falsifying of documents. To make sure we keep our hands clean, we usually don't do these things ourselves. Instead we hire freelancers, a whole underground network of people willing to do most anything for money. Most of them are criminals, but some are just ordinary men desperate for money.

Sometimes an assignment doesn't go as planned and a freelancer is called in to clean it up. That's what happened with my last assignment. One of the other members was assigned to recruit a man for a possible Senate position. The man was a partner at a law firm in Atlanta. He had no experience in politics, but we'd

158

been watching him. He had the right look, the right demeanor, and a complete lack of ethics—key attributes for a candidate. If he passed all our tests and met our criteria, we'd place him in office. We'd make sure he won the election so that he'd do what we needed him to do.

The member who was assigned to recruit this man had already met with him and he'd agreed to move forward with the plan. A memo was sent to his office, which outlined the next steps in the process. It was highly confidential and never supposed to be seen by anyone but the lawyer. But one day, his secretary was going through his mail and accidentally saw the memo. When we found out she'd seen it, a new assignment was made: Kill the secretary. I was the one who got the assignment. And I completed it. I *had* to. I wasn't given a choice. I didn't do it myself. I arranged to have it done by one of our freelancers.

When I got the assignment, I received a folder about this woman. Her name was Cheryl. I was given photos of her, which I handed over to the freelancer to make sure he got the right woman. But after seeing those photos, I felt like I knew her. I felt sick knowing what was about to happen to her. She'd done nothing wrong. She was just an innocent victim.

Right before the kill was supposed to happen, I tried to stop it. I couldn't go through with it. I called the freelancer, but it was too late. He'd already completed the job.

Later that week, I did more research on the woman and found out she was married and had a teenage son. I was devastated. I broke down. I couldn't believe what I'd done. I'd destroyed an entire family. The thought of that haunted me day and night for months. I barely slept. I felt immense guilt over it. I still do.

Two of my other assignments also involved killing people, but they were freelancers who threatened to tell our secrets. One of the men had served time for second degree murder and the other served time for sexual assault. I didn't feel as bad getting rid of them, but they were still lives. Two lives cut short because of me.

Again, I didn't do those jobs myself. I hired freelancers to kill those men. But sometimes hiring freelancers isn't an option. If a freelancer doesn't complete his assignment, it's your job to finish it. The organization considers that your penalty for not managing your freelancer effectively. The assignment becomes yours to complete, even if it's a kill assignment. In the past, some of the members weren't able to do it. When that happens, you're punished and the other members look down on you for not being strong enough or committed enough to the goal.

My father wanted to make sure that never happened to me, so he decided to prepare me for this task at a young age. I was 19 and home on summer break. I was working at Kensington Chemical, as I was forced to do every summer since the age of 16.

One day in July, my father sent me to Hartford to deliver a package to one of our clients. I asked why we couldn't just mail it instead, like we did with all our other packages. He said it contained sensitive information and he couldn't risk it getting lost in the mail.

The client's office was in a bad part of town, surrounded by old abandoned warehouses. My father told me to take my gun, just in case I ran into any trouble. I was trained to use a gun when I was just a child because my father had a lot of enemies who might come after me.

When I got to the building, I went to the back loading dock, which is where I was supposed to meet the man who was waiting for the package. But he wasn't there. It was six at night and the loading dock was closed up and the door to the building was locked. I turned around to go back to my car and saw a man standing about ten feet away from me. He had a gun pointed at me. He was around 30, wearing jeans and a black t-shirt. He had a scruffy face and his blond hair was sticking up in all directions. His eyes were bloodshot and he was very fidgety. I assumed he was high on something.

"Give me your wallet," he said.

I slowly reached around to my back pocket where my wallet was. I was wearing a suit. A black suit, white shirt, and a gray silk tie. My father had just bought me the tie and given it to me the previous day. He never gave me gifts so it surprised me, but I didn't question it.

I took my wallet and held it out to the man.

160

"Toss it over here," he said.

I purposely threw it long and to his side. As he watched it go past him, I whipped out my gun, which I had clipped to my waist, hidden by my suit jacket. When he turned back around, I had the gun pointed at him.

"Fuck!" he said when he saw my gun. He started shaking, the gun still in his hand.

"Go!" I yelled at him. "Get out of here!"

He shook his head. "I can't. I promised."

"Promised what?"

"If I don't do it, he'll kill her."

He was making no sense, which I attributed to the drugs. I assumed he was hallucinating or paranoid, making up stories. But the words 'he'll kill her' stuck in my head for some reason.

My heart was thumping hard and fast in my chest, adrenaline pumping through my veins, sweat trickling down my forehead. I forced myself to keep breathing at a normal pace in order to keep my hand steady, just like I'd been taught.

"Who's going to kill her?" I asked him. "Who are you talking about?"

He didn't answer. He just stood there, getting a firmer grip on his gun.

"Just take the wallet and go!" I yelled at him.

"I can't. I have to do it." He raised the gun until it was pointed directly at me. And then, just like when I witnessed my father shooting that homeless man, everything seemed to be in slow motion. I watched the man's finger pull back on the trigger, and out of pure survival instinct, I did the same, shooting directly at his chest.

The man stumbled back and hit the ground. But I remained standing. I quickly glanced down at my shirt. Nothing. Not even a trace of blood. How could he not hit me from just a few feet away?

Moments later I heard a car pull up behind me. I thought it was the police coming to arrest me after hearing the gun go off. But when I turned around, I saw that it wasn't a police car. It was a black limo. The driver got out, went around to the side, and opened the door.

My father stepped out of the limo and walked up to me. "Congratulations, son. You finally did something right."

He had a wide smile on his face. He never smiles.

"What are you talking about?"

"We'll discuss it in the limo. We can't be here."

"What about my car?"

"Someone is coming to get it. He'll drive it back to the office."

My mind raced, trying to figure out what had just happened. The man on the ground wasn't moving. He was dead. I'd killed a man. I'd taken a life. But I had to. It was self defense. One of us was going to die.

I clicked the safety on my gun and put it back in its holster. As I went to get in the limo, I stopped when a black car drove up next to us.

"Pearce," my father yelled from inside the limo. "Get in here. We're leaving."

I did as he said, and as we drove away I watched two men cloaked in black lift the body from the ground. Then we turned onto the street and the scene was no longer visible.

"What just happened?" I asked my father.

He'd opened the liquor compartment in the limo and was pouring himself a scotch. "You passed the test."

I didn't know what he meant, but I knew it was bad. Acid rose to the back of my throat and burned when I swallowed.

He pointed to the bottle of scotch. "Would you like a drink?"

"What test?"

"The test to see if you're man enough to perform your duties."

"What duties?"

"The duties you will be performing as a member."

When he said it, I remembered back to the day three years earlier, when I'd watched my father kill that homeless man in the alley. That was the day he told me about the organization. I'd tried to erase that day from my mind and pretend what he'd told me was all a lie, but this was a harsh reminder that it was true. I would soon be a member and be forced to do things I didn't want to do.

But I still wasn't sure what was going on. I asked my father once again to explain what had just happened behind the loading dock.

"How did you know that man would be there when I was?"

"I hired him." My father took a drink of his scotch.

"You hired him to shoot me?"

"Yes, but he wouldn't have killed you. His gun had blanks in it. But he didn't know that."

"That was all a setup?"

"Correct. And it went exactly as planned."

"You're saying you *wanted* me to kill him?"

"You had to know what it feels like. Now you'll be prepared for when you do it for real."

"For real? What I just did was real!"

"Technically, I suppose it was, but when you get an actual assignment it will be different. It will be premeditated. You'll have to plan it out. And if you don't plan right, you'll have to take over the assignment yourself and do what you just did. Only next time, if your intended target aims a gun at you, it won't have blanks in it. You can't hesitate, Pearce. You just have to shoot. Hopefully, now that you've done it once, you won't hesitate."

"The man said he had to shoot me or something would happen to her. What did he mean?"

"If he didn't complete the job, I would've killed his girlfriend."

"But he didn't kill me. So are you going after his girlfriend?"

"No. I don't need to. That was just an incentive I gave him to make sure he'd follow through on the job. Now let's talk about the assignments, which is the whole reason for the test."

He went on to explain how the assignments worked and how not completing them successfully would mean punishment and embarrassment for our family.

"I can't risk having you tarnish the family name," he said. "You're weak, Pearce. You always have been, despite all my efforts to make you strong. I blame your mother for that. She was always saying I should go easier on you. But no more. You're a grown man and you need to be treated as such. You need to embrace your responsibilities and make your family proud."

He continued to talk but I was unable to respond. I was too shocked to speak. I'd just killed a man for no reason other than my father wanting to teach me yet another one of his lessons. This time, how to kill.

I try to forget that day. Wipe it from my memory. But it never goes away. And whenever I get an assignment notice, it comes flooding back, along with all the other bad things I've done, like killing that secretary. I'll never forgive myself for that, or any of the other deaths I've caused or will cause in the future. I tell myself that it wasn't me who took those lives. That it was the side of me my father created. The dark side. Not the real me.

With my mind still on the assignment, I leave the office and go back to my loft. I sit on the couch, staring at the blank TV screen, imagining what they're going to make me do.

I don't want to be here. It's too quiet. Too empty. Too dark. I need to get out of here. I need to see Rachel. Being around her always lifts my spirits. Makes me feel like the world around me isn't so dark.

Or lonely.

Or hopeless.

CHAPTER SIXTEEN

RACHEL

There's knocking on the door. I turn the TV down. It's almost ten and I'm afraid to answer the door this late. I didn't hear Shelby come home so it can't be her.

The knocking continues. I go check the peephole and see that it's Pearce. What is he doing here? And why didn't he call first? Given how strict he is about manners, it seems odd that he didn't call before coming over.

I'm still upset with him for how he acted this morning, but when I open the door I can't help but smile. He's wearing the jeans and black polo shirt I picked out for him. They look good on him. Really good. His large shoulders stretch the fabric of the shirt and the band on the sleeve hugs his muscular arms. He needs to ditch those suits more often and show off that body of his.

"Hello, Rachel." He says it in a very formal way.

"Hello, Pearce," I say just as formally.

I wake up from obsessing over his body and come to my senses. Why is he here so late? To have sex again? Granted, it was amazing sex. I wouldn't mind doing it again. But I can't. I need to slow this relationship down and get the focus off sex. So if he came here for that, he's not getting it.

"I'm sorry to have stopped over uninvited, but I needed to give you this." He hands me the bag from the jewelry store that holds the vase he bought me. "And these." The hand that was behind his back appears, holding a dozen yellow tulips.

"Thank you. They're beautiful. Come on in."

He steps inside. "If you're busy, I can leave. It was inappropriate for me to stop by without calling."

He's still using that formal speech pattern. Last night and this morning, his speech was more casual, but tonight he's back to being formal and I don't know why.

"I'm not busy. I was just watching TV." I take the vase out of the box and set it in the sink, filling it with water. "You didn't have to get me more flowers."

"I wanted to get you your favorite. I didn't know your favorite color but the yellow reminded me of the dress you wore when I first met you."

I'm surprised he remembered that.

"I love yellow, but I like most any color." I put the tulips in the water, then place the vase on the kitchen counter next to the roses.

Adam never bought me flowers. He said they were a waste of money. Instead, he bought me plants, which he said were more practical. But to me they were work because I was stuck taking care of them.

"Do you want to sit down?" I motion him to the couch.

"I thought maybe I could take you to another movie." He points to himself. "I even dressed for it."

"I see that. You look good."

I smile as I say it, but he doesn't smile back. I'm not even sure that he heard me. He seems out of it. His eyelids are heavy and his shoulders are drooping. He looks exhausted. Work must've worn him out because he was full of energy this morning.

"It's late," I tell him. "Let's just stay here and watch TV."

He nods and we go sit on the couch. He's not being as affectionate as usual. He hasn't even kissed me. Something's wrong. He's distant and seems sad. Or depressed.

Without saying anything, I reach my arms around him and hug his chest, my head on his shoulder. He slowly puts his arms around me, hugging me back. He kisses the top of my head, then takes some deep breaths.

Something is definitely wrong. He's completely different than he was earlier. He was quiet in the car this morning, but now he's more than just quiet. He's upset about something.

"I don't know what I'm doing here." He said it so quietly it's like he was talking to himself.

I pick up the remote and turn off the TV. "What do you mean?"

"I couldn't be at my apartment and I didn't want to—"

"Didn't want to what?"

"Never mind. I just needed to see you."

I wanted to see him too, but not if it's just for sex.

"Pearce." I wait until he looks at me. "I need to know what happened this morning. The way you left like that, I thought maybe you were just...using me."

"No." He turns toward me and takes my hand. "Rachel, I would *never* do that. This morning had nothing to do with you. I was just angry that I'd been called into the office on a Sunday. I'd hoped to spend the day with you and instead I had to read contracts all day."

"Well, next time, you need to at least say goodbye. And a kiss would've been nice."

"You're right. I'm very sorry about that." He puts his hand on the side of my face and leans in and gives me a soft, gentle kiss. "That was for this morning."

I smile. "You didn't kiss me hello just now either."

His hand remains on my face as he kisses me again, a little longer this time. "Hello, Rachel." I feel his warm breath over my lips as he says it.

"Hi," I say, trying to keep control of my body, which is telling my head to rip his clothes off right now.

"Are there any other kinds of kisses I neglected to give you?" he asks in his deep sexy voice.

"I don't think so." I look into his silvery blue eyes, then down to his strong jawline which is covered in a thick layer of stubble. Damn, he's hot. Resisting him is going to be very, very hard.

"Then can I kiss you for no reason at all?" he asks.

"I suppose that'd be okay."

He kisses me again, this time a deep, fiery-hot kiss that makes my body want to repeat what we did last night. And this morning. But I can't.

I gently push him back. "Pearce, we need to slow this down. I'm not saying last night was a mistake. It was great, but I don't usually do that so soon into a relationship. I like to get to know someone better before we get to that stage."

He nods. "Okay."

That's it? I thought he'd insist we still do it while getting to know each other. He's probably used to having sex right away. Maybe even on the first date.

"So we're good?" I ask him. "We'll just continue dating?"

His lips turn up. "We have to. You have all these activities planned for me and I *did* agree to try them."

"That's true. When are we going out again?"

"I don't know. My work schedule is very unpredictable. I'll have to call you and let you know." He pauses. "But even when I don't have time to take you on a formal date, would you mind if I just came over? Maybe a couple nights a week after work?" He looks down at my hand and softly rubs it. "I like just being with you."

"Of course you can come over."

He lifts his head, smiling a little. "I promise to call next time."

"That would be good." I laugh as I look down at my pink sweat pants and white t-shirt. "It would give me time to clean myself up. I'm kind of a mess right now. I don't even have makeup on." My hair is also a mess. I tug on my ponytail, trying to straighten it.

He holds my chin, his eyes moving over my face. "You don't need to do anything. You're beautiful."

I glance away. "I'm just saying that you're probably used to being with women who are—"

"No." He shakes his head. "No other woman even compares to you." He laughs, but not in a funny way, but more of incredulous way. "It's amazing to me that you don't know that."

"Thank you." I glance away again. "That's very sweet of you to say."

He gets quiet. His hand drops from my face and he sits back on the couch, his eyes glazed over, like he suddenly remembered something and now his mind is elsewhere. What is going on with him tonight? He doesn't seem like himself. It's like something's weighing him down, causing him stress. I wish he would tell me what's wrong so I could at least try to help.

"Pearce." I touch his arm, waking him from his thoughts. "Are you okay?"

He looks at me like he's surprised by the question. That's strange. Does nobody ever ask him that?

"It was just a difficult day at work." He attempts a smile but I can tell it's forced. "But I'm fine now."

"Did you have dinner?"

"No. I wasn't hungry."

How could he not eat dinner? He'd have to eat a lot to fuel a body that big.

"I'd offer to make you something, but I doubt you'd want to eat canned tuna or mac and cheese. How about ice cream? I make a really good sundae."

"I don't eat ice cream."

"You don't? Why not?"

"I've just outgrown it. It's for children."

"It's not for children. It's for anyone."

"Perhaps. But in my household it was only allowed during childhood on birthdays. And after the age of 10, it wasn't allowed at all."

"Then that's your new thing to try today. Eating ice cream." I go in the kitchen and pull it out of the freezer. "Do you want it with crushed cookies? That's how I usually eat it."

"Rachel, I don't need ice cream."

"Nobody *needs* ice cream. It's a want. We'll skip the cookies and just have the ice cream."

I scoop it out into some bowls and bring them over to the couch. I hand him his. "It's chocolate."

He takes a bite. "Hmm. Yes, I remember eating this as a child. It's very good."

He takes another bite, and another after that, and soon he's finished the entire bowl while I'm only half done.

"I'll get you some more."

He doesn't tell me no so I fill up another whole bowl. He finishes that one just as I'm finishing my first.

"I think we've decided you like ice cream," I say.

"I think so too."

I take our bowls to the sink. I look over and see Pearce rubbing his temples. He looks so exhausted.

"Do you want to go lie down? You look really tired."

He gets up. "I should go. You have class in the morning."

Now that he's here, I don't want him to leave. I like having him here, and when he's not around I miss him. And I'd feel better if he stayed. Between that man coming by uninvited and my mom's comments about this being an unsafe neighborhood, I'm not feeling great about being alone tonight. I don't think Pearce should be alone either. Something's bothering him and it's worrying me. He says he's okay but I can tell that he's not.

"Maybe you could stay."

He looks surprised. "Stay, as in overnight?"

"Yes, but just to sleep. Nothing more."

Who am I kidding? The two of us in the same bed? With the attraction we have to each other? But I really want him here, so we'll just have to use some restraint when it comes to that.

"I didn't bring anything," he says.

"What do you need?"

"Something to sleep in."

"Just sleep in your boxers."

He's looking at me like I'm crazy. He's thinking the same thing I am. That we won't be able to control ourselves. Not after what we did last night and this morning.

"I don't know, Rachel. This may not be the best idea."

"I'd feel better if you were here. Shelby's not home and I'd just feel better if I wasn't alone tonight. Would you stay? Please?"

He smiles. "Of course."

I take him in my room and get ready for bed. I put on pajama pants and a t-shirt while he strips down to his boxers. I'm staring at his bare chest, lean and ripped and leading down to—I stop my eyes before they go there. What was I thinking? I can't be in bed with him like that!

"Are you getting in?" he asks.

He's in my bed now and I'm standing beside it, not moving.

"Yes." I get under the covers. We're facing each other, the glimmer from the streetlights filtering through the blinds. I notice he now seems much more awake. I am too.

"So. Rough day?" I ask him, trying to use conversation to keep our minds off what we really want to do.

"You could say that." Our bodies aren't touching but he slides his hand over to mine and holds it.

"Do you want to talk about it?"

"Not really."

"The sooner you tell me about yourself, the sooner I'll get to know you and the sooner we can. . . you know."

He laughs. "Then go ahead. Ask me whatever you'd like. I'll do my best to answer."

"Do you like your job?"

"No."

"Why not?"

"I'm not interested in the chemical industry. I would've preferred to start my own company and build it from the ground up."

"What kind of company?"

"I'm not sure. I've never allowed myself to think about it because it's not an option. I'm an only child, which means I'm the only one who can take over as CEO when my father retires."

"They could hire someone else."

"It doesn't work that way. My father would never allow that to happen. He wants to keep it in the family."

"Do you get along with your father?"

"Next question."

His tone was harsh and a little angry. I'm trying to get him to relax so I decide not to ask him more about his dad.

"What about your mom?"

"We usually get along. But we don't talk much so there aren't many opportunities to disagree or argue. Do you get along with *your* parents?"

"I love my parents more than anything, but they have trouble letting me grow up and that causes arguments. My dad doesn't say much, but my mom is constantly telling me she knows what's best for me. She's always telling me what to do. She doesn't understand that the life she has planned for me is what *she* wants, not me."

"What does she want you to do?"

"Move back to Indiana. Live in the same town as her and my dad. Get married and buy a house right next to hers. She has a whole list of things I'm supposed to do. Today she told me my ex-boyfriend stopped by. He's from my hometown. My mom loves him. She gave him my phone number. I haven't talked to him for over a year but it sounded like my mom was already planning the wedding."

"How long did you date him?"

"About a year. We went to the same college and dated senior year. He proposed right before we graduated."

Shit, I wasn't supposed to tell him that. Because telling Pearce about Adam will lead to telling him I can't have kids. And I'm not ready to tell him that.

"So he wasn't just a boyfriend," he says. "He was your fiancé."

"Yes, but we weren't engaged for very long."

"Can I ask why you broke off the engagement?"

"I didn't break it off. *He* did." I squeeze my eyes shut, frustrated with myself. I didn't mean to tell him that either. If I keep doing this, I'll end up telling him everything. Part of me wants to. I want to know if he's going to stick around after I tell him. Because if he won't, we should just end this now.

"How could this man possibly pass up the chance to marry you?"

I open my eyes and see Pearce smiling at me. I'm not sure what his question means. Is he just being nice? Or is he making some kind of statement about his feelings for me?

"It just didn't work out," I say, trying to get off the topic.

"Would you rather not talk about it?"

172

"Not tonight. Maybe some other time."

We're both quiet, then Pearce says, "So going back to your mother, what do you tell her when she tries to control your life?"

"Not much. I usually just keep quiet and let her talk." I pause. "The thing with my mom is that I feel like I can't stand up for myself because every time I try, she breaks down crying, saying she's just trying to help me and be a good mom."

"So she gives you the guilt trip."

"Big time. And I know exactly what she's doing, but I just let her do it because it's easier than fighting with her. Plus, I feel bad for her. She's never gotten over my sister's death. That's why she's so overprotective of me. She doesn't want to lose me too. But what she doesn't understand is that by being so overprotective, she's pushing me away." I pause again. "But honestly, I *do* love her. And my dad. Aside from being overprotective, they're great parents. And they're both really good people. They're always the first to help whenever someone needs it. Even a stranger."

"My father tries to control me," Pearce says. "But he's far worse than your mother. And he is *not* a good person. I'll just leave it at that."

I feel him tense up, his hand tightening around mine. I find another topic. A lighter topic.

"What's your favorite color?"

"Blue." I see his lips turn up. "Like the color of your eyes."

"Favorite band?"

"I mostly listen to classical music."

"Favorite food?"

"I think after tonight I'd have to say ice cream."

"Favorite book?"

"The Art of War."

"Seriously? That's not exactly fun reading."

"I don't read fiction. What's *your* favorite book?"

"I like a lot of different books, usually ones set in the past, given my love of history. Little Women is one of my favorites."

"And what's your favorite color?"

"Blue. But I have secondary favorites that vary by the season. Like right now I love orange. Orange leaves. Orange pumpkins. Okay, my turn to ask. What's your favorite place to visit?"

"Italy. I like all the small villages along the Mediterranean coastline. It's a beautiful area. The food is delicious. The people are friendly. And nobody knows who I am. I can walk the streets without being bothered."

"That happens here?"

Pearce told me his family is well-known but I wasn't sure *how* well-known. I hadn't heard of him until I read the poster promoting the lecture series.

"Unfortunately, it happens more than I would like. I get recognized a lot here on the East Coast. Not so much elsewhere. Of course, within the chemical industry everyone knows who I am, and my father is well-known in the financial world, so some people know me because of that."

"Do you travel a lot?"

"Not anymore. I used to travel during college breaks, mainly so I wouldn't have to go home." His voice trails off, but his comment, and his earlier one about his father, tells me he doesn't get along with his family, so much so that he doesn't even like being around them. There's a history there but I'm not going to ask him about it. It's clear he doesn't want to talk about it.

I ask the next question, not sure how he's going to react. "Have you ever been married?"

"Yes," he says simply. "When I was 22. It lasted a year."

"What was she like?"

"Quiet. Reserved. She mostly stayed at home and read books."

"Where did you meet her?"

He lets go of my hand. "At a dinner party at her parents' house."

"How long did you date her?"

He sighs. "Why are you asking about this? You already knew I was married. Are you trying to test me? See if I'll tell you the truth?"

He's angry. And he's right. It *was* a test and I don't know why I did it. I guess I don't trust him as much as I thought I did.

174

"I'm sorry, Pearce. I only asked because I couldn't understand why you didn't tell me you'd been married. That's kind of a big thing to leave out when you're getting to know someone."

He's silent, then says, "It was an arranged marriage. Our parents set it up. It's a common practice among wealthy families."

He says it like it's just a fact. No big deal.

"I didn't know that was still done. I know it used to be done all the time, but now it seems old-fashioned."

"For families like mine, it's tradition. And it's not that unusual. It's still a common practice in many parts of the world." He holds my hand again. "I don't want to talk about it. Next question."

"Pearce, this is something we have to talk about. If you're going to be forced into another arranged marriage someday, then why are we dating? Not that I'm thinking we'd ever get married but—" I stop. I was going to say that dating is generally a process used to see if you want to marry the person, but maybe that's not what it is to him. Maybe he just wants to date me for a few weeks, then move on to someone else. I don't think he's like that, but I'm not really sure.

"I'm not doing it again," he says forcefully.

"Not doing what?"

"An arranged marriage."

"Do you get a choice?"

"Usually not, but traditions have to end sometime and I've already fulfilled my obligation once. I'm not doing it again. Now can you please ask me a different question?"

His stress level is rising again. I need to calm him down.

"Have you ever had a pet?" I ask.

"No. And you?"

"I grew up on a farm. I had all kinds of pets. Dogs, cats, chickens, pigs. Well, we ate the chickens and the pigs but they were pets until they disappeared one day."

He laughs. "That's rather cruel."

"I guess. But it's a lesson you have to learn as a farm kid. Don't become friends with animals that will eventually end up on your dinner plate."

He laughs again. "I could see how that would be an important lesson."

"Have you ever been to a farm?"

"No. I never have."

"You're not missing much. I liked growing up there but I wouldn't go back and live that life. Okay, next question. Did you play any sports in high school?"

"Football."

"I should've known that. You're built like a football player."

He slips his hand under the hem of my shirt. It brushes against my skin, sending a shiver through me. "Do you know enough about me yet?"

"No. But nice try."

"Does this ban only apply to sex? Or any kind of physical contact?"

"Just sex. But I think if we do other stuff, we won't be able to stop."

"So I can't kiss you?"

"You can kiss me."

He leans over and kisses me just once. I kiss him back, which leads to him giving me another kiss. And another after that. The kisses continue, becoming deeper, more intimate, as his hand slowly slides up my shirt.

"Is this banned?" he asks over my lips as he caresses my breast.

"No," I whisper.

He lifts my shirt up and I sit up enough for him take it off. I lie back down and he puts his mouth over my breast, his tongue teasing my nipple.

I moan, begging for more. I don't know what other guys were doing, but they were doing something wrong because it never felt this way with them.

Pearce's hand slips down my pajama pants and under my panties. "How about this?" I hear him say. "Off limits?"

I shake my head. "No."

He continues pleasuring me with his hand until I'm beyond satisfied. I relax into the pillow, my body reveling in the warm, consuming afterglow.

Pearce lies on his back and puts his arm out, inviting me to lie next to him. But I'm not ready yet. I reach down and take him in my hand.

I hear his breath catch. "Rachel, you don't have to."

"I want to." And I do. I return the favor, then lie in his arms and fall asleep.

In the morning, I wake up and find myself wrapped all around him, our arms and legs entwined. I look up to check the clock.

"Pearce." I nudge him to wake him up. "It's six. What time do you need to be at work?"

He opens his eyes. "Right now."

"Sorry, I should've set the alarm."

He turns on his side to face me. "Thank you for letting me stay."

I run my hand over his bare chest. "You don't have to thank me. I'm the one who insisted you stay. And I'm glad you did. It was a good night. I learned a lot about you."

He kisses me. "But you still need to know more?"

I laugh. "Yes. A lot more."

He pulls me on top of him and kisses my neck. "There isn't much more to tell."

"I doubt that." I feel his muscular body beneath me, his warm skin. He's only wearing boxers and I can feel his arousal between my legs. Being in this position is far too tempting.

I move off him to the side. "Do you want breakfast? I have cereal and I think I have milk."

"I'm taking you to the grocery store this week. You never have anything to eat."

"Yes I do. I have all kinds of stuff."

"Your fridge is empty, and the only food you have in your cupboards is macaroni and cheese. You can't live on macaroni and cheese."

"I'm proof that you can. I eat it every day."

"Well, *I* don't. And if I'm going to be over here all the time, you need to stock the fridge. I'll pay for it. I cost a lot to feed."

I kiss his cheek. "I didn't know you were planning to be over here all the time."

He sits up on his side. "I'll be over here as much as you let me."

I smile. "Then I better stock up on food because I want you to come over more. And maybe spend the night again."

"I will definitely do that." He leans over and kisses me. "So that settles it. I'm buying you groceries."

"I'll make a list and we'll go shopping next time you're here."

I don't want him paying for my groceries, but right now I could really use the help. I'm barely making ends meet and there's no way I'm asking my parents for money.

"I need to get to work." He gives me a quick kiss, then gets out of bed and gets dressed.

When he's at the front door ready to leave, he gives me another kiss, this time a longer, sexier kiss, then says, "Goodbye, Rachel."

As he's walking away, I call after him, "Much better that time!"

He's already down the stairs. I laugh as I close the door.

My phone rings and I go in the kitchen to answer it. "Hello?"

"Hi, Rachel, it's Laura."

Laura manages the shelter. She usually doesn't call me so I'm surprised to hear from her.

"Hi, Laura. What's going on?"

"We're canceling the reading lesson this Saturday because we had a pipe break overnight and water went everywhere. There was a lot of damage and it'll take at least a week to clean everything up."

"Do you need me to help?"

"No, we have a crew coming in. I just wanted to let you know not to come in this Saturday. We transferred everyone to a different shelter but it's so crowded there that it wouldn't be worth trying to teach with all that noise."

"Okay, then I guess I'll see you a week from Saturday."

"It may not be cleaned up by then, but I'll keep you posted."

"Hey, I wanted to tell you that I met Jack Ellit yesterday."

"Who's Jack Ellit?"

"The man who funds the literacy program."

"Nobody funds the literacy program. Donations go into a general fund and get divided up later."

"He made it sound like he was a significant donor. He even said he'd look into converting space in the building next door into a classroom so we'd have a place to teach."

"I don't know what you're talking about, Rachel. I've never heard of anyone name Jack Ellit. And I've seen the list of donors. In fact, I've met most of them at fundraising events. That man must've been confusing our shelter with a different one."

"Yeah. He must have. Okay, well, bye."

She hangs up and I set the phone down, my hand shaking. Who was that man who was here? And why did he make up that story about funding the literacy program? He said he knew Laura. He knew that I volunteered at the shelter. He knew I was a student. How did he know all that? Is he watching me?

I let him into my apartment. I answered his questions. He knows all about me. He knows where I live.

What if he comes back? Who is this man and what does he want with me?

CHAPTER SEVENTEEN

PEARCE

By the time I drive home, get myself ready, then drive to work, it's 7:30, much later than my usual start time. My father is waiting for me in my office.

"You're late," he says, not bothering to say hello. He was facing the window but turned around when he heard me walk in.

"I'm not late. Most jobs start at nine, so by traditional standards I'm early."

I would normally just apologize for being late, but today I feel like fighting back. Talking with Rachel last night reminded me just how much my father controls me, not letting me have any kind of life. It's gotten to the point I've become numb to it. But last night, something sparked inside me and told me to fight.

"This job isn't nine to five," he says. "This job is your life and you will be here when I say to be here."

"As long as I get my work done, it shouldn't matter when I get here or when I leave." I go around him and sit at my desk.

He stands beside it, staring down at me. "Getting it done and doing it right are two separate things. Your work is satisfactory at best, which is why you need to be here putting in the hours to meet the level of performance I expect."

"If you feel I'm not performing up to par, fire me." I've never said that to him, but I've wanted to a million times.

He huffs. "Are you drunk?"

I almost laugh, but I keep a serious face. "No, I am not drunk. But I have a lot to do so I would appreciate it if you would let me get to work."

180

"You will be here at six tomorrow."

I don't answer. He likes having the last word so I let him have it. He turns and walks out the door.

God, that felt good. It wasn't much, but standing up to him with just those few comments was enough to give me some energy. Some life.

I notice a new stack of contracts on my desk. My father put them there because he knows how much I hate reviewing them. But right now I don't care. I'm still in a good mood from being with Rachel and I'm going to try to keep it going the rest of the day.

I check my phone and see the message light blinking. I listen to the messages. The first one is work related, but the second one is from Rachel. I call her back.

"Rachel, it's Pearce."

"Hi. I'm sorry to bother you at work but I need some advice. I wasn't sure who else to ask. Shelby's at work and I don't want to tell my parents this or they'll worry."

"Go ahead."

"Yesterday, a man came to my apartment. He said he donates money for the literacy program at the homeless shelter I volunteer at. He said he stopped by because he was trying to get to know all the volunteers. He was an older man and seemed okay so I let him in. He asked me all these questions about myself, and at first I thought he was just being friendly. But when he didn't ask much about the literacy program, I got suspicious."

I already don't like this story. It doesn't make sense. A financial donor would not show up uninvited at a volunteer's home. He could've easily met Rachel at the shelter when she's there working. And since she doesn't know this man, she never should've let him into her apartment. She needs to be more careful. She's far too trusting of people.

She continues. "Then this morning, Laura, the woman who manages the shelter, called to tell me something and I asked her about this man. She said he's not a donor. That she's never heard of him."

"Who is this man? Did he give you his name?"

181

"Yes. He said his name was Jack Ellit."

My temper flares, rage coursing through me. What the fuck was Jack doing at Rachel's apartment? I knew I couldn't trust him. I can't trust any of them. I thought he was different, but he's obviously not if he's going after Rachel. He must be following me and saw me with her.

"What should I do, Pearce? Should I call the police?"

"No. If the man didn't harm you or steal from you, the police won't do anything. What time do you have class?"

"At ten and one, and then I have to work at the museum until five."

"After work, I want you to go to my loft. Do you remember how to get there?"

"Yes."

"If I'm not home, George can let you in. I'll call him and let him know. And pack a bag because you're staying overnight."

"You don't think I'm safe in my apartment? You think he'll do something?"

"I'm not sure, but I'll check on this and take care of it."

"I don't understand. How would you take care of it?"

"I have a team of security experts I work with. When you have my kind of money, you have to be extremely cautious and hire excellent security. I'll have them see what they can find out about this man. But until I know you're safe, you're staying with me."

"Okay. Thank you. I really appreciate this."

"Call me back if you need anything."

As soon as she hangs up, I call Jack. His secretary answers.

"This is Pearce Kensington," I tell her. "I need to speak with Mr. Ellit. It's an emergency."

"He's away on business. He left for Dallas early this morning and has meetings all day. He'll be back tomorrow."

"I need a number where I can reach him."

"I can give you his hotel number but I doubt you'll get a hold of him. You know how he is."

What she means is that after his meetings, Jack will spend the evening drinking with clients and get so drunk he'll pass out in his room. He'll never hear the phone ring.

"When he gets back, tell him he needs to call me right away. This is urgent."

"Yes, Mr. Kensington. I'll make sure he gets the message."

"Thank you."

I consider calling him on his cell phone but that's only supposed to be used by Dunamis for official business. I'd face severe punishment if they found out I called his phone for something unrelated to the organization. And Jack doesn't have another cell phone for personal use. He doesn't like being able to be reached at all times. I don't either, which is why I don't have a personal cell phone. The last thing I need is another way for my father to be able to reach me.

If Jack's out of town, he can't do anything to Rachel but I still want her to stay at my loft. Until I know what he's up to, I want her with me, where I know she's safe.

The rest of the day I'm on edge, worried about Rachel and trying to figure out why Jack went to her place and if he plans to harm her in any way. I wonder who else besides Jack knows of my involvement with her. My father doesn't or he would've said something this morning. I hope only Jack knows. That's bad enough. I don't want any of the other members finding out about her.

As members, we're not supposed to date outside our social sphere, which means we're limited to dating wealthy women from powerful families. Currently there's no rule in place that forbids dating someone like Rachel because it's not necessary. None of the other members have any interest in dating someone of a lower social class. They're obsessed with image and status, and dating the right woman is part of that.

Still, Dunamis likes making rules, so just recently there was discussion to make a rule saying it's forbidden to date women who aren't approved by the members. But since it hasn't been an issue thus far, the rule hasn't been brought to a vote. So as of right now, I'm not breaking any rules being with Rachel. But if my father found out, he'd make sure the rule was put in place as soon as possible.

I call my loft at 5:30. Rachel is there but I'm not able to go home because my father scheduled a meeting at six. After the meeting, he leaves for a dinner party my mother's making him attend. If it weren't for that, he'd make me stay here under his watchful eye for several more hours. But since he's gone, I'm free to go.

When I get home, I walk off the elevator and instantly smile when I see Rachel there. She's in the kitchen making dinner. The entire room is filled with the delicious aroma of a home-cooked meal. It's warm and welcoming and I feel myself starting to relax.

"Welcome home." Rachel comes up to me and gives me a hug. "I made dinner. I hope that's okay. I stopped at the store on the way over."

"You didn't have to do that."

I keep her in the hug a moment longer. It feels good to hold her. It calms me even more. It's nice to come home and have someone here, especially when that someone is Rachel. I tell myself I like living alone, but truthfully, I don't. It's lonely and depressing. I'd much prefer to come home to *this* every night.

"I made baked chicken with mashed potatoes." She kisses me. "It sounded good so that's what I made."

"Thank you. It smells delicious."

"And I made my famous apple cobbler for dessert. You can go change clothes. Dinner will be ready in a few minutes."

I go in my room and put on the jeans and t-shirt Rachel picked out for me when we went to the mall. I'm getting used to the jeans, but I'm not used to wearing a t-shirt outside the gym.

When I come out of the bedroom, she's milling around my kitchen, finding the plates and silverware that I rarely use. She's wearing jeans and a deep orange sweater, her long dark hair pulled into a ponytail. I feel a smile forming again. I didn't smile once today at work, but then I see Rachel and it just happens.

"Everything's ready." She motions to the small round table just off the kitchen. I don't think I've ever sat there. I'm usually at work during dinner so I order something into the office. Or if I'm not at work, I go out for dinner.

Rachel has the table set, our food already portioned out on plates. The food and how it's arranged looks like a photo in a magazine. I didn't realize she was such a talented cook.

"You don't have any serving dishes so I just plated the food," she says. "Go ahead and sit down."

I hold her chair out for her. "You first."

She sits down and I kiss her cheek. "Thank you again for doing this."

"I liked doing it. It's nice having someone to have dinner with. When Shelby's around I eat with her, but she's hardly ever home."

I don't ask where Shelby is, because I don't want Rachel asking her questions. Shelby's probably having a hard enough time trying to keep her secret from Rachel and everyone else. Most of the associates don't have many friends for that very reason. They can't risk letting something slip, because if it did, their friend would be in danger. That's why I wish Rachel would stop being friends with Shelby. It's too much of a risk. Being with *me* is a risk too, but I can keep secrets. I'm not sure Shelby can.

"What do you think?" Rachel asks.

"Everything is excellent."

I'm not just being polite. It's an excellent meal. The chicken is moist and flavorful and the potatoes are creamy and buttery.

"It's nothing fancy like you're used to, but this is the type of food I grew up eating."

"It's much better than what *I* grew up eating."

"So did you find out anything about the man who came to my apartment?"

"No, I wasn't able to. I was in meetings all day. But I'll work on it tomorrow. You're planning to stay here tonight, right?"

"Yes. My bag is over there." She points to a small suitcase near the couch.

"You didn't bring much."

"It's just for one night."

"I think you should stay tomorrow night as well. Or as long as it takes to figure this out."

"Thank you for offering, but I can't stay here. You have things to do and so do I."

"If you don't stay here, I'll be forced to go stay at your place. I can't leave you alone at night. It's too dangerous."

She smiles. "Is that the only reason you want me to stay?"

"I admit I like having you here, but my main concern right now is your safety. If it makes you more comfortable, I'll sleep in the guest room. And you don't have to cook for me."

"I'll stay, but only until you find out who that man was. This is only temporary."

We finish dinner and Rachel serves us dessert. I don't really like sweets so I rarely eat dessert but she went to the trouble to make it so I eat it. And I'm glad I did. Her apple cobbler is better than desserts I've had from five star restaurants. It was warm from the oven and she topped it with vanilla ice cream.

After dessert, she gets up and takes our dishes.

"Let me clean up," I tell her. "It's only fair since you made dinner."

"We'll do it together." She brings the dishes to the sink and I clear the silverware and the glasses. This is another new experience for me. I've never cleaned up after dinner. I've never even *made* dinner so I had no need to clean up. I didn't even know how to load the dishwasher, but Rachel showed me.

When everything's put away, I scoop Rachel up in my arms and carry her to my bedroom.

I took her by surprise and she's laughing. "What are you doing?"

"It's question and answer time." I lay her on the bed. "I want you to hurry up and get to know me."

She's still laughing. "And why is that?"

I lie next to her and put my lips just above hers. "You know why." I kiss her. "How much longer do you think you need before you know me?"

"Maybe a few months?"

Months? Is she serious? My face must show my shock because her laughter continues.

"I'm kidding, Pearce. I don't know when it'll be, but I'll know when the time is right."

"Go ahead. First question."

She fires off questions even faster than last night. She's hurrying to get to know me. She wants to do it again just as much as I do. I'm not really sure why she insists on abstaining, given that we've already had sex, but I'm willing to wait as long as she needs.

I didn't think we were moving too fast, but she thought we were. I find it unusual because I'm used to having sex on the first date. Not that I would've done that with Rachel. I wanted to wait longer with her. And we did. We had several dates, and on each one of them, we talked for hours. In fact, in those few dates, I talked to Rachel more than I've talked to any other woman I've dated. So when we finally had sex, I didn't feel like we were rushing it. I didn't think she did either, until she told me she wanted to slow things down. But I like that she's that way. It's refreshing to be with a woman who isn't throwing herself at me, the way Rielle did that night at the bar. I'd known her all of five minutes before she invited me back to her place.

Rachel pauses to think of more questions, and as she does, I consider asking her some questions as well. She's told me a lot about herself, but she always skips over her college years in Indiana. I'm wondering if it's because of the man she was dating her senior year. The one who became her fiancé. I get the feeling there's a story there but I'm hesitant to ask her. I'd rather wait for her to tell me.

I answer the rest of her questions, but no matter how many questions she asks, she'll never know everything about me. Even if we were still together years from now, she could never know who I really am.

We talk for three straight hours but it seems much shorter than that. I've never been able to talk to someone for that long unless it was about business. And when I'm around my society friends, I try to avoid talking at all, because when I do, I have to watch my every word. Filter what I say. Make sure I'm coming across a certain way. But when I'm with Rachel, our conversation is easy and natural. I can talk without having to script my words in my head before I speak.

When I'm not talking, I like just listening to Rachel and watching her. When she tells a funny story, she smiles and laughs

187

and moves her hands around. When she says something serious or sad, the emotion shows on her face. She doesn't try to hide it.

The people I'm used to being around express zero emotion, or if they do express emotion, it's fake, intended to get a reaction out of whoever they're talking to. There's always a motive. They can't just have a normal conversation.

Around eleven, Rachel's eyes are struggling to stay open. "I think I need to go to bed," she says, yawning.

She gets in her pajamas and I get in mine, and once again, I fall asleep before midnight.

I could get used to this. Having Rachel here when I get home. Having dinner with her. Talking with her. Having her fall asleep in my arms. I never thought I could have this. And I probably can't. But I want it. I want this life.

CHAPTER EIGHTEEN

PEARCE

The next morning, I get up at five so I don't have to deal with my father scolding me for being late. I try to be as quiet as possible but Rachel wakes up as I'm putting my suit jacket on.

"Pearce?"

I go over to the bed and sit next to her and lean down to kiss her. "I have to go. Be careful today. And come back here after work. George will let you in."

She sits up and gives me a hug. "Thanks again for letting me stay here."

Her comment fills me with guilt because *I'm* the reason she can't stay at her own apartment. I'm the reason she's scared to be there. If it weren't for me, Jack never would've gone to her place.

I pull back to look at her, tucking her hair behind her ear. "You can stay here as long as you'd like."

She smiles. She's even beautiful first thing in the morning. That's another thing I could get used to. Waking up next to her every day.

"Any requests for dinner tonight?"

"Rachel, I told you, you don't have to make dinner. You don't owe me anything for staying here."

"We still have to eat and I like to cook, so it works out."

"Oh, I almost forgot." I stand up and take my wallet out. "I'll leave some money in the kitchen for groceries." I pull out three $100 bills.

She sees the money and laughs. "You're giving me three hundred dollars for groceries? For one meal?"

"I don't know what groceries cost. I've never gone shopping."

"I'll add that to the list of things you need to try. And just so you know, three hundred dollars would buy a lot of groceries."

"Take it and buy whatever you'd like, then keep the rest." I get up to leave. "I'll see you tonight."

I'm at the office at six sharp. My father is already there. He sees me in the hall and nods but says nothing. Not even a hello. That's his usual greeting. A nod.

At noon, I'm finally able to reach Jack.

"Hello, Pearce. My secretary said you wanted to speak with me."

"Yes. Right away." I'm trying to stay calm and not come out and accuse him of anything. That would get me nowhere. I need him to talk, and he won't do so if I make him angry. "Are you available now? I'll meet you at your office."

"No. Not the office. Meet me at my house in twenty minutes."

I agree to it, but find it odd he wants to meet at his house and not the office.

When I get to his mansion, he greets me at the door. "Follow me."

He takes me to a hallway that leads to the back of the house. He stops next to a painting on the wall and stares at it intently.

"What are you doing?" I ask him.

I hear a popping sound and see an opening in the wall. It's a hidden door, which many of the members have in their houses, but I've never seen one open like that. The painting must have a retinal scanner in it. It only opens with Jack's eyes so is more secure than a panel that uses a security code.

The door opens to a room with a bar and a poker table.

He goes to the bar and gets a drink. "Have a seat. You want a drink?"

"No." I sit at the table.

"My wife doesn't like it when I host poker games. She thinks us men get too loud, so I built this room. The walls are soundproofed."

It's a lie. If he wanted to play poker in the regular part of the house, he'd do it. He wouldn't let his wife stop him. Besides, this

190

house is at least 20,000 square feet. He could host a rowdy poker game without her ever hearing a sound.

I know what this room is. It's a safe room, meant to protect him if anyone comes to his house to attack him. There's a silver door behind him which I'm guessing hides a stash of guns and ammunition.

I get right down to business. "Why did you do it?"

He doesn't look confused or surprised. He knows exactly what I'm talking about. "Because I'm your mentor. I'm responsible for you. It's my job to know what you're up to."

"I'm not up to anything. And my friendship with her is none of your business."

"Is that what it is? A friendship? Because most of my female friends don't spend the night." He swigs his drink.

"Okay, yes, I'm seeing her. But it's not against the rules. I'm not doing anything wrong."

"They're *making* it a rule. You know that. You were at the meeting when it was discussed."

"Yes, but it hasn't gone up for a vote."

He sighs. "Pearce, I know how easy it is to fall for a beautiful woman. When it happens, you don't think straight. You make bad decisions. You do things you—"

"I'm not going to stop seeing her, Jack, so there's nothing more to say in that regard. Now why did you go over there?"

"I had to meet her. I also had my team run background checks on her and look into her past."

"Why would you—"

"Listen to me." His eyes lock on mine. "Trust no one. Especially a woman you're sleeping with. You have to be smarter about this, Pearce. You can't trust a woman just because she's beautiful or says the right things or is good in bed. I checked Rachel's history because I had to make sure she wasn't a reporter or a spy or an FBI agent. Luckily, my team found nothing to indicate she was anything more than what she claimed; a girl from a farm in Indiana. I went to see her at her apartment to confirm it, because paperwork can lie and identities can be stolen. Her reaction to a stranger coming to her door is telling. She believed

191

my story, invited me in, answered my questions, and her body language gave no indication she was lying. So she's just a regular college girl, which is all the more reason you should leave her alone."

"I'm not leaving her alone. I like her very much and I want to see where this goes."

"It'll never work. You know that."

"They haven't chosen anyone for me."

"Not yet, but they will. And in the meantime, go satisfy your needs with the associates. Stop wasting this girl's time. Let her find someone she can actually be with. Break this off now before it gets serious."

"It already *is* serious. I've never felt this way. I didn't think I could. I'm so used to feeling nothing and now—" I rub my forehead. "I just need you to leave her alone. If you had concerns about her, you should've had *me* check them out, not done it yourself."

"You're too close to her. If she'd had something suspicious in her background, you wouldn't have been able to see it."

"Well, she doesn't, so leave her alone."

"Pearce, I know you want a normal life, but that's not the life you were given. And you can't bring an innocent girl into our world."

Maybe he's right and I'm not able to see clearly right now, but I'm not ready to accept what he's saying. Not if it means losing Rachel.

"Give up the girl, Pearce, and focus on yourself. I told you I'd help you save that side of yourself you don't want to lose. The good side. But you need to stay focused in order to do that."

"Rachel already brings out the good side in me. She does it without even trying. I'm like a different person when I'm with her. I feel different. I act different. Being with her gives me hope. Makes me stronger. I even stood up to my father yesterday."

He leans back in his chair, his drink in his hand. "I'm advising you to stop seeing her. If you don't, you do so at your own peril. And hers as well."

"Are you going to tell them about her?"

"I don't need to. They'll find out on their own. Someone you know will see you with her and it'll get back to the members."

"Then I'll be more careful. I'll make sure we aren't seen in public."

"And you think she'll go for that?" He finishes his drink. "I have a wife and two daughters, so believe me, I know women. And I know they like to go out. Put on a nice dress. Be taken to dinner. Go dancing."

"Rachel doesn't mind staying home. She's fine with it."

"You're only saying that because you're trying to find ways to make this work. Rachel will want to go out, and when you tell her no, she'll find it suspicious. She'll start asking questions. She'll ask why you haven't introduced her to your friends and your parents. How are you going to answer those questions?"

"I don't know yet. I just know I have to keep seeing her."

He sets his glass down. "So this girl makes you happy?"

"Yes. Very much so." I smile just saying it.

He rolls his eyes. "Why do I always get the difficult ones?"

"What?"

"Never mind." He sighs heavily. "Pearce, I'm willing to keep this quiet. But only because the girl makes you happy. Given the life you're forced to lead, you deserve a few moments of happiness. But that's all it will be. If you pursue this, your happiness will be short lived. I guarantee this will end badly, and when it does, it will destroy you." He gets up and pours himself another scotch.

I don't believe him. I think he's being overly dramatic just to scare me into breaking up with her. "Are we done here?"

"No." He sits down again. "I got you a trainer to work on your physical strength. I don't just mean weightlifting or cardio. This man will teach you martial arts and how to use your body as a weapon. You can't always rely on a gun or a knife. Or a security guard. You need to be strong and know how to use your body to fight or to kill."

It's true. Sometimes all you have to fight with is your body, especially if your enemy turns out to be someone you thought was a friend.

"When does the training begin?"

"Next Monday. He'll be calling you to set up a time. A woman will also be contacting you. She's an expert in how the mind works and how to use it to your advantage. How to control your emotions. Facial expressions. Body language. Voice." He takes a drink. "You need to be a better liar, Pearce. You give too much away. And you need to learn not to react to things. Any questions?"

"No."

"Then I need to get back to the office." He gets up.

"Wait. I forgot to tell you, I got an assignment."

He sits back down. "What is it?"

"I don't know yet. I just got a notice that it's coming. I don't want to do it, Jack. I can't. Not after what they made me do last time."

"Relax. It could be something simple, like falsifying paperwork. Don't get worked up about it until you know for sure."

"And what if it's *not* something simple? What if it's a kill? An innocent?"

"Let your other side do it. That dark side will always be there as long as you're part of this. So use it. Let it take the blame for your actions. It's not you, Pearce. The real you had nothing to do with what happened to that secretary. The real you is not a killer. He's a good man. Remember that." He finishes his drink and stands up. "Let's go."

We leave the room and I go back to the office. The past few times we've met, Jack's given me so much to think about that I need time to sort it all out in my head. But today, the advice that stuck with me the most is to let the dark side do the assignment. It's not me. It never will be. I won't let it take over.

When I get back to the office, there's a note on my desk from my father telling me to call a new client, but there aren't any details about what exactly I'm supposed to talk to this man about. I go to my father's office to ask him about it. His door is closed, but he always has it closed so I open it and walk in.

I quickly shield my eyes and turn back around but my father saw me.

"Goddammit, Pearce!" I hear his voice behind the door I just closed. Then I hear a woman frantically talking.

My father was fucking his secretary against the desk and I just walked in on it. Good thing I didn't eat lunch or I'd be throwing it up right now. It's not like I don't know this happens. I know he cheats on my mother and I know he has sex in his office and probably elsewhere in the building. None of that is a surprise. But I've never actually walked in on him doing it.

"Pearce, get in here!" I hear my father say as his secretary walks out, trying to fix her hair as she scurries down the hall. She's probably around 28. She's only worked here a few months, but today will likely be her last day. My father always fires his secretaries after he fucks them.

I go in my father's office and close the door and sit on the couch on the far side of the room. "Remind me to never touch your desk again."

He goes around it and sits in his high-backed leather chair. "You find this humorous? Don't you know how to fucking knock?"

"She's a little young for you, isn't she?" I shouldn't have said that, but I feel like mouthing off to him today. I blame Rachel. She makes me want to fight my father instead of just sitting back and taking his abuse. "And next time, try locking the door."

He narrows his eyes at me. "I'm getting tired of this attitude of yours and it ends right now. I'm your father and your boss and you will treat me with respect."

"I find respecting you rather difficult after what I just saw."

He shoots up from his chair, his palms slamming down on his desk as he leans toward me. "Stop this right now! I will not stand for your insubordination!"

I decide to stop taunting him. I've taken it far enough for today.

"I came here to ask about the new client I'm supposed to call. Your note didn't mention any specifics about the goal of the call."

My change of topics takes him off guard. He stares at me, then slowly sits down.

"The client would like us to develop a proprietary chemical blend to be used in..." He continues telling me about the project and we pretend the earlier scene didn't happen. I thought he'd yell at me more about my behavior, but he didn't. I think he's so shocked that I spoke to him that way that he's not sure how to handle it. But he will. He'll find a way to get back at me. Try to find new ways to control me or punish me. And let him try. Because when he does, I'll no longer be standing idly by. I'll be fighting back.

As I'm exiting his office, my father says, "I'm leaving for Europe Thursday morning. I'll be gone for a few weeks."

I turn back and see him standing in front of me.

"A few *weeks*? Are you going on vacation?"

He never goes on vacation, but I don't know why else he'd be gone for that long.

"Of course not. This is for business. I'm meeting with potential clients in Europe. Cecil Roth set up the trip. He's introducing me to some of his contacts. I'm meeting him in London on Friday morning."

Cecil Roth is a fellow member. If he's doing this for my father, he must owe him a favor. Either that, or Dunamis is forcing Cecil to do this because they want to expand Kensington Chemical overseas for some purpose I don't know about yet. Members are told things on a need-to-know basis and as a new member, I'm not told much.

"You're coming as well," my father says, "but I need you to attend some meetings for me next week so you won't be leaving until the following week."

"I can't go to Europe."

He steps closer to me. "What did I just say about insubordination?"

I lower my voice. "I received an assignment notice. I'm not allowed to travel."

He steps back. "I see. It's too bad you won't be able to join us." He goes back to his desk and sits down. "Since you're staying here, I expect you to check on your mother while I'm gone."

"Of course. When will you be back?"

"The trip is scheduled for four weeks but if I'm done sooner than that, I'll fly back early."

"Four weeks is a long time."

"Yes. I'm not pleased about it, but between the meetings and the travel time to the various countries, I'll likely need the four weeks. If this trip results in our expansion overseas, then I suppose it's worth my time."

"I'll be sure to check on Mother during your absence. Now if you'll excuse me, I need to get back to work." I return to my office, elated I'm going to have an entire month without my father around. I'm sure he'll be checking in with me constantly and making me do his work but that's still better than having him here. I'll be able to leave work at a decent hour and spend more time with Rachel.

Just as I'm thinking that, my phone rings. It's the man I'll be training with at the gym. He wants to meet three times a week, which means I'm not going to have as much time with Rachel as I thought. Between the physical training and my training with the body language expert, I won't have much free time. But I'm committed to this training. I'm not letting that dark side of me take over. I always knew the good side of me was still there. I just wasn't sure it could survive. But meeting Rachel has made me want to fight for it. And in order to do so, I need to be strong and prepared.

I'm fighting a war. Not just with myself, but with my father and the other members. And I have to be ready for battle.

CHAPTER NINETEEN

RACHEL

Pearce just called me from work and told me that the man who came to my door *did* donate money to the shelter but that his donation was anonymous, which is why Laura didn't recognize his name.

Apparently, Jack is a very wealthy man, but eccentric and not all there mentally. He sometimes does inappropriate things, like stopping by my apartment uninvited. Pearce said Jack saw my photo at a fundraiser the shelter had last month. All the volunteers were featured in a display with our names and photos. For some reason, I caught Jack's eye and he tracked me down.

Pearce said he called Jack and told him to leave me alone but that Jack didn't even remember coming over here. So I guess he's just a confused old man. But Pearce advised me to still be careful because he's not sure what Jack is capable of. He may seem harmless, but if he has mental issues, you can't be sure.

It's 5:15 and I just got home from work and am wondering if I should just stay here tonight. I'd rather stay with Pearce, but I don't need to now so I feel like maybe I shouldn't. We just started dating and we need our space. Except I really want to see him. Maybe I'll just go over there tonight since he's expecting me, then the rest of the week I'll stay here.

I call my mom before I go because if she calls and I'm not here she'll have the police looking for me.

"Hi, Mom," I say when she answers.

"Honey, is something wrong?" She sounds panicked. I usually don't call her during the week so she probably thinks I'm dying. She always assumes the worst.

"Mom, I'm fine. I just wanted to let you know I'm going out tonight and won't be back until late. I didn't want you to call and worry because I wasn't here."

"Rachel, I don't want you going out at night. It's not safe."

She says it like she's talking to a five-year-old. Sometimes I think she acts that way because she lives in the past, like I'm still her five-year-old daughter. Like she wants to freeze time in that moment, before my sister got sick.

"Mom, I'll be with a friend."

"Two girls going out at night still isn't safe." She pauses. "Or are you going out with a boy?"

A *boy*? Again, I'm not five. I don't go out with *boys*. I go out with men. And Pearce is definitely a man. A tall, muscular, handsome man.

"Yes. It's a date." I didn't want to tell her that but it just came out.

"Who *is* this boy?"

The 'boy' term is getting on my nerves but I ignore it. "His name is Pearce. He's 25 and he graduated from Yale and got his MBA from Harvard. And now he's working for his father's company."

"Is this your first date?"

"No. We've been on several. He's really nice, Mom. I think you'd like him. He opens doors for me and buys me flowers. He even bought me a really nice vase. He's very mature and has good manners. And we can talk for hours. In fact, every time we go out we end up talking for hours and not even realizing it."

The phone's quiet.

"Mom, are you there?"

"Yes, honey. I'm just surprised how smitten you are with this young man."

At least she said 'young man' this time. The 'smitten' term has me smiling. I always think it's funny when she uses these old-fashioned words.

"Yes, I'm definitely smitten with him."

"Well, don't rush into anything. Take your time to get to know him. Don't do what your father and I did and get married twelve days after meeting each other."

She's not kidding. It really was twelve days. She was 20 and visiting her cousin in the small town my dad lived in. They met at the one and only diner in town. He saw her across the diner, went up to her, and asked her out. She said yes but they had nowhere to go in that small town so she just went and sat at his table and he sent the friend he was with over to sit with her cousin.

My dad said he knew the moment he saw my mom that she was the one. She didn't feel that way about him until their second date when he cooked dinner for her. He won her over with that meal. It wasn't anything special. It was just pot roast and potatoes, but she was impressed that he'd do that for her. Ten days later they got married. To me, it sounds completely insane to get married that fast but my mom said, "when you know you know." And they both must've known because thirty years later they're still together.

"We're not getting married, Mom. We're just dating. I like spending time with him."

"And what company did you say he works for?"

"Kensington Chemical. His family owns it. Have you heard of it?"

My mom didn't go to college but she knows so much about business that you'd think she had a degree in it. She's really smart. She read books and taught herself accounting and finance and whatever else she felt she needed to know. She manages the business side of the farm, doing all the paperwork, the taxes, the budget. And she follows business news, which is why I thought she might've heard of Pearce's company.

"Kensington Chemical is a very large corporation," she says. "And very successful. This man must be wealthy."

"Yes, his family is very wealthy. They're billionaires."

"Oh. I didn't think they were *that* wealthy. I'm surprised you're dating him."

"Why?"

"I can't imagine you two have anything in common. You come from such different lifestyles, different backgrounds. You had a modest upbringing and I'm sure his was very extravagant."

"It was, but that doesn't matter."

"Rachel, I know you said you're not interested, but I think you should give Adam another chance."

Adam? Is she serious? I've made it very clear I want nothing to do with him and yet she keeps pushing me to date him.

"Mom, I just told you I have a boyfriend."

"Honey, you only like that young man because he's different than what you're used to. And different is exciting and new, but once that wears off, you'll find you have nothing in common. It won't last. Someone like Adam is a better fit for you. You two have a lot in common."

"The only thing we have in common is that we grew up in the same town and went to the same school. That's it."

"You went to the same church. Had some of the same friends."

"That doesn't mean I should date him!" I'm trying to stay calm but it's nearly impossible. She's pushing all my buttons. Making me feel like a child. Acting like she knows what's best for me. Like I'm not smart enough to make my own decisions. It makes me want to scream, but I can't. I don't like yelling at my mom.

"Rachel, just calm down."

Now I really want to scream. I hate being told to calm down.

I take a breath. "I'm sorry. I didn't mean to yell. I just need you to understand that I have no interest in Adam. I'm dating Pearce and I really like him. I know you don't think so, but Pearce and I *do* have a lot in common." I want to say we both have controlling parents but I don't.

"I'm only asking that you talk to Adam on the phone. He's changed, Rachel. He's more mature. More responsible. He has a good job. He's looking at buying a house."

"How do you know so much about him?"

"Your father and I had him over for dinner last night."

Dammit. I can't believe she did that. She's leading him on. Now he probably thinks I'm interested in him. But why is he interested in *me*? Did he change his mind about having kids?

"Mom, you shouldn't have done that. I don't want Adam thinking I want to date him again."

"If you'd talk to him, you might change your mind. You have a history with him, Rachel. You shouldn't be so quick to dismiss him."

She just refuses to listen. She doesn't even care about what I want.

"The next time Adam is in town, I need you to tell him I'm not interested. I'm not kidding. I don't want to talk to him."

"Honey, I can't tell him that. You need to tell him yourself."

I feel my blood pressure rising, my head pounding. I'm so angry right now.

"Why can't you just do this for me?" I ask.

"I already told Adam you'd call him and I don't want to go back on my word. It'll make things awkward when I see him."

"You never see him. He lives in Indianapolis."

"He lives *here* now. He just moved back. So now I'll see him at the store and at church."

So that's why she wants me to be with him. Because if I married him, I'd live back in my hometown. She'd get what she wants and I'd be miserable.

"Fine. I'll call him. But only to tell him I'm not interested. And I'm not calling him today. I'll call him later this week. But if you see him, don't talk about me. I don't want him getting the wrong idea." I check the clock on the wall. "Mom, I really need to get going."

"Okay, honey. Be careful tonight. I don't want you getting hurt. I love you."

"I love you too."

I hang up, relieved I was able to make it through the call without screaming at her. I wish she could just be happy for me and not be so negative and controlling. She thinks she's helping, but she's not. She needs to let me be an adult and make my own decisions. I need to take risks and make mistakes. Maybe Pearce and I won't work out. Maybe he'll end up breaking my heart. But that could happen with any guy. And I'm willing to take that risk with Pearce more than anyone else. I may not know everything about him, but I feel like we have something special between us. I can't describe what that is exactly, but that's what makes me think our relationship might go somewhere. I've never had these feelings for anyone else and that has to mean something.

I go in my bedroom and quickly change into a light pink sweater and some different jeans. I grab my overnight bag and head out the door. I need to stop and get groceries on my way to Pearce's loft. I'm going to make him homemade pizza tonight. I bet he hasn't had many pizzas. Maybe he's never even tried one.

"Hey, Rachel." Shelby stops me as I'm going down the stairs.

"Shelby, I haven't seen you for days."

"Me? It's more like the other way around. I haven't seen *you* for days. Where have you been?"

"With Pearce." I smile.

Her face drops. "You're still dating him?"

"Yes. Why?"

"I just…" She seems flustered. "I thought you said he used you. After he dropped you off last Sunday, you said—"

"That was just a misunderstanding. He wasn't breaking up with me. His mind was just focused on work. That's why he was acting that way. But he came over later and we talked, and now everything's back to normal." I'm still smiling, but she's not smiling back. Actually, she looks kind of angry. "Shelby, what's wrong?"

"It's just…I just didn't think he'd date you for this long."

I laugh, even though I'm offended. "What's that supposed to mean?"

"Don't take this the wrong way, but you're not really his type. I mean, you don't exactly wear designer gowns and hang out at the country club."

"Shelby, where is this coming from? When I first met him, *you* were the one who kept pushing me to go out with him. You told me girls like us should be able to date guys like Pearce."

"Yeah, but I just meant you should go out with him. Like once or twice."

"So I can't be his girlfriend unless I'm rich?"

"He's calling you his girlfriend now?"

Now I'm really offended. "Yes. What's wrong with that?"

"I'm not trying to be mean. I just find it unusual. Rich people date other rich people. That's how it's always been and always will be."

"That's not true."

"Name one billionaire who married a regular person."

I roll my eyes. "I don't know any billionaires besides Pearce so I can't answer that question."

"You've met his rich friends. I bet his rich guy friends are all paired with rich girls."

I glance away.

"Rachel. You HAVE met his friends, right?"

I look back at her. "No."

She sighs. "This is what I'm trying to tell you. He's using you. You're not his girlfriend. You can't be, because you don't fit in his world."

I don't know why she's being so mean, but it's making me angry. "He's not using me. And I don't like you saying that about him. You don't know him like I do."

"You've known him for what? A few weeks? If that? You don't know him, Rachel. You don't know anything about him. He won't even introduce you to his friends. He's using you, and if you don't end this now, you're going to get hurt really bad."

Now she sounds like my mom. Why is everyone trying to ruin this for me? I was in such a great mood, excited to see Pearce later, but my mom and Shelby are determined to bring me down.

"Shelby, I'm not talking to you about this. I like Pearce and I'm going to keep dating him. And I'd appreciate it if you'd stop giving me advice about him. In fact, don't even talk about him at all. I'll see you later."

I hurry down the stairs.

"Rachel, wait!" I hear her behind me. "I'm sorry."

I keep going, out the door and to my car, fighting back tears. Why can't Shelby and my mom just let me be happy? Why do they have to bring up all these doubts and act like I'm stupid to think I could ever be with someone like Pearce? Is money really that important? I don't care about his money. It doesn't matter to me. And he doesn't act like it's a problem that I *don't* have money. It's not like he's ashamed of me. It's true he's never introduced me to his friends or his family, but he just hasn't had time to do it yet. And I'm in no hurry to meet them. Right now I just want to spend time alone with Pearce so we can keep getting to know each other.

I drive to the store and get to his apartment at 6:30. He said he'd try to get home by 7:30 so I start the pizza. But before I do, I turn on some music. He has a stereo system with speakers built into the ceiling. I find a radio station that plays popular music and turn it up and get to work. The music and the cooking put me in a good mood again and it gets even better when Pearce gets home.

He arrives with a bouquet of orange tulips, already in a vase. He has a black suit on with a dark gray tie. My heart skips a beat just seeing him walk toward me.

"You look beautiful, as always." He hands me the flowers.

"Thank you." I set the flowers on the kitchen table and when I turn around he's right there.

His big arms wrap around me and he leans down and kisses me, causing those sparks to ignite again. I need to speed up this get-to-know-him stage because I really want to be with him again. Maybe I should just do it. No, I can't. I don't want a relationship based on sex. It has to be more than that.

We kiss until the oven timer goes off. But he doesn't let me go.

"Pearce. I have to check the oven."

"How long will that take?"

I laugh. "A minute. Max." I walk over to the oven.

"Come back here when you're done."

But I don't have to because he meets me in the kitchen. "Would you like some wine?"

"I'd love some."

He pushes a panel on the wall and a door opens to a wine cabinet.

"I didn't even know that was there."

He points to the bottles. "What kind would you like?"

"You pick. I don't know much about wine."

He takes a bottle of red from the rack. "I never drink these. A bottle of wine should be shared and I never have anyone to share it with."

Is he kidding? He's a super hot billionaire. How could he not have anyone to share his wine with? I'm sure he's never had a problem getting women.

I take the wine glasses from the cabinet, then lean against the counter, watching him open the bottle. "Are you saying you don't date much?"

"I don't have time to date." He pours the wine in the glasses.

"But you're dating *me*."

"Yes. Because I like you. Very much. So much so that I never seem to have enough time with you."

His silvery blue eyes dance over my face. I love how he looks at me. It's so intense. His face doesn't show much emotion but his eyes do. And right now, they're honest, sincere. That wasn't just a line he was giving me. He meant what he said.

"I know what you mean," I tell him. "Whenever we hang out, the time goes so quickly."

"Which is why we're going to spend more time together." His arms go around me and he draws me closer.

I smile at him. "And how am I going to fit into your work schedule? You work like a hundred hours a week."

"I'm cutting back on my hours." He slips my hair behind my ear, leaving his hand there.

"Just for me?"

"Yes. Do you have any objections to that?"

I smile at his question, because he said it with such formality. He usually loosens up when he's around me, but sometimes he'll switch back and be very formal, probably because he's used to being that way with everyone else.

"Rachel?" He has a concerned look on his face and I realize I didn't answer his question.

I kiss him. "I have no objections to you cutting back on your hours. I think it's a good idea. You work way too much. And I would love to spend more time with you."

"Good." He steps back as the oven timer goes off again. "It sounds like dinner's almost done. I need to change clothes."

"Go ahead. I'll get everything set up."

When he comes back out of the bedroom, he's wearing jeans and a button-up shirt.

I smile at him. "You're liking those jeans, aren't you?"

"You seem to like them so I'm wearing them for you. But yes, I'm getting used to them." He glances over at the table where I have dinner set up. "The pizza smells delicious."

"I'm guessing you don't eat pizza very often."

"No, never."

"So it's another new thing for you to try. I made the crust from scratch. I hope you like it."

"Thank you for making dinner." He hugs me, which takes me by surprise. He's not really the hugging type. I'm usually the one initiating the hug. When he lets me go, he looks at me and says, "I like having you here. And not because you make me dinner."

I watch the expression in his eyes. They showed so much sadness when we first met, but now I see glimmers of happiness. I hope part of that is because of me, but if not, it doesn't matter. What's important is that some of that sadness is gone. I want him to tell me the cause of his sadness, but he's not ready to yet. If I had to guess, I'd say it's because he doesn't seem to have much in his life. He has work and more money than anyone I know, but he doesn't seem to have many *people* in his life. At least not people who care about him.

"Pearce, I appreciate you letting me stay here and I love spending time with you, but after tonight I need to go back and stay at my own place."

"You don't have to. You could live here."

He says it with a straight face, but I laugh, assuming he's kidding. "I can't do that. I'm not moving in with you. It's too soon."

"It's not moving in together. It's just two people living together. We'll be roommates."

I smile, still assuming he's kidding. "I can't afford rent at a place like this."

"Rachel, I'm serious. I don't like where you're living. It's not a good neighborhood. I worry about you."

"Now you sound like my mom. You don't have to worry about me. I'm fine." I lead him to the table. "Let's eat."

He pulls out my chair for me. "Would you at least consider moving to a safer area?"

"I don't need to," I say as I sit down. "I've never had a problem living there. And it's a good location. It's close to school and my job."

He takes the seat across from me. "When is your lease up?"

I serve him some pizza. "End of December."

"And then what are your plans?"

I feel his eyes on me as I take a slice of pizza for myself. "I don't know yet. It depends on where I get a job."

He nods, then directs his attention to his plate. He looks disappointed, like he expected me to say I was staying. But he knows I can't. I have to go to wherever I can find a job.

So what am I doing? Why am I getting involved with him knowing I'm leaving in a few months? When I met Pearce I thought we'd just go out a few times and that would be it. I never thought it would become anything more than that. But now it has. Now I have feelings for him and I don't like the thought of leaving him.

"Shall we toast?"

I look up and see Pearce holding up his wine glass. He's smiling, but now his eyes look sad. That glimmer of happiness is gone and I feel a pain in my chest. I think we both just realized that this relationship is only temporary. But neither one of us wants to address that. Not yet.

I pick up my glass. "What are we toasting to?"

"To the fact that I'm home from work at a decent hour, eating a home-cooked meal with the most beautiful woman I've ever laid eyes on."

I smile as we clink our glasses.

We sip our wine, and then we eat, and go back to pretending this relationship isn't headed for any kind of end. I think I'll just stay in that mindset for as long as possible. It may be a lie, but I like it much better than the truth.

CHAPTER TWENTY

PEARCE

Rachel made me dinner again tonight and I felt like I was living someone else's life. Someone who has a normal life with a woman he actually cares about and wants to be with. Someone who isn't consumed with work, but has a life outside of it. A real life.

God, I want that so bad. I never thought I did, but then I met Rachel, and ever since then I've discovered that it's exactly what I want. It's what I need.

For as long as I can remember, my life has belonged to someone else. My parents. The organization. My fake wife. I've never been able to make my own choices, and when I've tried, I've been punished for doing so. But now, I'm making the choice to be with Rachel and nothing has felt more right in all my life. Everything about her feels right. I feel like a different person when I'm with her. Like I'm finally being true to myself. Letting myself be the person I am, instead of the person I'm expected to be.

But she's leaving. Rachel is leaving after she graduates in December. Our relationship will end and my life will go back to being my career and nothing else. Knowing that, I should break up with her. I'm risking everything by dating her, and if it's going to end, I might as well do it now. I just can't make myself say those words. Instead of telling her to leave, I keep telling her to stay. Instead of accepting the fact that she'll be moving away, I hold out hope that maybe she'll stay. I would do anything to get her to stay, but at the same time, I can't hold her back from her dreams. I want her to be happy, and if that means leaving here to pursue those dreams, I won't try to stop her.

"How was dinner?" she asks.

"Very good. Thank you." I set my napkin on the table. She reaches for my plate but I pick it up, along with hers. "Let me clean up."

The phone rings as I'm taking the plates to the sink.

"Go ahead and get it," Rachel says. "There's not much to clean. I can do it."

I set the plates down and go into the bedroom. I don't know who's calling but I need privacy in case it's Jack or one of the other members. I pick up the phone on the nightstand. "Hello?"

"Pearce, it's your mother."

"Hello, Mother. Do you need something?"

She never calls unless she needs something.

"Yes. I need you to accompany me to a dinner party. It's not until the middle of October but I wanted to give you adequate notice."

"By then, Father will likely be back in town. He can attend the dinner with you."

"Possibly, but the dinner is on a Thursday and when I spoke with your father earlier, it sounded like he wouldn't be home until the following Saturday so I need to make alternate plans."

"I don't know if I can attend the dinner, Mother. I'll have to check my schedule." I despise these formal dinners. They last all night, and if my mother is attending, I'm guessing everyone there will be her age or older.

"Whatever else in on your schedule will have to be canceled. You're going to this dinner, Pearce. I can't show up without an escort, and since your father is out of town, you need to take his place."

"Where is the dinner?"

"At the Seymour residence. It's formal attire of course and dinner begins promptly at seven. But we'll need to arrive at 6:30 for cocktails. I'll call you next week to discuss the details."

"Mother, wait. Who else will be at the dinner?"

She sighs. "Pearce, I didn't memorize the seating chart. I need to go. We'll talk later. Goodbye."

211

She hangs up. It's just like I said. I'm never given a choice. I'm always being told what to do and when to do it. And I hate it, but it's all I know so I usually don't question it. But now, this dinner means I have one less night with Rachel, and since my nights with her are limited, I don't want to give one up to spend with my mother and the Seymours.

I don't care for the Seymours. Leland Seymour has always made me uncomfortable. He says things that always come out sounding like a threat. He's a member of Dunamis and owns MDX Aerodynamics, a large, international corporation that does a lot of work with the military. The Seymour family is extremely wealthy and they love letting people know it. They flaunt their wealth to the point of being obnoxious. They have two teenage daughters, Katherine and Caroline. Katherine's had a crush on me since she was 12. Now she's 15 and flirts with me whenever she sees me. She's just a child, but for some reason, she thinks I would date her. So not only will I have to deal with my mother and Leland Seymour, I'll also have to deal with Katherine.

There goes my good mood. All it takes is one quick call from my mother to shift my night from good to bad.

"Hey." I turn and see Rachel behind me. She's smiling. She has such a beautiful smile. Just seeing that smile shifts my mood back to good.

"You shouldn't be in here," I say, circling my arms around her waist.

"In your bedroom?" Her hands wrap behind my neck, her fingers moving gently through my hair. "Why?"

"Because you wanted to slow things down between us. And that will be very difficult to do if we stay in this room."

"We stayed in here last night."

"Yes. And it was very difficult."

She reaches up and kisses me softly on the lips, then backs away. "Thank you."

"For what?"

"For not pressuring me. I know you want to move this along, and I do too, but I want us to spend more time together first."

"I understand. But for now, let's spend time together in a different room."

She laughs. She has such a great laugh. It's light and happy and full of energy.

"I dished up some ice cream." She takes my hand and leads me to the tall stools that line the kitchen island. Two bowls of ice cream are sitting there. "I bought chocolate chip so you could try a new flavor. And there's a whole half gallon in the freezer so you can have some every night for the rest of the week."

She sits next to me, waiting for me to try it. I taste it. "It's very good."

It's odd to be eating ice cream. My parents would be embarrassed if they saw me eating such a childish dessert. My father probably hasn't had ice cream since he was a toddler. I was 10 the last time I had it and that was only because I begged my mother to let me have it one last time for my tenth birthday. My father forbid it, saying I was too old, but my mother snuck me a small bowl of it up in my room that night after my father had gone to sleep.

I set my spoon down. "So what are your plans this week?"

"The usual. Work and school." She smiles. "And hopefully, my handsome boyfriend will come visit me." She takes a bite of ice cream.

"And what if he came over every night this week?" I take the spoon from her hand and place it back in her bowl.

"Hmm. That's a lot of nights. And it's getting harder and harder to be around you without—"

I kiss her before she can finish. "Which is why we need to spend time together. You'll never get to know me if we're always apart. So what do you say? You won't have to cook. I'll bring dinner every night."

She mulls it over. "I like the idea, but I won't get any studying done if you're there."

"And why is that?" I bring her face to mine and kiss her. "I promise not to bother you." I kiss her cheek, then over to her ear. "I'll sit quietly on the couch."

She shivers at the feel of my breath. "If you're there, I'll want to join you on the couch."

I kiss her neck. "Then join me on the couch. You can sit next to me and study."

She closes her eyes, tilting her head and exposing more of her neck for me to kiss. "I guarantee I won't be able to study if you do this when you're at my apartment."

"Let's try it and see." I stand up and lift her off the stool.

"What are you doing?"

I carry her to the couch and set her down, then hand her one of my business books from the side table. "Go ahead. Pretend it's one of your textbooks."

She laughs. "Okay." She opens the book and starts reading.

I sit next to her, sweeping her hair aside and gently kissing her neck. Her body relaxes into the couch and her eyes fall shut.

"Yeah, this isn't going to work," she says, as the book drops to the floor.

I pick her legs up, setting them on the couch as she lies back. I lie over her and kiss her, this time on her lips. "I'm still coming over."

She pulls me closer and whispers, "I didn't invite you."

"I'm coming over anyway." My hand moves down her side, resting on her hip.

Before she can speak, I kiss her again, my tongue slipping past her parted lips. I've never kissed a woman as much as I've kissed Rachel. It's far too intimate for me. I always avoid kissing and move straight to the sex. But it's different with Rachel, and not just because sex isn't an option right now. It's different because I actually *want* to kiss her. In fact, whenever she's around me, I can't seem to stop kissing her. But I have to force myself to stop, because kissing her leads to wanting to do more with her, and she's not ready yet. I hope she's ready soon because it's killing me to wait.

Over the next couple weeks, I go to Rachel's apartment every night after work or she comes to my loft. We have dinner, then talk or watch TV or she studies while I catch up on whatever I

214

didn't get done at the office. We're getting into a routine and I like it. It makes me feel like I have a normal life. I know I don't, but for now, I'm pretending I do. My father is thousands of miles away and I haven't heard anything from the organization or Jack. I've been checking in with my mother, but other than that, I haven't talked to anyone from that part of my life. It's like I've left that life behind, at least for the time being.

It's now October and Rachel and I are spending the weekend at my loft. Friday night I order in a gourmet meal. The weather's getting colder, so I get the fireplace going. Rachel loves sitting in front of the fire, so we stay there all day Saturday, lying on the couch and watching movies. I've never watched so many movies in my entire life. I rarely even watch TV. But Rachel loves movies so I watch them with her, or I just sit and watch *her* as she reacts to the various scenes, sometimes smiling, sometimes tearing up, sometimes laughing. I love how she's able to put her emotions out there like that. I could never do that.

As I watch her, I realize that my feelings for her just keep getting deeper. It concerns me, but also makes me happy. It's nice to feel something for once in my life, especially something as good as this.

On Sunday night, it's cold and rainy outside and Rachel and I are snuggled up on the couch. I start kissing her and touching her, like I always do. I've learned what she likes and I love pleasing her. But I'd also love to go back to having sex with her.

She softly moans as we kiss. The sound, and the way she feels, has me turned on to the point that I can't hide it. I'm pressed into her and I know she feels me but I can't do anything about it. This happens whenever I kiss her. I normally don't react this way to a kiss, but I do with Rachel. And I don't care if she knows it. But I don't want her assuming my reaction is a sign that I'm pressuring her to go farther.

I lift up a little. "Maybe we should stop."

"Yeah." She nods, as she catches her breath.

I move off her and she sits up.

"I'm sorry," she says, her eyes on the floor.

I put my arm around her. "Sorry about what?"

"For not continuing this. In the bedroom. I want to. I really do. It's just that…"

I turn her toward me. "It's just what?"

"It's just that there are things you don't know about me and I'm sure there are things I don't know about you and—"

"Rachel, I understand. You don't have to explain."

She looks down at the couch. "I *do* have to explain. I haven't been completely honest with you."

"What do you mean?"

"Something happened to me that I don't like to talk about, but it affected me so much that I feel like you'll never really know me until you know this. I'm just not sure I want to tell you."

"Why?" I gently lift her chin up so I can see her face.

"Because it might change things. Plus, we're still early into our relationship and this is something we wouldn't worry about until way off into the future, but not telling you now seems…I don't know. Dishonest, I guess."

She's starting to concern me. What kind of secret is she hiding? Things are going so well between us, I almost don't want to hear what she has to say. But I can tell that she needs to say this and part of me wants to know.

"Go ahead, Rachel. Just tell me."

She moves back a little and shifts her gaze to the couch. "Remember when I told you I was engaged?"

"Yes." I don't want to hear this. Is she going to tell me she got married? And that she's *still* married? Has she been lying to me this whole time?

"I never told you why Adam broke off the engagement."

I sigh with relief. At least she's not married. "Go on."

"First, I need to make it clear that I never wanted to marry him. I didn't love him. I only accepted his proposal because I was…because I was pregnant."

She has a child? How could she not tell me this? Is the child living with her mother? Or her ex-fiancé?

"So you have a child," I say, trying to hide my anger. She should've told me this.

216

"No." A tear runs down her cheek. "I lost the baby. And then Adam broke up with me."

"Rachel." I put my arms around her and hold her against me. "I'm sorry."

She's quietly crying so I hold her tighter. I don't know what else to do. I'm the absolute worst person to spill your heart out to, and if this were anyone else, I'd be up getting a box of tissues, then hand them to the person and leave. I'm not comfortable in these situations. Then again, I've never actually been in this situation. I've never had anyone open up to me like this. And I've never done it myself, although I've told Rachel more than I've told any other woman I've ever dated.

"That's not all." She pauses.

"What is it?" I ask, getting concerned again.

"I don't want to tell you this," she says, still holding onto me, her head on my shoulder.

"Why don't you want to tell me?"

"Because I don't want this to end." Her voice is shaky.

"Why would it end?"

"It's just that…I know that you'll…" Her voice drifts off.

"Just tell me, Rachel."

She takes a breath. "Adam left me because my doctor told me that…that I can't have children."

That's what she didn't want to tell me? That she can't have children? Why was she so afraid to tell me that? It doesn't change anything between us. In fact, it's a good thing. I don't want children. As soon as I found out that any children I have would be forced to be part of the organization, I decided to never have them. I'd never want my children to go through what I've had to go through. If I had a son, he'd be forced into the life I'm now living. And if I had a daughter, she'd be forced to marry one of the members. Someone she didn't choose. I couldn't bear to see my own children's lives destroyed like that. And besides that, I'd make a terrible father. I had the worst role models for parents. I have no idea how to raise a child.

Even if I wanted children, I wouldn't give Rachel up because she can't have them. I can't believe her fiancé did. What the hell is wrong with him? He obviously didn't love her. Wait. What am I saying? That *I* love her? No. That can't be true. I haven't known her long enough for that to be true. I'm just saying that he never should have let her go because of that. I certainly wouldn't.

I still haven't said anything and realize I should just as Rachel pushes off me.

"Pearce, I understand if you want to end things between us. I know we're just dating, but I'm sure you'd rather date someone you could see a future with." She wipes her eyes and gets up from the couch.

I grab her hand. "Rachel, stop. Where are you going?"

"I need to leave."

I pull her down next to me. "You're not leaving. You haven't even let me say anything."

She nods. "Go ahead."

"I don't care that you can't have children. It doesn't matter to me."

She smiles weakly. "You're just saying that because I'm a crying mess right now."

"No." I hold her face with my hands and look into her eyes. "I'm saying it because *you're* what matters to me. Not the fact that you can't have children."

"I know you want them someday. Everyone does. And that's not something I could ever give you. Or any other man." She squeezes her eyes shut, trying to hold back her tears.

I sweep my thumb over her cheek. "Rachel, look at me." I wait for her to open her eyes. "That man is an idiot for letting you go. And hopefully you've noticed this by now, but if not, I will tell you that I am not an idiot."

She smiles a little.

"If you were mine, I would never make the mistake of letting you go. And although I know it's too soon to presume that you're mine, I most certainly would not end this relationship over the fact that you can't have children. I don't care about that. What I care about…is you."

She smiles completely now, tears running down her cheeks. "I care about you too."

I take her in my arms again and we stay there, not saying anything. After a while, she sits up and looks at me, hesitating.

"What is it, Rachel?"

"I just wanted to say that, um...I AM yours. I mean, if you want me to be."

I smile, moving the strands of hair off her cheek. "Of course I want that. I don't want anyone else but you."

"Are you sure?"

"I've never been more sure of anything in my entire life." And it's true. I just can't believe I admitted it. Out loud. But she needs to know how I feel about her.

She hugs me. "Then by default, you're mine. So tell that to all the girls who are constantly flirting with you."

I sit back so I can see her face. "Nobody's flirting with me. And if they were, I wouldn't notice. I'm too distracted by you and what you do to me."

"What do I do to you?" She bites her lip, smiling.

"I'm still trying to figure that out. I think you've got some kind of spell on me. I can't go two seconds without thinking about you."

"I have the same problem." She kisses me. "I think about you all the time." She rests her head on my shoulder. "Maybe we should go to sleep."

I kiss her forehead. "It's still early."

"Yeah, I guess it is." She sits back but takes my hand, gently rubbing it with her thumb. She's always touching me. My hands. My face. My shoulders. My hair. I usually hate it when people touch me, but I love it when she does. It soothes me, and when I'm not with her I crave her touch.

I notice the concerned look on her face. "Rachel, are you okay?"

She nods, her eyes on my hand as she runs her fingers over my palm. "I was so scared to tell you that."

"There was no need to be. You can tell me anything."

"I don't really have anything else to tell you. That was my big secret. It's the only one I have." She smiles at me. "You want to tell me yours now?"

219

My muscles tighten, my hand clenching up. If she only knew how many secrets I have. Secrets that are far worse than hers.

She releases my hand. "Did I hurt you? I'm sorry."

"No." I pick up her hand and place it back in mine. "I like it. I just forgot about something I had to do for work and it caused me to tense up."

"If you need to do some work, I can watch TV. I won't bother you."

"It's nothing that needs to be done right now. I'll do it tomorrow."

She lets go of my hand. "Turn around."

"Why?"

"Just do it."

I turn away from her and feel her hands on my shoulders. She starts gently massaging them, kneading the tense muscles. It feels amazing. The only massages I've ever had were sexual in nature and didn't relax me at all.

"How's that?" she asks.

"Good." I close my eyes as she increases the pressure a little. "*Better* than good."

Her hands remain on my shoulders and she adds slightly more pressure. "Is that okay?"

"Yes. It's perfect. But you don't have to do this."

"I want to. You're so tense and I want to make you feel better."

No one's ever tried to make me feel better. Not even my own mother. When I was a child and got sick or injured, my nanny took care of me. And she wasn't caring or nurturing in any way. She just did her job and left.

"When you're done, I'm doing the same to you," I say as Rachel's hands move down to my shoulder blades. God, it feels good. I can already feel the tightness in my muscles loosening.

She peeks around my shoulder and kisses my cheek. "Lie down so I can get more of your back. And you should probably take your shirt off."

I do as she says and her hands move over my skin in long, even strokes. Then she finds the tense spots and applies extra pressure, working the knots out. It might just be the best thing I've ever felt. She continues and I become so relaxed that I fall asleep.

"Pearce."

I open my eyes and see Rachel crouched down in front of me. I turn on my side to face her. "How long was I asleep?"

"About an hour." She brushes the hair off my forehead. "That massage really knocked you out. I didn't want to wake you up, but I think you'll be more comfortable in the bed."

I sit up and stretch a little. My muscles actually feel loose. They never feel loose. I'm always wound so tight I can barely breathe. I take a breath and notice my chest muscles are relaxed enough that I can actually inhale a deep breath instead of the shallow breaths I'm used to.

"You're really good at that," I tell her. "I feel great. Where did you learn how to do that?"

She shrugs. "I just taught myself. I can feel the tense areas I need to work on and then I just pay attention to how the person reacts and adjust the pressure."

"Well, you're very talented. I can't remember when I last felt this good. Probably never."

"Then I'll have to be sure and do that more often. You can't go around being that tense all the time." She holds her hand out to me. "Come on. Let's go."

We walk to the bedroom. She goes in the bathroom and gets ready for bed while I change out of my clothes. As I'm hanging my pants in the closet, I spot her overnight bag on the floor. I wish she'd reconsider my offer. I don't want her living in that run-down apartment in that dangerous neighborhood. I want her living here. With me. For her safety, but also because I don't want her to leave.

She comes out of the bathroom in a white tank top and pink and white striped pajama pants. She looks adorable and sexy at the same time. Her long brown hair cascades over her shoulders and her face is clean of any makeup. She doesn't need it. Her complexion is flawless and she has the most gorgeous face. It's perfectly symmetrical with high cheekbones like a model. Her eyes are bright blue and her lips are soft and full.

I step up to her, lifting her face up to mine. "God, you're beautiful."

She looks at me like I've lost my mind. "Pearce, I don't even have makeup on."

"You don't need it. You're gorgeous."

Her lips turn up into a shy smile. "Thank you. Let's go to bed."

I don't think she believes me. She really doesn't know she's beautiful? Has she never looked in a mirror?

"Pearce. Are you going to put pajamas on?"

I'm still staring at her face, but her question causes me to look down and see that I'm not wearing any pants. "Oh. Yes. Sorry, I was distracted."

She laughs and goes over to the bed. "I think pants would be a good idea."

"Yes. Of course." I go over to my dresser.

"So it sounded like your mom called earlier. I didn't mean to eavesdrop. I just heard you call her that when you picked up the phone."

"Yes, that was her." I find my pajama pants and slip them on. "She needs me to attend a dinner party with her in a few weeks because my father is out of town."

"I'd love to meet her sometime. And your father. Maybe when he's back from his trip, we could all go out."

Rachel can't meet my parents. They'd forbid me from seeing her. So how is this going to work? I can't keep her a secret forever.

I don't respond to her statement, but instead get into bed beside her. "Flip over." I pause, then say, "Oh, and take your shirt off."

"What?" She pretends to be shocked. "What exactly are you planning to do here?"

"You'll see." I motion to her tank. "Take it off, please."

222

She turns her back to me and slips it off, then lies on her stomach. "You don't have to do this. I'm not nearly as tense as you were."

"Maybe not, but it's an excuse to touch you."

She turns toward me and my eyes immediately shift down to her breasts. I'm trying not to make this sexual, but now that we're here in bed and she's topless, all I can think about is how much I want to be with her.

"You don't need an excuse to touch me," she says.

"Regardless, it's only fair that I reciprocate the massage, so flip over."

She does as I ask, lying on her stomach, her head on the pillow facing me.

I rest on my side, using one hand to massage her as I gaze at her face. She opens her eyes and sees me watching her. "That feels really good."

"It's not as good as you did, but you're the first person I've ever massaged so you have to lower your expectations."

"You've never massaged anyone?"

"No. You're the first, so if I do something wrong, just tell me."

She smiles. "Another first for Pearce Kensington. And you also had chocolate chip ice cream." She grabs my arm. "Oh, no! We forgot to eat it. It's still sitting on the counter. I should go clean it up."

"Don't worry about it. It's fine." I place her arm back by her side. "Now relax or you'll ruin the massage."

She smiles and closes her eyes.

I place my hand at the top of her neck, then run it down her spine, stopping when I reach her waistband. "How's that?"

"Good. *Really* good."

I do it again with a little more pressure.

"I think it's nice you do stuff with your mom," she says, her eyes still closed.

I don't know why she keeps talking about my mother. I'm trying not to think about her right now. Or anything related to that part of my life.

"You're a good man, Pearce."

223

I tense up when she says it because it reminds me of when Shelby said it, right here in this very room, right after she had sex with me. She said those exact same words. They weren't true then and they're not true now. I'm not a good man and I never will be. I do bad things. And I lie. I constantly lie. It usually doesn't bother me, but now I'm lying to Rachel and it doesn't feel right, especially after she opened up to me the way she did tonight.

I don't like lying to her. I want her to know me. All of me. But she can't. So as much as I don't want to, I have to continue to lie.

CHAPTER TWENTY-ONE

RACHEL

When I wake up, I notice I'm not wearing a shirt. I must've fallen asleep when Pearce was giving me the massage. That was so sweet of him. He didn't have to do that. He needed one way more than I did. I've never felt anyone that tense. His muscles were like rocks. Even after an hour of massaging him, he was still knotted up, but he was a lot better than when I started.

I wonder why he's so tense. He's only 25. He has plenty of money. A good job. So I don't know why he's so stressed. I guess it's just his personality. Some people internalize stress more than others. But it's bad for his health and I worry about him.

He's asleep now, his arm wrapped around my waist, his bare chest against my back. I'm glad I fell asleep without my shirt. I love feeling his warm skin against mine. But the front of me is cold, so I reach down and pull the covers over us.

"Don't go," Pearce mumbles, his arm tightening around me.

I relax into him again. "I'm right here," I whisper, although I'm pretty sure he's asleep.

He really doesn't want me to go. And not just tonight. He keeps asking me to move in with him. When he first asked me, I thought he was kidding, but he was completely serious and now he actually has me considering it. I'm just not sure I'm ready to take that step. I love being with Pearce, but I also love my independence and I'm not ready to give it up. So for now, we'll continue what we've been doing; sometimes I'll stay over here and some nights he can stay with me. Because I do love this. I love being in his arms, sleeping beside him. I feel like it's where I belong.

Our relationship took a huge step forward tonight. I finally told him I can't have children. I never in a million years thought he'd react the way he did. I thought for sure he'd end things with me, but instead he said the words I so desperately needed to hear. Words I should have heard from Adam, but never did.

Adam broke my heart, but tonight, Pearce put part of it back together. When he told me it didn't matter to him that I can't have children, I finally felt like I was okay. That I was normal and not defective, which is how Adam made me feel.

I don't think Pearce realizes how much that meant to me. His words made me feel something I never felt with Adam or any other man I've dated. It was love, pure and simple, and it took me by such surprise that I'm still wondering what this means. Am I in love with Pearce? I think I am. If not, I'm definitely *falling* in love with him. And I think he might be falling right along with me.

Shelby said if Adam had loved me, he wouldn't have cared that I can't have children. He'd still want to be with me. But he didn't. But Pearce does. So does that mean he loves me? I don't know. I don't think he knows either. I think we're both falling into something we're unsure of and not prepared for. And yet we just keep falling, waiting to see where we land.

Hours later I wake up to the sound of classical music. It's Pearce's alarm clock going off. I turn over and see he's already out of bed.

"Sorry about that." He comes out of the bathroom, a towel around his waist, leaving the rest of him exposed; his broad shoulders, muscular arms, ripped abs. Damn, he's hot. I can't hold out much longer. We have to do it soon. Really soon.

"It's okay," I say, as he turns the alarm off. "I need to get up."

He sits beside me on the bed and leans down to kiss me. He smells all fresh and clean from his shower. Extremely hard to resist.

"Good morning." He smiles at me. He has such a sexy smile. And a sexy voice. It's deep, confident, and makes him even harder to resist.

"How did you sleep?" I ask, trying to stay focused on something other than the sexual tension hovering between us.

"Excellent. That massage had me in such a deep sleep I feel like I've slept for days. I feel great. I'm usually dragging in the morning, but today I'm wide awake."

"Good." I notice his eyes on my chest and I look down and see I'm uncovered. "Oops." I lift the sheet over myself.

He laughs a little. "No need to cover up. I've seen them already. Several times, actually."

I smile. "Yes. I know."

"Would you like to use the shower? I'm done in there."

The past two days, I've showered in the guest bathroom down the hall while Pearce was using the shower in here. I told him it was just to save time but really it was because I didn't want to be anywhere near him while he was in the shower. I'd be far too tempting to walk in and join him.

"Um, no, that's okay. I'll just shower at home."

"It's a very nice shower. Multiple shower heads with various settings. I even have a heated towel rack so you'll have a warm towel when you get out."

"That does sound appealing compared to *my* shower, which barely trickles out water and is usually lukewarm, if not cold."

He stands up and extends his arm out toward the bathroom. "Go ahead. Take as long as you want. There's plenty of hot water. You won't run out."

"Okay." I shove the covers back, my arms crossed over my breasts as I walk to the bathroom. I know he's seen them before but I still feel self-conscious just walking around topless. I shut the bathroom door and pee and quickly brush my teeth. Then I kick off my pajama pants and open the glass shower door and step inside. The steam from Pearce's shower still hovers in the air, making it toasty warm. I attempt to turn the water on but there are all these levers and knobs and I'm not sure which one to turn.

"Um, Pearce?" I yell out the shower door.

"Yes," I hear him say from the bedroom.

"How do you turn the shower on?"

"I'll show you. Can I come in?"

"Yeah."

He comes in the bathroom and into the large walk-in shower, keeping his eyes on the tile wall and not my naked body. He puts his hand on one of the levers. "This one turns it on and this one adjusts the water temperature." He points to one of the knobs. "If you want to adjust the shower heads, just turn this left or right. Each one has three settings."

"Thank you."

He smiles as he looks me up and down. "You're very welcome."

"Hey." I swat at him. "You're not supposed to look."

"You didn't make that clear when you invited me in here."

"I didn't invite you. I just asked for your help."

"And I gave it to you." He leans down and puts his lips to mine for a very slow, very sexy, very deliberate kiss.

He's testing my will power. I'm naked. He's in a towel. We're in a shower. And his kiss is burning up my insides.

He stops suddenly and steps back out into the bathroom. "Mind if I shave while you're in there?"

"Um, no, go ahead," I say, stumbling on my words, my brain not fully functioning after that kiss. I start the water and adjust the temperature. Through the glass shower door, I see Pearce lathering up his face with shaving cream.

In the mirror, he catches me watching him and smiles, "How's the shower?"

"It's great." I turn a little so that all three shower heads are raining down on me. "Actually, it's pure heaven. So much better than mine. I'd love to have this shower."

"You could if you lived here."

I wipe the water from my eyes and see him running the razor over his face.

I decide to humor him. "How much is the rent?"

"How much do you pay for your current place?"

"Five hundred a month, plus utilities."

"The rent here is only a hundred a month, utilities included."

"Wow. That's a bargain. But I'd have to drive a half hour to class every day. That's a lot of gas money."

"Even with gas, it's still cheaper than your current place."

"That's true." I close my eyes as the water runs over my face.

"So what do you think?"

I hear his voice right in front of me. I open my eyes and there he is. No towel this time. Just him. Freshly shaved and looking completely irresistible.

"I need to think about it," I say, feeling breathless as my heart races in my chest.

He stands there, giving me an extremely sexy smile. I can't take my eyes off him. I try, but I can't. His body is amazing. I know he works out, but I'd like to know what kind of workout gets results like that. His body is hard. Solid. His muscles chiseled. I'm heating up even more just looking at him.

He steps closer, slipping his arm around my waist as he leans down and talks in my ear. "Would you like me to leave?" He trails soft, warm kisses along my neck as the water flows over us.

My eyes fall shut again as I shake my head, unable to respond verbally. I'm too focused on how good this feels. How turned on he makes me. How desperate I am for this to continue.

I feel his lips over mine as his hand travels slowly down my spine, just like when he gave me that massage last night, only this time there's no waistband to stop him and his hand keeps going, skimming over my hip and my backside. His other hand moves behind my neck, holding me in place as his kiss goes deeper. My body's on fire, exploding with sensations, which only intensify when his hand slips between my legs. He shows off his talent in this area once again, and moments later, I'm coming undone, finding it hard to remain standing as waves of pleasure roll through me.

His hand returns to my waist, holding me up. "Rachel."

I open my eyes and see him looking at me. "Yes."

"How well do you know me?"

I smile. "Well enough."

I'm still recovering from what he did to me, my body ultra sensitive to his touch. But I'm ready for more. I've held out long enough. I want this. I want this so bad.

"Are you sure?" he asks.

"Absolutely."

I loop my arms around his neck as he lifts me up and against the wall. I gasp as he thrusts inside me. I forgot how amazing he feels. Actually, I didn't forget, but I was trying to block it out so I could hold out longer and focus on the other aspects of our relationship. But I'm done holding out. My self control is gone, especially now, as I'm reminded how compatible we are this way. Not just our bodies, but the way he feels, the way he touches me. It's perfect. Like he knows me and knows exactly what I like.

I try to focus on each and every sensation, savoring them and wanting them to last. But it's overwhelming and all consuming and before I know it, I'm grabbing hold of him, calling out his name, begging him to keep going. The sensation overtakes me, sending me on another blissful ride of pure pleasure. It's intense, and like nothing I've ever felt with anyone else.

I keep hold of him as he finishes, then let him go as he sets me down. He wipes the wet strands of hair from my cheek and kisses me.

"You're right," I say. "This IS a great shower."

He chuckles. "Yes. In fact, I like it even more now. Are you done in here, or do you need more time?"

"I just need to wash my hair quick." He steps out of the shower as I reach for the shampoo. As I'm washing my hair, I realize we didn't use a condom. The last couple times we did this, Pearce insisted on wearing a condom, even though I told him I was on the pill. I hope he doesn't have a disease. He said he didn't, but maybe he was just saying that.

When I'm done with my hair, I shut the water off. Pearce opens the shower door and hands me a towel. "It's all warmed up for you."

I take it and wrap myself up in it. "Oh my God, this feels amazing. I love your heated towel rack almost as much as I love your shower."

"Another perk of living here," he says, as he walks out into the bedroom. He's still naked. After what we just did, he doesn't need to bother covering up with a towel. And I like him better without it.

230

I follow him into the bedroom. "Pearce, can I ask you a question?"

"Of course." He's at his dresser now, pulling out a pair of boxers.

"I don't mean to bring the mood down but just to be clear, you're clean, right? I mean you don't have any STDs, right?"

"No. Why do you ask?"

"It's just that last time you were pretty insistent on using a condom so I just wanted to make sure that—"

"I don't have an STD. I'm just so accustomed to using a condom that it's become a habit. I've actually never done it without one, other than just now."

"Really?" I walk over to him. "So I'm your first?"

He kisses me. "You're my first."

"Another new thing I've introduced you to." I kiss him back. "And this time it was me. I'm honored to be your first."

"I would love for you to be my second as well." He takes my towel and tosses it aside. "And my third. And many more after that." He backs me up to the bed.

"Pearce, you have to get to work. You'll be late."

"Work isn't going anywhere. You, on the other hand, will be leaving shortly. Therefore, my time should be spent with you."

And it is. We do it again, this time in the bed. Then he puts on his suit and tie and I put on my jeans and sweater and we say goodbye. I head back to New Haven and he heads to the office.

When I get to my apartment I practically skip up the stairs. I'm in such a good mood. And so happy. Maybe I *am* in love.

I open the door to my apartment, leaving my suitcase by the door. I go in the kitchen to make some coffee. As it's brewing, the phone rings.

I pick it up. "Hello?"

"Hello, beautiful."

I smile at his words and his deep, sexy voice. "Hi."

"I just wanted to make sure you made it home safe."

"I did, but thank you for checking. Are you at work?"

"I am."

"Well, have a good day."

"You as well. I'll see you tonight. I'm not sure what time, but I'll call you later and let you know."

"Okay. See you then."

"Goodbye, Rachel."

I hang up the phone and realize I'm still smiling.

There's a knock on the door and I go over to see who it is. It's Shelby. I haven't talked to her since that day we talked on the stairs and she lectured me about Pearce. I was really angry at her that day, but I'm over it now. I've stopped by her apartment several times since then, but she hasn't been around.

I open the door but she doesn't come in. She's just standing there, frowning, her shoulders drooping.

"Rachel, I'm really sorry. Are you still mad at me?"

"No." I hug her. "Not at all. Come inside."

She comes in, closing the door behind her.

"You want some coffee?" I ask as we go to the kitchen.

"Sure."

"So where have you been? I haven't seen you for a while."

"I've been staying at my parents' house. Helping my mom take care of my dad."

"How's he doing?"

"Same as always. I don't want to talk about it." She notices my overnight bag by the door. "Are you going out of town?"

"No. That's from last night. I stayed at Pearce's apartment."

"Oh." She gives me that look again. The same one she gave me on the stairs that day. A look of disappointment and worry.

I get some mugs from the cupboard. "Shelby, I know you don't like him, but I do. I really do. So please don't say any more bad things about him." She's quiet as I take the coffee pot from the warmer and fill our mugs. I hand her one.

"So what did you guys do last night?" she asks, sipping her coffee.

"We had dinner and then we talked." I get the milk from the fridge and pour some in my coffee. "I told him."

"Told him what?"

"I told Pearce that I can't have children."

"What? Why would you tell him that? Are you guys that serious? You're already talking about kids?"

"No. But I brought it up because I felt like he should know. I didn't feel right keeping a secret like that from him. And if he wanted to break up with me over it, I'd rather he do it now than later."

"So did he?" She almost sounds hopeful, like she wanted him to.

"No. Just the opposite. Telling him that just made us closer. You should've heard him, Shelby. He was so sweet. He said he didn't care that I couldn't have children and that the only thing he cares about is me." I smile. "He's such a great guy. He's caring and thoughtful and generous. He even offered to let me stay at his loft. He doesn't think this area is safe, and truthfully, it's not."

She's staring at me, looking even more disappointed. "What are you saying? You're moving in with him? Already?"

"No. I told me it was too soon. But I *am* considering it. I mean, I already go over there a lot or he comes over here so we're practically living together anyway."

"Rachel, no." She reaches over and puts her hand on my arm. "Don't do it. You need your own place. You don't need this guy controlling you."

I pull my arm away from her. "He's not controlling me. Why would you say that?"

"Because it's what guys like him do. They lure you in, saying all the things you want to hear, paying for things, buying you stuff. And before you know it, they take over your life, telling you what to do, where to live. You're like a possession to them. And then they get bored with you and toss you aside."

"What are you talking about? Pearce is not like that. He's not controlling me. And he doesn't treat me like a possession."

"He does. You're just too close to him to see it."

I try to stay calm even though I want to scream at her and tell her she's wrong and mean for saying these things. "I think you should leave."

She comes around the kitchen counter, her hands on her hips. "Why won't you listen to me? Dammit, Rachel, I'm trying to be your friend! I'm trying to look out for you!"

Why is she yelling at me? *I'm* the one who should be angry, not her.

"And why do you think you need to look out for me?"

She opens her mouth to answer, but then says nothing.

"What were you going to say, Shelby? That I'm some stupid naive farm girl from Indiana who isn't capable of making good decisions?"

"No! That's not what I said."

"You didn't have to. I know what you think of me. You're always telling me how innocent and naive I am and that—"

"I was just kidding around when I said that. It's a joke between us."

"Yeah, well, I'm tired of it and it's never been funny to me." I look at the door. "I think you need to go."

"Rachel, I know you don't want to hear this, but please, just listen to me. Pearce is lying to you. He's not the man you think he is."

"And how do you know that?" I ask, challenging her. If she's going to keep making these accusations about Pearce, I'm going to make her back them up. And when she can't, it'll prove she's lying and finally end this obsession she has with trying to get me to break up with him.

"Has he ever taken you out?" she asks.

"Yes. Of course he has."

"And where did you go?"

"We've gone out to eat. Had coffee. Gone to the movies. And we went to the mall."

"You did all that stuff here in New Haven. But what about the town where he lives, or works? Or the town where's he from? Has he ever taken you out in any of those places?"

"No, but I'm sure he will."

"It's not gonna happen, Rachel. He'll never take you any place where people he knows might see him with you."

"I'm sure he knows people in New Haven and he took me out *here*."

"Yeah, to dive restaurants his friends wouldn't be caught dead in. And the people in his social circle wouldn't go to the mall either. I bet he'd never even been there himself until you took him there."

I keep quiet because she's right. And what she's saying is true. Pearce and I hardly ever go out, and the few times we have, it's been to places he'd normally never go. Was that intentional? Did he only agree to go to those places because he wouldn't run into anyone he knew?

Dammit. Why am I listening to Shelby? Why am I letting her place doubts in my head about Pearce?

"Shelby, I don't want to talk about this anymore."

"Because you know I'm right. And if you want to test that theory, ask Pearce to take you out to dinner. Tell him you want to go somewhere nice that's near where he lives. Or ask him to take you to his favorite restaurant. See what he says. If he agrees to it, then maybe I'm wrong about him."

I set my coffee mug in the sink. "I have to get ready for class."

She takes off toward the door, but then turns back. "Ask him to introduce you to his friends. Just one. And see what he says."

"Goodbye, Shelby."

She leaves without saying goodbye, closing the door a little too hard. She's angry but she has no right to be. It doesn't make sense. Unless she's jealous that I have a guy like Pearce and she doesn't. But she doesn't seem like the jealous type, so I don't know what her problem is.

My phone rings and I smile, assuming it's Pearce calling to check in. "Hello?"

"Rachel? It's Adam."

My smile drops. "Adam. Why are you calling me?"

He laughs a little. "What kind of question is that? We're friends. And we used to be a lot more than that."

"Yes, but we're not now and I haven't talked to you in over a year."

"I meant to call you. I just didn't have time. I've been really busy. I don't know if your mom told you, but I opened an accounting firm here in town. It's not really a firm. It's just two people. Me and Dean Armison. Remember him? From high school?"

"Yeah."

"Anyway, Mr. Kizner finally retired so Dean and I are getting a lot of his clients. Business is going really well."

"That's good." I need to end this call. I don't want to talk to him. "Listen, Adam. I know my mom gave you my number but—"

"Yeah, I had dinner with your parents a few weeks ago. They were thinking of having me take over their books so your mom wouldn't have to do it. There are a lot complicated tax rules related to farming and it's hard to keep up with them."

So that's why he had dinner with my parents? To get their business? And here my mom thought he was just being nice. If anyone's deceitful, it's Adam, not Pearce.

"I need to get to class," I tell him.

"Then I'll call you later. I've been thinking about you a lot and I really want to talk to you."

"I don't think that's a good idea. I have a boyfriend."

"Your mom said you weren't seeing anyone."

I roll my eyes. Thanks a lot, Mom. "My mom shouldn't have said that. She knows I'm seeing someone. I'm sorry she misled you."

"Is it serious? You and this guy?"

"Adam, I'm not talking about this with you."

"How long have you been seeing him?"

"I really need to go or I'll be late to class. Good luck with your business."

"Rachel, wait."

"What?"

"I miss you. I'm going to come out there and see you."

"No. You're not coming out here."

"We need to talk. In person."

"There's nothing to talk about. We're not getting back together."

"Rachel, we dated for a year. We were engaged. You can't just throw that away. We need to give this another chance."

"I wasn't the one who threw it away. You did." I hate the way he always puts the blame on me, as if he's never the one at fault.

"That's not fair, Rachel. You can't tell me you don't understand why I reacted that way when you told me what the doctor said. I always assumed I'd have kids. And then you tell me I can't? I couldn't just agree to marry you after that. I needed time to think."

It's always about him. He's so selfish. I can't believe I ever dated this guy.

"I don't want to talk about this. Our relationship is over, Adam. I've moved on. I'm with someone else now."

"He'll break up with you when he finds out. You know that, right? No man will ever want you, knowing you can't have kids. I'm doing you a favor, Rachel. I'm still willing to be with you despite—"

"Goodbye, Adam. Don't ever call me again." I hang up before he can say anything else.

My eyes are full of tears but I straighten up and take a deep breath. I am not letting Adam's hateful words get to me. *No man will ever want me?* He's wrong. Because I have someone who wants me. Pearce wants me, despite the fact that I can't have children.

I check the clock. Class starts in ten minutes. How did it get to be so late? I grab my backpack and head out to my car, replaying that conversation in my head.

Was Adam really trying to get back together with me? Did my mom tell him I wanted to be with him? God, I hope not. I don't think she would come out and actually say that, but she must've hinted at it. She makes me so mad sometimes. I wish she'd just stay out of my personal life and stop trying to take over.

I'm so angry from Shelby's rant and Adam's call that I almost run a stop sign. I slam on the brakes, but instead of immediately stopping, the car stops when I'm midway through the intersection, the brakes making a loud screeching noise. Luckily, nobody's around and I make it safely through.

That's just great. Now I need new brakes. I knew I needed them. I have for months but I don't have money for brakes. I don't drive much and when I do it's usually only in town so I thought I could get by a few more months without fixing the brakes. But I can't wait any longer. It's too dangerous. I'll have to get another job to pay for it. The help wanted sign at the grocery store is still up. I'll get an application on my way home tonight.

This day started out so great. But it's going downhill fast. At least I'll see Pearce tonight. That's something to look forward to.

CHAPTER TWENTY-TWO

PEARCE

So far, this day has been one of the best days of my life. And that's not an exaggeration. The day kicked off with me waking up with Rachel in my arms after having the greatest night of sleep I've ever had. Then the shower, which I wasn't at all expecting. I thought I'd go in there and tease her and she'd tell me to leave. And when she didn't, I couldn't hold back long enough to make it to the bed. I didn't even bother with a condom. And the strange thing is, I didn't even think about it until she mentioned it, which is odd because I'm always extremely cautious when it comes to that. I don't want to get a woman pregnant. Then again, Rachel can't get pregnant so I'll never have to worry about that. But she said she's on the pill, so maybe she *can* get pregnant. When she said she can't have children, she didn't really explain why. Maybe she has some other medical issue she didn't tell me about.

After the shower we did it again, and by the time I left for work I was on a high. A Rachel high. I'm still feeling it now, at eleven o'clock. I got to work at nine this morning, which is the latest I've ever gotten to work. If my father were here, he'd punish me for my lateness. But he's not here. He's still in Europe. His office is dark and his door is closed. And the whole office feels lighter and brighter. Even the other employees seem to be smiling more. We're all happier without my father around.

At noon, I go to the gym to work out. Originally, my sessions were scheduled for after work, but last week I switched them to noon so I could spend my evenings with Rachel.

Since being with her, I finally sleep at night. I've had so much energy I've been upping the intensity of my workouts. I'm determined to get in the best shape I possibly can. I want to be strong. A fighter. I'm no longer going to sit back and let others control my life. Before, I didn't care. I had nothing motivating me. Nothing keeping me going. But now I do. Now I have Rachel and I will fight like hell to be with her.

I leave work at five, much earlier than normal. I go home and change clothes and pack an overnight bag. I called Rachel an hour ago to let her know when I'd be there. She was still at work and said she had to give a tour before she left. On my way to her apartment, I stop at my favorite Italian restaurant and pick up some food. I got way too much so she'd have whatever's left over for meals later in the week. I don't like that she doesn't eat well. Hotdogs and macaroni and cheese do not provide adequate nutrition. She doesn't like taking money from me but she needs to at least let me help her with groceries.

I arrive at her place with two large sacks of food. I knock on her door several times but she doesn't answer. But the door next to hers opens and Shelby appears.

"She's running late," she says, not looking at me as she unlocks Rachel's door. "She told me to let you in."

Shelby's wearing tight jeans and a short, boxy sweatshirt, her blond hair in a messy ponytail. She looks like she's still in high school, although according to Rachel, she's 22.

"How late will she be?" I ask Shelby.

She shrugs. "Maybe a half hour. She said the tour was running late. It was one of her old people tours. She said those people always have lots of questions."

I go inside with the bags of food and set them on the kitchen counter. I turn around and see Shelby right in front of me. I didn't hear her follow me in.

"Did you need something?" I ask her.

She narrows her eyes at me. "I told you to stop seeing her."

"And why would I listen to you?"

She huffs as she crosses her arms over her chest. "You're an ass, you know that?"

"Why? Because I'm dating Rachel and you don't approve? Well, get over it. It's none of your damn business."

"It IS my business. She's my friend and I care about her."

"So do I."

"No, you don't. You're using her and I don't know why. You could have any woman you want, so why her? Why Rachel?"

"I'm not using her. I told you, I care about her. More than anything. She's the most amazing woman I've ever met. She's kind and beautiful and intelligent and completely selfless. I can't get enough her. All I want to do is spend time with her. Make her happy."

Shelby's arms drop to her sides as she stares at me, barely blinking. "Fuck."

"Excuse me?"

"Fuck, fuck, fuck!" She starts pacing the floor.

"What's wrong? What are you doing?"

She stops right in front of me. "You love her, don't you? You love Rachel."

I don't know how to answer. Do I? Do I love Rachel? I'm not sure. I've never been in love, so maybe I am and don't know it. Shelby seems to think I am. But how would she know that? She doesn't. She's just saying that. But why would she say that? She doesn't even want me with Rachel, and telling me I'm in love with her isn't going to make me break up with her.

"Fuck!" Shelby says it again. "You're in love with her? How is that even possible? I thought guys like you didn't fall in love. Isn't there a rule against that? I'm sure there is. That place is nothing but rules."

She's referring to the organization, which she shouldn't be. She should never talk about them, even when she's doing official business as an associate.

"Don't talk about them," I tell her. "Especially here."

She places her hands on her hips. "Just admit it. You love her."

"I'm just dating her. I never said I was in love."

"You don't have to. It's written all over your face. You have that same lovesick look that Rachel has." She turns to start pacing again but I hold onto her arm.

"Wait. Rachel's in love with me?"

She rolls her eyes. "Oh, please, like you didn't know this?"

"No. I didn't. She's never told me that. Why do you think she's in love with me?"

"Because of that." She waves her hand at my face. "That look you guys get whenever you talk about each other. Your eyes light up and you get that stupid smile on your face. It's like you can't control it. It's fucking annoying."

"She's not in love with me. We haven't known each other that long."

"I know, right?" She walks in the living room and plops down on the couch. "I thought maybe I was wrong. That maybe Rachel just thought she was in love because you're rich and hot and can sometimes be charming."

I smile at her backhanded compliment as I go over and sit in the chair that's next to the couch. "Just sometimes?"

She rolls her eyes again. "Don't flatter yourself. Everyone knows guys like you turn on the charm when you need to impress a girl. I thought Rachel would be able to see through your games, but instead she fell in love."

"I'm not playing games with her."

"Oh, really?" She shifts so she's facing me. "Then why are you stringing her along knowing you can never be with her?"

I glance down, rubbing my forehead. "If I want to be with her, I will. It's not their decision."

"It sure as hell is." She moves closer to me and nudges my shin with her foot. "Pearce."

I glance up again. "What?"

"You know you can't be with her. It'll never happen. And if you really loved her, you'd let her go. If you keep waiting, you'll hurt her even more when you leave her."

"I'm not leaving her. I'm going to find a way to make this work."

"So you're going to marry her?"

242

"I don't know. I haven't thought about it."

"Bullshit. I know you've thought about it. And you're really okay with not having kids someday?"

"I've never wanted children, so the fact that she can't have them isn't a concern for me. And it wouldn't be even if I *did* want them. I would never leave her because of that. It wouldn't even be a consideration. I love her too much to—" I stop, realizing what I just said.

"See? What did I tell you?" Shelby's staring at me again. "This is so messed up. You're seriously thinking of having a future with her?"

"Of course I am. I love—" I stop before I say it again. "Fuck."

"Yeah." Shelby sinks back in the couch. "Exactly what I said."

I sigh. "I didn't mean it that way. It's not a bad thing. I just wasn't expecting it. It's all happening so fast and I'm not ready for it."

"Well, you better *get* your ass ready and figure out what the hell you're going to do because you're going to be in deep shit if they find out about her."

"I don't need a lecture. I'm quite aware of the consequences."

"So what are you going to do?"

"I don't know yet."

She jumps up from the couch. "*I* do. I'm not letting her do this. I don't care if you two are in love. Love can be broken. She can find someone else. I'm not letting her get wrapped up in the world of Pearce Kensington and your asshole friends and psycho father."

I stand up. "How do you know my father?"

"Like you didn't know your dad uses the service? You think he doesn't cheat on your mom? Seriously?"

"Of course I know he cheats on her. And I know he uses the service. I just didn't know you'd been with him." I feel sick knowing my father and I shared the same woman. She's young enough to be his daughter. What the hell is wrong with him? "Why did you say he was psycho?"

"Because he's into all that kinky shit, like—"

"That's enough. I don't need to hear it."

"It was after I was with you, if that makes you feel any better."

"He wasn't the one who…" I point to her wrists.

"Tied me up and held me hostage?" she says, nonchalantly, like she's separated all emotion from that incident. It's what girls like her do in order to be able to keep doing what they're doing.

"Did he do that or not? Tell me the truth."

She shakes her head. "No. It was someone else. Your dad doesn't have time to have sex all day. And he's old. I don't think he could do it that many times in a day."

"Okay, stop." I put my hand up. "Don't talk about it."

She walks away from me toward the window. "Going back to Rachel, I've already told her you're lying to her and I'm going to keep telling her until she believes me. I know it'll hurt her to find out about you but it's for her own good. The sooner she gets away from you, the sooner she can—"

"No." I meet Shelby by the window. "Don't do it. I promise you, I will keep her safe."

"You and I both know you can't promise that. If they find out about her, they'll hurt her."

"They won't. I'll protect her. I won't let anyone near her."

"You're not thinking straight, Pearce. Your judgment's clouded by Rachel and the feelings you have for her. That's why I need to intervene before the two of you take this any farther."

I hold her shoulders. "You will do no such thing. You understand? Stay out of it."

She glances at my hand on her shoulder. "Are you threatening me?"

"No." I step back, taking my hands off her. "But I'd like to propose a deal."

She eyes me suspiciously. "What kind of deal?"

"Your father. What does he need? How much money do you need for his medicine?"

Her face softens a bit. "It doesn't matter. The medicine isn't helping so he isn't even taking it anymore."

"Then what does he need? I'll do whatever I can."

"He's dying. There's nothing you can do."

"How much time does he have left?"

244

Her eyes are tearing up, but she takes a deep breath, fighting the urge to cry. "A few months, maybe. The doctors don't know for sure."

"There must be something I can do."

She shakes her head, wiping her eyes. "Your money won't help. He's at the point where he's just waiting to die." She's crying now, her head down so I can't see her face. "I just wish he didn't have to suffer. He's in so much pain. And the doctors can't seem to help him. They've tried everything."

I place my hand on her shoulder, gently this time. "Shelby. Listen to me. I will get him help. I will at least ease his suffering until the end."

"You can't," she says, sniffling.

"Yes, I can. I know people. People who could help him."

She lifts her head to look at me. "What do you mean?"

"I know a man. A doctor. He's young, but very good. He's extremely smart. He believes in challenging conventional medicine and is working to create new treatments and drugs for conditions that haven't responded to traditional medicine. He can't cure cancer but I'm almost certain he could give your father something for the pain."

"Who is this guy? And how do you know him?"

"His name is Dr. Logan Cunningham. I met him when I was going to Harvard. He was in medical school at the time. We were friends. From the first time I met him, I was impressed by his brilliance. When he graduated, he went to Europe to train under some very innovative doctors who are also looking for new and better treatments."

"So he lives in Europe?"

"No. He recently moved back to the states. He's living in Boston. I haven't talked to him since last summer but I know he'd be willing to help your father. And I would cover any costs that are incurred."

"Is this Cunningham guy one of you? I mean, is he part of—"

"No, he's not a member. He doesn't even know it exists."

"And you really think he could help?"

245

"Yes, but the treatment won't be something that's FDA approved. His treatments are ones he's either developed himself or with the other doctors in this group he's been working with. The general public doesn't have access to them."

"So they're dangerous?"

"All drugs can be dangerous. Even ones that have been approved. They all have side effects. So yes, your father would be taking a risk, but at this point, he might be willing to try anything."

She nods. "Yeah, he would. My mom and I would too. We're desperate to help him."

"Then let me do this for you. Let your father know that a doctor will be coming to see him. I'll contact Logan and let you know when he'll be there."

"I want to be there too. I want to meet him before he does anything to my dad."

"That's fine. But I assure you, you have nothing to worry about. And I'm almost certain that Logan will be able to help. Now, will you help *me* by not turning Rachel against me?"

She sighs. "Okay, but you have to promise me she won't get hurt."

The front door opens and Shelby and I turn to see Rachel walking in. "Hey. Sorry I'm late."

"It's no problem," I say. "Shelby let me in and we've just been talking."

Rachel hangs her coat on the rack and comes over to me. "What did you talk about?"

Shelby answers. "Pearce is going to have one of his doctor friends see if he can help my dad."

"Really?" Rachel smiles at me as I put my arm around her. "Who is it?"

"A man I met when I was going to Harvard."

"He might be able to help my dad with his pain," Shelby says. "And Pearce offered to pay for any expenses."

Rachel reaches up and kisses me. "That's so nice of you."

"Yeah, it is," Shelby says. She's really selling me here. I didn't expect her to do that. I just wanted her to leave Rachel and me alone. But I'll take the support. It's far better than the alternative. "Well, I should be going. Your dinner's getting cold."

"Why you don't stay?" Rachel asks her. She looks at me. "Did you get enough food?"

"Yes, there's plenty. You're welcome to join us, Shelby."

"No thanks. I already ate and I have things to do."

"Okay." Rachel walks Shelby to the door. I hear her quietly talking to her, "Thanks for letting him in…and being nice to him."

I walk to the kitchen as she shuts the door. "So are you ready for dinner?"

She runs up to me. "I have to kiss you first. I missed you."

My chest warms hearing her say it. It's nice to be missed. Nobody ever misses me. Nobody cares enough to. Nobody but Rachel.

"I missed you too." I kiss her and keep kissing her because it's never enough. We make our way to the bedroom, and by the time we're done, I'm sure our dinner is ice cold.

"I need to go out and get us some dinner," I say. Her naked body is wrapped in mine and we're both still catching our breath.

"We'll just reheat what you brought over. It smells really good."

"I didn't know what you wanted so I bought half the items on the menu."

She laughs. "You could've just asked me. But for the record, I like most anything. I'm not a picky eater."

She rests her head on my chest as I stroke her hair. She has the softest hair and it always smells flowery.

"Did you have a good day?" she asks.

"The beginning and end were excellent. The middle was just was okay." It's true. The best parts of my day are when I'm with Rachel. "Did you consider my offer?"

"To move in with you?" She rubs her hand over my chest.

"Yes."

"I'm still considering it."

"Is there anything I could do to sway your decision?"

She looks up at me. "I want to. I'm just confused."

I sit up slightly, leaning against the wall since she doesn't have a headboard. "What are you confused about?"

"Us."

"What about us?"

"I don't know what this is….this relationship of ours. I don't know how serious we are, or where this is going. But I *do* know that I have all these feelings for you and it scares me and excites me all at once."

"Why does it scare you?"

"Because I keep thinking it's too soon to feel this way. Like maybe I'm reading it wrong or that the feelings aren't real."

"Do they *feel* real?"

"Yes, which is why it's so confusing."

"Rachel." I cup my hand around her face, looking into her eyes. "I feel the same way. I've never felt this way about anyone but you, and part of me doesn't understand it. But it doesn't change how I feel. It doesn't change the fact that I—"

She sits up a little. "That you what?"

My hand remains on her face, my eyes locked on hers. "That I love you. I love you, Rachel."

She looks surprised, but she's smiling. "I love you too. But I thought it was just me. I didn't know you felt the same way."

"It's not just you."

She climbs on top of me and hugs me, her warm skin covering mine, her soft hair falling over my shoulder. I hold her against me and kiss the top of her head.

"I love you," I tell her again.

It's another first for me. Saying I love you. I've never said those words to anyone.

"I love you too," she says.

And there's another first. Nobody has ever told me that. Not even my parents.

"That's the first time someone's said that to me." Did I just say that out loud? Shit.

She sits up. "Really?"

I clear my throat. "Yes."

"Not even your parents?"

248

"We don't say things like that in my family."

Sadness comes over her face. "They should have said that to you. A long time ago. But since they didn't, I'm saying it now. I love you, Pearce. And I mean it with all my heart. It doesn't make sense and it confuses me and makes me want to doubt it. But it's how I feel and I can't change it and I don't want to."

"Then don't. Don't doubt it. Don't change it. Just let it be. Just love me, and let me love you."

I bring her back into me, our bodies pressed together, my arms wrapped around her.

This is it. This is one of those moments when you can't imagine things getting any better. When everything seems perfect and right and almost too good to be true. I never thought I'd have such a moment, but here it is.

I'm with the woman I love. I truly, deeply, with all my heart, love Rachel. And even better, she loves me back.

It couldn't get more perfect than this.

CHAPTER TWENTY-THREE

RACHEL

I just told Pearce that I love him. I knew I did but I was too scared to admit it to myself, so I was definitely too scared to say it out loud to him. But then he said it to me, so I said it back. It felt good to finally tell him how I feel and to hear he felt the same way.

When he told me nobody had ever told him they love him, not even his parents, I almost cried. It broke my heart to know that he's 25 and hasn't heard those words until I spoke them just now.

I'm starting to understand why Pearce has such sadness in his eyes. Such loneliness. Such pain. But I think it's more than his family making him feel that way. I think there are other things too. I wish he would tell me what those things are, but he's not ready to, or maybe he doesn't want to. Maybe he doesn't want to go back and relive whatever it was that put that sadness and loneliness in his eyes.

"Hey." I kiss his cheek and rest my head on his shoulder.

He kisses my forehead. "Yes?"

"I love you."

He smiles. "I love you too."

"Let's go eat. Then maybe we'll come back here later and do this again."

He pulls me closer and kisses me. "Or we could just do it again right now."

"I'm starving. We need to refuel." I push off him and climb out of bed. "And after that, I need to do some reading for class."

"Are you making me go home tonight?" He shoves the covers aside and gets up.

"No. I want you here."

"Good." He hugs me from behind and kisses the side of my neck. "Because I wasn't leaving."

"Yeah, I assumed if you came over I wouldn't be able to get rid of you."

His lips tickle my neck. "You say that like it's a bad thing."

I laugh and squeeze out of his arms.

We get dressed, then go in the kitchen and reheat our dinner. Then we curl up on the couch together and read. I read my textbook and he reads one of my history books about the Revolutionary War. He doesn't watch much TV and I only get a few channels, none of which he would watch. When he *does* watch TV, it's usually sports or financial news.

Later we return to bed and I fall asleep in his arms. I want to fall asleep with Pearce every night, so maybe I should just move in with him. If I did, I couldn't tell my mom. She'd be ashamed of me for living with a guy I'm not married to. But I'd have to tell her. She'd know I wasn't living here when I didn't pick up my phone.

In the morning, Pearce isn't in bed and I wonder if he already left for work. But then I hear him in the other room.

"Pearce?" I call out.

He walks into the bedroom, carrying a bouquet of yellow tulips and a dozen long-stem red roses.

"Good morning." He sets the flowers down and kisses me.

"What's all this?" I point to the flowers.

"I bought you some flowers. I noticed you didn't have any."

"The other ones died. But you didn't have to get me more."

"Of course I did. You like flowers, so I had to make sure you had some. I'll get you as many as you'd like. I'll fill your entire apartment with them."

"These are more than enough. Thank you." I hug him. He smells good, like he already showered. And he has on different clothes; jeans and the white polo shirt he bought when we went shopping. "You went all the way back to your loft to shower and dress?"

"No. I showered here and had an overnight bag in the car." He smiles. "I was confident you'd let me stay over."

"You don't lack confidence, that's for sure." I kiss him. "Let me get ready quick and then I'll make you breakfast."

"It's already made. I picked it up when I was out getting the flowers."

"You did?" I race out to the kitchen and see a small tray of pastries, some fresh fruit, coffee, and orange juice.

I hear him behind me. "I decided against getting eggs. They don't travel well."

"This is perfect." I sit on one of the barstools and take a sip of coffee. "I usually just have a piece of toast."

"Rachel, you need to buy groceries. You hardly have anything in your refrigerator. I gave you money for groceries, so why didn't you go shopping?"

I take a croissant. I don't know where he got this stuff but it looks delicious. I bite into the croissant. It's flaky, buttery, melt-in-your-mouth goodness. "These are amazing."

He sits on the barstool next to mine.

"Rachel, why didn't you buy groceries?"

"I will. I just…I had to use that money for something else."

"What?"

"The electric bill," I mumble, embarrassed to admit I didn't have money to pay for it myself.

He sighs as he gets his wallet out. "Take this and buy some food." He puts three $100 bills on the counter.

"I'm not taking your money. I'm getting another job."

"Is that why you have this?" He holds up the application I picked up yesterday.

"Yes."

"You're going to work at a grocery store? That pays almost nothing. After taxes you'll be lucky to make a hundred dollars a week."

"Probably more like fifty. They only need someone a few hours a week to fill in for people who call in sick or go on vacation."

"Do your parents know you're struggling like this?"

"No. And I'd never tell them. That would just prove to my mom that I can't live on my own and need to move back with them. And that's not going to happen." I pop the lid off one of the orange juice cups and hand it to him. "Here. And take a pastry. They're delicious. Where did you get these?"

He moves the orange juice aside and slides the money closer to me. "Take this."

"I don't need it."

He gets his wallet out again. "If you don't take it, I'll just keep adding to it until you do." He sets another hundred dollar bill down.

"Pearce, don't."

"You still haven't taken it." He puts another hundred down. "I've got plenty more where that came from. We could do this all morning." He sets another bill down, and then another.

"Okay, stop." I pick up the bills and count them. "That's seven hundred dollars. I don't need that much for groceries."

"Then use the rest for something else."

I hold up the bills. "Fine. I'll take this, but only because I need new brakes. And I'll pay you back when I—"

"Brakes?" He holds my arm. "What brakes? Car brakes?"

"Yes. I need new ones but I've been putting it off because I didn't have the money."

He swivels my barstool so I'm facing him. "You've been driving around in a car with bad brakes?"

"It's not a big deal. I'll get them fixed."

"Do they even work? Are you able to stop?"

"Yes." I swivel back toward the kitchen and take another pastry. "But it's kind of a delayed stop."

"A delayed stop? Rachel, you could've killed yourself!" He gets up and walks around the counter, standing in front of me as I remain seated at the bar. "You're not driving that car until it's fixed."

"Then how do you expect me to get to class?"

"I'll rent you a car. One that has working brakes. I'll have your car brought to the garage I go to. The mechanics there are excellent. They'll put in new brakes and check to see if anything else needs to be fixed."

He picks up the phone on the wall and calls someone.

"Pearce, what are you doing?"

"Calling my secretary. She has the number for my mechanic." He talks to her and takes down the information, then hangs up.

I go over to him. "Pearce, stop. I can do this myself. I don't need you to do this for me."

"This can't wait. It needs to be done today. You never should've been driving that car knowing the brakes were bad. Why didn't you tell me this?"

"Why would I tell you?"

"Because I would've given you the money!"

"Why are you getting so angry?"

"Because you're driving around in a car without brakes!"

"It has brakes. They're just worn out. And I didn't feel right asking you for money."

He raises his voice. "Rachel, I'm a fucking billionaire. Just ask me for the money! When your life is at risk, you set your pride aside and you take the goddamn money!"

"Just stop, okay? I don't like your tone and I don't like the fact that you're taking over like this. You're overreacting."

"Overreacting? You're driving around in a car without brakes!"

I feel like he's lecturing me and I hate being lectured.

"I have to get ready and you have to get to work. I'll see you later." I storm off to the bedroom, shutting the door behind me.

"Rachel. Come back here."

I sit down on the bed. I need a moment to calm down. I know Pearce is only trying to help, but the way he's doing it makes me feel like I'm a child. Like I'm not responsible or competent or capable of doing anything for myself. It's how my mom makes me feel every time I make a mistake. She doesn't let me fix it. She just takes over.

A few minutes pass and I assume Pearce left. I haven't heard any noise in the kitchen since I stormed out of there. I shouldn't have done that. I'm so bad at arguing. I always run off instead of just talking it out. Now I feel bad. Pearce was just trying to be nice and I yelled at him for it.

"Rachel, can I come in?" It's Pearce. So he didn't leave. I guess he was waiting for me to come out.

"Yes."

He opens the door and comes over and sits next to me. "I'm sorry."

I climb on his lap and hug him. "Don't be. You were only trying to help."

"But I didn't. Instead I took over. It's what I do. I see a problem and I fix it. And the thought of you driving around without—"

"I know. It's dangerous. I should've fixed it weeks ago." I scoot back on his lap. "And you're right. I could've asked you to loan me the money."

"I would've given it to you." He tucks my hair behind my ear. "Any time you need something, just ask."

"I have trouble accepting help, even when I know I need it. My mom was so overprotective when I was growing up that now I have this strong need to be independent. To be free to make mistakes without being judged or rescued. So when you took over like that, I felt like I used to feel with my mom. Like I *still* feel whenever she tries to take over my life."

"Rachel, I'm not trying to take over anything. I want you to be independent. I like that about you. I just panicked when I imagined your brakes going out and you getting hurt." He pauses. "I suppose this is a problem of being in love."

"What do you mean?"

"When you love someone, you'll do anything to keep them safe. And you don't always think straight. I didn't react well earlier and I'm sorry for that."

"I didn't react well either."

"I should've asked you instead of telling you, so I'm asking you now. Would you please allow me to take care of this for you?"

I kiss his cheek. "Yes. But I'm giving you the money back. If you're taking care of the car, then I don't need the money."

"Keep it. And use it to fill that damn fridge up." He smiles. "I'm getting tired of starving whenever I come over here."

"Hey!" I push on his shoulder. "You're not starving. You're just huge and you eat a lot."

"Maybe so, but the fact remains that you need to buy groceries."

"Okay. I will. Except now I don't have a car."

"Get dressed and we'll go to a rental place." He checks his watch. "I just need to cancel a meeting." He lifts me off him and gets up. "I need to go make a call."

"Pearce, just go. I'll see if Shelby can give me a ride to campus later. I don't want you getting in trouble at work."

"I won't get in trouble." He leans down and kisses me. "I own the company."

He walks out to make his call. Sometimes I forget that he's a billionaire who will someday take over one of the largest companies in America. When we're together, I don't think about that. To me, he's just Pearce. My boyfriend. The man I love.

We go to the rental place and pick out a car, then he heads to work. I go to class and when I get back to my apartment for lunch, my car is already gone. Someone probably picked it up right after Pearce called the garage.

Now I'm relieved he's doing this for me. My car probably has all kinds of problems that need to be fixed. And if I'm going to let him spend money on me, I'd rather have my car repaired than have him buy me an expensive gift, like a necklace or earrings. Those things are nice, but having a safe, reliable car is far more important.

After lunch, I call Pearce. "Hi. I was just checking in. Did you hear anything from the garage?"

"Yes. They found several issues and have to order in some parts. They probably won't have it ready for a few days."

"What's wrong with it?"

"I don't know all the details. They faxed me a list of items. I can show it to you later. Rachel, I'm sorry but I have a meeting I'm late to. I have to go."

"Okay. Have a good afternoon. I love you."

"Goodbye." He hangs up without saying 'I love you' back. He probably doesn't want to say it at the office in case people are listening.

The week goes by and Pearce comes over every night after work. He keeps hinting I should move in with him, but I like being close to school. I told him I'd stay with him in December, once classes are over. And I'll continue to stay with him until I figure out what I'm going to do after graduation. We still haven't talked about that, but I've thought about it a lot. I don't want to move away from Pearce, but I can't give up a job opportunity because of a boyfriend. We'd have to be more than that, and I don't see that happening anytime soon.

On Friday, I go to Pearce's loft to stay for the weekend. George, the security guy, knows me now and we're becoming friends. His job can be kind of boring, sitting in that security booth all day, so sometimes, like today, when I'm waiting for Pearce to get home, I go out and talk to George. He always tells me jokes. He has twelve grandkids and they love jokes so he has enough to fill a book. They're silly jokes but still funny. I've even used some of them on my tours. They're a big hit with the seniors.

Pearce gets home from work at six. I didn't make dinner so he has it delivered. He always does this when I'm over there, and although the food is delicious, I don't know why he won't take me out. I don't want to bring this up at dinner, but later, when we're cleaning up the dishes, I decide to say something.

"Pearce, why don't we go out tomorrow night?" I take his plate from him and put it in the dishwasher.

"Where would you like to go?"

"Out for dinner." He hands me our glasses and I add them to the dishwasher and close it up. "You could take me to your favorite place."

He clears his throat. "I'd rather stay in."

Once again, he refuses to take me out. I don't understand it. But I don't want to fight about it.

"Then we'll have dinner here, but maybe we could invite a couple of your friends over so I could meet them."

"I don't have friends." He walks around me to the table and pushes our chairs in.

I go over to him. "Of course you have friends. You always tell me about the social events you go to. You must have friends you see there."

"They're acquaintances, not friends."

"Pearce, why won't—"

"We're NOT having anyone over." He says it forcefully as his body tenses up.

I step back. "Um, okay."

I don't know what happened just now but I didn't like it. It's like the Pearce I love disappeared and was replaced by someone else. And that someone scared me. I didn't like his tone or the way his body went rigid when I suggested we have people over.

The room gets quiet. He's staring down at the floor. I take another step back and he notices.

"Rachel, I'm sorry. I didn't mean to raise my voice."

"It's not just that. You became almost...I don't know how to describe it. I've never seen you react that way."

He pulls me into his arms. "I'm sorry. I had a long day at work and I'm tired. And as for having people over, maybe we could do it some other time. I feel like we don't get much time together so the time we *do* have I want to spend with just you."

I look up at him. "But eventually you'll introduce me to your friends, right?"

"Like I said, I don't really have friends, but—"

"Pearce, just agree to it."

He hesitates. "Yes. I will introduce you to some people."

I feel somewhat better that he agreed to it, but I still think his initial reaction was odd. And he seems very reluctant about doing it.

I return to the kitchen and pick up the takeout containers and toss them in the trash. "Oh, I forgot to tell you. The shelter finally got the okay to reopen so I'll be going there tomorrow morning."

When I turn back around, he grabs hold of my arm. "I thought you weren't doing that anymore."

"Of course I'm doing it." I look down at his hand on my arm. He's acting strange again.

"But you said it was closed for repairs."

"It was, but everything's fixed now so they reopened the shelter last night."

"I don't want you going there." He uses that forceful tone again.

I yank my arm from his grasp. "Well, I'm going there, so you'll have to get over it."

"Then I'm going with you."

I seriously do not understand what his problem is when it comes to my volunteering at the shelter. And his attitude about this is starting to make me angry.

"Pearce, you're not going with me. I don't need a chaperone."

"You can't go there alone. It's too dangerous."

"You say that about everything and I'm getting tired of it." I leave the kitchen and go into the living room. "I know the world is a dangerous place, but that's not going to stop me from going out in it and helping others. So I'm sorry if you don't like it, but I'm going to keep working at the shelter."

"Why are you doing this?" He walks over to me. "Why can't you just volunteer somewhere else?"

"Why are you acting this way? You know I love working there, so why would you try to take it away from me?"

His body is even more tense than before, like he's trying hard to hold in his anger. "That shelter is in a bad part of town. Drug dealers wander the streets and there are murders there all the time. You are NOT going there."

That's it. I can't handle him telling me what to do. I go to the closet and get my coat.

"What are you doing?" Pearce asks.

"Leaving. I can't be around you when you're like this." I quickly put on my coat and grab my purse. "I'll see you later."

"Rachel, wait!" He stops me at the elevator. "I'm trying to help you. I don't want you getting hurt."

"I know you don't. But I don't need you to protect me." The elevator opens and I get on.

"Are you coming back here tomorrow?"

I pause. "I think I'll just stay at my place. I have a lot to get done at home."

"Rachel, don't be angry. Just stay here and we'll talk about this."

"I can't. I need to go."

As the elevator door closes I see the sadness in his eyes. I don't like being the cause of that sadness but he can't try to control me like that. I like working at the shelter and he can't take that away from me just because *he* doesn't like it. Our relationship won't work if he's going to be that way.

The next morning I go to the shelter. I have a new student to teach as well as my regulars. But given how tired I am, I'm not sure how good a job I'm doing. I can't seem to stay focused.

I didn't sleep much last night. I was up thinking about Pearce. And missing him. I'm used to having him next to me, so now when he's not, I toss and turn, looking for him.

I don't like fighting with him and I hated leaving him like that. But I felt like I didn't have a choice. I'm not giving in to his demands and I didn't want him spending the rest of the night trying to convince me to change my mind, which is why I didn't answer when he called me last night and this morning.

When I'm done at the shelter I go back to my apartment building and find Pearce waiting there. He's standing next to his car, wearing a suit and a black overcoat.

I go up to him. "Hi."

"Hello, Rachel." His formal tone is back. I haven't heard him talk that way for a while. "I wasn't able to reach you by phone. I wanted to let you know that I have to go into the office today. If you need to reach me, just call my office number."

I nod. "Okay."

260

He leans down and hugs me. "I love you."

Both the hug and his words warm my heart and dissolve any remnants of anger I felt toward him. Even though we're sort of fighting, he still drove all the way over here, completely out of his way, to talk to me. And to tell me he loves me and give me a hug, two things I know he's still not comfortable doing. And yet he still did them.

He lets me go and gets back in his car.

"Pearce, wait," I say before he closes his door.

"Yes, Rachel?"

"I love you too." I pause. "Can we talk about this?"

"There's no need to. We'll always disagree on this issue so there's no use discussing it." He hesitates, then gets out of the car again. He takes my hand. "I know I could've reacted better last night, and I apologize for raising my voice. But my feelings remain the same. I love you, Rachel, and because of that, I will always be concerned about your safety." He looks at the area around us. "I don't like you living in this neighborhood and I don't like you going to that shelter. And although you disagree with me, I am not going to hide my opinions on these matters. I want you to know how I feel, even if it does nothing to change your mind."

"Pearce, I understand where you're coming from, but I'm not going to stop going to the shelter."

"Yes. I know." He lets go of my hand. "I need to get to the office."

As he's getting in the car, I ask, "Do you want to have dinner tonight?"

He smiles, which he hasn't done the entire time he's been here. "Yes. I would like that very much."

I smile back. "What time will you be home?"

"Probably around five."

"I feel like cooking something. I'll stop at the store on my way over there." I lean in the car and kiss him. "See you later."

"Yes. I'll see you tonight." His face brightens, the sadness in his eyes now gone.

As he drives away, I feel relieved that we ended this fight before it got out of hand. Adam and I used to fight all the time, over the littlest things, and it drove me crazy. I felt like we were still in high school.

I'm not going to do that with Pearce. I want this relationship to work, and in order to do that, we need to fight like adults and talk things out and be okay with the fact that we won't always agree.

I'm actually glad Pearce didn't give in just now. I liked that he was honest in telling me his feelings, but that he still respected mine. And I liked that we were able to settle this in a calm, mature way.

Our fights may not always end this way, but the fact that this one did is a good sign. It makes me feel better about our relationship and makes me think that maybe we could have a future together.

CHAPTER TWENTY-FOUR

PEARCE

It's the middle of October, which means my father will be home from his trip soon. I'm dreading his return. I feel like I've been on vacation these past few weeks and now it's about to come to an end. I'll have to go back to working all hours of the day and night, as well as weekends, which means I'll have less time with Rachel. That makes me dread my father's return even more. I'm used to seeing Rachel every day, and I want that to continue. I need it to. I can't go a day without seeing her. I love her more each time we're together. I love everything about her. And when she's not around, I feel this sense of loss, like something's missing.

Last weekend, we had a fight. That would normally cause me to break up with a woman, but I had no desire to do so with Rachel. The thought didn't even cross my mind. We worked through our disagreement and came out stronger because of it.

Our fight was about her work at the shelter, and although I hate that she works there, I realized that I can't force her to quit. If I do, she won't want to be with me. She's independent and strong-willed and I like that about her. But I still worry about her safety. The shelter is located right next to the alley where my father shot that homeless man when I was 16. I've heard rumors that some of our freelancers train there, shooting homeless people so that they're better prepared to successfully shoot the intended targets of their assignments.

If that rumor is true, I don't want Rachel anywhere near that place. I don't want her near our freelancers and I definitely don't want her near that alley. I also don't want her around the drug deals, thefts, and stabbings that I know occur in that neighborhood.

But Rachel refuses to listen to my concerns, so I sent one of my security men to keep an eye on her while she was there. And I'm going to *keep* sending him there every time she volunteers. I'm not going to tell her this because she'd get angry. Besides, she doesn't need to know. This way, we both get what we want. She continues to volunteer there and I feel good knowing she's safe.

As the week goes by, I prepare for my father's return by catching up on the work I didn't get done. I don't see Rachel until much later in the evening, but it's better than not seeing her at all.

It's now Thursday night and I have to go to that dinner party with my mother. I pick her up promptly at six and we drive to the Seymour mansion. I hope Katherine won't be there. This dinner will be bad enough. I don't need it getting even worse by having some love-struck teenager following me around all night.

When we arrive at the mansion, the cocktail hour has already begun and my mother takes off to go talk to her friends. I get myself a bourbon, and as I'm leaving the bar, I spot William Sinclair, Royce's brother. He must've drove down here for the party. He's currently living in Boston, attending Harvard Business School.

I've always liked William. He's quiet, studious, intellectual. Royce is the complete opposite. He cheated his way through college and spent all his time drinking and partying.

I make my way over to William and ask him how school is going. He tells me about his classes and we compare notes about some of the professors.

"It looks like you have an admirer." William nods toward the side of the room. Katherine is standing there, staring at me. She's 15, but she looks more like 12. She's very thin with no curves and a flat chest. She's wearing a simple black dress, her long, straight-blond hair framing her childlike face which she's covered in makeup in an attempt to look older.

"I think it's past her bedtime," I say, turning back to William.

He chuckles. "She's had a crush on you for years. Maybe she'll get over it when they move."

"I didn't know they were moving."

"They're moving to New York. Westchester County. But I think the move isn't for a few more months." He drinks his scotch. "So aside from your teenage admirer, do you have a woman in your life?"

As much as I want to tell everyone about Rachel and how great she is and how much I love her, I can't. She has to remain a secret, at least for now.

"No," I say. "They're waiting until more time has passed from the divorce."

"I wasn't referring to your future wife. I was asking if you were dating someone."

"There's nobody around here I'd want to date." I glance around the room at the women my age. They're all daughters of members, so are on the approved dating list, but I don't find any of them attractive. I've gone out with some of them and slept with some of them, so it's not like I didn't give them a chance. I played by the rules. Dated the right girls. And all it did was make me realize I don't want them. I'm tired of these rich, spoiled girls who spend all their time shopping and gossiping about each other. I want Rachel, and now that I have her, she makes all other women unattractive to the point I don't even notice them.

"Royce's wife has been picked," William says. "We'll be voting on it at the next meeting, but I'm sure she'll be approved."

"Who is it?"

"Victoria Lissfeld."

Victoria is a tall, thin, dark-haired woman who has made a career out of spending her father's money. She graduated from college but has never had a job and never will. Instead, she spends all her time shopping. Buying herself diamonds and designer clothes that she hopes will impress her friends, thus expediting her rise to the top of the social ladder. She's shallow, spoiled, and self-absorbed. A complete nightmare. When we were younger, people used to call her Victoria Witchfeld.

I can't help but laugh. "How unfortunate for Royce."

"Yes, I know. I don't like her either, but if you think about it, the two of them are perfect for each other. She's just as obsessed with her image as Royce is. The problem is she's not good for him. Royce could stand to have his ego brought down a few notches and Victoria's not the one to do it. She's already building him up. Trying to make him a star. She's hoping his political career will turn into more than just a Senate position."

"Does she really think they'll pick Royce for president?"

"It's already being discussed. And Royce would do anything to make it happen. He'd much rather be president than a senator."

"I can't imagine Royce being married."

"He doesn't have a choice now. His wife has been picked."

Bells start chiming throughout the room, indicating it's time for dinner. William and I make our way to the dining room. The servers start showing us to our seats. I'm brought to a chair near the end of the long table, expecting my mother to be seated next to me. But instead, I see her a few seats down. There must be a mix-up. If I'm taking my father's place, I'm to be seated by my mother. It's protocol.

"Hello, Pearce." I look over and see a tall brunette around my age standing next to me.

"Hello." I shake her hand.

"I'm Sydney St. James. It's nice to meet you."

I glance down the table and see my mother smiling at me. This was a set-up. I'm not taking my father's place. I'm here as Sydney's date. I should've known my mother was up to something. I never attend these events with her. If my father doesn't go, *she* doesn't go.

"Shall we sit down?" Sydney waits for me to pull out her chair. I do, and then seat myself.

"I'm surprised we've never met before," she says, turning toward me. She's wearing a tight black dress that's cut low enough to show off her breasts without being considered improper for a dinner party.

"It's not that surprising. You live on the West Coast. I don't get out there much."

"So you know who I am."

"I know your father. Owner of SJS Shipping. One of the largest shipping companies in the world."

266

"That's correct. And you're the future CEO of Kensington Chemical, soon to be one of the largest chemical companies in the world."

"I doubt that. We've just recently started exploring our overseas options."

The servers appear again, bringing in the first course. There will be at least four courses, maybe five. This is going to be a very long evening.

The hours pass by and my mind is on Rachel the entire time. I'm not even listening to what's-her-name. Sydney? Yes, that's it. She's talked this whole time, mostly about her studies abroad. There's nothing wrong with her. She's beautiful and seems to be well educated. She's just not for me. I have absolutely no interest in her.

During the final course, I feel her hand rubbing my thigh. She lowers her voice and says, "When this is over, let's go back to your place."

I remove her hand from my leg. "I need to take my mother home, then go into the office."

"You're working this late at night?"

"I've had to take over my father's responsibilities while he's away, so I've been working nonstop." It's a lie. I'm not going to the office, but I needed an excuse so she wouldn't show up at my loft later.

"It won't take long." Her hand returns to my thigh, moving up to my crotch.

"Stop." I say it under my breath as I take her hand and hold it under the table so she doesn't put it back on my leg.

The man next to her asks her something and she turns toward him to answer. I release her hand and she finally keeps it to herself. Luckily, the man keeps her engaged in conversation until we're excused from dinner.

I meet my mother at the front door, not saying anything as we wait for our coats to be brought to us. When we're in the car and have been driving a few minutes, she finally speaks.

"So I noticed you were talking to Sydney St. James."

"You don't have to pretend, Mother. I know you were setting me up."

"Enough time has passed since your divorce. Your father is already talking with the other members about who you should marry. I'm simply intervening before they make their choice. You don't want your father picking someone. If you find someone before he does, you'll at least have some say in who you'll be spending your life with. Sydney is a beautiful woman. And very intelligent. I think you two would be perfect together."

"I don't need you or Father finding me a wife. I don't even want to get married again."

"Of course you're getting married. That isn't a choice. Appearance is everything, and when you take over the company you need to appear to be a mature, responsible family man with the proper wife and at least one child, hopefully more."

I'm quite aware of the plan for my future and yet my parents continue to remind me of it every chance they get, probably because they know it infuriates me. They get some kind of sick pleasure out of torturing me, especially my father. I think my mother actually thinks she's being nice by finding me someone like Sydney. She knows my father will pick someone I hate just to spite me.

"I'm not interested in Sydney," I say, as we sit at the stoplight.

"You didn't spend enough time with her. You should've taken her back to your loft."

I look at my mother, shocked that she would even suggest such a thing. She notices me watching her, but keeps her eyes on the front of the car.

"I'm not naive, Pearce. I know how people your age act. You skip the dating and move straight to the sex." She smooths her skirt, then adjusts her gloves. "So what was stopping you? You didn't find her attractive?"

I'm still staring at my mother, not believing we're actually having this conversation. I've never even heard her use the word 'sex' before tonight.

"The light is green," she says pointing to it. "Hurry up."

I face forward again and proceed down the road.

"You didn't answer my question," she says. "Do you find Sydney attractive?"

"Yes. But I just met her. I wasn't going to take her back to my loft."

"You're running out of time, Pearce. If you don't find someone soon, your father and the other members will. They plan to have someone picked before the end of the year."

My pulse spikes. "What? Why didn't he tell me?"

"Because he doesn't want you choosing someone before *he* does."

"But the members always choose. They wouldn't let me choose Sydney even if I was dating her."

"That's not true. The members are more lenient than you think. If you found a compatible mate who was a good fit with our family, both on a personal level and a business level, they would allow the marriage. And Sydney comes from a family that fits well with the Kensingtons on both accounts."

"But Father made it sound like I had no choice."

"He just said that so you wouldn't try to find someone. Or, heaven forbid, that you would find someone from the outside and marry her without our consent. Your father knows you have a rebellious streak, and he knows that when given the choice you'll always go against his wishes. So he makes sure choices aren't an option."

"Does Father already have a woman picked for me?"

"If he does, he hasn't told me. But I know that he's looking. If the Seymour girls were older, he'd pick Katherine. She already likes you and her family is a perfect fit, at least in regards to helping Kensington Chemical. Katherine's father could help us obtain new contracts that would greatly expand the business."

"Katherine is 15. I'm not marrying a teenager."

"Which is why she's not being considered. And Victoria Lissfeld has already been chosen for Royce Sinclair."

"I would never date Victoria Lissfeld. I can't stand that woman."

"There aren't that many eligible women your age, Pearce. You should really consider giving Sydney a chance. I have her number.

You could drop me off at home and give her a call. Perhaps invite her to your loft."

I can't believe my mother is telling me to have sex with a woman I just met. I want to tell her about Rachel, but I can't. If I did, she'd tell my father and he'd have me married off to the first single socialite he could find. He'd make me marry another lesbian, if that's all that was available. Anything to keep me away from Rachel.

We're at the house now. I've chosen to ignore my mother's comment about Sydney, but as I'm walking her to the front door she pulls out a business card. "Sydney's number is on the back. Call her and ask her to dinner. She's only in town for the week. And don't tell your father about this. If he knew I was interfering, we'd be fighting for months."

I take the card and kiss her cheek. "Goodnight, Mother."

"Goodnight, Pearce."

I wait until she's inside, then get back in the car and speed off. I'm completely on edge, knowing my father is actively trying to find me a wife. What if he's already found someone? This can't happen. I'm not marrying some woman my father picks. If I'm marrying anyone, I'm marrying Rachel. Maybe I should. I could secretly marry her before I'm forced to marry someone else. It's not like I haven't considered proposing to her.

I wonder if Rachel would accept my proposal. We haven't dated that long, but we love each other and I don't want to be with anyone but her, so why wait?

What would happen if I married her? What would the organization do? Would they punish me for not following orders? And what would the punishment be?

I need to talk to Jack. It's past ten, but the man never sleeps so I'm guessing he's awake right now. I'll just stop by his house. It's improper to show up unannounced, especially at this hour, but Jack isn't one to follow proper social rules so maybe he'll be okay with it.

When I arrive at his mansion, the security guard calls Jack to see if he'll allow me inside. He does, and I drive through the gate to the front of the mansion.

Jack greets me at the door wearing a white fencing suit and holding a face mask and a sword.

"Pearce, what a surprise." He shakes my hand. "Come on in."

I go inside. "It's a little late to be fencing, isn't it?"

He walks down the hall and I follow him. "I don't live my life by the clock. I do things on my own time schedule." He goes into a large open room. There's another man there in a fencing suit. Jack waves him away. "We're done here."

The man leaves and Jack goes over to a table and picks up a glass of scotch. The bottle is sitting next to it, half-empty. I don't know much about fencing, but I'm guessing it's not good to be getting drunk while shoving a sword at someone or dodging the swords coming at you. But that's Jack. Unconventional. A risk taker.

"Would you like a drink?" He holds up a glass.

"Actually, yes. I could use a drink."

He chuckles. "That bad, huh?" He pours it, then hands it to me. "Let's have a seat."

We sit down on some chairs set up on the side of the room.

"So what brings you by this evening?" He wipes the sweat off his forehead, then takes a drink.

"I was out with my mother earlier."

"And how is Eleanor? She's such a beautiful woman. She should've ended up with me instead of your father. I would've given her a much better life than Holton." He crosses his legs and swirls the scotch in his glass.

I almost drop my drink. "What are you saying? You used to date my mother?"

He waves his hand around. "Years ago. I was maybe 25, 26. I can't remember. When you drink as much as I do, your memory fails. Most people would find that a problem, but not me. I prefer to live in the present, not the past."

"How long did you date my mother?"

"How the hell should I know? I just told you my memory's shit." He stops to think. "Maybe a few months. And despite my memory loss, I do remember a few nights from those months."

271

He winks. "Your mother was quite the wild one, if you know what I mean."

I cringe. "Jack, please. I don't want to know."

"Yes, I suppose that would make you uncomfortable to think of your mother and me that way. The point is, I would've made a much better husband for her than Holton. And your father knows that, which is just another reason why he hates me."

"Why would he hate you? He married her, so he won."

Jack huffs. "Bullshit. He didn't win. He didn't even have to try. She was chosen for him, and only because her father made some kind of deal with Holton's father. The members approved it and it was done."

"Why didn't *your* father try to get her?"

"My father didn't give a flying fuck who I ended up with." He shrugs, causing some scotch to splash out of his glass. "In the end, it all worked out. Martha's a good wife and given me two beautiful daughters. She's just not Eleanor." He winks again.

"Well, my father still ended up with her, so he has no reason to harbor any ill will toward you."

"Holton despises me because your mother still has a spark for me. She always has." He smiles. "In fact, we might've had a reunion or two over the years."

I almost drop my drink again. I came here to talk about Rachel, not get a history of my mother's past sexual encounters.

"My mother cheated on my father? With *you*?"

"I'm sure it wasn't just me. The women are just as bad as the men, Pearce. They cheat just as much as we do. *My* wife certainly does."

"My mother doesn't seem like the type who would do that."

"Children can never see their parents for who they really are. Anyway, you were saying something about being out with Eleanor."

"Yes, we went to a dinner party at the Seymour residence and—"

"Is Katherine still begging for your attention?" He laughs. "Is she in high school yet?"

"Yes. To both of your questions. As I was saying, my mother had me attend the dinner with her, but only so she could set me up with Sydney St. James."

"Ahh, yes. Beautiful woman. I've never met her but I've seen pictures of her. She went to Princeton, I believe. And she's around your age. You two are an excellent fit. Eleanor did well choosing her." He takes a drink.

I set down my glass. "I'm not interested in Sydney."

"Why the hell not? She's certainly better than anyone your father would pick. And she's definitely better than your first wife. What was her name?" He holds his finger up in the air like he's thinking. "The lesbian girl. What was her name?"

"Kristina. Could we stay on topic here?"

"Yes, go ahead." He gets up to refill his scotch. "So what's wrong with Sydney?"

"Nothing's wrong with her. I'm just not interested in her. I already have a girlfriend."

"Who is it?" He sits down again.

"Rachel. You know her. You went to her apartment."

"No." He shakes his head. "You're not dating her. You might be having sex with her, but you're not dating her."

"I AM dating her and it's becoming more serious. That's what I'm here to talk to you about. I'm thinking of maybe...proposing to her."

He slams his glass down on the table and shoots up from his chair. "Are you out of your fucking mind?"

I stand up so I'm on his level. "I love her and I want to marry her."

"Yeah, well, I'd love to skydive while fucking Miss America but it ain't gonna happen. There are some things that just aren't possible and this is one of them. So get your head out of your ass and face reality. You're not marrying anyone who isn't approved. And your Indiana farm girl isn't on the list. You have plenty of beautiful women to choose from and you're going to pick one of them to marry. End of discussion." He plops back down in the chair.

"Listen to me." I remain standing, glaring down at him. "I'm marrying Rachel, despite what you or anyone else says. I thought *you* of all people would support me on this, Jack. You do what you want. You never follow their rules. So why should I?"

Jack bursts from his chair. "Because you'll get that girl killed! Is that what you want? You want her dead?"

A chill runs through me. He's lying. He's only saying that to scare me into staying away from her. They wouldn't kill her. Not if she were my wife. She'd be one of us. They couldn't kill her.

"Is that what you want, Pearce?" Jack's yelling at me, his face so close to mine I feel his spit when he talks. "Is it?"

"No! Of course not!" I back away. "But they wouldn't do that. Not if she were my wife."

"They sure as hell would."

"How do you know that? Have they done it before?"

"No, because you're the first idiot to even consider doing something like this. I may not follow all the rules, Pearce, but I do when it comes to picking a wife. We belong to a society that's closed off to outsiders. You let someone from the outside in and you risk destroying what they've worked so hard to build. They won't let that happen."

"Other members have married women who aren't part of it."

"Yes, but those women are all wealthy socialites who fit with someone like you. And they're carefully screened before they're allowed in. Some aren't even told about us. Their husbands keep it a secret for the entire marriage."

"Rachel would keep quiet. She wouldn't tell our secrets. I know she wouldn't."

"If she knew your secrets, she wouldn't want to be with you. Do you really think she's the type of girl who wants to be married to a killer?"

"I'm not a killer," I say through gritted teeth. "The freelancers did it. I didn't. And I was forced to give them the order."

"Yes, but you also killed a man yourself. You shot him dead."

"How do you know about that?"

"Your father bragged about it for months after it happened. He was quite proud of you."

274

That was the one and only time he was proud of me. It took killing a man to make my father proud.

"Then I won't tell her. She doesn't need to know about that side of my life."

"Do you really think you can keep a secret like that?"

"I have to if it'll keep her safe. Do you think it will? If I don't tell her about Dunamis, would they leave her alone?"

"I have no idea. Like I said, this has never happened before. But Pearce, keeping a secret like that will never work. As a member you can be called to fulfill an assignment in the middle of the night. How are you going to explain that? And what are you going to tell her when you have to leave to go to one of our week-long meetings?"

"I'll tell her it's for work. She already knows my work schedule is very demanding."

"And when you come home after an assignment, a broken mess like you were after killing that secretary? How are you going to explain that?"

"I won't. I'll just revert back to my other side. The good side. That's the only side Rachel will see. You said you'd teach me how to keep that side separate and I'm determined to do that."

He sighs and sits down again. "You're a damn fool, Pearce. You're putting yourself at risk and you're putting that young woman at risk."

"Nothing will happen to her. I'll keep her safe."

"You can't. If you do this, you're risking her life."

"Then help me protect her. You have more power than I do. Convince them to let me be with her."

"That would mean putting *myself* at risk. Why the hell would I do that?"

"Because you don't believe in their rules. You're sick of them controlling us. Taking away our choices. Our freedoms."

"That's true, but I don't have a death wish. I only fight battles I know I can win."

"There are ways around this, Jack. We just need to figure out what those are. Please. I'm begging you to help me. I love this woman more than anything. I'll do whatever it takes to be with her."

His jaw moves side to side, his fingers tapping the table next to him. He's thinking, so I wait.

Finally, he speaks. "I don't know what it is about you, Pearce, but for some reason I've got a soft spot for you. Maybe because I always wanted a son and you're the closest thing I've got to one. But you're still fucking annoying. So goddamn persistent. Stubborn. Rebellious. You never listen. Don't follow rules. Always questioning things. Taking risks you shouldn't be taking." He chuckles.

"What? What's so funny?"

"You sound just like me. No wonder I like you." He shoves up from his chair and stands in front of me. "Fine. I'll help you. It's the worst goddamn decision I've ever made and I'm sure I'll regret it, but what the hell? I'm old. I'll be dead soon. Might as well go out with a bang. Give those bastards something to remember me for. And doing this will piss off Holton, so all the better."

I shake his hand. "Thank you. You have no idea how much this means to me. So what's the plan? What should I do?"

"If you're serious about marrying that girl, you'll have to do it before they make a rule forbidding it, and you can't let them find out about it until after it's done."

"So how do I do this without them finding out?"

"Give me some time to think about it. I'll get back to you. Now get the hell out of here. I need a shower." He sniffs his arm. "This suit stinks."

I leave and go out to my car, smiling the entire way. This is really going to happen. I'm going to have a future with Rachel. Now all I have to do is convince her to marry me. Soon. And in secret. And I can't tell her why.

This could prove to be a challenge.

CHAPTER TWENTY-FIVE

RACHEL

It's Friday night and I'm going to Pearce's place to spend the weekend. He went to a dinner party last night so I didn't see him. It was just one night apart and yet I missed him like crazy. I guess that proves I'm in love. I never missed Adam this much.

When I get to Pearce's loft, I go up the elevator and when the doors open he's there waiting for me, holding a bouquet of red tulips.

"Hello, Rachel." He smiles.

"Hi." I jump into his arms and hug him. "I know it's only been a day, but it seems like forever since I saw you." I kiss him, then let him go.

He hands me the tulips. "For you."

"Thank you." I kiss him again.

"There's a vase on the counter." He leads me over to the kitchen. Next to the vase is a bottle of champagne and two glasses.

"Are we celebrating something?"

He takes the flowers from me and sets them down, then slips his arms around my waist. "I'm celebrating that you're here." He kisses me. "With me." He kisses me again. "All weekend."

"We're always together on the weekend."

"And I look forward to it all week."

I smile at him. "I love you."

"I love you too." He hugs me, his arms tightening around me, but not too tight. I taught him that and it makes me smile each time he does it. He's so determined to do it right, but truthfully, I'd take any kind of hug he wanted to give me.

"Are you hungry?" He points to the counter behind me. "I have some menus over there. You can pick whatever you'd like."

"Why don't we just go out?"

"I'd rather stay in. Restaurants are crowded on Friday nights and I didn't make reservations anywhere."

"You're Pearce Kensington. I'm sure just saying that name gets you a table."

He gives me a kiss. "I'd still rather stay in."

I lean back and look at him. "But we always stay in. Couldn't we just go out tonight? We've never been to any of the restaurants around here."

He straightens up. "Rachel, I don't feel like going out. I don't know why we can't just stay in."

This is so frustrating. Why does he always refuse to take me out? I don't want to start a fight over it so I let it go.

"Then let's do something else. I'm not ready to eat yet."

"What kind of something else?" He kisses me as he slowly undoes each button on my shirt.

"Let's go to the bedroom," I say as I undo his belt.

"You read my mind," he whispers in my ear.

After being apart last night, we're dying to be together. Our lips crash together as we undress each other on our way to the bedroom.

The sex is fast and frantic, and when we're done we sound like we've just run a sprint, our chests heaving as we try to catch our breath.

"Okay, now I'm hungry," I say.

He laughs. "What would you like?"

"I don't know. I'll have to go check out those menus."

"I'll get them and bring them in here. Would you like something to drink? I could open the champagne."

"Water is fine. We'll save the champagne for later."

While he's gone, I pull the covers over me. He has the most comfortable bed and the softest sheets I've ever felt. I always sleep well when I stay over here. I reach over to the nightstand and turn on the light. I look down and notice my bracelet on the floor. I took it off during the sex because I didn't want it rattling around on my wrist. I get out of bed, and as I'm picking up my bracelet, I spot something glimmering on the floor under the headboard. It's tiny and I can't tell what it is. I scoot under the bed and grab it and pull it out. I hold it up to the light.

My breath catches in my throat as a chill runs through me. It's an earring. A silver angel wing earring with a tiny fake diamond in the center. It's Shelby's earring. The one she lost.

Shelby was here.

In this bed.

With Pearce.

I drop the earring, my hands shaking. What does this mean? They obviously slept together, but when? How long ago? Is he still seeing her? Is he cheating on me with Shelby? Is that why they always act so strange around each other? Is that why he's helping her dad? Is that why she keeps trying to get me to break up with him?

The sting of betrayal shocks my system, making me feel like I can't breathe. Pearce has been lying this whole time. Lying. Cheating. Telling me he loves me when he really doesn't. Why would he do that to me?

"Rachel?" Pearce walks around the bed, holding the glass of water. He stands over me. "Rachel, why are you on the floor?"

I quickly stand up. "I have to go." I grab my clothes and run in the bathroom. I get dressed as fast as I can, tears rolling down my cheeks.

Pearce is talking on the other side of the door. "Rachel, what's wrong? Why are you leaving?"

Once I'm dressed, I swing open the bathroom door and race past him but he catches my arm. "Rachel, stop. What's going on?"

I rip my arm back. "Don't touch me!"

He steps in front me. "Why? What's going on? I don't understand. Why are you crying?"

I go around him and pick the earring off the floor. "Because of this!" I shove it in his hand.

He holds it up, confused. "What is it?"

"An earring! I found it under your bed. It's Shelby's earring!"

He looks at me and his expression says it all. I've seen that look before. My first boyfriend in college cheated on me, and when I found out and confronted him about it, he had that same look that Pearce has right now. That look of guilt, of being caught.

"You had sex with Shelby?" I ask just to see if he'll admit to it.

"Rachel, it's not what you're thinking."

"So you didn't have sex with her? Is that what you're saying? Then how did her earring get under your bed?"

He doesn't answer.

"Pearce, just tell me. Did you have sex with Shelby?"

He sighs. "Yes. But it was a long time ago."

My chest is aching as I try to breathe. I grab the earring from him. "Shelby lost this back in September. She noticed it was missing the day I met her. Right before I met *you*. Which means you had sex with her right before you met me. That wasn't a long time ago, Pearce!"

"Rachel, I'm sorry, but—"

"Is this still going on? Are you still seeing her?"

"No! Of course not!"

"Why should I believe you? You lied to me! You acted like you didn't know her. Like you'd never met her."

"I *didn't* know her. I promise you. It was a one-time thing. We'd both had too much to drink. It was a mistake."

"I don't believe you. And even if that were true, you should've told me." I storm out of the room with him right behind me. "I'm leaving. And don't bother calling me. This is over." I grab my purse off the counter next to the tulips and the champagne. There's also a box of chocolates there that I hadn't noticed earlier. He had this whole romantic weekend planned and now it's ruined.

I hurry over to the door, a sniffling, sobbing mess.

"Rachel, please. Don't go. Let's talk about this."

"There's nothing to say. Just leave me alone." I get on the elevator, pushing the button over and over.

He joins me just as the doors are closing. "Don't do this, Rachel. Don't end this."

"It's already ended. It ended the moment I found that earring."

"That happened before I even knew you! And nothing has happened since. Ask Shelby if you don't believe me."

The elevator door opens and I race out to the parking garage. Pearce doesn't follow me. I get in the car and drive off. I'm crying so much I can barely see the road. How could he do this to me? And how could *Shelby* do this to me? I thought we were friends.

When I get back to my apartment, I stop at Shelby's place and bang on her door until she answers. I storm inside her apartment and take the earring from my pocket.

"Rachel, what's wrong? You seem mad."

"THIS is what's wrong!" I hold up the earring. "I found your missing earring. And guess where it was?"

She takes it. "I don't know. Where?"

"Under Pearce's bed!"

She stares down at the earring. "Oh."

"You slept with Pearce and you've been lying to me this whole time!"

"I didn't lie to you. I just didn't tell you. There was no reason to. It was one time and it happened before he even met you." She walks into the kitchen and sets the earring on the counter.

"That's it? That's all you have to say?"

"What do you want me to say? That I'm sorry? Because I didn't tell you? Why would I tell you that? I knew it would hurt you if I did. You love Pearce, and it hurts to think about the guy you love being with someone else. I was trying to protect you, Rachel."

"I don't need your protection! I need the truth!" I'm crying again. Completely sobbing. "Just tell me the truth."

Shelby comes over to me and hands me a wad of tissues. "Come sit down."

I follow her to the couch, wiping my tears as I sit.

"This is the honest truth," she says. "Pearce and I met the night before I met you. We both had too much to drink and we ended up going back to his place. When I woke up the next morning, I left and never saw him again until you introduced me to him."

It's the same story Pearce told me, so maybe he wasn't lying. Maybe it really was just one drunken night. A mistake.

"And you haven't been with him since?" I ask, sniffling.

She shakes her head. "No. I promise you I haven't."

"What else do you know about him? What are you not telling me?"

"What are you talking about?"

"You keep telling me to stay away from him, like you know something about him you're not telling me."

"I only said those things because I've dated rich guys in the past and they didn't treat me well. They were assholes who thought they could do whatever they wanted just because they had money. I assumed Pearce was the same way, but I know now that he's not. I see how happy he makes you and how well he treats you and—"

"I broke up with him," I say, my voice shaky, tears falling again. "I told him it was over."

"Because of *me?*"

"Because he didn't tell me about you. He lied to me."

"But when you confronted him, did he tell you the truth? Or did he deny it?"

"He didn't deny it. He said the same thing you did. That you were both drunk and that it was just one night. Before he met me."

"Then he told you the truth. He could've lied, Rachel, but he didn't."

"He never would've told me the truth if I hadn't found your earring. I can't believe all this time he knew you and he never told me."

"If he told you, he'd have to explain how we met. And he didn't want to do that. Because it doesn't matter. We never went out. Never dated. It was one night. And it was before he even knew you existed." She sighs. "Rachel, you can't break up with him over this. You love him. I know you do."

"Yes, but he can't hide stuff from me."

"Was this really something you wanted to know? Look how upset you are right now."

"This was something he should've told me." I glare at her. "And something YOU should've told me."

"If I'd had a relationship with him, then yes, I should've told you. But that's not what it was. It was a drunken one-night stand. It was a mistake, and when I saw him again, I didn't see any reason to tell you." She pauses. "Rachel, I know you don't want to hear this, but a guy like Pearce has been with a lot of women, so chances are, he'll at some point run into one of them. And if you're with him when he does, do you really expect him to tell you he slept that woman?"

"No. But if I don't know her, it's different. I know you. You're my neighbor and my friend, so he should've told me."

"Would you do the same if it were the other way around? If you slept with one of his guy friends but didn't know it was his friend until Pearce introduced you, would you admit to him that you'd slept with his friend?"

I sigh. "Probably not."

She's right. If it'd just been a one time thing, I probably wouldn't tell Pearce.

Just minutes ago I was fuming mad, but now I'm not sure how I feel. Maybe I'm making more out of this than I should. It was one night. Before he met me. So should he have told me? Or was it better that he didn't? We're both adults. We both have pasts, and I knew his past included a lot of women. I just didn't know Shelby was one of them.

"So what are you going to do?" she asks.

"I don't know. I don't want to break up with him, but I also need to be able to trust him and I'm not sure that I do. Sometimes I feel like he's hiding stuff from me. He still won't take me out anywhere. It's like he doesn't want people seeing us together. It's starting to really bother me. And then when I found that earring, I felt like it was a sign telling me not to trust him. If he didn't tell me about *you*, what else isn't he telling me?"

"You guys need to talk and work this out. He loves you, Rachel. And I don't mean just a little. I mean like deep-in-his-soul loves you. Like he would literally fall apart if he lost you."

"How do you know that?"

"Because I can see it in his eyes when he looks at you. My dad looks at my mom the same way and she's the love of his life. Not many people have that kind of love and when it comes along you can't just throw it away. You have to fight for it."

"I love him too. The same way." I dab my eyes with the tissue. "I love him with everything I am. And I don't want to lose him."

"Then don't. Talk this out so you can get past it." She nudges my arm. "And then have really awesome makeup sex."

"I should go call him."

"No. Never call a guy during a fight, especially when he's in the wrong. Make him come to you. He needs to grovel and beg for your forgiveness. Bring you flowers."

"He's not going to do that. Not after I told him it's over."

"A man like Pearce doesn't give up that easily, especially given how much me loves you. When guys are in love, they're totally pathetic. They'll do anything to get you back. Just wait. I bet he's here within the hour, knocking on your door with a bouquet of roses in his hand."

"Then I better get over there." She walks me to the door. "I *am* still mad at you."

"I know. And you have every right to be. I'd feel the same way, except if I were you, I probably would've punched me. You want to punch me?" She sticks her face out. "Go ahead. I can take it."

I half smile. "No. I'm not going to punch you."

"I hope knowing this doesn't make things weird between us."

"It's weird, but I'm going to try not to think about it."

She hugs me. "Good luck with Pearce."

I step into the hall. "You just hugged me. You never hug me."

"You needed one. I only give them when necessary, unlike you, who hugs everyone she meets." She pushes me toward my door. "Now get over there. And clean up your face. You're a mess."

She shuts her door and I go in my apartment and check my answering machine. It's blinking red and says it has ten messages. I'm sure they're all from Pearce. As I'm about to listen to them, someone knocks on the door. He's here already? That was fast.

I wipe the remaining tears off my face as I walk to the door. I open it, but instead of Pearce being there, it's Adam.

"Adam. What are you doing here?"

"I came here to surprise you." He hugs me and I notice a suitcase sitting next to his feet.

I push away from him. "No. Adam, you can't stay here. You need to leave."

He takes his suitcase and walks past me into my apartment. "I'm not leaving. I just got here." He sets his suitcase down and looks me up and down. "You look great. Even better than the last time I saw you, which was what? Like six months ago? I saw you at church last Easter, but you left before I could talk to you."

"Adam, I mean it. You need to leave."

"Rachel, why are you acting this way?" He comes up to me, standing too close. "I thought you'd be happy to see me." He leans in toward my face.

I shove him back. "What are you doing?"

"Giving you a kiss. I missed you."

"Listen, Adam, I don't know what my mom told you, but I'm not interested in getting back together with you. I have a boyfriend now, and even if I didn't, I wouldn't want us getting back together."

"Rachel, I know you don't mean that. You and I have a history. We love each other. We belong together."

"I didn't love you. I only thought I did because I was pregnant and I thought that meant that I *should* love you. But I didn't." I take a breath. "Why would you even want me back? You broke up with me."

"I've done some thinking and realized there are other ways we can have children. I'd rather have my own, but since that's not possible, I'm willing to adopt. I've already looked into it and—"

"Adam, you're not listening to me. I don't want to be with you."

"We just need time to reconnect. I'll be here all weekend. We can do whatever you want." He places his hand on the side of my face, but instead of comforting me like it does when Pearce does it, it makes me tense up. "Come on, Rachel. I'm giving up a lot to be with you. The least you could do is act grateful."

I push his hand off me. "Stop touching me. I don't want this. You. Us. I'm sorry you came all the way out here, but you need to leave." I walk to the door and open it and see Pearce standing there with his hand up, like he was getting ready to knock.

"Rachel, I—"

"Is that him?" Adam meets me at the door.

"Who's this?" Pearce asks me, his eyes on Adam.

Adam steps in front of me. "I'm her fiancé. And we're trying to have a discussion here so you need to go."

"You're not my fiancé," I tell him, nudging him aside so I can see Pearce. "This is Adam," I tell him. "My EX-fiancé. He was just leaving."

Adam turns me toward him, his hands gripping my shoulders. "Rachel, you barely know this guy. You've dated him for what? A couple months? I've known you since kindergarten. I know your family, your friends. I know everything about you."

"You don't know anything about me."

"Of course I do. How could you say that?"

"If you knew me, you'd know how much I hurt when we lost the baby." I'm tearing up as I say it because it still hurts. "And you'd know how devastated I was when I was told I could never have a child." I sniffle and wipe my tears. "And you'd know how much I needed you after it happened. Yet you went and took a job in Indianapolis. You left me, Adam, when I needed you the most. You never even called or came back to see me."

"I thought you needed some time alone."

"Which just proves we were never even friends."

"Take your hands off her," Pearce says to Adam.

He glances up at Pearce, noticing his large stature and big muscles. Adam slowly lowers his arms to his side.

"Just leave," I tell Adam. "And don't come back."

He just stands there.

Pearce steps closer to Adam. "She asked you to leave."

Adam looks at me like he expects me to change my mind. When I don't, he storms into the apartment and grabs his suitcase.

286

On his way out, he stops at the door and says to me, "You and him will never last. And when you don't, I won't be waiting for you."

He takes off down the stairs.

I stand there, completely stunned that he showed up here like that. He really thought I wanted him back? He didn't even apologize after I told him how much he hurt me. How could he not even say he was sorry?

"Rachel." Pearce is still in the hallway. "May I come in?"

I nod. "Yes."

Maybe I shouldn't let him in. I'm supposed to be mad at him and not want to see him. But right now, he's the only person I want to see. The only person who can make me feel better.

We go inside and I stand there, still sniffling. Pearce is across from me, lacking his usual confidence and seeming hesitant.

"I know you're angry with me and probably don't want me touching you, but I would really like to put my arms around you right now. I think you need that, and since there's no one else here, maybe—"

"Yes."

That one word is all it takes for him to wrap me in his arms. I can hear his heart beating really fast. He's nervous. Scared I'm going to reject him. Afraid I'm going to tell him to go away and never come back, like I did to Adam just now. But I wouldn't do that to Pearce, because I love him way too much. And because he cares about me more than Adam ever did. And loves me more than Adam ever could.

Pearce loves me so much that I can feel it whenever we're together. I can hear it in his voice and see it in his eyes. Even Shelby can see it.

And now he thinks he's lost me. The only person who ever looked him in the eye and said I love you.

I know he lied to me, but I want to forgive him. I don't want to let him go.

"Pearce, we need to talk."

He slowly drops his arms and steps back, and when I look at him I see his eyes are red and watery. This big strong man who

287

never shows emotion is brought to tears because he thinks he's lost me.

"Rachel. I'm sorry. I hope that you can forgive me, but if not, I at least had to say goodbye. You left and I..." He takes a breath. "I didn't get to say goodbye."

I take his hand. "Don't say it."

"Don't say what?"

"Don't say goodbye. I don't want you to."

He looks confused. "You don't?"

"No. I'm still hurt that you lied to me, but I also love you and want to be with you. So...I don't want you to say goodbye."

He takes me in his arms again, holding me tighter this time. "I'm so sorry I hurt you. It was never my intention. I love you so much. I would do anything to keep you from hurting. All I want to do is make you happy."

He's going to make me cry again if he keeps this going.

"Speaking of that, I forgot something." He lets me go and heads back out the door.

What is he doing? And where is he going?

He comes in with a grocery sack. "It doesn't make up for what I did but I know it makes you happy, and I thought that even if you wouldn't let me inside, I could at least leave this at your door."

He hands me the sack. Inside are a package of chocolate chip cookies and two quarts of ice cream, one vanilla and one chocolate.

"I bought both flavors because I've noticed you sometimes like to mix them."

I smile. "You went grocery shopping?"

'Yes. It was another first for me. That's what took me so long to get here. I wasn't sure where they sell these items but an elderly gentleman helped me out."

Okay, now I'm crying. Imagining Pearce searching all over a grocery store looking for this stuff is just too sweet. He even got my favorite brand of cookies.

"What's wrong?" he asks, concerned. "You don't like it? I should've just got flowers."

"No." I drop the sack and hug him. "I don't want flowers. This is so much better."

"I tried to time it right so that some of the ice cream would be melted when I got here. I know how you like to let the cookies soak up some of the ice cream."

I pull back to look at him. "How did you know that?"

"I watch you, so that I learn what you like." He brushes my hair back and rests his hand behind my ear. "I also watch you because you're beautiful. And because I love you and can't take my eyes off you." He kisses my forehead. "Whatever I have to do to get you to forgive me, I will do it."

"I want us to talk. I want to talk about the things we haven't talked about because I was too afraid to bring them up. I didn't want to start a fight so I kept putting it off. But in order for this relationship to keep moving forward, we need to talk about these things."

"Go ahead."

"Let's have our ice cream first."

After all that's gone on tonight, I need some time to gather my thoughts before talking to Pearce. I make us both a cookie sundae and we're quiet as we eat. The ice cream calms me down from the stress of this crazy night and when we're done eating, I'm ready to talk.

"Pearce, I want you to take me out."

"Out where?"

"Somewhere you would normally go. Like your favorite restaurant or a coffee shop near your loft. You never take me anywhere and it's making me think you don't want us to be seen together. Like you're trying to hide me."

"I'm not trying to hide you." His tone tells a different story.

"Pearce, no more lying. Tell me the truth."

He sighs. "The truth is, I've been trying to shield you from that side of my life. The side in which I'm known only as Pearce Kensington, the billionaire. Holton Kensington's son. The future CEO of Kensington Chemical. I'm not allowed to be myself when I'm in that world. Instead, I'm just a name. A name that people pay attention to and respect, but only because there's a great deal of money behind it. I don't like that side of my life and I don't think you would either, which is why I've kept you out of it. I would like more than anything to take you out and show you off, but it's not that simple. The world I live in is all about appearances, and that includes being seen with the right people. You wouldn't believe how the people around me gossip. It's sickening really. And childish. And yet they still do it. If I'm out having a drink with a woman and someone sees me, within a day, everyone knows. I have no privacy, which is why I prefer to stay home."

"So you don't want your friends knowing we're dating?"

"These people aren't my friends. They're just people I know. People I'm forced to be around because of my name and my wealth. It's a very small social circle and outsiders are not allowed in."

"And I'm an outsider. Because I'm not wealthy?"

"Yes. And as wrong as it is, they wouldn't treat you well. They'd judge you and say things they shouldn't say, both to your face and behind your back. I don't want you to have to endure that. I don't want those people anywhere near you."

"But maybe once they got to know me, they'd accept me."

"They'll never accept you. It's just how they are."

"Well, I'm not afraid of them and you don't need to protect me from them. I want to go out, Pearce. Not right now, but tomorrow night. I want you to take me to dinner at a place you'd normally go. Would you do that?"

He hesitates. "Yes."

"I also want to meet your parents. It doesn't have to be right away, but maybe before the end of the year."

"Fine. Before the end of the year."

"Do you think your parents won't like me? Is that why I've never met them?"

"My parents don't like anyone. Including me."

I hold his hand. "That's not true."

"What other demands do you have?" He says it jokingly.

I smile. "That was it. Well, maybe one more."

"What is it?"

290

"Can we make up now?"

He kisses me. "I thought you'd never ask."

He walks me to the bedroom. And we make up. Several times.

CHAPTER TWENTY-SIX

PEARCE

Last night was bad. I never wanted Rachel to know about Shelby. I knew it would hurt her to know I'd been with her friend. But what hurt her even more is that I didn't tell her, not just about the fact that I'd slept with Shelby, but that I knew her and pretended I didn't.

If Rachel only knew how many other secrets I have. Would she forgive me if she ever found out? I don't think she would. I think I'd lose her forever. I thought I'd lost her last night and it had me in a state of panic. I drove to her place, willing to do anything to get her back, but worried it might be too late.

When I saw Adam there and saw how he treated her, it took everything in me to control my rage. Even after she told him how much he'd hurt her, he still didn't care. I wanted to kill him, or at least beat him unconscious. But that would've upset Rachel and I was already in enough trouble with her.

Thank God she forgave me. We made up last night, and today we're even closer than before. I never thought fights were a good thing, but I see now that sometimes they can help a relationship. Finding out about Shelby caused Rachel to open up to me about the other issues that were bothering her, mainly the fact that she knows I've been keeping her out of the other side of my life. I tried to explain to her as best I could why I've done that. I couldn't tell her about the organization, but I was honest about the realities of my life and how the people in my world will never accept her. I felt bad saying it, but it's the truth and she needs to know what she's getting into by being with me.

It's not an easy life and I have no idea how she'll react to it once she's immersed in it, but like she said, I can't protect her from everything. She'll eventually have to meet my family and the other people in my life. I just wasn't ready for her to do so, but now I don't have a choice. She's been asking me for weeks to take her out, and I kept saying no, but last night she wouldn't take no for an answer, so I finally agreed to it.

It's now Saturday night and we just arrived at Rolheim's, a steak restaurant I used to go to a lot before I met Rachel. I've never seen any of the members here. Most of them live along the coast and don't come up here to eat. But I could easily run into someone else who knows me. If it happens, I'll just have to deal with it. I can't hide Rachel forever. If we're going to have a future together, people will eventually find out about her.

We have dinner without any problems. In fact, it's enjoyable. The food is delicious and Rachel looks beautiful as always. It's nice to finally be on a real date with her where I'm actually taking her out.

We finish dessert, and as I'm setting money out for the check, I hear a voice I recognize. I look over and see Royce walking toward me.

"Kensington. Good to see you." He turns to Rachel. "And who is this beautiful woman?"

"Rachel," she answers, shaking his hand. "Rachel Evans."

"Royce Sinclair."

"How do you know Pearce?" she asks him.

He glances at me. "Pearce and I go way back. Our families are friends. We went to Yale together. Lived in the same dorm. So how do *you* know Pearce?"

"We met at Yale," I say before she can answer. "Rachel attended a speech I was giving."

"So you go to Yale?" he asks her.

"No. I'm in grad school at Hirshfield."

"Royce, we'll have to talk later," I say to him. "Rachel and I need to be going."

"Yes, of course. I should get back to my seat. Victoria's waiting. Did you know I'm seeing Victoria Lissfeld?"

"Yes, your brother told me." I stand up. "I'll call you next week and we'll catch up. Perhaps we could meet for drinks."

"Yes, let's plan on that." He smiles at Rachel. "Goodbye, Rachel. It was a pleasure meeting you."

She smiles back. "You as well."

I go around the table and pull out her chair and help her with her coat.

"He seems nice," she says.

"He's not. He's just good at putting on a show."

She picks up her purse. "I need to use the restroom quick before we leave."

"Certainly. It's by the door. Go ahead. I'll meet you there."

She leaves and I make my way over to Royce, who's on the other side of the dining room. Victoria spots me as I approach the table.

"Pearce, what a surprise," she says. "I haven't seen you since your parents' party last summer. How have you been?"

"I'm good." I don't ask how she's doing because she'll ramble on for an hour. I turn to Royce. "Can I speak to you for a moment?"

We walk to a hallway at the back of the restaurant. "What is it?"

"Don't tell anyone about her. I mean it. Not one word."

"Why? Who is she? I don't recognize the name."

"She's not one of us. She's just out here going to school. She's from Indiana."

He smiles. "Your father's going to kill you. I hear he's been trying to find you a wife."

"Yes, I know. Which is why I need you to keep quiet about this."

"Hmm. I don't know."

"Royce, don't be an ass. I've covered for you more times than I can count. You owe me."

"Do I?" He smirks. "Because I don't think I do. But let's discuss it. Are you free tomorrow?"

"No, but I'll make time. When do you want to meet?"

"Three. At my place."

"I'm busy at three. Make it seven."

"Fine. Seven. And bring me a bottle of scotch. The good kind."

I walk off, furious that he's going to blackmail me in exchange for keeping quiet. But it's what we do. We blackmail each other to keep our secrets hidden. Royce claims to be my friend, but he'd turn on me in a second. They all would. Every single person I know. The only person in my life that I trust is Rachel. With everyone else, I have to constantly be on guard and use bribes and blackmail to keep people in line.

I meet up with Rachel just as she's leaving the restroom. We go back to my place and finish our evening. I try to focus on Rachel, but all I can think about is Royce. I don't trust him to keep Rachel a secret.

I still haven't heard anything from Jack. I'd like to think I can trust him, but I know better than to trust someone who's part of the organization. He said he'd help me, but he could've just been saying that to appease me. For all I know, he could be plotting ways to break up Rachel and me, instead of finding a way for us to be together.

On Sunday morning, I ask Rachel if she'd like to go out for breakfast. She happily accepts the offer, thrilled that I'm going out in public with her again.

When we get in my car, I spot my cell phone on the floor. It must've fallen out of my pocket last night. As a member, I'm expected to have my phone on me at all times in case they call. And last night, it wasn't with me. Shit.

Rachel sees me pick it up. "You have a cell phone?" She reaches for it. "Can I see it? I've never seen one up close."

I hand it to her, keeping my eye on it in case it goes off. If she answered it, who knows what would happen? It wouldn't be good.

She hands it back to me. "I wonder if those will catch on and someday everyone will have one."

"I'm sure people will want one once the price comes down. Right now they're too expensive."

"Do you use it much?"

"No. I only use it for work." I glance at it and notice a message waiting. I never get messages. I'm not supposed to, because I'm supposed to answer the phone when they call. And I didn't. Shit, I'm in trouble. Deep fucking trouble.

"Someone called last night," I say to Rachel. "I need to check this."

I get out of the car and shut the door. I walk off to the side of the parking garage and call in to hear the message. I'm asked for my member number so I punch it in and listen to the recording.

"Member services has been notified that this message was unable to be delivered directly. The rules state that you must have your phone with you and turned on at all times. Failure to do so could result in punishment. Call us immediately to receive your assignment. This concludes the message."

I shove the phone in my pocket and get back in the car. "Rachel, I'm sorry but something came up at work. I have to go into the office. I need to take you home."

"Would you mind if I just stayed here? I need to study and your place is so much quieter than mine."

I hesitate, because I was planning to do this assignment from home, but I guess I could go into the office and do it.

"Of course." I fake a smile. "Would you like me to walk you back inside?"

"You don't need to. Go ahead and go. Do you know what time you'll be home?"

"No. So don't worry about dinner. And I'm sorry about breakfast. I'll call and have something delivered."

"That's okay. I'll just make something." She leans across the seat and kisses me. "Don't work too hard. I love you."

"I love you too."

She steps out of the car and goes inside. She's being very understanding about this. She's always understanding regarding my work schedule, which is another reason I love her and can see a future with her. Not many women would put up with my schedule. In fact, the other women I've been with used to whine and complain when I had to work late or on the weekends. I couldn't take it, which is why I could never sustain any kind of relationship with them. But Rachel is very independent and doesn't demand that I be with her at all times. She's content spending time alone.

When I arrive at the office, nobody's there. Our employees often come in on the weekends to catch up on work, but usually not on Sunday mornings. I'm relieved no one's here. I can't be around anyone right now. I'm nervous about this assignment, assuming it's going to be bad.

I go in a conference room and make the call. When it picks up, I punch in my member number, then wait as the phone rings repeatedly. I'm not supposed to hang up. The rule is you stay on the line until someone answers. After about a minute, I hear a man's voice. He asks me to restate my member number, then he goes through the security questions that confirm my identity. Before the man gives me my instructions, I ask him if I'll be punished for not having my phone with me. He says I won't be because it's a first time offense, but if it happens again I *will* be punished.

I have no idea who's on the other end of the phone and I'm not allowed to know. I've never been told who gives the assignments. I assume it's one of my fellow members, but I don't recognize the voice so I really don't know.

I listen closely to the instructions. My body relaxes as I realize this isn't a kill assignment. Instead, it's an order to cover up the inappropriate activities of a man we placed in the Senate a few years ago. He's up for re-election soon and he keeps getting himself wrapped up in scandals involving prostitutes. We'll rig the election to make sure he wins, but reporters or the public could get suspicious if this man wins despite his unsavory behavior. He's a conservative with a wife and three children, so his voting base won't stand for his philandering. I'll fake some documents and interviews, discrediting the women he was with, and all will be well. His wife and the public will be led to believe he never did those things and he'll go on to win the election without question.

Perhaps it's wrong that this man gets away this behavior, but to me, this is nothing. Everyone I know cheats on their wives and the members all use prostitutes. We just call them associates. So covering this up for the senator doesn't bother me. It's probably the easiest assignment I've had, which makes me think the next one will definitely be a kill assignment. But I'll worry about that later.

After I get all the details, I call up one of our freelancers who is skilled in the various tasks that need to be done; getting rid of police reports, creating fake statements from the prostitutes saying they were lying about being with this man, making fake recordings of these girls trying to blackmail the man for money. It's so easy to manipulate the truth. That's why I never believe anything I see on the news or read in the papers. If the organization is able to distort the truth this way, then I know for sure that others are doing it as well.

By five o'clock, my work is done and I call and check in with Rachel. She's working on a paper for class. I tell her I'll take her out for dinner when I get home. But before I do that, I have to meet with Royce. I'm supposed to meet him at seven, but I don't want to wait around for two hours so I'm going to stop by his place now.

He lives in a luxury townhouse in Westport. I check in at the gate. The guard calls Royce and he gives him the okay to let me in. I assumed he would, despite my early arrival. Royce is very proper when it comes to following etiquette rules, but only with other people. He's not that way with me. If it's just the two of us, we set the formalities aside. We spent four years at college together and have seen each other at our worst. There were lots of drunken nights. Lots of girls. Lots of things we shouldn't have done, but did anyway. We know each other's secrets and I guess that makes us friends, although I'd rather not have friends like him. He's only a friend when he wants something. And he always wants something, which is why I try to avoid him.

"You're early," he says when he opens the door.

"I didn't want to wait until seven." I walk into his townhouse. It's 4000 square feet so more like a house. It's too formal for my taste, with marble everywhere and white pillars separating the entryway from the living room. Tapestry rugs line the floors, expensive paintings hang on the walls, and long flowing drapes hide the windows. The decor fits Royce's personality. Formal. Over-the-top. Filled with objects that show off his wealth and status.

My loft is much more casual and has a more masculine feel. Dark wood panels cover the floors and simple shades hang from my windows. I have just a few framed black and white photos on the walls whereas Royce's walls are filled with oil paintings in ornate, antique frames.

"So tell me about this new girl of yours." He sits down on his all-white couch, resting his feet on the glass coffee table. He's wearing a robe so I'm trying not to look at him.

"Could you put something on before we talk? Why are you wearing a robe at this hour, anyway?"

He smiles. "I had company earlier."

"Who? Victoria?"

He rolls his eyes. "God, no. That woman's horrible in bed. She has a decent body but she doesn't know what to do with it."

"But you're still going to marry her?"

"Of course I'm going to marry her." He tightens the tie around his robe. "She was picked for me. I don't have a choice."

"Did your father pick her out?"

"No. He hates Victoria. So does Mother. But given that I'm going to have a political future, Victoria was the right fit. The higher-up members chose her. My parents weren't allowed to have input."

The higher-up members are never seen. They meet separately from the rest of us and make the final decisions on things. Since they have a political future planned for Royce, they have to choose just the right wife for him. One who will work well in a political environment. They wouldn't trust the judgment of the other members for something like that, which is why they handpicked Royce's wife.

"So back to business," he says, his robe slipping a little, exposing part of his leg.

"Royce, please put some clothes on. I can't talk to you like that."

"Fine." He gets up. "I'll be back in a minute."

While he's gone, I go down the hall to use the bathroom. When I come out, I walk by one of the guest rooms and notice something on the floor. The door is half closed, but I open it and see ropes scattered across the thick beige carpet. In the middle of the room is a four poster bed.

I go in the room and pick up the rope. It's the same width as the red marks on Shelby's wrists. I knew it was him. I fucking knew it.

I take the rope and storm into the living room. Royce is waiting at the bar, now in suit pants and a white button-up shirt. He doesn't dress casual. He only wears suits.

"Where'd you go?" he asks, pouring himself a drink.

"What is this?" I toss the rope at him.

He grins. "What? Are you thinking of tying up your girl? I'd highly recommend it. I have some extra rope if you need it."

I get up in his face. "I'm not tying up anyone, at least not against her will."

"What are you talking about?"

"You tied up one of our associates and wouldn't let her leave."

"And your point is?" He takes his drink and goes back in the living room and sits on the couch.

I walk over to where he's sitting but remain standing. "It's against the rules and you know it. They do their job and they leave. They're not even allowed to spend the night, let alone all day."

"Who the fuck cares? They're hookers. We can do what we want with them. I don't know why they even have that rule."

"You hurt the girl. She had marks all over her arms. You abused her."

He shrugs. "So I was a little rough. Big deal. I'm sure she's had worse done to her."

I take the drink from his hand and slam it down on the table. "You don't treat them like that, you understand?"

"Wait a minute. How do you know all this? Did she tell on me?"

"No. I saw her after she'd been with you. I saw her arms and the bruises. She tried to cover them up but I saw them. She wouldn't say who did it, but I had a feeling it might be you. And now that I know it is, you're never fucking doing it again. To her or anyone."

"And you really think you can tell me what to do?" He picks up his glass from the table. "I do what I want to do. I don't take orders."

"You will when the members find out about this. Do you really want their punishment?"

"I'm not being punished, because they'll never find out. I have ways to keep you quiet, Pearce. I did some research on that girl you were with and she's even worse than I thought. Some hick from the Midwest? A farm girl? Seriously?" He laughs. "I admit she's fucking gorgeous, but if the members found out you were dating her, your punishment would be a thousand times worse than mine for tying up an associate. Your father would probably kill you before they even had a chance to punish you."

"There's no rule that says I can't date her."

"There doesn't need to be because we're all smart enough to know better. Except for you. You're not actually serious about this girl, are you?"

I don't answer.

He sits up. "You're kidding me, right?"

I sit across from him, not looking at him.

"Do you have some kind of death wish, Pearce?"

"They're not going to kill me for marrying an outsider."

"Marry?" He bolts up from the couch, spilling his drink. "Have you lost your fucking mind? You can't marry that girl."

"I can if no one finds out."

"What are you saying? You're eloping? So you already proposed to her?"

"No. But I'm going to."

I didn't plan to tell him this and now I regret it. Why did I tell him this? What was I thinking?

"How long have you known this girl?"

"Since early September. But I love her and I don't want to wait to marry her. I *can't* wait. If I do, I risk having them find out and trying to stop me."

301

He paces the floor, rubbing his hand over his face. "I always thought out of the two of us, I was the risk taker, but you're clearly taking over that role. Even *I'm* not stupid enough to do something like that."

"I already married the woman they chose. I'm not doing it again. I never thought I'd find a woman like Rachel, and now that I have, I'm not letting her go."

He stops pacing and stares at my face. "Shit. You're really in love with this woman."

"Is it that obvious?"

"Yes. Which means it's going to be difficult to hide."

"What are you saying? That you'll keep my secret?"

"I don't know." He returns to his spot on the couch, putting his feet up on the table. "I must say, I *am* intrigued by the danger of it. I get an adrenaline rush just thinking about what they might do to you. So in that respect, I might keep your secret just to find out what they'll do to you after you marry her."

I shake my head. "Thanks a lot, Royce. You're a real friend."

"I already told you not to do it. That was me being your friend. But you didn't listen to me so now I'm interested in seeing how this plays out. Nobody's ever done this before. So what's your plan?"

I don't want to tell him about Jack's involvement, because doing so would be putting Jack at risk. There's a good chance Royce would spill that secret to the others and then Jack would get in trouble and could no longer be my mentor.

"I'm still working on the plan," I tell him.

He swigs his drink, then sets his glass down. "I know what to do."

"What?"

"You take this girl to Vegas and get married, and while you're there, you send out an announcement about your engagement. Send it to all the major newspapers, the news channels. Let everyone know. Then start planning the wedding. A big elaborate spring wedding. And invite the media and maybe a few celebrities."

"Why would I do all that?"

"Because the public will eat it up. The billionaire marrying a regular girl? It's a fairytale story. Plus, you're both annoyingly attractive, which will make for good photos for all the media outlets. The bottom line is that if you're popular with the public, the members can't harm you. Or the girl. They won't risk it, at least not right away. Not while the spotlight is on you. And by the time the press dies down, maybe they'll accept this woman. It's highly unlikely, but I'm trying to be positive here."

"But the members could easily find out that I got married in Vegas. That's public record."

"You're not thinking, Pearce." He holds two fingers in the air. "Two things. First is that you can easily conceal public records so that they can't be found. We do that all the time. And second, it doesn't matter if the members know the truth. Because by the time they find out, you'll have already alerted the media about your engagement and it will be too late for them to stop it. Given that you've already been married and divorced, it would look bad if you broke off your engagement. You'd look irresponsible, incapable of making a decision and sticking to it. Your father can't have a person like that taking over his company. He needs you to appear stable and reliable. So he'll be forced to go along with your engagement and pretend to be happy at the wedding." He smiles. "The more I think about this, the more I love it. Now I kind of wish it were me instead of you, except my father isn't the tyrant that yours is, so it wouldn't be nearly as fun." He gets up and goes back to the bar. "You haven't said anything, Pearce. What do you think?"

I'm quiet as I think about his plan. Royce never did well in school, but when it comes to scheming, he's a master. His plan is perfect. Brilliant, really. It would force the members to allow my marriage to Rachel. And they wouldn't dare try to harm her, not with all the media attention she'll be getting. Even after the press dies down, it would be reckless of them to even attempt to harm her. If anything ever happened to her, reporters would become suspicious, asking questions and doing investigations, which could lead to them finding out about us. The members wouldn't want to risk exposing themselves like that.

"I think it might actually work," I say, meeting him at the bar.

"Of course it will work. But you'll need my help. Someone has to cover for you while you're off getting married." He takes a drink of his scotch.

"You'd do that for me?"

"I will if you keep your mouth shut about the associate."

I take a moment to consider it. I'd really like to report him, but truthfully, they may not even punish him. They may decide it's not worth it. And then Royce would become my enemy. He'd destroy my future with Rachel.

"You can't do it again," I tell him. "If you tie up a girl, she has to agree to it. You can't hold her against her will."

"I couldn't even if I wanted to. I have Victoria bothering me now. She checks in on me constantly and has a key to my place. These days I'm lucky if I can get an hour with a girl."

I try to hide my smile. William's right. Victoria is a perfect match for Royce. She'll keep him in line, or she'll at least try. She knows about the associates, but she won't want him using them. She likes controlling things as much as he does, and it sounds like she's already trying to control Royce, which is good. He needs it.

"So you're really going to help me with this?" I ask.

He slaps me on the back. "Sure. Why not? Like you said last night, you covered for me plenty of times. I owe you. And as long as you keep quiet about the associate, we shouldn't have any problems." He pours some bourbon into a glass. "So when is this secret marriage going to happen?"

"I'm not sure yet. I need to give Rachel more time. If I proposed to her today, I don't think she'd say yes."

"You can't wait much longer."

"Yes. I know. Maybe in a couple weeks."

He hands me the glass of bourbon. "Drink up."

"No, thank you. I have to go."

He sets the glass down. "You owe me a bottle of scotch. We had a deal."

"Yes. Sorry, I forgot." I walk to the door. "I'll have one sent over. Goodbye, Royce."

I leave and go out to my car. This day has gone far better than I imagined it would. When I left Rachel this morning, I was preparing to get a kill assignment, but it turned out to be a simple cover-up. Then I was prepared to fight with Royce, but instead got a plan for marrying Rachel that might actually work, along with his offer to help. This is turning out to be a very good day.

It turns out to be a good *week* as well. Monday morning, my father is back at work but tells me he has to go out of town again. Some of the potential clients he met with have agreed to do business with us, so my father is going back to Europe to work out some deals. Normally I'd have to go as well, but he needs me to take care of things here, which means I have another few weeks of freedom. More time to spend with Rachel.

So that's what I do. I see her every night and stay at her place on the weekends. We even go shopping again at the mall. I'm starting to like the jeans, so I got another pair and Rachel picked out some casual button-up shirts for me to wear because I only own dress shirts which don't look right with jeans. If my parents saw me dressed in these clothes, they'd be horrified. But they'll never see me wearing them. I usually only wear them when I'm at home or over at Rachel's apartment.

I feel like I'm living a double life and I wonder how much longer I can keep this going. Royce and Jack are the only people who know about Rachel, and so far, they've both kept my secret. Jack has been traveling for business so I haven't been able to meet with him. Royce has also been out of town so I haven't talked to him either.

When my father finally returns, he's so busy catching up on work that he has no time to question me about what I've been up to while he was away. And surprisingly, he doesn't criticize the work I did while he was gone. He has no reason to. My performance actually improved without him here, even though I was working fewer hours. In fact, all of the employees were more productive without my father around. It just shows that his overbearing management style hinders performance and hurts the company. Of course I could never tell him that.

With my father back in the office, I've had to return to working long hours. Some nights I'm there so late I'm unable to see Rachel because she's asleep by the time I leave to go home. I miss seeing her. I've grown accustomed to working normal hours and spending the rest of my time with Rachel, and I want that again. I just haven't yet figured out how to make that happen.

It's now the middle of November. Time is going way too fast. In just a few short weeks Rachel will graduate, and after that I don't know what she plans to do. I know she's looking for jobs, but as far as I know, she hasn't applied for any yet.

We need to start discussing our future. I definitely want to marry her and I think she wants that too, but I'm worried she'll want a long engagement, at least a year, maybe more. But we don't have that kind of time. I need to marry her before Dunamis makes a rule forbidding it.

My other concern is that Rachel will insist on meeting my parents before agreeing to marry me. She keeps asking when I'm going to introduce her to them, but I'm not ready to. I know they'll be furious so I keep avoiding it. If I could avoid it forever I would, but that's not possible. I need to face reality and stop living this secret life with Rachel. Which means I need to make some very big decisions, very soon.

CHAPTER TWENTY-SEVEN

RACHEL

It's Thursday and I'm at Pearce's loft. My afternoon class was canceled so I came here to work on a paper. I get so much more done here than at my own apartment. Pearce's place is super quiet and toasty warm. My apartment is noisy and always freezing because the heat barely works.

It's now six and I thought Pearce would be home by now, but he's not. He just called and said he was running late and that he'd take me out for dinner after he finished up at the office.

Pearce's father got back into town last week and he's making Pearce work all the time. When his father was gone, Pearce cut way back on his hours and I got used to having him around. But now it's back to the way it was when I first met him, where he works nonstop and I hardly ever see him. In fact, this past week I only saw him once, and that was just for a few hours late Tuesday night.

While I wait for Pearce, I decide to watch TV. I settle into the couch and turn on the TV, but then notice the elevator door opening. I jump up to greet Pearce, but it's not him. It's a man who looks like an older version of Pearce, along with an older woman. They're both tall and thin and very well dressed. The man is wearing a black suit and tie, and the woman is in a sleek black dress, topped with a black wool coat.

I stand in front of the elevator. "Hi. Can I help you?"

The elevator opens right into Pearce's loft, but you have to punch in a security code to access this floor and Pearce has never said who else has the code besides him and me. He obviously knows these people, and given how similar the man looks to Pearce, I'm guessing these are his parents. Wait. His parents? I'm not prepared to meet his parents! I'm not even dressed nice. I'm wearing jeans and a sweater and have my hair in a ponytail.

The man and woman walk past me into the living room, looking me up and down.

The man speaks. "I think the better question is, who are *you* and why are you here?"

"She's the maid, dear," the woman says. She directs her attention to me. "How much more time do you need? We could go wait elsewhere until you're done."

"Um, no, I'm not—"

"Is Pearce here?" the man asks, interrupting me.

"No. He'll be here shortly. Are you his family?"

The man goes over to the bar. "I don't see why that's any of your business, but yes. We're his parents."

This is very uncomfortable. They think I'm the cleaning lady? Do I look like the cleaning lady? Why don't they know who I am? I know I haven't met them before, but I thought Pearce would've at least told them about me.

I go up to his mother. "It's nice to finally meet you. I'm Rachel. Pearce's girlfriend."

"Pearce's what?" The man drops the glass he was holding and it shatters on the hardwood floor.

"His girlfriend," I say, hesitantly. Pearce obviously didn't tell them about me.

"Pearce doesn't have a girlfriend," the man says, as he walks back over to me. "And if he did, it certainly wouldn't be you." He eyes me up and down, looking disgusted with my appearance.

I'm trying to be nice, but I already don't like this man. And I don't think I like his wife either. She, too, looks disgusted at my appearance. I don't understand. I'm not dressed up, but I'm not exactly unkempt. I'm wearing a red sweater and my best pair of jeans, but they're looking at me like I'm covered in dirty rags.

"How long have you been seeing him?" the woman asks.

"A few months." I say it softly, suddenly afraid to talk to them. They're very intimidating.

"Months?" The man almost yells it. "That's not possible. If Pearce was seeing someone, I would've known about it. I've had him—" He stops and clears his throat. "I know everything Pearce does, and if he was seeing someone, I would be the first to know."

I say nothing, figuring it's best to keep quiet.

The woman straightens up and lifts her chin, her eyes peering down at me. "What is your name, dear?"

"Rachel."

"Last name," the man orders. "Nobody cares about a first name."

I swallow. "Evans. Rachel Evans."

"Where are you from?" he barks. "And what do your parents do?"

"I'm from a small town in Indiana. My parents have a farm."

He huffs and walks away. "You have got to be kidding me. Is this some kind of joke?" He heads toward the kitchen. "Pearce, are you in here?" He checks the bedroom. "We don't have time for your jokes and I'm not finding your humor to be the least bit funny."

"He's not here," I say. "He said he'd be home around seven, or maybe before, if he finished his work."

The man comes back and stands by his wife. "Pearce is at the office?"

"Yes," I answer.

"When I left there, his office door was closed and the lights were off. I assumed he was here."

"Well, when I talked to him earlier he was at the office."

The man takes his wife's arm. "Eleanor, let's go." He points to me. "I suggest you leave as well. You shouldn't be here."

"But I—" I stop when I hear the elevator door open. I turn and see Pearce standing there, holding a bouquet of red roses, wearing the big smile that's always on his face whenever he greets me.

"Pearce!" His father storms over to him. "Why is this woman in your apartment?"

Pearce drops the flowers, his expression one of sheer panic and shock. "Father, what are you doing here?"

"Your mother and I were going to—never mind. We have other things to discuss, such as who this woman is and why she's here in your apartment."

I wait to see what Pearce will say. But he's standing there, still in shock, not saying anything.

His father speaks again. "She claims to be seeing you. Is that true?"

Pearce looks at me. He can tell how nervous I am and how tense his parents are making me. He goes past his father and puts his arm protectively around me.

"This is Rachel Evans. And yes, we *are* seeing each other and have been for several months." He gently rubs my arm, trying to help me relax. "Rachel, these are my parents, Holton and Eleanor Kensington."

I nod. "Yes. We met earlier."

The man I now know as Holton glares at Pearce. "You think this is funny?"

"This isn't a joke, Father. I'm telling you the truth. Rachel is my girlfriend."

"Why didn't you tell us about her?" his mother asks.

He keeps his eyes on his father. "I think we both know the answer to that."

I'm starting to understand why Pearce never introduced me to his parents. They're not nice people. Not even a little. They're not even nice to their son. They both look like they're about to strangle him. I don't get it. He's 25. A grown man. They shouldn't be getting this upset about who he's dating.

"Get her out of here," Holton orders. "And then you and I are going to have a talk."

Pearce holds me tighter against his side. "She's not going anywhere. If anyone's leaving, it's going to be you."

I can hear Pearce breathing hard and feel the tension in his muscles. He's nervous or angry or both.

"Holton." Eleanor turns to him. "Perhaps we should stay. I'd like to learn more about Rachel."

I can't tell if she's being nice. I get the feeling she isn't. I feel like her decision to stay is so she can get information about me to use against me later.

"I don't think that's a good idea," Pearce says. "I think you two should go."

"Eleanor is right." Holton grins, and not a friendly grin, but a smug grin, like he's determined to do the opposite of whatever Pearce wants. "We need to learn more about this girl. We're going to dinner."

His mother half smiles at me. "I assume you'll want to change clothes and freshen up a little."

Pearce takes my hand. "We'll be right back."

We go in his bedroom and he shuts the door. "Rachel, forgive me for their behavior. They never should have spoken to you that way."

"Why didn't you tell them about me?" I whisper, even though I'm sure they can't hear us.

"Because I knew they would react this way. They're very judgmental and controlling and completely unreasonable. I knew they wouldn't approve of you. I told you that."

"I know you did but I guess...I just didn't think they'd be that...rude. Sorry. I shouldn't say that about them."

"No, you should. They *are* rude. They just don't see it that way. They act this way to anyone who doesn't fit in our world. I told you they don't accept outsiders."

"What are we going to do? Should we go to dinner with them?"

"No. I'll just tell them to leave."

He turns to go but I hold him back. "Wait. Maybe we should go. Maybe things would get better if we all sat down and talked."

"They won't. If anything, they'll get worse before they get better. But if you want to go, we'll go."

"Maybe we shouldn't. Now I'm changing my mind. They really hate me. I'm sure they don't want to have dinner with me."

"They'll make us go to dinner eventually. We might as well get it over with. I'll go out and wait with them while you finish getting ready."

He returns to the living room while I change clothes. I stay here so often that I keep some of my clothes in Pearce's closet. Luckily, I had a dress to change into. It's not that great of a dress, but it's better than wearing jeans.

I can hear Holton in the other room, scolding Pearce like he's a child. I can't hear everything he's saying, but his tone is harsh and condescending. No wonder Pearce avoids his family. I don't know how he puts up with this. Maybe his parents aren't always like this. Maybe they're only acting this way because *I'm* here.

I go in the bathroom and put on more makeup. Then I take my ponytail holder out of my hair and let my natural waves fall over my shoulders and down my back. I brush it out a little and spritz some hair spray over it. That's good enough. I don't want them waiting forever for me to get ready.

When I leave the bedroom, I see the three of them sitting on the couch. They all stand up as I approach.

Pearce smiles and comes up to me. "You look beautiful."

"Thank you," I say quietly.

His parents say nothing. They just stare at me with disgust. When Pearce said people in his world wouldn't approve of me, this isn't what I expected. I thought they'd either ignore me or fake being nice. I didn't think they'd actually come out and express their disapproval so openly like this.

Holton insists we all ride together in his black Mercedes. Pearce and I sit in the back seat and he holds my hand the entire way. His father keeps glancing back at us in the rearview mirror and mumbling things under his breath.

Holton takes us to a very fancy seafood restaurant. The hostess says it will be an hour wait, but when Holton says his name we're immediately seated.

While we wait for our food, Pearce talks to Holton about work, probably hoping to get his father's mind off his anger toward me. But it doesn't work. Holton keeps throwing mean, almost threatening, looks my way and Eleanor tries to avoid looking at me at all.

"Are you done with those financial reports?" Holton asks Pearce.

"No. But I'll get there early tomorrow and get it done."

"You'll go there tonight and get it done. The morning's not soon enough."

"You don't arrive at the office until six. I'll have them ready by then."

"You'll have them ready when I tell you to have them ready. And I want them ready tonight." Holton has been ordering Pearce around like this since we arrived at the restaurant. And when he's not ordering him around, he's insulting him or criticizing him.

Pearce's jaw tightens as he takes short shallow breaths. I hate seeing him so stressed. No wonder his body is always wound so tight. I take Pearce's hand under the table, hoping it will calm him.

Pearce and his father continue to talk about work, and when there's a short break, Eleanor asks me about school. I tell her a little about Hirshfield but her eyes wander to whoever's behind me, like she's lost all interest in what I have to say.

"Rachel is an expert in American History," Pearce says, trying to get her attention back. "She works at a museum and gives tours. She tailors each tour to her audience. I went on one of them and it was excellent."

"Speaking of museums," Holton says. "Your mother ran into Rielle last week at a benefit for the art museum. Rielle was asking about you."

"Father, we were talking about Rachel's job. Perhaps you'd like to ask her about it."

I prepare for Holton's question, but instead of asking me about the museum, he says, "My son was in a relationship with Rielle, and likely still is." He smirks. "I hope you didn't think you were the only woman in his life."

"Father, that's enough!" Pearce lets go of my hand. "You and I need to step outside. I'd like to speak to you alone."

Just as he says it, our food arrives, so Pearce and his father remain at the table. My meal looks delicious, but I don't have much of an appetite. Holton and Eleanor have me so uptight my stomach hurts. I eat what I can, in between Eleanor's questions.

"Who is your designer?" she asks, patting the edge of her mouth with her napkin.

"I'm not sure what you mean."

"Your clothes. Who styles you?"

She knows I don't have a stylist so why is she asking? Just to prove how wrong I am for her son? How I don't fit in his world?

"I'm my own stylist." I say it with confidence. I've had it with their put downs. They already don't like me, so what do I have to lose by sticking up for myself?

"What salon do you go to?"

"I go to one near campus. It's very small. I'm sure you've never heard of it." I smile at her, and I'm going to keep smiling through the rest of dinner. Maybe I can kill them with kindness. "I like your earrings," I tell her. "They're beautiful."

She touches the large square diamond on her left earlobe. "Holton bought them for me for our twentieth wedding anniversary."

"Do you like expensive jewelry?" Holton asks me as he cuts into his salmon with his fork. "Is that why you're pursuing Pearce?"

"Father, stop it!"

I rub Pearce's arm and whisper to him. "It's okay." I direct my attention back to his father. "To answer your question, Mr. Kensington, no, I am not interested in expensive jewelry. I'm dating your son because I think he's a kind and caring man and I enjoy spending time with him. You're very lucky to have him for a son."

Holton huffs. "You obviously don't know him." He stares at Pearce. "He's a complete disappointment as a son."

I want to reach across the table and slap him. How dare he say that. How could he even *think* that?

Pearce seems unaffected by the comment, like he's used to his father's abuse. But I'm not used to it and it makes me furious.

"Your son graduated from both Harvard and Yale. You can't possibly tell me you're not proud of him."

"Rachel," Pearce says quietly, urging me not to continue this.

"He was only admitted to those schools because of my connections," Holton says. "And because of the Kensington

314

name. A name he disparages when he refuses to work hard and put in the time and effort needed to grow our company."

I can't believe he just said that. He really thinks Pearce doesn't work hard? Is he serious? I know I should keep quiet, but I can't. "Your son works harder than anyone I know. How can you even—" I stop when Eleanor interrupts me.

"When do you graduate?" she asks.

I take a moment to compose myself. "December."

"And what are your plans for after graduation?"

"I'm hoping to get a job at a museum in New York."

"They won't hire you," Holton says. "The Manhattan museums hire only the best. There are candidates far more qualified than you. Ones who attended an Ivy League school."

Pearce sets his fork down. "If you continue this, Father, Rachel and I will be leaving. We came here for you to get to know her, not to insult her all evening."

"I will do as I please," he says. "And you will not disrespect me by speaking to me that way."

Pearce turns to me. "Rachel, would you like to leave?"

He says it calmly, but his face is red with anger. We've only eaten half of our dinners, but it would probably be good to get out of here. Pearce's temper continues to rise the longer we're here.

"Maybe it would be for the best." I turn to his mother. "Unless you'd like us to stay, Mrs. Kensington."

"No. Leave," Holton says. "I've had enough of my son's insubordination. And Pearce, you need to go into the office and get those reports done."

Pearce ignores the comment and stands up, pulling my chair out for me.

I smile at his parents. "It was very nice to meet both of you." It really wasn't, but I was brought up to be polite, even to people as hateful as this.

Eleanor nods while Holton just continues eating. As we're leaving the table, Pearce stops suddenly. I turn back and see Holton has a tight hold on Pearce's arm.

"End this," he says through gritted teeth. "Now."

Pearce rips his arm back and places it around me, then leads us to the coat check. He's fuming mad so I keep quiet as the woman goes to get our coats. The hostess calls us a cab and we wait in the bar for it to arrive. Pearce is quiet and tense and still very angry, so I just sit next to him and hold his hand.

A few minutes later the cab shows up and takes us back to Pearce's loft. When we get inside, we take off our coats and he leads me to the couch to sit down.

"I'm very sorry about tonight," he says.

"I'm sorry, too. I didn't know your father treated you like that. I couldn't take hearing him say those things to you."

"I don't care about myself. I'm used to it. But I won't stand for him or my mother treating you that way."

"Well, you warned me. I just didn't believe you. I've never met anyone like them."

"Everyone I know is like them. That's why I've tried so hard to keep you away from that side of my life."

"But if we're going to be together, I'll have to be part of it. I won't have a choice."

"I know," he says with a heavy sigh, almost like he's questioning our future together. Is it because of *me*? Does he think I won't want to be with him because of his parents? If so, that's not true at all.

I move closer to him. "Pearce, what happened tonight doesn't change anything. I love you and I want to be with you. I don't care what your parents, or anyone else, thinks."

"Rachel." He pauses, like he's not sure he wants to say whatever he's about to say.

Wait. Is *he* the one who's changing his mind about us? Is he going to break up with me? Is that why he was so quiet while we waited for the cab? And why he barely said two words on the ride here? Was his parents' reaction to me enough to convince him to end our relationship?

I wasn't prepared for this. I wasn't even thinking about it. I thought he'd fight for us, not just do what his parents told him to do. But now, I think he's about to end this.

CHAPTER TWENTY-EIGHT

RACHEL

"What is it, Pearce?"

He holds my hands. "I've been thinking about you, and us, and where I see this relationship going."

He pauses again and it's making me nervous.

"And?" I say, my heart beating fast.

"I need to know if we're on the same page."

"Okay. So what are you thinking?"

"I want a future with you." He looks directly at me as he says it. "And I need to know if you feel the same way."

So he's not breaking up with me. He's doing the opposite. Telling me he wants a future with me. Future, as in marriage?

"Wait, you're not—"

"No." I must look anxious because he smiles and says, "I don't have a ring in my pocket. But yes, when I said future, I meant marriage. What are your thoughts about that?"

I don't answer right away. Because what *are* my thoughts about that? I love him and I want to be with him, but I'm not ready to commit to marrying him. At least not yet.

"Rachel?" He squeezes my hand, a concerned look on his face. "What do you think?"

I need to answer him. It's not a hard question. He's not asking me to marry him tomorrow. Just sometime in the future.

"I feel the same way," I say, still shocked we're even having this conversation. Where did this come from? Why is he bringing this up now? Tonight?

"I was hoping you'd say that." He hugs me to his chest. I feel his body relax and wonder if it's because he's away from his father or because he's relieved at my answer about our future. This is the first time we've talked about it and I think he was worried I'd tell him I didn't feel the same way. That I wasn't sure I wanted a future with him, especially after meeting his parents.

"But it's kind of crazy, isn't it?"

He pulls back and looks at me. "Why would it be crazy?"

"Because we haven't dated that long."

"I love you, Rachel. And you love me. So what does it matter how long we've known each other?"

"I guess it doesn't."

"When I know I want something, I don't wait for it. I go after it and get it. And I think I've made it very clear that I want you in my life."

His words have my mind racing to figure out what this means. Is Pearce planning to propose to me? Soon? Am I ready for that? It's not that I haven't thought about it or don't want it. I'm just not sure that I'm ready. This isn't what I planned. I was supposed to graduate and move to New York, not get married and stay in Connecticut. What would I do for a job? I'd be married to a billionaire, so I wouldn't need a job but I'd still want one. I wouldn't want to sit around doing nothing all day.

"Rachel." Pearce is now sitting back, watching me. "Why are you so quiet?"

"Sorry. I didn't mean to be." I get up from the couch. "I think I'm going to head home."

As much as I'd love to spend the night with him, I need to go back to my apartment and think about this. I didn't know we'd be talking about marriage tonight and I'm suddenly feeling very anxious. I'm also a little excited. And a little happy. But also scared. My emotions are all over the place.

He stands up. "Is something wrong? Are you still upset because of my parents?"

"No. I just need to go back to my apartment and get some things done before class tomorrow." I turn away but he catches my wrist.

318

"Are you sure there's nothing wrong?"

"Nothing's wrong." I kiss him. "I just need to go home." I walk back to the bedroom and get my overnight bag and meet him at the elevator. He has a worried expression on his face, so I set my bag down and hug him. "I love you." I give him a kiss. "Before I go, I need to say something, and I need you to listen very carefully."

He nods. "Go ahead."

I set my eyes on his. "Don't you ever listen to your father. You are the smartest, hardest working person I know. You're also kind and generous and thoughtful and so many other great things. And if your father can't see that, then he's completely blind. He should be beaming with pride having a son like you."

Pearce is quiet. I can't tell what he's thinking. I know he isn't comfortable talking about his father, but I had to say something. I don't want Pearce ever believing his father's hateful words.

His hands reach up and hold my face. He leans in and presses his lips to my forehead. "I love you," he breathes out. "So much." We stand there a moment, then he lowers his lips to mine and kisses me. "Call me when you get home so I know you're safe."

"I will." I hug him one last time, then go down to my car. As I'm driving back, I think about that dinner and how Holton treated Pearce and the awful things he said to him. My parents have never said such hateful things to me. They wouldn't talk that way to their worst enemy.

When I get home, I call Pearce to let him know I made it. Then I tell him again how much I love him. I don't think it's possible for him to hear it too many times. After growing up with parents like Holton and Eleanor, Pearce needs to know what it's like to be loved and I'm going to be the one to show him.

After witnessing that scene at the restaurant, I feel like I understand Pearce better. I now know why Pearce has so much sadness in his eyes. Why he always seems so tense and stressed. And why he looked so surprised when I first told him I love him. Even now, he looks surprised when I tell him I love him, like he can't imagine why anyone would. It breaks my heart.

For the rest of the night, I think about Pearce and what it would be like to have a future with him. And the truth is, I don't know what it would be like. I know nothing about his world and how it works. But I'm not sure that matters. What matters is that I love him. And that *he* loves *me*. He treats me better than I've ever been treated. He's gentle and caring and affectionate and considerate and protective and loving. When I close my eyes and think of him, I can see us together years from now. I can see us married and living in a house and maybe having a child. Despite what my doctor said, I still hold out hope that maybe he was wrong and that I actually could have a child someday. And I would love to have that child with Pearce.

The more I think about a future with Pearce, the more I want it. And maybe that future will start sooner rather than later. Like Pearce said, if we love each other, why wait?

Before I go to sleep, I call Pearce one more time to say goodnight. It's midnight, but I know he's still up. He only sleeps a few hours a night unless I'm there with him. Maybe I should've stayed with him tonight. He needs to sleep. He's been so tired ever since his father got back to town and made him go back to working sixteen hour days.

Pearce's phone rings and rings but he doesn't answer. I can't imagine he'd be asleep and not hear the phone. I hope he's not at the office. I call there just to check.

"This is Pearce," he says when he answers.

"Pearce, it's Rachel. What are you doing at the office? It's after midnight."

"I have to get these reports done for my father."

"The reports can wait. You need to sleep."

"It won't take me long to finish these. A couple hours, if that."

"A couple hours? Pearce, by the time you get home, you'll only get a few hours sleep before you have to get up for work."

"It's fine. I'm used to it." I hear some papers shuffling. "Is something wrong? Why are you calling so late?"

"Nothing's wrong. I just wanted to say goodnight. And that I love you."

"I love you too." I'm silent and he laughs a little. "Was there anything else? Not that I'm not happy you called. It's just that it's late and you should probably get to sleep."

"Yes, I, um, had something else to say."

"Go ahead."

"I felt bad about racing out of your place like that. You probably thought it meant something and I don't want you getting the wrong idea. I just needed some time to think."

"Rachel, it's fine. I understand. I brought that up out of the blue and I know you weren't expecting it. But it's how I feel and I wanted you to know. I hope you didn't feel like I was pressuring you in any way."

"No. Not at all. I'm glad you brought it up." I pause. "I thought about what you said tonight and…" I'm not sure how to say this so I turn it back on him. "Pearce, do you ever picture us in the future? I mean, do you ever see images of us in your head, together, years from now?"

"I do. All the time."

I smile. "I do too. I mean, I did tonight. I pictured that. Us. Together."

The phone is quiet, but then I hear him again. "What are you saying, Rachel?"

"I'm saying that I want this to continue. I want a life with you, Pearce. I know I need to figure some things out, like what I'm going to do after I graduate and where I'm going to work. But right now, I'm not worried about any of that. We'll figure it out later. Right now, I just need you to know that I don't want this to end. I love you, and I don't want to be with anyone else. Ever."

There's silence on his end of the phone and I start to worry that I said too much. I wasn't saying he had to propose to me anytime soon. I just wanted to let him know I want to be with him. I didn't want him to doubt it, which I thought he might after I ran out on him like that.

He finally speaks. "Would you mind if I came over?"

"Right now?"

"I know it's late, but I have to see you."

"But what about work?"

"I'll come back here in a couple hours. I'll still have time to get the reports done before my father gets here."

"I could just meet you at your loft."

"I don't want you out driving this late. It's not safe."

I smile. I'm starting to like how he worries about me. It just shows how much he loves me. "Come on over. I'll wait up."

In record time he's at my door, a huge smile on his face. He comes inside and wraps his arms around me, tightly, but not too tight, exactly how I taught him.

I hug him back, my head resting on his chest, hearing his strong, fast heartbeat.

"God, I love you," he says, not letting me go. "I love you so much it scares me."

I lift my head up to look at him. "Why does it scare you?"

"Because I don't want to lose you." His voice is quiet, his hand gently pressing my head back to his chest. "I'm afraid of losing you," he says in almost a whisper.

"You won't lose me, Pearce. I just told you I want to be with you."

"I know. I just—" He stops.

"You just what?"

"Nothing," he says, his voice trailing off.

We make our way to the bedroom and just lie there, quietly, on the bed. Pearce is holding me in his arms, which he always does, but it feels different this time. It feels more protective, like he won't let any harm come to me. I don't know why, but he always acts like he's worried something bad might happen to me. Maybe it's just because he's rich, and money tends to attract bad people. Maybe he's had trouble in the past. It's another part of his world I haven't yet been exposed to. And although I realize there might be risks that come from being with someone with his kind of wealth, I don't worry because I know he'll keep me safe. He'd do anything for me. I know he would. And I would do anything for him.

I feel his hand move down my arm. I look up and he kisses me. Soft, sweet kisses. I can feel his love in each and every one. When I first met him, our attraction to each other was so intense, I worried our relationship would be nothing more than sex. We

322

still have that intense attraction, but our relationship is so much more than physical. I think it always has been. There was something between us that first time we met. A connection I couldn't really explain. And I loved the way he looked at me and listened to me, giving me his full attention, like I was important, even though he'd just met me. Unlike his parents, Pearce has never judged me for not having money and that says a lot about him as a person.

I never believed in love at first sight, but now I do. I think part of me fell in love with Pearce on that first day we met. I just wasn't aware of it at the time.

His kisses and caresses eventually lead to sex and then we fall asleep. Pearce set the alarm to go off at 3 a.m. so he can get back to work. I wish he didn't have to go. He's so tired. He needs to rest. But he doesn't want to deal with his father throwing a fit if the work's not done.

In the morning, I wake up and he's gone. I didn't even hear him leave. I turn to check the time and see a note sitting on my nightstand. It's from Pearce and reads, *Have a wonderful day. I'll come by your place after work. I'll bring dinner. See you soon. I love you.—Pearce.*

I read it again, smiling as I do. And the smile remains as I shower and dress and do my hair.

As I'm eating breakfast, I check my answering machine and notice a message from my mom.

I call her back. "Hey, Mom, it's me."

"Hi, honey. I couldn't reach you last night and then I remembered you said you were with Pearce."

"Yeah, I got back late. I didn't want to call and wake you up."

"Did you have a nice evening?"

"I finally met Pearce's parents. They stopped over last night and we all went out for dinner."

"How did it go?"

"Not well. They don't approve of me."

"That's not surprising."

"Mom! What's that supposed to mean?"

323

"Honey, I'm not referring to you, personally. I just meant that we aren't wealthy. I'm sure his family expects him to be with someone within his social class."

"Well, they need to get over it because Pearce and I are very happy and we have no plans to break up." I pause. "In fact, we've been talking about the future."

"Rachel, what are you saying? Are you engaged?"

"No." I smile. "But I might be soon."

"How soon?"

"I'm not sure. I just know Pearce is thinking about it."

"Honey, you're not ready for that. You've only dated him a few months."

"You dated Dad for twelve days."

"Which wasn't long enough. We should've waited longer before getting married."

"Why? What difference would that have made? You've been happily married for thirty years."

"Yes, but your father and I got married in a different era. These days people date for a year or two, then spend a year engaged. It gives them time to get to know each other."

"I don't need all that time. I already know Pearce."

"I doubt you know everything about him."

"Maybe not, but I know I love him and that's what counts."

"You said you loved Adam and look how that ended."

"I wasn't in love with him. I just thought I was. I didn't know what love was back then, but now I do. Mom, I really do love Pearce and I don't want to wait to have a future with him."

"You need to slow this down and give yourself time to think. I don't want you rushing into something."

"Let's not talk about this. We obviously disagree and I don't want to fight."

"Honey, I didn't mean to—"

"Please. Just talk about something else."

She sighs. "I wanted to ask you when you'll be arriving for Thanksgiving."

"I'm not sure yet."

"Rachel, it's next week. You need to get a plane ticket."

"I know. But I need to talk to Pearce first."

"Why would you need to talk to Pearce?"

"Because I…" I don't even want to say this. I know she'll be upset, but she needs to understand that I can't always have every holiday with her. "Mom, I was thinking I'd just stay here."

"Oh." She sounds sad. "So you're not coming home?"

"It's not that I don't want to. It's just that I'll be home again at Christmas and it's expensive to fly home for just a few days."

"Rachel, you know your father and I will pay for it. I'll get the ticket for you. Just tell me when you want to leave."

I need to fess up and tell her the real reason I want to stay.

"Mom, I know you want me home but…I want to spend Thanksgiving here. With Pearce. I don't want to leave him all alone with his parents. They're horrible people. They're verbally abusive and I don't want his holiday ruined by them."

"I didn't know things were so bad for him. I'm sorry to hear that."

"I didn't know how bad it was until I met his parents. You wouldn't believe how they talk to him. They didn't say one nice thing to him the entire evening. And his father…all he did was criticize Pearce. He shouldn't have to put up with that at Thanksgiving."

"Have you talked to him about this? About his plans for Thanksgiving?"

"No. I assume he's planning to be with his family, so I guess I need to talk to him before I decide anything."

"Why don't you bring him here? He's certainly welcome and it would give your father and me a chance to get to know him."

"Really? You wouldn't mind if I brought him home for Thanksgiving?"

"Of course not. Honey, why would you even think that?"

"Because you always act like you don't approve of him."

"I never said that. I just wanted you to be careful and not get hurt. But I can tell how much you love him. You've been talking about him nonstop for months so it's about time your father and I meet him."

"Thanks, Mom. I'll talk to Pearce and get back to you. I have to run to class. We'll talk later."

I'm so happy she reacted that way. And that she wants Pearce to come home with me. I can't wait for them to meet him. I know they'll love him as much as I do.

CHAPTER TWENTY-NINE

PEARCE

I got back to the office at 3:45 this morning and just finished the reports. It's 5:50 and my father usually arrives promptly at six. I leave the reports in his office, then go back to my desk and call Royce. It's time to do the plan we discussed. We never agreed on the timing but I can't wait any longer. Now that my father's met Rachel, he'll do anything to keep us apart.

I just hope Royce doesn't back out of the plan. He's the only one I know who can help me with this. Jack doesn't know about it, and even if he did, I know he wouldn't help me. It's too risky, and although he likes taking risks, I don't think he'll take one when it comes to this. There's too much at stake.

But Royce? He loves taking risks. The bigger, the better. He's reckless and always has been. He craves the excitement that comes with doing something he shouldn't, so I know he'll help me.

His phone rings repeatedly until he finally picks up.

"Hello?" He sounds groggy. I'm sure I woke him up. He doesn't have a job so he can sleep as late as he wants.

"Royce, it's Pearce."

"Pearce?" I hear a loud noise, like he's fumbling for his clock. "It's not even six o'clock. Why the fuck are you calling me at this hour?"

"What are you doing today?"

"You called to ask what I'm doing today? Do I need to remind you what time it is?"

"I need your help. I'll explain later, but for now I need to know if you can go into the city with me."

He groans and then I hear him yawn. "Why? What's this about?"

"I'll tell you when I get to your place. Can you do it or not?"

He sighs. "Yeah. I'm going there anyway. I have to meet with my speech coach at two."

Royce is already being trained for his future as a politician. That's his "job" if you want to call it that. Part of his training includes being taught how to give speeches. He's also being trained in how to perform in debates and answer questions from the press.

"That's perfect. It will give us an excuse."

"An excuse for what?" he asks, yawning loudly into the phone.

"An excuse for why I need to go into the city. I'm going to sit in on your speech practice. You wanted my opinion and that's why I'm going with you."

"What the hell are you talking about? Is this a dream? Am I even awake?"

"Listen to me. If my father calls you, tell him you asked me to go to Manhattan with you to critique your speech. Then tell him we're going out for dinner and drinks."

"Why would I—"

"Royce! Just do this for me. You said you'd help me."

"This is for that girl, isn't it?" He yawns as he talks.

"We'll talk about it later. Now will you do it or not?"

"Yes, fine. Do you really think your dad will call me to check your story?"

"I know he will."

He laughs. "The man treats you like a five-year-old. Is he ever going to let you grow up?"

"Get up and get dressed. I'll be over there at eight." I hang up before he asks me any more questions. I can't talk about this here, especially since my father will be arriving any second.

"Pearce."

I look up and there he is, standing at the door to my office. He's going to yell at me about Rachel. I'm surprised he didn't call me last night and do it.

"Good morning, Father. I left the reports on your desk."

"Yes. I saw them. For once, you actually did a halfway decent job on them."

I nod, acknowledging his compliment. To most people, it wouldn't seem like a compliment, but for him it is. This is odd. Why is he complimenting me instead of yelling at me?

He motions to me. "Weren't you wearing those clothes at dinner last night?"

And here it is. He's going to accuse me of spending the night with Rachel and then he'll order me to never see her again.

I glance down at my white shirt and gray striped tie. "I didn't have a chance to go home and change. Those reports took me all night."

"Good. I'm glad you're finally putting in some effort. Doing some real work for a change."

I ignore his insult and focus on the fact that he still hasn't asked me about Rachel. It's making me nervous. Why hasn't he said anything about her?

"I talked to Jack last night," he says.

Jack? Why would he call Jack? He hates Jack.

He continues. "He said that woman you were with is nothing more than a fling. A physical relationship because you were bored with the associates."

I say nothing. I have no idea what else Jack told him so it's best if I keep quiet.

"So was that just some game you were playing?" He sounds angry now. "Pretending you were actually with that woman simply to upset your mother and me?"

"I didn't expect you to stop by. It took me by surprise and I didn't know how to explain her to you."

He watches my face, searching for any clues that I'm lying. "Well, I won't stand for it again. You should have sent that woman home."

I take a folder from the stack on my desk. "I need to finish some things so if you don't mind, I—"

"I understand you want variety, Pearce. You're young and the world is full of beautiful women. Even a man my age can't help himself sometimes. But you need to use better judgment. Keep it hidden."

As someone who has sex with his secretaries here in the office, he's the last person who should be giving me advice on that. But I play along.

"Yes, Father. I'll try to be more discreet."

He checks behind him to make sure nobody's around. "There's a vote coming up at the end-of-the-year meeting."

He's referring to the organization. At the end of the year, we always have a weeklong meeting where things are discussed and voted on.

"A vote about what?"

"The rule we've proposed that says our members can only be involved with women on the approved list. I'm not referring to sexual flings like you had with that woman, although that too is frowned upon. What I was referring to is an actual relationship with a woman. The proposed rule will only allow for relationships with women who have been approved."

My pulse races, but I fight back any kind of response, my face expressionless.

"That doesn't seem necessary," I say. "No member has ever shown interest in a woman who didn't fit the criteria."

"Actually, Randolph's son, Ezra, was seeing a waitress last summer and his father didn't find out until months later."

"And what happened?"

"Ezra had already called it off with the woman by the time his father found out. Of course his father still punished him."

"Why was he punished? There's no rule against what he did."

Shit. Why did I say that? I know why he was punished. Dammit! I try to backpedal my way out of this. "What I mean is that maybe Ezra wasn't aware of the rule since it's not official."

He huffs. "Everyone knows the damn rule. Ezra just chose not to follow it. Which is why we need to make it official. Now he, and all the other members, will be *forced* to follow it. In fact, I've suggested we take the vote at the next meeting rather than wait until the end of the year. Everyone will vote yes so there's no need to have a discussion about it."

I nod, struggling to hide the anxiety building inside me. Now I definitely have to go through with my plan. If I don't, I'll lose Rachel forever. But what's going to happen when they find out what I've done? My parents will probably disown me. Take away my inheritance. But what concerns me even more is what the other members might do to me. If they'll punish me, and if so, what that punishment will be.

"Go home and change, Pearce. You're a mess."

"I will. I just need to finish up a few things first."

"You need to go now. Our employees will be here soon and I don't want them seeing you in a wrinkled shirt."

"Fine." I stand up. "But I won't be coming back today. Royce called me last night and asked if I would sit in on his coaching session. He wants an outside opinion of his public speaking skills and I told him I'd do it."

My father crosses his arms, his eyes narrowed. "You should've asked me first."

"I didn't think I needed to. We both know Royce plays a critical role in their future plans. Therefore I assumed you would approve of this, and perhaps even encourage me to help him."

My father considers it. He values the organization as much as he values our company and he'll do most anything to help them achieve their goals. Getting Royce elected to the Senate in a few years is one of their goals so I know my father will go along with this. But since he didn't suggest it, he has to ponder it and act like he's doing me a favor by agreeing to it.

"So you're going into the city?" His question is his answer. He's letting me go, but he won't come out and say it.

"Yes. We're spending the day there, and after his coaching session we're going out for dinner and drinks."

"Very good. I'm pleased that you're renewing your friendship with Royce. He has a very bright future in politics and it would be good if you were associated with him."

I knew Royce was the right person to help me with this. In fact, he's perfect. My father sees Royce as someone who will help boost the Kensington name, which is of utmost importance to him. When I was an undergrad at Yale, my father forced me to be friends with Royce because even back then, the organization was eyeing him as a possible political candidate. My father always wanted me to go into politics but since I wasn't chosen, he wanted me to be friends with someone who was headed down that path. Because politicians have power and prestige—two things my father already has, but always wants more of.

I grab my coat, then stand at the door in front of my father. "I'll check in with you later to see if you have any questions regarding those reports."

"Tell Royce I said hello."

"I will. Goodbye, Father." I walk past him into the hall and hurry out to my car.

As I'm driving away from the office, I feel a sense of exhilaration. I just lied to my father and he believed me. He can always tell when I'm lying but today he couldn't. I guess all those sessions with the body language coach are finally paying off. If I can fool my father, I can fool anyone.

Jack lied to him too. I'm surprised he did it. I hadn't even considered that my father would call him. But my father knows Jack keeps a close eye on everyone around him, including fellow members. I'm sure my father assumed Jack was spying on me. Or maybe my father asked him to. That sounds like something he would do. Luckily, Jack didn't tell him the truth. I wonder if Jack's spying on me right now. I check behind me but nobody appears to be following me. If Jack knew what I was doing, I'm sure he'd try to stop me, and since he's not, he must not be watching me.

So now my plan begins. I don't know if it's going to work. I have no idea if Rachel will agree to it. But I'm going to try. I'm going to do more than try. I'm going to convince her to do it. Because if I don't, we'll never have another chance to do this again. They're voting in a few weeks, or maybe even sooner if my father gets his way. And if they vote yes, I won't be allowed to be with Rachel. There will be an official rule against it and I don't want to even know the punishment for breaking that rule. But as of today, there is no rule, at least not an official one. So this is my only chance. We have to do this. And we have to do it soon.

When I arrive at Royce's townhouse, he tells me my father has already called to check my story. It infuriates me the way he keeps tabs on me like that. But I let it go, refusing to let it put me in a bad mood. I knew he'd call Royce. It's not like it was a surprise.

I sit down with Royce and explain why the plan we discussed must be done now and not later. Then we go over the details.

"They're still going to punish you," he says, as he puts on his tie. When I arrived, he'd showered but was still in his bathrobe. He takes forever to get ready. He's always been like that. I don't know what the hell takes him so long.

"They can't punish me," I tell him. "That's why I need to hurry and do this. As of right now, there's no rule forbidding it."

"And when has that stopped them?" He adjusts his tie in front of the large framed mirror that hangs above the bar. "If they want to punish you, they will."

"Then I'll take the punishment. They can do whatever they want to me. I don't care. All I care about is being with Rachel."

He takes his suit jacket from the back of the couch and slips it on. "They could fuck with your company. Your father would kill you if that happened."

"Royce, I'm not going to worry about what-if scenarios. We're doing this. And whatever happens after that, we'll figure out later."

He stands in front of me. "And what about *me*? I have a lot at stake here."

"You're the one who wanted to take the risk. Are you changing your mind? Afraid of them now?"

He straightens up. "No. Of course not. I'm not afraid of anyone, especially them."

It's a lie. He tries to pretend he doesn't care, but I know he fears them. If he didn't, he wouldn't be getting a rush out of doing this. His fear of what they might do if they found out the truth makes this all the more exciting to him.

"I'll do all I can to minimize any damage that might come your way when this is over," I say. "But if we stick to the plan, they'll have no reason to suspect you had any part in this. For all you knew, it was just a guy's weekend in Vegas. You do that all the time. They'll think nothing of it."

"I suppose you're right." He smiles. "And I do get a trip to Vegas out of it. Maybe I'll stay there and skip out on Thanksgiving. I'm supposed to go to Victoria's house for dinner. Bond with the future in-laws. All that shit." He shakes his head.

"Are you tired of Victoria already?"

He shrugs. "It could be worse. She'll make an adequate wife. I've made it clear I won't be faithful to her and she accepts that. I *will* have to have children with her to fit the role of the family man politician, but I'd planned to have children anyway. I didn't really care who the mother was."

I pat him on the back. "You're so sentimental, Royce."

He goes to the bar to get a drink. "Some of us are smart enough to know better than to actually fall in love with a woman."

"Believe me. I didn't plan on this."

It's only eight in the morning but he's pouring himself some scotch. "So what's it like?"

"What?"

"Being in love." He chuckles. "Because I guarantee it's not going to happen to me. I'll make sure of it."

I smile as an image of Rachel pops in my head. "I can't quite put it into words. All I can say is that she makes me happier than I've ever felt. And she's so damn beautiful. Not just on the outside. She's also a beautiful person. Sweet, kind, caring. I've never met anyone like her and I'm certain I never will again. Whenever I'm around her I'm—"

He interrupts me, coughing on his drink and putting his hand up. "Enough. I can't listen to this. Do you hear yourself? And you should see your face. You look like one of those lovesick idiots you always see in movies. Only it's worse because you're not acting. This is real. I've never seen you like this, Pearce. You sound like a damn woman." He swigs the rest of his drink. "We need to get out of here before you start crying or get your period."

I laugh. "You need to fall in love, Royce. It'd be good for you."

He takes his coat from the rack by the door. "If I ever fall in love, just kill me. My life will be over."

I meet him at the door, preparing to tell him he's wrong. That being in love makes you feel like your life is just beginning. But then I change my mind. He wouldn't understand. He has no interest in falling in love or being in love. He likes being with a different woman every night. I used to like it too, back when I was younger. But then it got tiring. I wanted more than just sex. But I accepted that as my life and never thought it'd be any different. I didn't even think real love existed. Until I met Rachel. The woman who taught me how to love. The woman who fills my thoughts. Fills my heart. Makes me want to do better. Be a better man. And hopefully, the woman who will soon be my wife.

When we get to the city, we go to Royce's apartment, which is on the upper west side of Manhattan. He shares the place with his brother, William. They use it whenever they're in the city. But since William's in school at Harvard, he doesn't get down here much so Royce has basically made the place his own, changing the decor to fit his taste.

After I leave Royce, I head down to the diamond district. I want to get Rachel the perfect ring and that could take all day. I'll know the perfect ring when I see it. Rachel and I have never talked about engagement rings, but I know what she'd like. Or I at least think I do. Actually, I'm not getting what I know she'd pick out because I know she'd choose too small of a diamond. And the wife of Pearce Kensington cannot have a small diamond. It wouldn't look right and people would talk. Plus, I want her to have a beautiful ring with a large diamond that shimmers and sparkles as much as she does. She brings so much light into my life that I feel like it radiates off me whenever she's around. And I want that radiance to be proudly displayed on her finger when she's my wife.

My wife. Shit. What if she says no? What if she says she's not ready? That she needs more time? We don't have more time! We have to do this now. We can't wait. But I can't tell her why, so how am I ever going to convince her to do this?

Three hours later, I find the perfect ring. I also buy her diamond earrings and a diamond necklace. Then I go to Fifth Avenue to finish my shopping. On the drive into the city this morning, I called my personal shopper and arranged to have her meet me here. She already has things picked out when I arrive at each store. Some casual clothes for Rachel to change into when we arrive. A beautiful assortment of lingerie for our evenings together. And finally, the dress. There are several options to choose from and I pick the one I know Rachel will like the best.

By the end of the day, I'm exhausted. All of my purchases, except for the ring, are packed away on the Sinclair jet that Rachel, Royce, and I will be taking to Vegas. Royce is coming along so people will believe our guys' weekend in Vegas story. We won't be sharing that story until we're already there. And when we call our families, we'll make sure we sound extremely drunk. Like we got drunk while still in New York and decided to take Royce's jet to Vegas. This isn't unusual behavior for Royce, but it is for me. I normally wouldn't do something like that, but Royce has a way of persuading people to do things they normally wouldn't do, which is why I think my father might actually believe my story. And he shouldn't be too upset by it. After all, he wanted me to be better friends with Royce, which is exactly what I'm doing, or what he thinks I'm doing.

I checked in with Royce this afternoon and he said he already had people working on the press release that will be sent out once Rachel and I are married. The announcement will appear on all the news outlets before we even get back to Connecticut.

The press release will announce that Rachel and I got engaged, not married, and that our wedding will be in the spring. Only our families and the organization will know the truth. I'm only telling the organization because if I'm already legally married, they can't forbid it. It'll be too late. And as Royce pointed out, my father won't try to stop the fake wedding in the spring because it would reflect poorly on me. I need to appear mature and responsible, and calling off an engagement would make me look like I'm neither one of those things. My short marriage to Kristina got me enough negative press. I can't afford to have any more.

Around four, I head back to Connecticut. Royce remains in New York. We'll meet up at the airport later tonight, as long as everything goes as planned.

I go back to my loft and pack my bag, then shower and shave and put on a suit. If I had more time, I'd plan a big, elaborate proposal, but that's not possible now, and truthfully, I don't think Rachel would want something big and elaborate. She'd prefer something simpler, and hopefully that's just me in a suit with a ring, because that's all I have time for.

At 5:45 I knock on her door, my heart pounding. I'm nervous. Extremely nervous. Not about marrying her, but about her answer. Because if she says no, this will be the end for us. And it can't be. I need her in my life. I won't even have a life if she's not in it.

She didn't have to work at the museum today so she's been home for a couple hours. I called her and told her I was heading over. She thinks we're just going on a date. Out for dinner and maybe a movie.

When she opens the door, I feel myself smiling. One of those big, idiotic smiles that happen automatically every time I see her. It just confirms how much I love her. How much she lightens my dark, lonely world. How much she fills me with happiness.

"Pearce." She smiles and pulls me inside her apartment. It's overflowing with tulips in vases scattered around the room. I ordered fifteen dozen in different colors and had them delivered earlier today.

Rachel looks beautiful as always. She has her hair down in long, soft waves and she's wearing the blue dress she wore on our first date. It's more of a summery dress that's sleeveless so she's wearing a white cardigan sweater to cover her arms. She doesn't have many clothes, but she will soon. If she's my wife, she can have all the clothes she wants.

I pull her into my arms and kiss her. She smells like lavender from the soap she uses. I love that scent. I find it calming, probably because I associate it with her.

"I see you received the flowers," I say.

"Yes. And thank you. They're gorgeous. But why so many? It looks like a floral shop in here."

"You like tulips."

She smiles at me. She doesn't need me to explain. She knows I tend to go overboard on things. And hopefully, she'll keep that in mind when I pull out the ring.

"Why are you so dressed up?"

I kiss her. "I'm not dressed up. I always wear a suit."

"Not on our dates. Did you come here straight from work?"

"I wasn't at work today."

"You weren't?"

"No. I was shopping."

"Shopping?" She laughs. I love her laugh. "You hate shopping."

"Yes. But it had to be done."

"What did you shop for?"

"I'll tell you in a minute. First, I have to ask you something."

"Okay. Go ahead."

My heart is now pounding even harder. I try to control my breathing, but she notices the up and down movement of my chest.

She takes my hand. "Pearce, are you okay?"

"Yes." I take a breath, trying to calm my nerves. I just need to hurry up and say this. If she says no, I'll spend the rest of the night trying to change her mind. And if she still says no? Shit. She can't say no.

"Pearce, go ahead." She looks worried. I don't want her to be worried. I want her to be happy.

I take both her hands in mine, and just the feel of our hands joined together relaxes me and I'm able to speak.

"Rachel. From the first moment I saw you, I knew I had to meet you. And once I met you, I knew I had to get to know you. And once I got to know you, I couldn't let you go. Because I knew I loved you. I knew it a long time ago." I take a breath, my eyes not leaving hers. "I can't even begin to tell you how much you mean to me. You've changed my life. You've brought light into my darkness. You've made me experience happiness for the very first time."

Tears are now running down her cheeks, but she's smiling. I hope that's a good sign.

"I love you, Rachel, more than I can even describe. I didn't know love like this existed until I met you. That's why I know, without a doubt, that you're it. You're the person I'm meant to be with. The person I want beside me for the rest of my years." I let go of her hand and reach into the pocket of my suit jacket. Tears continue to fall down her cheeks as she watches me take the box and hold it out in front of her as I get down on one knee.

"Rachel." I open the box. "Will you marry me?"

She doesn't even look at the box. Any other woman would be inspecting the ring. But not Rachel. This isn't about the ring. This is about her and me, so her eyes remain on mine.

"Pearce." She's crying and I'm not sure what that means. Is she sad because she's going to turn me down?

It seems like hours go by as I await her answer.

Then I see her slowly nod, her smile growing wider. "Yes, Pearce. I would love to marry you."

I shoot up off my knee and bring her into my arms and hug her, tighter than she likes, but I can't help it. She said yes! This kind, beautiful, loving, caring, smart, amazing woman agreed to marry me.

When I finally let her go, I present the ring to her once again. This time, she looks at it.

Her eyes widen. "Oh my goodness. That's the biggest diamond I've ever seen!"

I take it out of the box. "It's not that big. It's only four carats. I would've bought a bigger one but you have small hands and I didn't think it would look right." I slip it on her finger. It fits perfectly. She left one of her rings in my loft last week so I brought it with me to the jewelry store so I'd get the right size.

She holds her hand up. "It's beautiful."

I smile. "Not bad for someone who doesn't know how to shop."

She wraps her arms around me and kisses me. "The ring is perfect. But any ring you would've picked would've been perfect because it came from you. I love you, Pearce. I love you so much."

Every time she says that, I feel this warmth in my chest. She's the only one who's ever said that to me and she says it all the time. It's like she's trying to make up for all those years I never heard it. I love her for that. I love how she cares about me. The *real* me, not the person I portray to the rest of the world. I love that she doesn't care about the money or the status or my name. None of that matters to her. She doesn't even know that side of my life. She only knows this side, the one I share only with her.

Her love for me is true, real, genuine. The old me would've doubted that, but the new me doesn't. I have no doubts when it comes to her. What we have between us is real. I feel it deep within my soul and I never want it to go away. Which is why I don't know what I would've done if she'd said no to me tonight. I couldn't lose her. I can never lose her.

She smiles at me. "I can't believe we're doing this. But I'm so happy we are. I can't wait to spend the rest of my life with you."

My heart starts thumping hard again. "I'm glad you said that because I feel the same way. Which is why I have something else to ask you."

"Go ahead."

I take hold of her hand. "Let's go sit down."

"Why?" She looks worried again. "What's wrong?"

"Nothing's wrong." I walk us to the couch.

When we're seated, she says, "Pearce, just say whatever you wanted to say. You're making me nervous."

I look down at our joined hands, then back at her face again. "Remember how we said that if we love each other, there's no reason to wait to get married?"

She nods. "Yes."

"Do you still believe that?"

"Um, I don't know. I guess I do."

"So if I said I wanted to marry you tomorrow, you'd agree to it?"

She laughs, assuming I'm joking. "Sure. Why not? I love you and I can't wait to be married to you."

"Good. Because I want us to get married tomorrow."

CHAPTER THIRTY
Thirty-Six Hours Later

PEARCE

I wake up with Rachel tucked inside my arms. She's still asleep. I take a moment to look at her. She's so incredibly beautiful.

I kiss the top of her head, waking her. "Good morning."

She opens her eyes and lifts her head up to smile at me. "Good morning."

I kiss her again, this time on her lips. "I love you."

"I love you too." She kisses me back then rests her head on my shoulder.

"What would you like to do today?"

"Stay here. With you."

"We could go out tonight. Have dinner. Maybe see a show."

"Or we could stay here in bed." She kisses me as her hand moves over my chest. "Order room service. And make our own show."

"That sounds perfect." I run my hand along her curves, feeling the softness of her skin. "But I thought I should at least offer to take you out since you've never been here before."

"The casinos don't interest me. And we can see a show some other time." She sighs happily. "Right now, I just want *you*."

"You have me." I kiss her. "Forever."

A smile fills her face, extending all the way up to her bright blue eyes. "That makes me very happy."

I kiss her hand, just below the sparkling four carat diamond ring perched atop her finger. "That's all I want. For you to be happy. And I promise I will do everything possible to make sure that you always are."

"You don't have to do anything, Pearce. As long as we're together I'll be happy." She closes her eyes, that smile still on her face.

She really means it. She really can be happy with just us. She doesn't need designer clothes, expensive jewelry, or a mansion to be happy. She just needs us.

"Shall we have breakfast?" I ask her.

She looks at me, her hand wandering below the sheet. "I'd rather do something else first. With my husband."

"Well, then, Mrs. Kensington." I ease her onto her back. "That's what we shall do."

We spend the rest of the day in bed. We haven't left this room since after the ceremony. The wedding was yesterday in a small chapel near the Vegas strip. Royce was there, along with a showgirl he met earlier that day. She was still wearing her outfit from the previous night's performance, complete with a bright blue feather headpiece.

It was a true Vegas wedding. Something I never thought I'd do in a million years. But desperate times call for desperate measures. This wasn't the wedding I wanted for Rachel. I wanted her to have her dream wedding in a beautiful setting with flowers and candles and whatever else she would want. And that's exactly what she'll get in the spring when we do this again.

I told her about my plans for a second wedding last Friday night, explaining that, given who I am, I'm expected to have a large, formal wedding. I told her it would be a high-society event that would receive a lot of media attention. As for my plans for this weekend, in order to get her to go along with it, I had to explain why we had to hurry up and get married and do so in secret. I couldn't be entirely truthful, because that would mean telling her about the organization. And I can't do that. So instead, I used my parents as the reason we had to elope. I was completely honest with her and told her how my parents disapproved of her and probably always would. She needs to know this, because my parents will never change and Rachel needs to be okay with that. And she was. After meeting my parents the other night, she knows they have no interest in my happiness. But *she* does. Rachel is the only person in my life who wants me to be happy, so when I told her my parents would do anything possible to keep us from getting married, she agreed to elope with me. She didn't want them interfering with our future.

As for her own parents, she considered calling them to tell them what we were doing but then decided against it. She knew they'd be disappointed and she didn't want them trying to talk her out of it. Rachel loves her parents and has a strong need to please them, but she also wants her independence and they're reluctant to give that to her. In some ways, our situations are similar. My father tries to control me and her mother tries to control her, but in different ways. Both of us fight against their control, wanting to follow our own path in life without their interference. It's this shared goal that helped make this secret wedding possible. She wants to be with me as much as I want to be with her and we didn't want our families interfering with that.

Neither one of us has even mentioned our families since getting married. Right now, we're trying to remain in this blissful state, locked inside a luxury suite on the top floor of a five-star hotel, high above the Vegas strip. Our every need is catered to so we can simply relax and savor these last few hours together before we have to return to real life.

When we *do* return, it's going to be hell. I knew that before we did this, but I wouldn't let myself worry about it. But now it's almost time to go home and I'm starting to panic. I have absolutely no idea what's going to happen. I know it's going to be bad, but I don't know *how* bad. Rachel's parents will be upset, but mine will be livid. Beyond outraged. I can't even imagine what my father will do. If he could kill me, he probably would, but I'm his only son and he needs me to take over the company someday, so killing me isn't an option. But he can make me wish I were dead.

As the room darkens and evening rolls in, I hold Rachel in my arms and she nestles against my side, her hand moving softly over my chest.

"Pearce, relax," she says, sensing my worry. It's like she can read my mind. She senses my stress and knows my mind is on my father. "It'll all work out."

343

If only that were true. She always tries to see the positive side of things, and I love that about her. But she wouldn't be so positive if she knew the truth. She doesn't know the whole story. She doesn't know the real reason why we're not supposed to be together. She doesn't know about the members. The organization. The rules, and what can happen if you don't follow those rules.

Worst of all, she doesn't know me. Not all of me. Not the real me. She has no idea what I've done or what I'll be forced to do in the future. I have to live that side of my life in secret. I don't like hiding that from her, but I can't tell her. I can never tell her.

And so, my life will remain a secret, as it's always been.

But at least now, I have happiness.

At least now, I have love.

At least now, I have Rachel.